Reviewers' Choice Awards for Career Achievement
in Urban Fantasy

"Keri Arthur's imagination and energy infuse
everything she writes with zest."
—CHARLAINE HARRIS

Praise for *Full Moon Rising*

"Keri Arthur skillfully mixes her suspenseful plot with
heady romance in her thoroughly enjoyable alternate
reality Melbourne. Sexy vampires, randy werewolves,
and unabashed, unapologetic, joyful sex—you've gotta
love it. Smart, sexy, and well-conceived."
—KIM HARRISON

"*Full Moon Rising* is unabashedly and joyfully sexual in
its portrayal of werewolves in heat . . . Arthur never fails
to deliver, keeping the fires stoked, the cliffs high, and
the emotions dancing on a razor's edge in this edgy,
hormone-filled mystery . . . A shocking
and sensual read, so keep the ice handy."
—*TheCelebrityCafe.com*

"Keri Arthur is one of the best supernatural romance
writers in the world."
—HARRIET KLAUSNER

"Keri Arthur's Riley Jenson series just keeps getting better and better and is sure to call to fans of other authors with kick-ass heroines such as Christine Feehan and Laurell K. Hamilton. I have become a steadfast fan of this marvelous series and I am greatly looking forward to finding out what is next in store for this fascinating and strong character."
—*A Romance Review*

Praise for *Dangerous Games*

"One of the best books I have ever read. . . . The storyline is so exciting I did not realize I was literally sitting on the edge of my chair. . . . Arthur has a real winner on her hands. Five cups."
—*Coffee Time Romance and More*

"The depths of emotion, the tense plot, and the conflict of powerful driving forces inside the heroine made for [an] absorbing read."
—*SFRevu*

"This series is phenomenal! *Dangerous Games* is an incredibly original and devastatingly sexy story. It keeps you spellbound and mesmerized on every page. Absolutely perfect!"
—*Fresh Fiction*

Praise for *Embraced by Darkness*

"Arthur is positively one of the best urban fantasy authors in print today. The characters have been well-drawn from the start and the mysteries just keep getting better. A creative, sexy and adventure filled world that readers will just love escaping to."
—*Darque Reviews*

"Arthur's storytelling is getting better and better with each book. *Embraced by Darkness* has suspense, interesting concepts, terrific main and secondary characters, well developed story arcs, and the world-building is highly entertaining. . . . I think this series is worth the time and emotional investment to read."

—*Reuters.com*

"Once again, Keri Arthur has created a perfect, exciting and thrilling read with intensity that kept me vigilantly turning each page, hoping it would never end."

—*Fresh Fiction*

"Reminiscent of Laurell K. Hamilton back when her books had mysteries to solve, Arthur's characters inhabit a dark sexy world of the paranormal."

—*The Parkersburg News and Sentinel*

"I love this series."

—*All About Romance*

Praise for *The Darkest Kiss*

"The paranormal Australia that Arthur concocts works perfectly, and the plot speeds along at a breakneck pace. Riley fans won't be disappointed."

—*Publishers Weekly*

Praise for *Bound to Shadows*

"The Riley Jenson Guardian series ROCKS! Riley is one bad-ass heroine with a heart of gold. Keri Arthur never disappoints and always leaves me eagerly anticipating the next book. A classic, fabulous read!"

—*Fresh Fiction*

By Keri Arthur

GENERATION 18

KERI ARTHUR

DELL
NEW YORK

Generation 18 is a work of fiction. Names, characters, places, and incidents either are the product of the author's imagination or are used fictitiously. Any resemblance to actual persons, living or dead, events, or locales is entirely coincidental.

2014 Dell Mass Market Edition

Copyright © 2004, 2014 by Keri Arthur
Excerpt from *Penumbra* by Keri Arthur copyright © 2005, 2014 by Keri Arthur

Published in the United States by Dell, an imprint of Random House, a division of Random House LLC, a Penguin Random House Company, New York.

DELL and the HOUSE colophon are registered trademarks of Random House LLC.

Originally published in different form in paperback in the United States by ImaJinn Books, Hickory Corners, MI, in 2004.

This book contains an excerpt from the forthcoming novel *Penumbra* by Keri Arthur. This excerpt has been set for this edition only and may not reflect the final content of the forthcoming edition.

ISBN 978-0-440-24659-6
eBook ISBN 978-0-8041-7955-3

Cover design: Lynn Andreozzi
Cover illustration: Juliana Kolesova

Printed in the United States of America

www.bantamdell.com

9 8 7 6 5 4 3 2 1

Dell mass market edition: September 2014

GENERATION 18

ONE

BEING A SPOOK WASN'T AT all what Samantha Ryan had expected. Long nights, sleepless days, yes—she'd faced that, and worse, during her ten years as a state police officer. In her time with State, the agents of the Special Investigations Unit had breezed in and out of situations, always on edge, always on the move, always looking like they loved what they were doing. So the sheer and utter boredom that filled ninety percent of her new job with the SIU had come as something of a shock.

She sighed and shifted slightly, trying to find a comfortable position on the icy metal step. *Watch the back door,* Gabriel had said. *Make sure the vamps don't hit the blood bank from the alley.* This despite the fact that, in the five previous robberies, the vampires had always gone in through the front door.

So why the hell would they change a successful MO now?

They wouldn't. He knew that. She knew that.

She rubbed her eyes wearily. She could hardly

argue, though, as he was her senior and in charge of the investigation. And with intel stating that this blood bank would be the next one hit, she couldn't argue with orders that were little more than covering all the bases.

What the intel wasn't saying was whether it was actually vampires doing these robberies. Hell, with recent estimates saying that at least thirty percent of newly turned vampires were unable to control their bloodlust, human blood had become a hot commodity. Combine that with the recent spate of deaths brought about through infected blood in all the major hospitals—leading to a proliferation of private blood banks where people could stockpile their own blood—and you had the perfect opportunity for those wanting to make a quick buck.

So here she sat, in the cold night, on a cold step, waiting for robbers who weren't likely to appear, while her goddamn partner watched the front door from the warmth of the car.

Bitter? *Oh yeah.*

He was certainly making good on his statement that he would never work with a partner. Whenever possible, he left her in her box of an office doing paperwork, or sent her on inane errands. This was her first "real" duty in the three months since her transfer, and she suspected she was here only because Byrne had given him a direct order to take her.

The wind picked up, running chilly fingers through her hair. She shivered and flicked up the collar on her coat. Overhead, the starlit sky was beginning to cloud over. The rain they'd been predicting for days was finally on the way. She could smell the moisture in the breeze, could feel the tingle of electricity running through the night air, charging her body with an odd sense of power.

Why she could feel these things was another point of concern, though it was one she kept to herself. There were only two people she trusted enough to sit down and talk to, anyway. The first was Finley, who was the head researcher for the SIU. While she didn't really know him all that well—the only time they'd ever crossed paths was when he was doing either tests or research on her—he probably knew more about her than anyone else alive. Or, at least, knew more about her biology. If anyone had any chance of understanding why these things were happening, it would be him. But Finley was still on leave, recovering from the injuries he'd received in the bomb blast three months ago. The second person was her goddamn partner, and *he* was harder to nail down than a snowflake in a storm.

And he wasn't just keeping his distance on a professional level, but on a personal one as well. Given how well they'd gotten on during their investigations of her former partner's disappearance, she'd thought they could at least be friends. Obviously, she'd been very much mistaken.

God, how bad was it when he wouldn't even go for a cup of coffee with her?

"Sam, you there?"

His warm voice whispered into her ear, so close she could almost feel the caress of his breath across her cheek. Except that he was tucked nice and warm in the car half a block away.

She was tempted, very tempted, to ignore him. But she'd spent ten long years as a cop doing the right thing, following all the rules—including keeping in constant contact when on watch. Even when her partner was being a bastard and deserved to suffer, it was a hard habit to break.

"What?" But her tone left no doubt of her mood. He'd left her sitting here so long her butt was almost frozen to the step. If he expected civility, he needed a brain transplant.

"Just checking if you're still awake."

Yeah, right. Like *she* was the one sitting in the nice, warm car. "The cold's doing a fine job of that, thank you very much."

He paused. "Do you want to swap for a while?"

She raised her eyebrows. Just for an instant, the compassion in his voice reminded her of the man she'd known before she'd become his partner. "You got coffee onboard?"

"Freshly brewed."

And he hadn't offered her any until now? It was lucky he'd equipped the two of them with only stun rifles, because she was very tempted to march right over and shoot him. "Sure you can spare a cup?" she said tightly. "I mean, you oldsters need some sort of stimulant to keep you awake at this hour of the night, don't you?"

"Do I take that as a yes or a no?" His warm voice held an undertone of annoyance.

But she was way past caring at this particular moment. "That depends."

"On what?"

"On whether you intend to freeze me out, figuratively or literally."

He made no immediate reply and she waited, wondering what he'd do now that she'd finally called him out. Down toward the Main Street end of the alley, she heard a soft thump, as if someone had jumped off a rooftop, and a dog yelped somewhere to the left of that—a short, sharp sound that spoke of fear. She frowned and stared into the darkness. The electricity filling the night stirred, running over her skin, standing the small hairs at the back of her neck on end. Heat followed quickly. Then her senses exploded outward, and she was tasting the night.

A kite creature walked toward her.

"Sam—"

She jumped and quickly pressed the earphone, cutting him off. He'd once told her the kites hunted by sound and movement. She wasn't about to chance the creature hearing his voice, no matter how unlikely that might be.

The kite came into view. It almost looked like a large white sheet, except that it had feet and talon-like hands. The creature hesitated as it neared the steps, sniffing the night like a dog. It turned milky-white eyes in her direction. She controlled the urge to reach for the stun rifle and remained still.

After a moment, it lumbered past, moving to the other end of the alley. Avoiding the yellow wash of the streetlight, it slunk around the corner and disappeared. She rose and picked up her rifle before switching the earpiece back on.

"A kite just made an appearance in the alley. I'm about to follow."

"Negative. You're not equipped—"

Sam snorted softly. "Neither are you, partner. You continue to keep watch on the blood bank, and I'll see what the creature is up to."

"Stun guns won't—"

"Gabriel, remember imperative one?" The SIU had

become aware of the kites only five months ago, but since then, the creatures had reached the top of the SIU's extermination list. With an edge in her voice that imitated his own, she continued, "Find and stop all kites, regardless of the cost."

"That doesn't mean you have to do a suicide run when you're not properly equipped to deal with them."

"Please credit me with a little bit of sense. I'm merely going to see what the thing is up to." She stopped at the end of the alley and carefully peered around the corner. The kite lumbered across the road.

"I'm calling for backup," he said, his voice terse.

The kite disappeared around the corner of the opposite street. She ran across the road and then edged forward, keeping to the shadows of the three-story apartment building.

"Fine." It only made sense. "I'll keep in contact."

"You'd better," he growled.

She grinned. She might well pay for it later, but damn, it felt good to annoy him.

She reached the corner, but the kite was nowhere to be seen. Wondering how the creature could have moved so fast, she frowned and glanced up—and found it. The loose skin around its arms flapped lightly as it climbed crablike up the wall.

The wind tugged at her hair, throwing it across her eyes. She brushed it back and listened to the sounds beneath the soft cry of the wind. Two men were talking, their voices harsh and grating. A radio near the top of the building played classic rock. Between the two came the squeak of a bed and a whispered good night. These were all sounds she wouldn't normally have heard but now did thanks to the odd sense of power flowing through the night.

The creature seemed to be headed for the apartment in which the radio played. She watched it for as long as she dared. When it stopped and pressed a taloned hand against a window, she turned and ran for the building's front door.

"Gabriel, the kite's about to break into a top-floor apartment on the corner of Gibb and Macelan streets."

"Help's on the way. Stay where you are."

The words had barely whispered into her ear when she heard the sound of glass shattering. A heartbeat later the screaming began. Sickening visions swam through her mind—bloodied images of the street bum she'd found three months ago, his body a mass of raw, weeping muscle stripped of skin.

She swallowed heavily and pounded up the stairs. "Negative. It's attacking. I'm in pursuit."

"Damn it, you're not equipped to deal—"

"Just get backup here quickly." She pressed the earphone, cutting him off again. She didn't need to hear what she could and couldn't do. Not when a man's life was at stake.

Two flights . . . three. She leapt over the banister and up the remaining stairs. People milled in their doorways, their eyes wide and fearful. Not one of them appeared willing to investigate what was happening to their neighbor. City living, she thought, sucked. But then, would neighbors in suburban areas be any more willing to risk investigating screams as horrifying as the ones currently shattering the silence? She suspected not.

She slithered to a stop outside the apartment door

and glanced back at the pajama-clad crowd. "SIU, folks. Go back inside and lock your doors."

The crowd melted away. With her laser held at the ready, she stepped back and kicked the door. Wood shuddered, splintering. She booted it a second time and the door flung open, crashing back on its hinges.

The kite was in the middle of the living room, its sheetlike form covering all but the stranger's slippers. His screams suddenly choked off, and all she heard was an odd sucking noise. Blood seeped past the flaccid, winglike sections of the creature's arms, forming pools that seemed to glisten black in the darkness.

She raised the stun rifle and fired at the creature. The blue-white energy bit through the darkness, flaring against the kite's leather-like skin. If it had any effect, she couldn't see it.

She switched her aim to the creature's oddly shaped head and fired again. The kite snarled and looked up. It had no mouth, she saw suddenly. It was sucking the stranger's flesh and blood in through pores on its skin.

She shuddered and fired again, this time at its eyes. The creature snarled again, the sound high-pitched and almost batlike. Then it shook its head and jerked upright. Bloodied strips of half-consumed flesh slid down its body and puddled at its feet. Her stomach churned, but she held her ground and kept on firing at the creature's eyes. It obviously wasn't stunning the kite, but it *was* doing something, because the kite's movements were becoming increasingly agitated.

It screamed again, then turned and stumbled toward the window. She edged into the apartment. The kite smacked into the wall, then flung out an arm, feeling for the window frame. It was almost as if it had lost all sonar capabilities. So maybe the weapon *had* addled its keen senses.

It grasped the window frame, felt for the other side to position itself, then dived through the shattered glass. Sam ran over to the window and leaned out. The kite was floating back to the street, its arms out wide, loose skin stretched taut to catch the light breeze. She pressed the earphone again.

"Gabriel, the kite is now on Macelan Street, heading west."

"Do not go after it. I repeat, do *not* go after it. Stay in the apartment."

Her smile was grim. If the tone of his voice was anything to go by, he was madder than hell. He had a right to be, she supposed, but what else could she have done? Let the kite devour the stranger?

Not that her intervention had saved him. She turned away from the window and dug out the marble-sized crime-scene monitor—the latest gadget from the SIU labs. She hit the activate button, then tossed the CSM into the air. It hovered for several seconds, then the light flickered from red to green, indicating it was now recording. She ordered it to do a sweep of the premises for record purposes. The monitor obeyed, panning around the room, taking in the doorway she'd kicked open, the window and the body. Then it returned, hovering several feet away from her.

"The kite smashed through the living room window and attacked the victim at three fifteen a.m. I— SIU Officer Ryan—intervened and drove the kite back through the window." She showed the monitor her badge, then walked across the room to squat beside the body. "The victim is male, probably mid-sixties."

The CSM dropped closer to the body, capturing the bloody details of the murder. What remained of the victim's flesh hung in strips, almost indistinguishable from the remnants of his red-and-white-striped pajamas. His eyes were wide, his mouth locked into a scream—a look of astonished horror that was now permanently etched into his features.

Why this man? Why not the two men talking in the apartment below, or the woman who'd just joined her partner in bed? She glanced up and studied the room.

The kite had come straight to this apartment, so it had obviously wanted this man specifically. What they now had to find out was why.

Sam rose and walked over to the shelving unit. The CSM followed her, a small limpet that recorded her every move, protecting her from future accusations of mistakes. Or possibly damning her, if she *did* screw up. Mentally shrugging, she dug a set of gloves out of her pocket and put them on. Then she turned off the radio and ordered the CSM to pan across the photos lining the shelf.

Each photo contained the same four men, either fishing, drinking, or standing around a barbecue. All of them looked to be at least fifty or sixty. She glanced again at the body. The victim was bald, save for a few scraggly wisps of white near either ear. He wasn't in any of these photos, then. Maybe he'd been the one taking them?

She picked up one framed photograph, then turned at the sound of footsteps. Gabriel entered, his gaze sweeping the room until he found her.

"I could put you on report for your behavior to-night," he said, stopping just inside the doorway.

Though his face was impassive, his hazel eyes were stormy with anger and, surprisingly, a touch of fear. She debated ordering the CSM to stop recording, then shrugged and let it continue. Procedures stated that any and all activity at a crime scene had to be recorded. If that included being told off, then so be it.

"Do it. Maybe then you'll get your wish and be rid of me." She hesitated. What was the point of arguing about it here? There were far more important matters at stake—like why the kite attacked this man. "Do you know who our victim is?"

For an instant, it looked as if he might continue with his reprimand. Then he shoved his hands in his pockets and walked across to the body. "Male, in his mid-sixties, obviously." He glanced around the apartment. "And fairly well off. Those paintings are by Kyle Parker."

She glanced across to the stylized landscapes. To her admittedly untrained eye, a three-year-old could have done a better job. And yet Parker's paintings sold for millions.

"If he could afford those, he should have installed better security."

"Security doesn't usually stop the kites."

"No, only decapitation or the sun can do that." She frowned down at the body. According to the SIU labs, the kites were some sort of offshoot of the vampire family tree. The SIU researchers were desperate to get their hands on a live specimen for testing, but as yet no one had figured out a way to capture one. "This wasn't a random attack. The kite came straight to this apartment."

"Maybe the victim was the only one moving around."

Sam shook her head. "There was movement in several apartments, but the creature ignored them all and came straight here."

Gabriel frowned. "There's been no evidence that the kites can be programmed to kill certain individuals."

"But there's been no evidence that they can't, either."

"True." He studied her for a moment, his hazel eyes intense. "How did you drive the creature away? Stun rifles don't work on kites."

"No, but they definitely don't like it when you fire it at their head. It seems to affect their ability to echolocate."

He raised his eyebrows in surprise, but any comment he was about to make was cut off as a wristcom—a two-inch-wide communications and minicomputer unit worn around the wrist—beeped. His, not hers.

He hit the unit's interface with more force than necessary. "Stern here," he said, with more than a hint of impatience in his voice.

Given the tightening of his already annoyed expression, the news obviously wasn't good.

"What?" she said, the minute he'd hung up.

"It looks like our serial killer has struck again. Byrne wants me to investigate."

Me, not *we*, she noted—and wondered if, in fact, Stephan had said that, or if Gabriel was locking her out again. "Where this time?"

"Elwood."

She raised her eyebrows. If it was the same killer,

then he was certainly showing no preference for area. So far, he'd killed in Toorak, Broadmeadows and now Elwood. And it was more than just miles that separated the three suburbs; each one occupied a different rung on the social ladder.

"What about the blood bank stakeout?"

"Briggs and Thornhill have taken over."

Lucky them. But she'd seen the two working together before, and she had no doubt that Briggs would be considerate enough to offer her partner some hot coffee long before his butt froze to the step.

"So let's go investigate."

Gabriel's gaze narrowed, as if he'd sensed the hint of sarcasm underlying her words. "You disobeyed orders and came after the kite. Now you're stuck with this case, I'm afraid."

But if the kite hadn't attacked, he would have found some other reason to keep her away from the murder investigation. Had it been anyone else, she would have sworn it stemmed from distrust—of both her and her ability to cope with the job—but he'd already told her it wasn't so much her, but partners in general. It was almost as if he distrusted *himself* more than her or any partner he might be assigned.

Not that *that* thought made any sense at all—unless, of course, something had happened to his other partners. Something *he* felt responsible for. Maybe that was something she needed to check out, because it would certainly go a long way toward explaining things.

Of course, it was also something he should tell her, but, obviously, the man had a stubborn streak a mile wide. Either that or he thought telling her it wasn't about her, but about partners in general, *was* explanation enough.

"Well, at least it's better than filling out endless rounds of paperwork."

His brief smile held a grim edge. "You've been with the SIU for just on three months. You've yet to go through full training. Don't expect to be treated as anything more than a trainee."

She snorted softly. "Don't worry. Any expectations I might have had have *long* since died."

Anger flared briefly in his eyes. Then he glanced at the hovering CSM and his face became impassive once more. "Keep in contact. I'll see you back at the office."

He turned and walked away, his movements sharp and agitated.

She stared at the door for several minutes after he'd disappeared, then turned and walked across to the bedroom to see what she could find.

GABRIEL SHOWED HIS ID TO the black-clad police officer keeping watch, then ducked under the yellow crime-scene tapes. The rotating red and blue lights of the nearby police vehicles washed across the night, splashing the otherwise somber, glass-walled building with color.

Like so many other buildings constructed in the area recently, this one had no real character. Its only purpose was to provide a decent view for those wealthy enough to afford an apartment so close to the city and the beach. He glanced up—ten floors in all. Surely, this time, they'd find a witness.

His brother walked down the steps as Gabriel approached. Stephan was a multi-shifter, capable of taking the form of any human male he touched, but the shape he mostly wore these days was that of Jonathan Byrne, the head of the SIU. Gabriel raised his eyebrows in surprise. It was unusual for the SIU director to become involved in routine investigations such as this. Something had to be up.

Byrne stopped in front of him, his blue eyes narrowed. "Where's Ryan?"

Gabriel shrugged, even though he knew his nonchalance would only irritate his brother more. Right now, he didn't really care. "Handling the kite murder."

Stephan shot an aggravated look at the two police officers standing nearby and Gabriel smiled grimly, knowing their presence prevented Stephan from saying too much. It was well known that Byrne had little to do with his six assistant directors. Being too familiar now might just blow Stephan's cover.

"Damn it, Stern, you're supposed to be partners."

"I don't want or need a partner." And his brother, more than anyone, should have understood why.

"Andrea died a long time ago," Stephan said softly, an edge of compassion in his voice.

"Mike didn't." Gabriel tried to control the almost instinctive rush of anger, but the desire to hit someone, anyone, was so fierce his fists clenched. "Death comes in threes, Byrne. I'm due one more."

And come hell or high water, that was *not* going to be Sam.

Stephan studied him for a long moment, then shook his head and headed back to the building. Gabriel fell into step beside him. The matter of his partner might have been dropped, but it was definitely not forgotten. Yet this was one battle of wills his brother was *not* going to win.

"Why are you here?" he asked as they entered the building.

"As a personal request from Frank Maxwell."

Maxwell was the Federal Minister for Education, and one of the few friends the real Byrne had actually had. As such, he'd posed a very real threat to Stephan as he tried to secure his new identity. Luckily, the two men had seen little of each other in the last year, so any differences Maxwell might see in Byrne now would surely be put down to time and the pressures of a new job. "Why?"

"It's his son who's been murdered."

Gabriel glanced at his brother in surprise. "A male? Are you sure it's the same killer and not a copycat?"

Stephan's smile was grim. "You'll see when we get there."

Which could only mean the clinical brutality of the previous attacks was evident here too. Gabriel eyed the police officer guarding the express elevator and frowned. The same officer had been guarding the doorway after Jack bombed Sam's apartment. Odd that he was here now, too.

"Is Marsdan on the scene?" Gabriel asked softly.

Stephan met his gaze and shook his head minutely. The young officer stepped aside as they approached the elevator. Gabriel glanced at his name tag: Sanders.

"Tenth floor, sir?"

Gabriel nodded, noting that Sanders's eyes were a deep, unfathomable green that somehow seemed older than his years. It was almost as if the soul behind the eyes had seen more than one lifetime.

The officer pressed the button, then stepped clear as the elevator doors slid shut. Stephan raised an eyebrow at Gabriel. "Why ask about Marsdan? He's a beat cop, not homicide."

Gabriel shrugged. "That officer was working with Marsdan when Sam's apartment was bombed."

"He might have been transferred."

"Maybe." Or maybe he was just getting suspicious in his old age. Still, it wouldn't hurt to check why that officer was here, when he had the time. "How old was Maxwell's son?"

"Twenty-five, same as the others."

The elevator came to a stop and the doors opened. The hallway beyond was pale blue, offset by gold carpeting. Four doors led off the hall, and a police officer stood guard at the far end. Gabriel glanced up at the ceiling. CSMs were stationed at regular intervals, tracking them silently.

"You requested the building's security tapes?"

Stephan nodded. "Copies have already been sent back to your office."

"Good." Gabriel stepped into the apartment. The place was huge, and the floor-to-ceiling glass flanking two sides of it only added to the feeling of space. What few inner walls the apartment had were pale blue, but the carpet and the furniture were white. Another CSM hovered in the middle of the room, red light flashing to indicate it was recording.

Gabriel showed his badge to the monitor, then said, "Our victim obviously didn't have any kids, not with all this white furniture. Do we know his name?"

"Harry. And no—there are no kids, no wife, and, as far as Frank knew, no girlfriend."

Gabriel raised an eyebrow. "What about a boy-friend?"

"It's a possibility. Frank was rather brusque when I asked if there was any particular woman his son might have been seeing."

The body lay on one of the white sofas. As long as you didn't look below the waist, it would be easy to think Harry had merely died in his sleep. His arms were crossed, his face peaceful. There was no terror, no hint that he'd known he was about to die so brutally.

"Cause of death?" Gabriel asked, despite the fact that it was obvious. No man could lose both his penis and testes and survive the resulting shock and blood loss unless he had medical help *really* fast.

"Same as the others—blood loss. There's an ashtray full of cigarette butts on the dining table, too."

"Same brand as before?" Gabriel squatted to inspect the gaping wound. The blood staining the leather no longer smelled fresh, and the wound itself was beginning to blacken.

"Yes. We've scanned for prints, but our killer was wearing gloves again. All we got was a latex smudge."

"Hmm. There's one difference, at least. Our killer has shown no real precision with his knife work here. He's basically just hacked it all away."

Stephan snorted softly. "I suppose it's a hell of a lot easier to part a man from his penis than it is a woman from her womb and ovaries."

"True. But all three victims were obviously unconscious before the murderer operated, so why take care with the women and not with young Harry here? There are several deep nicks on his right inner thigh."

"Maybe our murderer gets a perverted pleasure from gutting women and wants it to last longer."

Gabriel frowned. Something in that statement didn't sit right. The murderer had been meticulous in every detail so far, so why would he change anything just because this victim was male? The sheer number of cigarette butts at every scene very much suggested that the murderer had sat back and watched the blood pour from his victims. And that, in turn, perhaps suggested that he enjoyed the death more than he did the cutting.

Gabriel rose and then hesitated. On the back of the sofa, near Harry's right hip, a hair glinted softly in the light. It wasn't one of Harry's. His hair was red, the same as the other two victims. This was blond and long, with a dark root.

He dug a glove out of his pocket and carefully picked up the hair. "Got a bag?"

Stephan dug one from the crime kit on the table. "Maybe he did have a girlfriend."

"This could still be male. Long hair is fashionable in the rave scene at the moment. I'll run a check on Harry's acquaintances and see what I can find."

Gabriel secured the bag in the crime kit and turned back to the sofa, certain there was something still to be found. In the previous two murders, the killer had been careful not to leave anything behind. No hair, no prints, nothing that might give him away.

But this time he'd been less than precise with his cutting. So maybe, just maybe, he'd been less than precise with his cleanup. Gabriel studied the position of the body for a long moment, then walked around to the back of the sofa. Blood had soaked through, contrasting starkly against the white, embroidered material. Oddly enough, the thick carpet showed signs of a recent vacuuming.

He frowned and studied the crisscrossed suction patterns on the carpet. Only the small section between the sofa and what looked to be the bathroom had been touched. Near the bathroom door, a faint footprint marred the lush white expanse.

"How many people have been in the apartment since the body was discovered?" he asked, squatting near the print.

"The usual—the two State officers who attended the original call, the building super who let them in and us. Forensics is still on the way. Why? What have you found?"

"A print." He glanced up at the CSM. "Record image and location of print."

The black sphere responded immediately, zipping across the room to hover inches from his head. "Image recorded," a metallic voice stated.

"Resume original position." He knelt to study the print. As he did, he noticed a slight stain near the door. Liquid of some sort had been spilled near the door frame. He touched it lightly; the carpet fibers were dry and stiff, almost as if they had been glued together. He sniffed his fingers. The faint but unpleasant mix of urine and rotten eggs had him screwing up his nose in distaste.

"Jadrone," he muttered, coughing to ease the sudden sting in the back of his throat.

"What the hell was Harry doing taking something like Jadrone? Frank's family is human, not shifter."

"Which means maybe our killer is some kind of shifter." It would certainly explain why no one had noticed any strangers hanging about in the two previous murders—particularly if their killer was a multi-shifter. Multis weren't the norm, but they weren't exactly rare, either. *That* title went to shifter-changer hybrids, of which his old man was one—although he certainly wasn't on any record as such. But *that* was due more to careful record erasing than his status actually being missed.

In either case, Gabriel doubted if the killer would be taking the stuff himself. Jadrone was designed to ease the inevitable bone and muscle ailments that afflicted most shifters late in life, but it also had an unpleasant side effect. After several months of continual use, the ability to tell truth from fantasy blurred. And their killer was too practical, too careful, to be on some Jadrone-inspired trip.

So why in hell was there Jadrone on the floor?

"The government took Jadrone off the market a year ago," Stephan said. "It shouldn't be too hard to track through records and find out who's still taking it."

Gabriel smiled grimly. It might not be too hard, but it was a task he had no intention of doing. Sam could. It would keep her out of his way a while longer. Her anger and frustration had been all too evident in her smoke-shrouded blue eyes tonight. A few more pushes, a few more inane tasks, and she'd be asking for a transfer. All he had to do was convince Stephan it was for the best.

He rose and continued on into the bathroom. The stark whiteness was practically blinding—it had to be hell on the eyes when the sun was shining. A slight breeze stirred the hairs at the back of his neck. He glanced at the ceiling to make sure it wasn't the air-conditioning and then turned. A hole had been cut into the thick glass wall.

"Monitor, record bathroom evidence." As had been the case in the two previous murders, this hole was barely big enough to fit his fist through, and the edges were razor sharp, suggesting they'd been cut with a laser.

"Any thoughts on these holes?" Stephan asked from the doorway.

Gabriel shrugged, then stepped out of the CSM's way. "Escape route, maybe?"

"If the killer's using Jadrone, he can't be a shapechanger."

"No." Jadrone was as deadly to shapechangers as it was helpful to shapeshifters. No one knew why—though Karl, a good friend of Gabriel's and one of Australia's top herbal scientists, thought it might have something to do with body chemistry. "Nothing's making much sense in this case."

"Well, it had better. If the killer keeps to his current schedule, you have precisely twelve hours before he strikes again."

Twelve hours to find someone as elusive as a ghost. What could be simpler? "It would be a damn sight easier if we could find some sort of pattern. Other than being the same age and having red hair, the victims have nothing in common."

"The answers are there. All you have to do is find them." Stephan hesitated, then smiled grimly. "And I want Agent Ryan brought in on this one."

Gabriel stared at his brother, wondering why he was so determined to see him and Sam teamed up. "No."

"That's a direct order, Stern."

And it was one he had no intention of ever obeying—
if only because Sam had red-gold hair, the same as
the three victims. She might not be twenty-five, but
he wasn't about to risk her safety. Not with his track
record.

"Are you listening, Stern?"

"I'm all ears, sir."

Anger flared briefly in Stephan's blue eyes. "Good.
Report to me hourly."

Stephan turned and walked away. Gabriel stared
after him for a long moment, then glanced up at the
CSM. "Position of autopsy team?"

"Entering the building now."

"Good. Resume original monitoring position."
Gabriel followed the monitor back out to the living
room. The answer was here somewhere. He could
feel its presence, like an itch he couldn't quite scratch.
He stared blankly at the corpse for a long moment
and then turned.

Why had the killer vacuumed? And why just the
section behind the sofa?

Frowning, he crouched down, studying the vacuum
marks intently. Something had to have been spilled or
dropped here. Why else vacuum? He shifted slightly
and caught sight of something glittering deep in the
white pile. He carefully plucked it out—a shard of
glass. Then he ran his fingers through the carpet. A
plate-size section near his feet felt damp. He sniffed
his fingers again. Ginger and lemon, mixed with
something spicy he couldn't define. Its touch burned
across his skin.

He knew the scent. *Heat,* the latest rage in per-
fumes and one designed solely for female use. The
manufacturers claimed it made the wearer irresistible

to men—a claim that had proven so true that the government was considering putting the perfume on the illegal substances list. Oddly enough, when used by a male, Heat lived up to its name in an entirely different way, burning where it touched.

Harry had no wife, no girlfriend. No reason to buy Heat.

So the killer was female, not male.

TWO

SAM LEANED BACK IN HER chair and rubbed her forehead wearily. She'd had an almost constant head-ache for the last two days, and sitting for hours in front of a com-screen certainly didn't help. Nor did the lack of sleep. In fact, that was probably the cause.

But if she slept, she dreamed. Though she couldn't remember what those dreams were about, she always woke drenched in sweat, with her heart pounding at the walls of her chest as if trying to escape. And al-ways, *always,* there was a name dying on her lips.

Joshua.

Why, she had no idea. She had no friends by that name. She'd never even met a Joshua, so why dream of him? And why were those dreams always so full of fear?

Sighing, she opened her eyes and stared blankly at the com-screen for several seconds. It was seven thirty in the morning. She should go home and get some rest. Shower, at the very least. But her apart-ment didn't seem right anymore. It was too sterile, too neat. The builders and painters had restored the living area after the bombing three months ago, but no one could ever replace all the knickknacks and books she'd collected over the years. And the apartment just wasn't the same without them.

Maybe she should sell it and start anew. Hell, she'd done it before. She'd left the orphanage with nothing more than the clothes on her back and a hand-drawn picture of her mother. At least she now had a job and a decent amount of credits to fall back on—and given that her apartment was in a posh part of town, it could fetch a small fortune in any sale. A fact Gabriel had noted more than once, and always rather suspiciously. But it wasn't as if she hadn't tried her damnedest to uncover who'd left her the apartment in his will. According to the solicitor involved, part of the terms of the gift were anonymity—and that was frustrating, especially when she could remember nothing at all about her parents or her early life.

She picked up her coffee, took a sip, then said, "Hey, Iz."

The com-screen blinked to life. Dizzy Izzy, a hot pink fur-ball that was the current cartoon rage, stared at her while slowly swinging the end of a purple boa. "Yes, sweetie?"

"Can you do a quick search for Assistant Director Stern's former partners? Minimal detail—who and where they are?" Izzy's foot tapped for several seconds. "Results onscreen."

Two names flashed up—Andrea Morris and Michael Rose. Both dead. And *that*, she thought grimly, was probably the reason for his current determination not to have another partner. Yet even though she could understand his fear, it made his behavior no less annoying.

"That other search you requested is completed," Izzy added.

"Split screen, and show results."

"Can do."

The screen split in two. One side held the images of the four men she'd downloaded from the CSM, and on the other, their names and addresses, courtesy of the Motor Registration Board. Fortunately, they insisted motorists update their license photos every two years. As a State Police officer, there'd been countless forms to fill out before she could access the MRB's information. The SIU, it seemed, was more powerful. She'd yet to find a system she *couldn't* get into.

"Do a complete background on those four men, as well as our murder victim, Peter Lyle. Concentrate on current work details and banking activities."

Izzy frowned, and the boa went into overdrive. "That'll take time, sweetie."

"I know. Proceed."

"You're the boss."

"Only in this shoe box," she muttered, then turned as the door opened. Gabriel walked in and dumped a file on her desk.

She eyed it wearily. "What's that? More of the newly turned to be cataloged?"

"No. I want you to do a search and find out who's still being prescribed Jadrone."

She raised her eyebrows in surprise. "Why?"

"Because we found traces of Jadrone in Harry Maxwell's apartment."

"Harry Maxwell? Frank Maxwell's kid?"

Gabriel frowned and sat down on the edge of her

desk. Given her office was little more than a glorified broom closet, he practically loomed over her. "Yes. Do you know him?"

"Sort of. Jack and I often ran across him during our shifts."

"Doing what?"

"He was a regular at Maximum."

Gabriel raised a dark eyebrow. "I've never heard of it."

"Really? A major outfit like the SIU doesn't know about the existence of a dive like Maximum?"

"The SIU might well be aware of it—I simply said that *I* wasn't. This organization has hundreds of investigations underway at any one time. I'm certainly not aware of all of them—just the ones my department are responsible for."

A perfectly reasonable answer, except for the fact that, from what she'd seen over the last few months, both Gabriel and Stephan lived and breathed work— whether it was for SIU or for the Federation. Not that she was much better, but, hell, they had friends, a family. A choice.

And probably the only reason neither of them knew about Maximum would be because it hadn't come into the SIU's sphere until now. Which was understandable, given that Maximum was more a vice squad problem than SIU.

"It's an underground rave house. Popular with the gay scene, and for those seeking prescribed or illegal drugs."

"So Harry was a user?"

"He's what I term a prescribed druggie. He used to hit up on Jadrone."

"But Jadrone has no effect on humans."

"Which can only mean that Harry wasn't entirely human, because he got blasted pretty regularly."

Gabriel frowned. "But even shifters have to take it daily for several months before it has any effect—at least in terms of blurring the line between fantasy and reality."

"So says the government, but take a large enough dose and the hallucinogenic effects are pretty immediate."

He studied her for a minute, his hazel eyes intense and unreadable. "Why was he never pulled in?"

"He was. Several times. But Frank Maxwell knows all the right people. The department kept dropping the charges."

"Did you know his supplier?"

She hesitated. "No." In truth, she did—but if she told Gabriel, she'd remain stuck in this shoe box for yet another day. "But I can find out if you want."

"I want. I've got nine hours before the killer strikes again."

I've got, not *we've* got. He still wasn't letting her in. "Anything else?"

His sudden smile was almost predatory. *Here it comes,* she thought. *The inane task to end all inane tasks.*

"I want you to get a list of everyone who's bought Heat in the last month, then contact every one of them to see if any of them happen to know Harry Maxwell."

She stared at him. "But that could take days! Heat is the perfume world's flavor of the month."

"Then you'd better get started, hadn't you?"

He rose and left, but not before she'd caught the amused glint in his eyes. "Damn you to hell," she muttered, and kicked the door. Easy to do when she was so damn close to it. It slammed shut with wall-shaking force.

"Hey, careful!" yelled the guy in the neighboring shoe box.

She snorted. She'd probably woken the old bastard up. Her office was in an area the SIU called the vaults, but was more commonly known as the black hole. Once in, never out—or so the saying went. It was a cataloging area and generally reserved for those close to retirement or no longer able to cope with the pressures of the SIU. Gabriel's excuse for putting her here was lack of office space elsewhere.

Of course, *his* office was large enough for four desks.

He was obviously trying to piss her off enough to quit, and, in part, he was succeeding. But she wouldn't quit, and she wouldn't ask for a transfer, if that was what he was after. She'd ride it out, if only because being his partner gave her access to a whole new range of computer systems. And one of them surely held some clue to her past—although it wasn't as if she'd actually made use of the SIU's system yet. She hadn't dared to risk it, given her initial three-month probationary period. But with that now almost ended, she had to take the chance—just in case Gabriel succeeded in getting rid of her.

She leaned forward and picked up the folder. Inside she found photos and the crime scene report. She thumbed past the photos, barely bothering to look at them, and then scanned the autopsy results.

Interestingly enough, no traces of Jadrone had been found in Harry's system. Which meant he couldn't have had a fix for at least a week. But Harry was a junkie. If he'd been off Jadrone for any longer than three days, he would have been a mess. Frowning, she sorted through the papers and found the follow-up report. He'd showed up for work, on time, every single day.

She'd seen Jadrone junkies being weaned off the drug. Harry shouldn't have been able to piss on his own, let alone get up and go to work.

Maybe she should head down to Maximum and find old Max, the owner and chief supplier. "Izzy, I need two more searches."

The pink fuzz-ball reappeared on the screen. "I'm stressing out here, darlin'."

"You'll live. I want a complete list of everyone who's bought Heat in the last month."

The purple boa became a blur. "Why don't you ask for the moon to turn blue? Hell of a lot easier."

"Tell me about it," she muttered. "The other search I want done is for all available information on the following names." She hesitated and dug the birth certificate out of her drawer. After unfolding it, she added, "Meg More, Mike Shean, David Wright, Jeremy Park, Alice Armstrong, Rae Messner, Mark Allars and Fay Reilly. That's a priority-one search. All channels."

The purple boa stilled. "By what authority?"

"Gabriel Stern, Assistant Director, badge number 5019."

"The director has a note online to be informed if you request information on these eight names."

The only way Gabriel could have known about the birth certificate was if he'd been snooping through her desk. She certainly hadn't mentioned it. "Then inform him and get on with the search."

"Search underway. It may take the whole day, sweetie."

And she wasn't about to hang around waiting. "Save all the results to my personal folder and scan a copy onto disk." Working with Jack for so many years had taught her to be careful. Computers could be hacked into, and data erased or changed. But if you made a hard copy of everything, you at least had a backup.

"Consider it done. Have a nice day."

"Yeah, right." She rose and stretched. A shower and a few hours' sleep were her first priority. Then she'd head to Maximum and have a cozy little chat with Max. Harry had been a reliable customer for at least three years. And if Max didn't know how Harry had come off the drug with no side effects, no one would.

She grabbed her bag and headed out the door.

GABRIEL ENTERED HIS OFFICE, YANKED off his tie and tossed it across the arm of the nearest chair. Then he loosened the top two buttons on his shirt and walked across to the autocook. "Coffee, black, two sugars."

He whistled tunelessly until the coffee was ready, then walked across to his desk and sat down.

"Computer on."

The com-unit hummed softly. "Good afternoon, Assistant Director."

"I want a complete background check on Harry Maxwell. Priority one."

"Proceeding. The search results for Anna Jakes and Raylea Burns have also been completed."

"Split screen and show results."

"Proceeding."

He leaned back in his chair and sipped the steaming coffee. They'd begun using decent beans in the AD's machines of late, and the coffee actually tasted like coffee, rather than the bitter metallic substitute that was used in the rest of the SIU's machines. It was a nice change.

The com-screen came to life, displaying the bloody images of the first two women killed. Underneath the photos were their histories.

He scanned through them both quickly and frowned. They'd been born on the same day, in the same military hospital.

"Display the birth certificates for both women."

"Displaying."

The two documents came onscreen. He raised his eyebrows. A birthday wasn't the only thing they'd shared. They also had the same mother. So why hadn't Emma Pierce raised her daughters? And how could both girls be listed as being born at ten fifteen p.m. if they had the same mother?

"Who was the attending obstetrician on the births?"

"Dr. Frank Lloyd."

"Where can I find him?"

"Dr. Lloyd is the resident physician at the Hopeworth Military Base."

Hopeworth was something of a black hole when it came to military bases. Little was known about its activities, and it was one of the few areas the SIU computers could not access. Officially, Hopeworth was a weapons development area. Unofficially . . . who knew?

But why would they want a full-time obstetrician? Were the staff so bored that the base was experiencing a population explosion?

"Dig up Harry Maxwell's birth certificate, and see what you can find on Emma Pierce." If Emma worked at Hopeworth, there wouldn't be much to find. The base guarded the identity of its personnel almost as fiercely as its activities. It was surprising that they'd let the birth certificates slip out—although, perhaps because both children had been adopted, they'd been forced to do so.

"Agent Samantha Ryan has just requested a priority-one access-all search."

"Indeed?" He smiled. So she'd finally decided to search for the eight names listed on the birth certificate he presumed Jack had given her—a certificate he knew about *only* thanks to the fact that he'd gone through her drawers a few days ago after seeing her hastily hide it one afternoon. He had begun to wonder if she'd ever take the risk. Of course, he could have told her all about *one* of the four men on that certificate—Mark Allars had been a friend of his father's for a very long time, after all—but for the time being, he was keeping his silence. She'd undoubtedly be furious that *he* hadn't mentioned knowing Allars, but, damn it, the old adage of leading a horse to water was correct. He could push all he wanted, could lead her to names, but in the end it wouldn't matter unless she truly *wanted* to uncover her past. "The search is approved. Post a copy of the results to me, but otherwise continue."

The key to who—or perhaps what—she was lay not in the present, but in a past she couldn't remember. He was certain of that much. But it wouldn't do him any good to do the research, because he had no idea what might or might not trigger her memory. She *had* to be the one to look, which was why he'd allowed her full computer access in the first place—something that went against all SIU rules.

The computer blinked to life again. "No current information is available on Emma Pierce."

He frowned. "What do you mean?"

"No purchases have been made with credit cards in the last month. No transactions within bank accounts. The utilities to her home have been cut due to nonpayment."

"No death certificate was issued?"

"The death records have been scanned. There is no match."

If she wasn't dead, then what the hell was she up to? "Last known address?"

"Fourteen Errol Street, Melton."

His frown deepened. What would someone like Emma Pierce, who'd obviously been employed by the military and should have retired with a nice, fat pension, be doing in a place like Melton? The government had bought out a good portion of the suburb some ten years back, with the aim of providing both the poor and the homeless with someplace cheap to live. Or, as the critics of the move had observed, with a dumping ground. Out of sight, out of mind.

"Was she in government or private housing?"

"Government-funded."

"Is there a husband or living relative listed on file?"

"There is no marriage certificate on record, and no listing of immediate family available."

"No record of parents?"

"Her parents were killed in an automobile crash

sixty-two years ago. Emma Pierce was listed as their only child."

"Do a complete background check on Emma Pierce. Post a copy of all the results to wristcom 5019."

He finished the rest of his coffee and rose. Time to go to Melton and pay a visit to Emma Pierce.

SAM CLIMBED OUT OF THE car and glanced skyward. Gray clouds stormed across the sky, so low it felt as if she could reach out and touch them. Electricity burned through the air, tingling across her skin and through her soul.

She took a deep breath and, for a moment, imagined the power of the storm filling her body, strengthening her. Changing her.

She frowned, wishing Finley would hurry up and return from sick leave. She really needed to talk to him. She needed to understand the changes that she sensed were happening.

Thunder rumbled. It was a sound she felt rather than heard. A sound that seemed to vibrate through every cell in her body. Fear rose in her heart, but she thrust it away. For now, there was nothing else she could do, because there was simply no one she could talk to.

She reached back and grabbed her jacket off the backseat, then climbed out. The car locked automatically when she slammed the door shut. She turned and studied the concrete, slab-sided building. It didn't look like much—not in daylight, anyway. But at night, the blue-painted concrete became the perfect canvas for all sorts of computer animation. And it attracted creatures as weird and as wild as its graphics.

Slinging her jacket over her shoulder, she walked up the half-dozen steps and opened the front door. In her ten years as a cop, she'd never known this place to be closed—even though it only had a license to operate at night.

Smoke drifted past her body, thick and somehow cloying. With it came the smell of hopelessness. Jack, her now-dead ex-partner, had often asked her to define what she meant, but it was something she found hard to explain. Even at night, when the place was full of people and noise and life, the smell was there. It was a scent of desperation, perhaps. Or maybe it was the smell of death hovering close. So many of the people who came to Maximum were on a downward spiral to oblivion.

She closed the door but didn't move farther inside, allowing her eyes time to adjust to the darkness. The place was quieter than usual. There were only a half-dozen people in the front bar, either wearily nursing drinks or hiding in the darkness of the booths to her right. Josie, the gum-chewing, red-haired bartender, stood at one end, looking as disinterested as the rest of the patrons.

She walked across the room. "Hey, Josie, is Max around?"

Josie's golden-brown eyes jumped into focus. "Officer Ryan. It's been a while."

Her pupils were large, her speech somewhat slurred. She wondered what Josie was taking these days. "That it has. I need to see Max."

"You here to haul his ass downtown?"

Sam smiled thinly. "If I were, would I be talking to you, giving Max time to run?"

Josie sniffed. "That's okay, then. He's upstairs."

"Thanks. I remember the way."

Josie nodded vaguely and went back to polishing, a somewhat erotic smile touching her lips. *Mind's Eye*, Sam thought, catching the candy-sweet scent as Josie moved. It was, in many ways, an aphrodisiac for the brain. Wondering which patron Josie was having mind-sex with, Sam headed through the door into the main area of the club.

The huge dance floor lay in darkness. Her footsteps echoed against the wood, the beat a tattoo that set her nerves on edge. Wishing she'd brought something more than a stun gun, she made for the rear stairs and ran up to the next floor.

Max's office lay at the end of the long corridor. She stopped and eyed the shadows warily. With the approaching storm running liquid fire through her veins and seeming to expand her senses to new heights, she knew that no one lay in wait. And yet something felt *wrong*.

She half-raised her wristcom to call for help, but stopped. Calling Gabriel for help wasn't the answer. He'd only berate her for coming here in the first place.

Besides, there was probably nothing more at stake than a case of nerves. This was the first time she'd come to Maximum without Jack by her side.

She took a deep breath and released it slowly. Jack might be dead, but her life was no less complicated. And in truth, she missed him. Missed having someone to talk to, to laugh with. In the darkest hours of the night, she couldn't help thinking that even a friendship based on a lie was better than no friendship at all.

But that feeling of wrongness wasn't going away—and she knew from long experience it was better to be safe than sorry. Frowning, she pressed the wristcom's locator button, giving the SIU her immediate position. Then, stun gun in hand, she walked toward the door.

It opened before she got there. Max's obese figure loomed large in the doorway, his smile flashing in the gloom.

"Officer Ryan. Pleased to see you again."

His tent-sized Hawaiian shirt was buttoned up wrong, and he wore no shoes or socks. She held back a slight grin. Maybe she'd interrupted something. "Yeah, right. Back up, Max."

He held up his hands and backed away from the door. She checked left and right before entering. Max was the only human in the room.

But he wasn't alone.

She glanced up. The office ceiling was a good fifteen feet high and made entirely of glass. Vines twisted their way across a network of wires, and flowers hung in chains, dripping pink and red petals to the floor. Budgerigars flittered through the greenery, bright splashes of yellow and blue. One of them was a shapechanger, but the birds moved too fast to define which one.

"They have to be hell on the furniture," she commented. "Why the sudden fixation on budgies?"

Max shrugged. It sent ripples running across his flesh, like waves in an ocean. "They amuse me. Besides, I have plenty of money to spend."

She kicked the door shut and leaned back against

it. "Then why not try weight reduction surgery? You might live longer."

His answering smile was gentle. "They won't operate. They say I'm too large."

"So sue them."

"I am." He moved around the desk and squeezed his frame into a chair the size of a two-seater sofa. "Now, I'm presuming you did not come here to discuss my weight . . ."

"No. But first, where's Morris?" Max's ape-sized bodyguard was rarely more than two feet from his side.

"I sent him for a walk."

Wanted a little privacy with his budgie friend, no doubt. Though from what she'd heard, he normally didn't mind having an audience. "Tell me about Harry Maxwell."

Max returned her gaze evenly. No surprise there, though. When he wanted to, he could act with the best of them.

"I haven't seen him in over a week."

"When was the last time you *did* see him, then?"

"Last Thursday."

"And did you sell him any Jadrone?"

"No." A bead of sweat formed on his forehead.

"If you didn't sell him Jadrone, what did you sell him?"

The bead rolled down his cheek. Max swatted at it heavily. "I don't—"

"Do drugs, illegal or otherwise," she finished for him. "Yeah, I've heard the song before. Just tell me the truth."

He shifted in his chair, and metal groaned in the brief silence. "I didn't sell him anything. Honest."

"Then his abstinence must be putting a strain on your finances. He was one of your best customers, wasn't he?"

Max made no comment, just stared at her somewhat sullenly.

"Have you tried to find out where he is?"

Fingernails, almost lost in the envelope of flesh hanging over them, began to beat a rhythm against the desk. Nerves rather than anger.

"Yes."

"And?"

His hand edged toward the left side of the desk. "He said he didn't need me no more."

She raised an eyebrow. "He had a new supplier?"

"No. He said he didn't need the drug no more." His hand moved again.

"We both know he was a junkie. And we both know he could never have given it up cold turkey." She hesitated, saw a budgie dive-bombing her head and ducked. Bird shit splattered across the door just inches from her ear. "I don't think your bird likes me, Max."

He made no comment, but the look in his brown eyes suggested she wasn't on his list of favorite people either. It wasn't exactly a surprise. She'd hauled his ass downtown more than a dozen times over the years.

It was more than that, though. She crossed her arms and regarded him steadily. There was something going on here, something she couldn't quite define. But it had something to do with the shapechanger whose presence fairly itched at her skin.

"You know Harry's dead, don't you?" she said,

keeping her voice conversational. "He was victim number three of a serial killer."

Max jumped, and for the first time she saw fear, true fear, leap into his eyes. He hadn't known about Harry.

And the murder scared the shit out of him.

He knew the killer, she thought, watching the glittering beads of sweat roll down his cheeks. Or at the very least, knew who Harry was with the night he was murdered.

Dodging the dive-bombing budgie, she walked to the desk. Placing her palms on its surface, she leaned across it until her nose was only inches from his.

This close, he smelled of sweat and fear and sex.

"Tell me who Harry was with the night he died, Max."

He licked his lips, tongue lizard-like in his agitation. "I don't know what you're talking about. I told you, I haven't seen Harry in over a week."

God, this close his breath literally reeked. He'd obviously been overdoing the garlic and onions again. "But you know someone who has seen him since then, don't you?"

He didn't deny it. He merely sat and sweated some more.

"I want to know who, Max."

"I can't." The denial came out a strangled whisper.

She leaned back a little, more to get a dose of fresh air than anything else. "I'm not the beat police anymore, you know. I'm SIU. I don't have to follow the rules. I can beat your fat ass to a pulp and no one would ever question me."

He moved his hand again. She unclipped her stun

gun and shoved it under his nose. "I'd really love for you to go for the weapon under your desk."

He raised his hands and leaned back in his chair, and she frowned. Something about this felt wrong. Despite the fact that he dealt in death for a living, there was no way in hell Max would get mixed up in something like the serial killings. It just wasn't his style.

So why wouldn't he talk? The budgie, maybe?

"That your girlfriend up there, Max? Why don't you invite her down for a chat?"

His gaze jumped to the ceiling, and his growing look of horror was one she didn't understand.

"What do you mean?" he whispered.

"I mean that mean-looking blue bird who keeps trying to shit all over me. She the jealous type, perhaps? Or doesn't she know about the sidelines you have going?"

"Yes. I mean, no." Max hesitated, licking his lips. "She's not my girlfriend."

But they were involved at a basic level, at least. Why else would he smell of sex?

"The sooner you tell me what you know, the sooner you and your girlfriend can get back to business."

His cheeks reddened slightly, and he looked like a kid caught lying to a teacher. "I can't tell you anything, Officer."

"Then maybe I'll have to interview your girlfriend." She clicked the safety off and aimed the stun gun at the ceiling. "I'll shoot every one of them if that's what it takes."

She wouldn't, but Max didn't know that. And he'd seen Jack in action often enough to think she meant what she said.

Max sighed and rubbed his eyes, looking suddenly defeated. "She means it."

For several seconds nothing happened. But the birds flying above her head seemed less frantic. Something blue and green fluttered to her left, briefly catching her attention. But it was only a couple of the birds coming to rest on the edge of Max's desk. Actual birds, not a shapechanger.

Power ran across Sam's skin, a faint tingle that burned a warning into her soul. The shapechanger was on her *right*.

She turned, stun gun rising. But she wasn't fast enough by half.

Something smashed into the side of her head and the lights went out.

THREE

ERROL STREET SAT IN THE heart of government-
owned housing. Gabriel slowed the car, searching for
numbers on the shabby-looking brick-and-concrete
residences.

Twelve . . . fourteen. He stopped and climbed out.
The wind swirled around him, thick with the scent of
rain. He glanced skyward. The clouds were black and
looked ready to burst. He reached for his coat, shrugging it on as he walked across the road.

Number fourteen was different from its neighbors
in that no one had tended the garden for at least a
month. Weeds twined their way through the imita-
tion picket fence, crowding the sad-looking roses,
and what there was of the lawn had died some time
ago.

The house itself was little better. The porch drooped
at one end, as if the foundation had given way. Several of the front windows were smashed and had
been roughly boarded up. The second story looked
thrown on, and sections of the tin roofing rattled

noisily in the wind. Gabriel walked up to the front door and rang the bell. He waited several minutes for someone to answer. When there was no response, he knocked loudly. Still no one came to the door. He stepped back and studied the second story. No lights; no sound.

The house looked and felt deserted.

He walked around to the back. Several sweaters and skirts hung on the line, flapping forlornly in the wind. If the bird shit caking the side of one navy skirt was any indication, they'd been there for a while.

The back door was locked. He stepped back and kicked it open. The handle gouged out a large chunk of plasterboard from the wall behind the door and dust flew high, making him sneeze.

Clothes lay scattered on the laundry floor—whites separated from colors, but both piles gathering dust. He stepped past them and into the hallway.

The air smelled stale, as if the house had been locked up for a long time. He turned right and found himself in the kitchen. A loaf of bread sat on a board near the sink, so green it was almost unrecognizable. A carton of milk sat nearby—and even from where he stood, he could smell its pungent sourness. Someone had prepared breakfast and not come back to clean up.

Both the dining room and the living room were empty of life. The stairs were at the back of the house, but on the first step, he stopped. No light filtered down from above. Darkness hunched at the top of the stairs like some demon waiting to pounce. But it wasn't the lack of light that stopped him. It was the smell. Meat, long gone rancid.

Death waited above.

He slowly climbed the stairs. Darkness wrapped around him, as heavy as a cloak. On the top step, he hesitated, waiting for his eyes to adjust. Shapes loomed out of the blackness—several bookcases lining the walls on either side of the doors.

The odor came from the room on his left. He walked through the doorway.

Emma Pierce sat up in bed, her body supported by several cushions, watching a TV that no longer worked. Her eyes were still open, her jaw hanging loose. Her skin had a waxy look to it, pale cream in color tending to green near her neck. A tray, containing a half-eaten slice of molding toast and a cup of what looked to have been coffee, sat by her side.

Her death obviously wasn't recent. And given how cold it had been lately, she could easily have been dead for over a month. Bodies tended to deteriorate far slower in lower temperatures. While her death appeared to be natural, he couldn't take any chances. Not when Emma Pierce was related to at least two murder victims.

He called in an SIU cleanup team, then put on some gloves and walked over to the window, opening the blind. Light flooded into the room, highlighting the decay—human and otherwise. Several envelopes sat on top of the drawers next to the bed. He picked them up. Bills, mostly. But one envelope caught his eye, because the return address was Hopeworth.

He tore it open. It was a letter from Dr. Frank Lloyd, asking Emma to contact him immediately. The request was dated August 17—the day after the first murder. He wondered if there was a connection—and if Hopeworth knew anything about it. Not that they were likely to tell him. The people at Hopeworth were something of a law unto themselves. He put the letter in his pocket and opened the first of the drawers. Neither the drawers nor the room itself gave up any further secrets.

In the second bedroom, he discovered a wardrobe full of clothes—modern stuff, not the type worn by most women in their fifties. Someone else had stayed in the house with Emma, and for some time, if the range of apparel was anything to go by.

So where was that person now? And why hadn't she reported Emma's death to the authorities?

He searched the remaining bedroom, but he didn't find anything else, so he went back downstairs.

He was in the kitchen when the pain hit. Fire flashed through his brain and sent him stumbling forward. He grabbed the counter, holding on as the kitchen danced around him. Sweat rolled into his eyes, stinging, blurring his vision. For an instant, everything went black.

Then it was gone, as swiftly as it had come. Leaving him with the certainty that Sam was in trouble.

"Assistant Director, are you okay?"

He swung around. Michaels stood in the doorway, regarding him with concern.

"No. I think the smell finally got to me." He took a deep breath, fighting the urgency beating through his veins. "The body's upstairs."

"Foul play evident?"

"No, but look for it. I want cellular analyses included."

Michaels frowned. "That'll take some time."

"Emma Pierce has nothing but time. Get the sweepers into the second bedroom, too. Someone else has been staying here, so see if you can pick up any DNA traces."

Someone had cared enough to stay here and look after Emma as death approached. So why hadn't she cared enough to report the death and bury her?

Michaels nodded. "You want us to contact you if we find anything?"

"Yes. Send the results through as soon as you have them."

"Right." Michaels headed for the stairs.

Gabriel tapped the wristcom's contact button, then said, "Place a call to the SIU." The screen went blank for a moment, then the SIU's digital secretary answered.

"Christine, have we got a location signal on Agent Ryan?"

"Sector Five. One-five-six George Street, Fitzroy."

"Anything of importance at that location?"

"It is commonly known as the rave district."

Gabriel swore softly. While he'd asked her to investigate who might have supplied Jadrone to Harry, he hadn't expected her to practically run out the door the minute he'd left her office. "Any reports of trouble in that area?"

"None, sir."

No reports of trouble, no indication that Sam herself was in trouble. So why was he so certain that she was? "Christine, send someone to collect my car. I'm heading out to join Agent Ryan."

"Yes, sir."

As the connection broke, he walked outside and called to his alternate shape. Power surged, burning through his body, snatching away sensation and pain as every nerve ending shuddered, twisted, to find new form. Then the sensation died, and an odd sense of emptiness followed. A heartbeat later, he was a hawk soaring skyward, heading toward the city.

SMOKE TICKLED SAM'S THROAT, MAKING her cough. She tried to swallow, but her mouth was dry, empty of saliva. Her throat felt raw, parched, as if she'd scalded it. Even her lungs burned.

She groaned and rolled onto her back. Moisture ran past her ear, tickling her scalp. She swatted at it and her fingers came away damp. It was a sticky dampness, like blood.

Why was she bleeding? Had someone hit her over the head? Maybe the budgie had been armed with a big brown club. The image made her smile, but only for a second. Smoke swirled, thicker than before, catching in her throat.

Urgency began to beat through her, but it was distant, muted, as if fighting its way through a veil.

She opened her eyes. The budgies flew above her, their movements frantic, panicked. High-pitched cries of terror itched at her ears as they desperately sought an exit. One that the shapechanger must have blocked after her departure, because there was no trace left of a changer in the room.

Frowning, Sam turned her head. Across the room fire roared, gold and red. It not only reached bloody fingers toward the ceiling, but was spreading swiftly toward the desk and the fat man. A fat man whose shoes had started burning.

"Please," Max said, his voice a mix of hysteria and urgency. "Help me."

The flames were beginning to reach his trousers.

His legs jumped and twitched, as if in time to the silent music of the fire.

"Officer Ryan! Get up! Help me! Please!"

The desperation in his voice bit through the fog enveloping her mind. She groaned and rolled onto her hands and knees. Her stomach heaved, jumping into her throat, and sweat beaded her forehead. Heat flashed across her skin, followed quickly by an icy chill.

Swallowing heavily, she inched forward. The flames raced up Max's trousers. *Too fast,* some dim part of her mind protested. Max wore only natural fibers— wool usually. Only some form of accelerant would make his clothes burn so quickly. She sniffed the air and caught a trace of gas.

She swore and reached the wall, inching herself upward. It was like moving through glue, as if her mind and her limbs were on separate planes. Snagging the fire extinguisher from the wall, she pulled out the safety catch, then pressed the lever and turned. Foam gushed from the nozzle—a blue-white cloud that arced across the room like cannon-blasted snow.

Max screamed when it hit him—or maybe he'd always been screaming and it just hadn't registered until now. The flames hissed as they died, and the smoke in the room became thicker. She coughed, her vision blurring with the tears streaming down her face. When she could no longer see the flames eating Max, she turned the extinguisher on the rest of the fire.

The door behind her flew open. Men dressed in black and gold ran in, hauling silver snakes that reared up and spewed water at the flames. Her vision wavered. She dropped the extinguisher and reached out for the wall. It danced away, laughing.

Then the floor rushed up to greet her.

OUTSIDE THE DARKENED AMBULANCE IN which Sam sat, someone slammed a car door. The noise vibrated right through her, then reached into her brain and squeezed tight. She groaned and held her head in her hands. Any minute now, it was going to explode. A head could take only so much pain, and hers had surely reached saturation point.

She wouldn't mind so much if it were only her head, but her whole damn body ached just as fiercely, and her stomach felt about as steady as an umbrella in a windstorm. If she moved, she'd puke—no doubt about it.

Footsteps approached the ambulance. They rebounded through her brain like a freight train. Then the rear door opened and light flooded in.

She hissed and squeezed her eyes shut. "Shut the door, damn you."

The door closed softly. She took a deep breath, waiting for the pain behind her eyes to subside a little. The ambulance creaked as someone sat on the seat opposite. The earthy scent of exotic spices, mixed with the warm freshness of the sun and the wind, washed over her. *Gabriel*, she thought, and bit back another groan. That was all she needed right now. Her damn partner, here to witness the mess she'd made of a simple questioning.

She leaned back against the ambulance's cool metal wall, not opening her eyes, not wanting to see the anger in his.

"You okay?" His voice was little more than a whisper, devoid of emotion.

"No," she muttered. "I feel like shit."

He was silent for a second, but she could feel his gaze on her. Assessing. Watchful.

"The doctor said he wants you in the hospital."

"The doctor can go to hell." And she'd told him as much, several times already. She needed rest, not endless pokes and prods from curious medical staff.

"He says you're lucky to be alive."

She didn't feel lucky. She wiped the sweat from her forehead and opened her eyes. He was leaning forward, chin resting on his interlocked fingers, regarding her with an odd expression in his warm hazel eyes. Had it been anyone else, she might have thought it was concern.

"I asked them not to call the SIU."

One dark eyebrow arched upward. "They didn't."

Then why was he here? Checking up on her? She regarded him for a moment, then closed her eyes again. The rolling in her stomach was getting worse. The last thing she felt like right now was any sort of confrontation with her so-called partner. She just wanted to go home, to hide in the darkness. To forget the image of the blackened mess that Max's legs had become. "Any word from the hospital about Max?"

She could almost feel Gabriel's frown. "If Max is the proprietor of this dump, then yes. Third-degree burns, but nothing unsalvageable."

"Is he conscious?"

"No."

Damn. She needed to talk to him, needed to know why his girlfriend had tried to kill them both.

"Do you remember what happened?" he said.

She snorted. As if she could forget. "Yeah, I was attacked by an angry budgie."

His surprise rippled around her. "A shapechanger?"

"And probably a hooker, if I know Max. She was the one who clubbed me. When I woke, the office was on fire, and so was Max."

He was silent for a moment, yet his gaze swept over her, a touch that seemed both calculating and troubled. "Do you think she administered the Jadrone?"

She opened her eyes. "Max was given Jadrone? Why on earth would she do that? He's human."

"Not Max. You."

She blinked. "Me?"

He nodded. "Enough to kill, apparently. The doctor can't understand why you're still sitting here."

She stared at him. Not so long ago, her late partner, Jack, had said she wasn't human. She hadn't wanted to believe him. She had hoped it was yet another of his lies.

Jadrone didn't affect humans. It certainly couldn't kill them. But it killed shapechangers outright, and it could certainly kill shifters with a high enough dose. Her stomach rolled again, and sweat broke out across her brow. She put a hand to her mouth, battling to hold back the rising tide.

Damn it, she *was* human. The Jadrone *shouldn't* be affecting her.

"I'm going to be sick," she muttered. Gabriel grabbed a nearby container and shoved it under her mouth. Just in time. When she'd finished, he silently offered her a towel. She wiped her mouth and closed her eyes, leaning back again. "I need to sleep."

"No." There was a hint of alarm in his voice. "Not for the next twelve hours."

Not sleep for the next twelve hours? What drug was *he* on? "Just take me home, Gabriel. I'll answer all your damn questions after I've gotten some rest."

"If you rest, you'll die." His voice was tight, hinting at anger, barely suppressed.

She met his gaze. "What do you mean?"

"I mean that there's enough Jadrone in your system to kill several shifters. The doc wants you in the hospital. He doesn't know why you're still breathing, let alone conscious, but he's certain that if you do slip into sleep, you may never wake up."

"No hospital. And he's already told me I'm not going to die. He only wants to run tests on me." And she had no intention of being anyone's lab rat. Not for the sake of the doctor's curiosity, anyway. But . . . damn it, if she wasn't human, then what the hell was she? A changer who couldn't shapechange? And even if that *were* true, how would the budgie have known? For all intents and purposes, she presented as a human. It was only that unknown chromosome, and Jack's mysterious words, that suggested anything else. So why had the budgie tried to kill them? What had the fat man known—and what had *she* seen— that had forced the budgie's hand?

"What did you do or see in that office?" Gabriel's question mirrored her thoughts.

"I don't know." She rubbed her forehead wearily. "We were discussing Harry. Max knew something, something he was afraid of."

"Max was Harry's supplier?"

She nodded. "Jack and I used to bust him regularly. It didn't seem to make a great deal of difference to his business."

"Small-time supplier?"

"Medium. Max liked his freedom too much to ever get involved with the big syndicates."

Gabriel was silent for a moment, then he reached out, gently wiping the sweaty strands of hair away from her forehead. His touch felt so wonderfully cool against her fevered skin, it was all she could do to resist the temptation to lean farther into his caress. "You'd better come back to my place. It's safer, at least until the Jadrone has vanished from your system."

One minute he couldn't wait to get rid of her, and the next he was acting like he cared. What was going on with him?

"Haven't you got a murderer to catch?"

"Yes, but I can access the necessary reports from home. Can you walk?"

Just thinking about it made her stomach turn. "I'd keep the bucket handy."

"What about the sunlight? How badly is it affecting your eyes at the moment?"

"At the moment, it's not. Mainly because there's no light here in the ambulance."

A smile tugged the corners of his full lips. "But if you were outside, you'd be screaming, right?"

"Just a little."

"Then we'd better use the ambulance as transport." He raised his hand and tapped the wristcom's interface.

She closed her eyes, listening to the rhythm of his speech rather than his actual words. There was something very soothing in the resonance of his voice. Something that made her just want to drift—

"Sam!"

The word leapt through her brain and jarred every

nerve ending. She jumped, then opened her eyes and glared at him.

"What?"

"You were going to sleep."

"I was just resting my eyes, for God's sake."

"Yeah, right." He hesitated. Someone climbed into the front of the ambulance and the engine roared to life. "Tell me what happened in the office just before you were knocked unconscious."

"Nothing happened. Max wouldn't tell me anything, so I suggested his bird come down so I could talk to her."

"Did he tell you she was up there?"

"No, but I sensed her presence the minute I walked in."

"So she wanted her presence kept a secret?"

"Looks like it. Setting a fire to kill the two of us was going a trifle overboard, though."

"Not if she was involved with Harry as well as Max."

"Max usually has to pay for his fun, but I very much doubt Harry had to. And either way, it's *still* an over-the-top reaction." Her frown deepened. "I got the impression Max knew who Harry was with the night he died, but I got knocked out before he could say anything."

Gabriel leaned back and regarded her thoughtfully. "What makes you think Harry was with someone? There's no mention of it in the initial reports."

"I asked Max the question. He said he didn't know, but he was lying. He was so scared I could almost taste it."

"Then maybe Max was involved."

She shook her head. "That's not Max's style. He'll

push death in the form of drugs, but he'd never get involved in something like these murders. Max has standards, lines he won't step over."

"What did he say about supplying Harry with Jadrone?"

"Harry told him he didn't need the drug anymore."

Gabriel arched an eyebrow in surprise. "That's not possible—not if Harry was as addicted as you say."

"I know. He must have found some other drug to sate his need."

"Supplied, perhaps, by our mysterious shape-changer. Anything else you remember about her?"

"Yeah, she tried to shit all over me."

He smiled. "Birds shit when they're scared. Fact of life."

"And do you suffer this problem, Assistant Director?"

His smile widened, lending warmth to his angular features. "Hawks don't scare as easily as budgies."

Didn't scare at all, from what she'd seen. In the brief time they'd known each other, they'd been shot at, bombed, even gassed. The only time she'd seen the slightest hint of fear in Gabriel's eyes was when his brother Stephan had gone missing in the explosion at the SIU headquarters. Family mattered more than personal safety, it seemed.

His wristcom buzzed into the brief silence. He gave her an apologetic look, though she wasn't entirely sure why, then answered it. And the warmth lingering on his face quickly disappeared.

"What?" she said, the minute he hung up.

His expression was grim as he glanced at her. "It would seem our serial killer has just accelerated her schedule."

FOUR

GABRIEL LEANED SIDEWAYS AND BANGED on the communications hatch. The small door opened and light flooded in. Sam hissed.

"Change of direction. Head for 280 Elizabeth Street."

The ambulance driver nodded and the hatch closed, enclosing them in darkness once again.

"Who are you dumping me with?"

Though her voice was even, her underlying anger was something he could almost taste. She was so pale she looked like death, and the thought chilled him. He didn't want to lose another partner, but he almost had, yet again. "What makes you think I'm dumping you?"

"Well, maybe because you've used any and all excuses to keep me away from everything except paperwork?"

"I've done it for your own safety."

"Yeah, right. Tell that to someone who hasn't spent ten years with the State Police."

"And the mess you made interviewing Max proved just how capable you are as an SIU officer, didn't it?"

It wasn't a fair statement. Had their positions been reversed, he doubted if he'd have coped any better. And the Jadrone would definitely have killed him.

Her hands clenched briefly by her sides. It was the only sign of the fury he could feel pouring from her. "One of these days you're going to have to trust me."

"I do trust you." With both his and his brother's lives. He just didn't trust fate.

Not that he had much choice at this particular moment. As much as he *did* want to dump her somewhere safe, he actually couldn't. There were only two people he'd trust with her safety. And of those, Karl was still on vacation with the family, and Stephan had a series of high-level meetings to attend.

"Then start acting like you do," Sam countered. "Stop giving me inane tasks and start giving me some real work." She raised a hand, as if to stop his answer, then closed her eyes and leaned back against the ambulance wall. "It doesn't matter. Forget about it."

He watched a trickle of sweat roll down her pale cheek. "Sam, 280 Elizabeth Street is where the murder happened."

She opened her eyes, and her smoky-blue gaze swept him from head to foot. Then a slightly bitter smile touched her lips. "Ah. You can't dump me. You haven't got anyone you trust to watch over me."

She was altogether *too* perceptive. "Are you sure you're up to this?"

"I think the question should be are *you* sure I'm up to this?"

"Well, it wouldn't be a good idea to puke all over the evidence," he said, half in jest.

Her gaze narrowed. "I won't puke. I won't even comment, if that's what you prefer."

He grimaced. It was times like these, when all the laughter, all the warmth, had died from her face, that he really regretted what he had to do. Stephan was right; they did work well together. But two people had died simply because they'd had the ill fortune to be his partner. She would not be the third.

The ambulance jolted to a stop. She winced.

"Watch your eyes," he said, then opened the door.

The light flooded in, and though she made no sound, her eyes narrowed to little more than slits through which he could see the glimmer of tears. He climbed out, then held out a hand. After a slight hesitation, she accepted it and got out.

Above, the sky was leaden, the clouds so heavy they looked ready to burst. Thunder rumbled—an ominous sound that vibrated through his body.

She stopped and breathed deeply. Electricity tingled across his fingers where they touched her arm, a sensation that was warm rather than threatening. It was almost as if she were sucking in the power of the storm itself.

"You okay?" he asked.

Though she was still unsteady on her feet, she definitely looked better than she had five minutes ago. But that didn't really surprise him. When her feet had been cut to the bone by laser fire, she'd still managed to walk, when most people would have been unconscious.

"Yes." She took another deep breath, and color began to warm her cheeks. "Let's go."

She shook off his hand and walked unaided into the building. But despite the show of strength, her hand trembled when she punched the elevator button.

"Maybe you should stay down here and wait," he suggested, indicating the nearby bench.

She gave him a wry smile. "You're not getting rid of me that easily now."

He was beginning to see that. He followed her into the elevator and pressed the button for the twenty-third floor. The doors closed and the elevator zoomed upward.

She gulped at the sudden movement, and sweat began to redarken the red-gold strands of hair near her temple. She leaned back against the wall and closed her eyes, her full lips pursed. Fighting her stomach, he thought.

She had guts; there was no doubt about it. If he had been in the market for a partner, he certainly couldn't have found a better one.

The elevator came to a smooth stop. Once the door had opened, he led the way through the foyer. Two State Police officers guarded the door at the end of the corridor. He dug out his ID and flashed it at them. The two men stepped aside, allowing them access into another corridor.

The metallic odor hit almost immediately. The bloodshed had to be bad if he could smell it this far away from the body.

A third officer glanced up from a com-unit. "AD Stern?"

Gabriel nodded. "And Agent Ryan."

The detective glanced at Sam and almost instantly dismissed her. Either he wasn't very perceptive or he didn't care for female officers. Or maybe he was just plain stupid. Gabriel looked at the man's ID. "What have we got, O'Neal?"

"A woman, mid-twenties, in the reception area. Multiple knife wounds to the throat and stomach. Apparently she's the resident doctor here."

"Time of death?"

"Estimated to be around twelve-thirty."

During lunchtime, so they probably wouldn't find many witnesses. "No sign of forced entry?"

The detective shook his head. "No witnesses so far, either."

"What about the security cameras?"

"Several. We're investigating them now."

"I want copies sent to my office."

The detective nodded, and Gabriel continued to the small reception area.

It was worse than any of the previous murders. Blood had sprayed across the white walls, and splashed over the cheerful flowery patterns on the carpet and across the pristine whiteness of the reception desk. The body lay between the desk and the sofa, one hand outstretched, reaching for the nearby phone.

He glanced at Sam. She was sheet white. "Why don't you sit while I check out the body?"

"Why? Afraid I'll fall over and contaminate the crime scene?" She crossed her arms and glared at him mutinously. His anger surged, made worse by the fact that he had only himself to blame for her reaction. If he hadn't treated her like shit, she wouldn't be flinging it back at him. "Check the damn desk, then. See if there's anything there."

She nodded, and he squatted beside the body. Overhead, the CSM buzzed. "ID, please."

"Assistant Director Gabriel Stern and Agent Sam Ryan, SIU," he replied absently.

There was nothing patient, or gentle, in this woman's death. The murderer had slit her throat before gutting her—and had probably done so while she was still alive. There was tape stretched across her mouth and a look of terror permanently etched on her face. If it was the work of the same killer, something must have gone terribly wrong. Either that, or the madness that had set the killer on this path was getting progressively worse.

"It's not madness; it's anger," Sam said softly.

He looked up. She wasn't even looking at him, but somehow, she seemed to read his thoughts. It was almost as if there was some kind of connection between them—yet that was impossible, given that he'd learned to raise shields so strong that not even his twin could share his thoughts. "What do you mean?"

She motioned almost absently toward the victim as she continued to leaf through the paperwork on the desk. "The murderer was angry with this woman. There was no care taken here, no time. Look at the way the victim's throat was slashed. Another eighth of an inch, and our killer wouldn't have even hit the carotid."

He swept his gaze around the room. No ashtray full of cigarettes was sitting on any of the tables, and there was no immediate evidence that the killer had even stayed to watch this victim die. In fact, the only thing linking this victim with the other murders was the hole in her gut and the color of her hair.

"Why the anger here, though?" He glanced back at

Sam, interested in hearing her observations—or was it something else? Not the training of a cop, but a perception coming from her developing psychic talents? The clouded look to her eyes certainly suggested it was the latter. "Why not with the previous three victims?"

"That's presuming it's the same killer."

He nodded. She pursed her lips, her gaze finally rising from the desk and sweeping the room.

"Maybe in this case, it's something as simple as the white coat the victim is wearing." She hesitated, frowning. "I don't think the killer was expecting a doctor."

He frowned. "Yet the precision of the wounds on the first two victims indicates the killer has some sort of medical background. Our killer might even be a doctor. Why react so strongly against a fellow practitioner?"

Her gaze came to rest on his. Her blue-gray eyes were suddenly unclouded and amused. "Find the answer to that and you might just find your killer."

True. He rose and crossed to the windows. Outside, rain had begun to sheet down, and on the street below, men and women scurried for cover. This street was always busy—surely someone, somewhere, had seen *something.*

The killer hadn't cut an escape hole in the smoke-colored glass, so if he or she was a shapechanger, the killer certainly hadn't escaped that way this time. He headed into the doctor's office to check the windows there, but there was nothing. Nor did anything appear disturbed or out of place in the room itself. Meaning their killer had come in and out through the

front doors—either in human or nonhuman form—
and *had* to be on the security tapes.

He returned to the reception area. Sam was looking through the diary.

"Anything?"

She shook her head. "No appointments during
lunch. Looks like the postman had just been here,
though." She motioned toward a stack of mail, half
of which had been opened.

"We'll track him down, see if he saw anything." He
frowned and studied the corpse for several seconds.
"Someone must have seen the killer leave this time. If
she left in human form, she would have had blood all
over her."

"Has anyone checked the restrooms?"

"You up to it?" The trembling in her hands had
definitely eased and color was back in her cheeks.

She nodded and walked from the room. He squatted next to the body again. It didn't make any sense.
The killer had been so careful up until now, so why
do this? And why accelerate the time frame? He
scanned the room to check if they'd missed anything,
but there was nothing he could see. He swore softly
and thrust a hand through his hair as he pushed to
his feet. They needed to catch this psycho before he
or she killed again, and yet there was nothing—
absolutely nothing—here that could help them.

His wristcom beeped. "Yes?" he said, scanning the
room yet again.

"Think you'd better come down to the restroom."
Sam's voice was devoid of all inflection, giving no
hint as to what she'd found. "On my way."

He made his way over to the main door. O'Neal
stared at his com-unit, viewing the security tapes.

"Anything?" Gabriel said.

O'Neal shook his head. "Nothing yet."

"Did anyone check the restrooms either on this floor or on the floors above and below?"

"No, sir. Not yet."

Slack as well as dumb. Gabriel shook his head, took off his plastic glove and dumped it in the nearby bin. Then he headed down the hall to the restrooms. Sam was waiting outside the ladies'—which could have meant their killer was a female, as the presence of Heat at the last crime scene seemed to imply. Or maybe it was simply a case of the ladies' room being closer.

"What did you find?" he said, the moment he saw her.

"A few spots of blood splattered across the mirror. A bloodstained sweater wrapped in plastic and stuffed deep into the trash can." She pushed the door open and entered. Her movements were still slow, but becoming steadier.

He could only shake his head in amazement. She shouldn't even be alive, for Christ's sake, and here she was, walking and talking almost normally. Whatever race she was, it was a damn strong one.

"So our murderer came down here to clean up?"

"It would appear so."

The trash can's cabinet door stood ajar. The plastic bag was easy enough to see, wedged about halfway down. A CSM hovered nearby, light flashing to indicate it was recording.

He put on fresh gloves, reached into the bin and grabbed the plastic bag, holding it by two fingers in an effort not to foul whatever prints might be available. Blood smeared the plastic inside and out.

"Military green," she murmured. "Available in any disposal store."

"Yes." He tapped his wristcom and called O'Neal, instructing the young detective to bring the crime kit down. Then he glanced back at her. "Where are the blood spots?"

She pointed to an arc of five microscopic spots. Maybe the murderer had flicked her hair, spraying droplets across the mirror, but how had Sam spotted them? *He* could barely see them, and his hawk-sharpened senses were more attuned to things like this.

"The murderer is desperate." Sam stared at the spots, her expression becoming distant once again. "She knows we're closing in. She needs to get the job finished. Needs to fulfill promises made."

Her voice was as distant as her expression. He'd seen this type of thing before—the SIU employed several psychics who could read the emotions that lingered in otherwise empty rooms. But Sam had been tested repeatedly for psychic gifts, and she had repeatedly come up negative. That is, until she reached the SIU, where she'd registered as a neutral—a feat that should have been impossible.

Finley had said that it implied her abilities were so strong that she was able to void all the tests done on her.

"What promises?" He kept his voice soft, not wanting to jar her out of her trancelike state.

"To the dead." She hesitated, frowning lightly. "To her twin sister."

Emma Pierce was listed as an only child, but she was also adopted. So it might be worth checking to see if a mistake had been made. "Why is she killing these people?"

"They should not exist."

Her breathing was becoming too shallow, too quick. As much as he needed the insights, he couldn't let her continue. Not while she was still clearing the Jadrone from her system.

"Sam." He touched her arm lightly and she jumped.

Her gaze leapt to his, her expression confused and just a touch frightened. "What happened?"

"You were reading the room. Or the emotions in the room."

A shudder ran through her. "It felt like I was an observer in someone else's dream. I could see and hear what was going on, but I couldn't intervene."

He touched her cheek, gently wiping away a drop of sweat. "I think those psychic gifts you don't have are starting to come to the surface."

She stared at him and then shook her head. "Impossible! I was tested."

"The tests can be skewed. I think we should do more."

She reeled back as if he'd hit her. "No more tests. You promised!"

"I also promised to help you get answers about your past. That isn't going to happen unless you start cooperating."

"No." She crossed her arms, her look mutinous. "The last batch of tests almost killed me. I won't do any more."

She was talking about the tests that the bastard she'd once called her partner had performed. "Jack didn't care about you, only what you were and how he could use you."

"And are you so very different, Assistant Director?"

The barb struck home and his anger surged. O'Neal chose that moment to walk into the room, but he stopped abruptly, his gaze darting from Gabriel to Sam.

"Everything all right, sir?"

"Fine." Gabriel somehow managed to keep his voice even. "We found a bloody sweatshirt in the trash can. There is blood sprayed across the mirror. I want samples taken from both and sent to the labs ASAP. And next time, O'Neal, kindly make sure you do a proper sweep of the crime scene."

The detective flushed and nodded, and Gabriel shoved his hands in his pockets and walked from the room. He heard Sam murmur something to O'Neal, then her footsteps as she followed.

He punched the elevator button. She stopped behind him, her gaze burning deep into his back.

"If you've got something to say, then say it," she said. "Don't take your anger out on other people."

Normally, he didn't, but she had an uncanny knack of seeing what others didn't, and it both irritated and alarmed him. He turned to face her.

"I'm not Jack. I'm not using you for my own purposes. If I were, I'd keep you as a partner."

She crossed her arms, her expression cynical. "And that's supposed to make me feel better?"

It wasn't supposed to make her feel anything. "Sam, that birth certificate Jack gave you might be a fake."

"I know that."

"Then you should realize that the only true clue we may ever get lies in uncovering whatever that unknown chromosome in your system is. Remember, someone looped Finley's computer to stop us from accessing the test results. They may very well have bombed Central Security for the same reason." He hesitated, then added, "Damn it, Sam, don't you *want* to know what you are?"

She rubbed her arms and stared at him for several moments. "*Who* I am, yes. *What* I am? I don't know." Her voice was soft, face troubled. "I really don't know."

"Then you'd better decide quickly. People died because of the secrets in your past. How many more have to do so before you find the courage to face what you might be?"

She stiffened. "You're a bastard, do you know that?"

"Maybe I am. But at least I'm a realistic bastard."

They waited in silence for the elevator, then got in and headed back to the ground floor. She led the way out of the building. The rain pelted down, a cold gray curtain that quickly drenched them both. Not that she seemed to take much notice as she marched up the street to the nearest cab rank.

"What now?" she muttered, once they were both inside the cab.

"Now we go back to my place and view the security tapes from both Harry Maxwell's building and this one." The address he punched into the console was hers—she'd catch a cold, or worse, if she stayed in her current clothes, and he didn't have anything that would even come close to fitting her.

"Well, gee, don't *you* know how to show a girl a good time?"

He ignored the sarcasm in her voice. "We'll stop

and get some takeout, too. There's not much in the way of edible food at my place."

"There's a surprise."

She crossed her arms and stared out the side window, angry as all hell and fighting not to show it. He ran a hand through his wet hair and half-wished he could take back the words he'd said in anger. But, damn it, if she didn't start investigating just who and what she was, all hell could break loose. Her psychic gifts were coming to the surface. Why that was happening now, when she was almost thirty, he didn't know. But Sethanon had feared the emergence of those gifts enough to place at least one guard on her—though, oddly enough, he seemed reluctant to harm her physically.

It made no sense. Nothing about her past made any sense.

But he had a bad feeling they'd better start finding some answers. Jack had warned them that a war was starting, a war in which Sethanon planned to subjugate the human race as well as any nonhumans who sided with them, and he had a feeling Sam was a key to what might happen. Why else would Sethanon be so interested in her? And if she *was* a key, then he sure as hell was going to keep forcing her to chase her past and the memories she'd lost. Because they could be very important for everyone's survival. So perhaps she was right. Perhaps he *was* no better than Jack.

Except that she'd liked Jack. And she sure as hell did not like *him*.

Which was a damn shame, because if she weren't his partner, he would have been tempted to take her in his arms and kiss her senseless.

* * *

SAM LEANED BACK IN THE chair and stretched. She'd been sitting at this console for close to ten hours and her butt felt numb. As numb as her mind.

She rubbed her forehead. The ache had set in behind her eyes again, and her stomach was beginning to cramp—probably as a result of all the coffee Gabriel had given her in the last few hours.

It was time to give her eyes another break. Sighing, she turned away from the console. His apartment wasn't what she'd expected. Given his long hours, and the time he spent working on Federation projects, she'd expected his apartment to be sterile—a place where he came to sleep and regain strength, and nothing more.

Situated in Parkville, opposite the grand old Royal Park, the two-story apartment block was a carefully renovated remnant of the Victorian age. Gabriel owned the whole top floor, and the view from the front windows was a sea of green. It was like living in the treetops, she mused, and wondered if that was why he'd bought it. Perhaps it appeased some need in his hawk soul.

The color scheme within the apartment complemented the leafy view, with sandstone-colored walls and faded turquoise doors and frames. Brightly patterned rugs were scattered across the polished floorboards, topped by dark blue leather sofas that had seen better times. It reminded her of the southwestern décor in Stephan's house and yet, oddly enough, there were no photos of Stephan here—no photos of *any* family. Maybe it was a precautionary measure. Maybe he didn't want to risk anyone breaking in and discovering just whom he was related to. Certainly that information wasn't available on any computer; she'd checked the SIU files some weeks back.

Gabriel himself used the com-unit in the kitchen. His long legs, crossed at the feet, were stretched out under the table. No doubt he'd wander back in soon with more coffee to keep her awake.

The com-unit pinged softly. The tape had finished rewinding. She turned around. "Fast-forward to twelve fifteen, then play."

The murderer must have arrived sometime between then and twelve thirty. The doctor had patients booked up until twelve. Allowing the usual ten or fifteen minutes per patient, the last appointment would have walked out around twelve fifteen. The postman—or woman, as was the case here—had walked in at twelve eighteen, and the doctor had been alive and alone.

"Playing," the com-unit intoned.

She leaned sideways against the desk, propping her head up with her hand. This was the fourth time she'd watched this particular run of film. She could just about cue each person.

Yawning hugely, she watched the postwoman, dressed in a yellow raincoat, carry a handful of letters and a small parcel into the doctor's office. On the far edge of the screen, a man in a badly cut blue suit headed toward the stairs. Nothing further happened for a good five minutes; then the lunchtime rush began.

The yellow-clad postwoman walked back out. She glanced at the clock. Twelve twenty-two. After that, nothing. People moved in and out of the foyer, but no one went near the doctor's office. The initial report set the time of death as twelve thirty-one—nine minutes after the postwoman had left. Given the extent of the doctor's wounds, and the fact that she'd died reasonably quickly, it was doubtful whether the postwoman could have been involved. Besides, there wasn't a speck of blood to be seen on her uniform.

"Rewind tape to twelve twenty-two."

The computer hummed briefly. "Tape rewound."

"Find an ID on this woman." She pointed to the postwoman. Her details were probably in the initial report, but Gabriel had the folder and she didn't want to walk across the room to check.

"Search started."

She yawned again and glanced at her watch. It was nearly two o'clock. Surely Gabriel would let her go home soon and get some rest. Twelve hours had just about passed and she seriously needed sleep. Her brain felt like mush.

The tape continued running. She leaned on her hand again and watched it. People flowed through the foyer. A sandwich trolley came out of the elevator and was briefly mobbed by those few who didn't go out for lunch. She rubbed her forehead again, trying to ease the growing ache between her eyes. It didn't help.

"Gabriel, have you got any painkillers?"

"Yep. Hang on, and I'll get you some." His chair scuffed against the floorboards, then his footsteps moved across the kitchen. She returned her gaze to the screen. And saw the doctor walk out of the office.

At twelve forty-eight.

Seventeen minutes after she'd been murdered.

FIVE

THE KILLER WAS A MULTI-SHIFTER, Sam thought, staring at the woman on the screen. The counterfeit doctor wore a knee-length white coat and carried a plastic bag in her right hand. She kept her head down, loose brown hair all but covering her face, and headed quickly for the stairs.

"Rewind tape one minute, then freeze," she said, and glanced up as Gabriel walked into the room. "I think I've found your killer."

He handed her two painkillers and a glass of water, then leaned over the back of her chair and studied the image frozen on the com-screen.

"A shapeshifter?"

"A multi-shifter," she corrected, "not that it comes as much of a surprise. You said in your report that you suspected a shifter was involved."

He squatted down beside her chair, his face almost level with hers. "We suspected it, but this is the first evidence we've found to confirm it."

She frowned. "You found nothing on any of the other tapes?"

"No." His breath washed warmth across her face. "No evidence of anyone going in. The only form of exit appears to be the small hole cut into the bathroom windows."

"But that makes no sense." If the killer was a multishifter, how the hell was she getting away from the crime scene if not through any doors? "A small hole cut in a window points toward a shapechanger, not a shifter. Can someone be both?"

"Yes, but there are only three registered in Australia, and all those are accounted for."

"But isn't it possible that one or two have been missed?"

"Maybe." He scrubbed a hand across the dark line of stubble on his chin. "Did anyone enter the office close to the time of the murder?"

"The postwoman, but she came out at twelve twenty-two. I've begun an ID search."

"Good. Have you checked the tapes for the seventh floor?"

"Not yet."

He looked at the screen. "Display tape seven. Fast-forward to twelve forty-eight p.m."

The screen went blank. Gabriel went against current trends, having no character as the face of his com-units. No time for fun, she thought, even for something as minor as that.

The seventh-floor tape began to roll. The counterfeit doctor came into sight, quickly disappearing into the ladies' restroom. She was out four minutes later, hair wet but tied back off her face and still wearing the white coat. The elevator answered her call almost immediately. The doctor joined several other people already standing in the lift and was whisked away.

"Why keep the coat?" She met his gaze. "Why not dump it with the sweater?"

"Maybe she had nothing else to wear."

"But why not? This woman is meticulous. She gets in and out of crime scenes without being spotted—at least not until now. She knows there are security cams watching, and she knows how to get around them. Her timing with the doctor was perfect. So why wouldn't she pack a change of clothes?"

A smile touched his lips. "There's a limit to what you can hide when you shift form, you know."

She raised her eyebrows. "There is?"

He nodded. "Clothes don't change. Nor do watches, or shoes or bloodstained sweaters. The body image is all that shifts."

"But what about shapechangers? You grow feathers and talons, for Christ's sake. And I've never seen you wearing size-ten boots in your hawk form."

His smile widened, touching the corners of his eyes. "Nor will you. The rules vary for changers. No one knows why. It's just a fact that whatever we carry on our person becomes integrated within the animal persona."

"Weird." She frowned at the screen for a moment. "But that still doesn't answer my original question."

"You suggested in the doctor's office that the killer was angry. Maybe she didn't bring a change of clothes simply because she thought she was in control—until confronted by the doctor wearing a white coat."

"So our killer has an unpleasant history with doctors, might be a doctor herself, and is definitely a multi-shifter." She met his gaze. This close, flecks of green gleamed in the warm hazel depths of his eyes. "How many multi-shifters has the SIU got on file?"

"Worldwide? Several hundred, at least."

"I thought you said multi-shifters were rare."

"They are, compared to the number of regular shifters."

"Yeah, right." What other half-truths had he fed her? "How many of those have twins?"

He shrugged. "Twins run in families. It's not a side effect of being a shifter."

"So the first thing we do is search the files and see how many multi-shifter twins we have on record."

The warmth fled from his face. "The first thing *you* do," he corrected softly. "After you get some sleep, that is."

He was locking her out again—not that she was entirely surprised. He'd warned her of his intentions, after all.

"You can push as far as you like. I'm not quitting and I'm not giving up." Despite an effort to keep her voice flat, a hint of anger crept in. It was tempting, *so* tempting, to add that she wasn't going to die on him like his other partners had, but she held back. Maybe it was cowardice, or maybe it was instinct, but something suggested it was better *not* to say anything until he did.

He didn't reply, but simply rose to his feet and held out a hand.

She ignored it and rose. She brushed past him, trying to ignore the tingling warmth that resulted from such a brief contact, and walked over to the coffee table to collect her bag. "There's a cab rank down the street. I'll catch a ride there."

"It's two thirty in the morning."

"And I'm a cop with a gun. I think I can manage to survive a three-minute walk in the dark."

"I have no problem driving you home."

"But I have." She snorted softly, then added, "You can't play it both ways, Gabriel."

He raised an eyebrow. "I am merely offering you a ride home. Nothing more, nothing less."

"Yeah, right."

"Fine," he muttered, and made an oddly violent motion with his hand. "Go, then."

She walked out. And, for the second time in twenty-four hours, slammed a door shut with wall-shaking force.

GABRIEL GRABBED HIS COAT, THEN set his apartment's alarm sensors as he walked out the door. Once he reached the street, he changed shape and soared into the night skies.

He had no doubt Sam could survive the three-minute walk to the cab rank. Under normal conditions, he'd expect her to survive just about anything the streets could throw at her. But in the last twenty-four hours she'd been given an overdose of Jadrone and had had very little sleep. Her reflexes, strength, even alertness would be compromised. If someone *did* actually want to take her out, it would be the perfect time.

He spotted her within minutes—an angry-looking shadow striding toward the cab rank. He circled slowly while she climbed into the vehicle, then followed it through the quiet city streets.

She got home without incident. He waited until the

lights went on in her apartment, then wheeled away and headed for his brother's place in Toorak.

A bleary-eyed Stephan opened the door as Gabriel walked up the steps.

"Do you know what time it is?" Stephan asked.

"Yeah. It's time for a drink." Gabriel stopped on the top step and regarded his twin steadily. The shadows under Stephan's eyes were darker than ever, but at least he no longer looked like death. "Why are you up?"

"Lyssa's been throwing up half the night."

Gabriel raised his eyebrows. "She's close to term. Shouldn't the morning sickness be over by now?"

"It should be. And the term 'morning sickness' is definitely a misnomer." He stepped aside. "Let's go into the study."

Gabriel followed Stephan through the marbled entrance hall. It was hard to believe that only three months ago, this house had been little more than a crater in the ground. Everything was the same, right down to the knickknacks that lined the bookcase shelves.

Stephan closed the study door and walked to the bar. "Whiskey?"

"Double. No ice."

Stephan raised an eyebrow. "Trouble with the case?"

"No."

"Then what?"

Gabriel accepted his drink and swallowed half of it in one gulp. The liquid burned its way down his throat, hitting his stomach with the force of a hot brick. Not wanting to answer that particular question just yet, he said, "How are things going with Lyssa?"

Stephan shrugged. "As well as can be expected, given I was fucking another woman for six months."

"She could hardly blame you when that woman was her exact replica."

"Not exact." Stephan grimaced and took a long drink. "There were differences in behavioral patterns when I think about it. I should have picked them up."

"Hindsight is a wonderful thing."

"And all-hours puking isn't. Her feeling like hell isn't helping the situation." He swirled his drink around in his glass for a moment. "So, why are you here?"

"Because I hate being a bastard."

Stephan sat on the sofa and crossed his legs. "We're talking about your treatment of Sam?"

He nodded.

"Then the solution is simple. Stop being a bastard."

"The solution is simple, all right. You can transfer her to another section. Or another agent."

"I've already told you that's not going to happen."

Gabriel met his brother's gaze. Stephan smiled, though the smile never touched his eyes.

"You work too well together, Gabriel. It's almost instinctive, the way you two interact, and that's extremely rare."

"My partners have a horrible tendency to die in the line of duty. I told you the last time it happened that I will not go through that again." He downed more whiskey.

"If she is fated to die, it will happen, whether or not she's your partner."

Gabriel finished the whiskey and slammed the glass

down on the desk. Thrusting his hands into his pockets and unable to keep still, he began to pace.

"It damn well almost happened today."

Stephan frowned. "I read a report that mentioned her involvement in a disturbance at a nightclub. The owner's in intensive care." He hesitated. "Did she put him in there?"

"No. She went there to interview him, as he was apparently Harry Maxwell's regular Jadrone supplier."

Stephan's frown deepened. "Harry was human. Jadrone shouldn't affect him."

"That's exactly what I said. But according to her, Harry was a regular user—and one she'd busted frequently. The only reason he never ended up with a rap sheet was because Frank kept getting the charges dropped."

"But Frank's human, and I'm pretty sure his wife is, as well."

"And according to Sam's profile, she's also human, but she was given enough Jadrone to kill an elephant changer and it affected her the way it would affect any changer. The doctors who looked after her have no idea how she actually survived."

"The fact that she was given Jadrone suggests that whoever did the administering knew she was something other than human. And that begs the question: how? Especially given you, as a changer, should have sensed the changer in her."

"I know." Gabriel paused, thinking back to what she'd said. "I think the answer to why she was drugged is simple. According to Sam, she ordered the owner to tell his girlfriend to change shape. Yet the owner hadn't told her his girlfriend was amongst the other birds flying around."

Stephan frowned. "But why was she given Jadrone rather than simply being left to die in the fire like the owner?"

"That I don't know, and I'm afraid she was too loopy from the Jadrone to really remember anything useful about the attack."

"But you'll question her when she's recovered?"

"Of course." Gabriel walked across to the window and stared at the moon-washed garden. "Something else happened today, though. Something that worries me."

"What?"

He hesitated, wondering if he was doing the right thing coming here tonight, talking about this with his twin. If nothing else, it would open old wounds between them.

"I was in Melton when the attack on Sam happened," he said, after a moment, "but I felt the blow to her head, and the pain of the Jadrone burning through her body, as if it were happening to me."

"Well, well," Stephan murmured.

Well, well, indeed. The ability to link minds, to psychically share thoughts, or, in this case, emotions and pain, was very rare—a bond seldom found outside the domain of twins. But it was a connection he didn't want with Sam—or anyone else. Not even his twin.

"So we come to the real reason you're here tonight," Stephan continued softly. "You are being forced to face what you have denied for so long."

He turned and faced his brother. "Apparently so."

Stephan's expression held very little sympathy. But

then, Gabriel wasn't expecting a whole lot from him. Not when it came to something like this—something that had caused a rift between them for years.

"I told you it would happen someday. You cannot keep denying one part of your soul forever—not without consequences."

"And you're saying this link with Sam is a consequence of denying my link with you?"

"I'm saying it's possible. You may have developed shields strong enough to keep me out, but I am far from the strongest telepath there is."

"This isn't telepathy. This is something else."

"Then perhaps it's simply a rerouting of your talent."

"It's not. It's unlike anything I've ever experienced—"

"You've experienced nothing," Stephan said, his voice sharp. "You closed yourself psychically when Andrea died, and you haven't allowed that part of yourself to experience *anything*."

He turned away from the anger—the accusation—in Stephan's expression. "And you know why."

"Denying what you are will not change the events of the past. It will not bring Andrea back to life."

"Don't you think I realize that?"

"Then why do you cut yourself off? Why bury yourself in your work? Why give nothing of yourself to your friends or family?"

"You're a great one to talk about not burying yourself in work. How often do you see Lyssa?"

"Not often enough, that's for certain." The anger in Stephan's voice was stronger. "But at least *I* have a wife and a child on the way. You have nothing."

"I have friends." Though his brother, who *should*

have been closer to him than anyone else, couldn't really be counted as one of those.

"And a family," Stephan retorted. "Yet when it comes to your dreams and desires, you confide in neither."

Because he had no dreams. No desires. Only a wish to someday glide upon the wind and see where it might take him. "It's safer that way."

"Safer for whom?"

Safer for everyone—himself included. "I didn't come here to dissect past decisions."

"You never do," Stephan retorted, "but you might want to start talking to someone. If Sam has breached your defenses and somehow created a link that is strong enough for you to feel her pain, we need to know how. And why."

"That's part of the reason I'm here. I want the Federation labs to go through her test results and see what they can find."

"What do you hope the Federation labs can find that Finley couldn't?"

"The origin of that unknown chromosome. Maybe even the reason why, at the age of nearly thirty, she's beginning to develop psychic abilities."

A human normally developed psychic skills during puberty, and she was well past that. That it *was* happening now suggested nonhuman origins—as did her reaction to the Jadrone. Most nonhumans were slower in development, and for changers and shifters, at least, puberty hit at about thirty. And while Sam had all the physical characteristics of an adult, Finley's tests had showed otherwise. So why hadn't those tests also revealed a nonhuman link? Or did Finley's tests only look for the obvious? Maybe they needed to go deeper. Much deeper, and look for things like gene-splicing.

"Send the disk to Martyn. He'll take care of it."

"I'm also sending her to Doctor O'Hearn." O'Hearn was a nonhuman and rare species specialist, and though she wasn't strictly in the Federation's employ, she often worked closely with both them and the SIU. "I want the Federation to pick up the cost."

"Are you intending to ask Sam to join the Federation?"

"No. We can't afford to, not until we know more about her."

"Keeping her as a partner would be a surefire way of discovering more about her. Certainly better than trying to get rid of her."

"I'm not trying to get rid of her," Gabriel said, a note of frustration in his voice. "I never said I wanted her out of my life. I just don't want her as a partner."

"But you said it once yourself—Samantha's work is her life. Get rid of her as a partner, and you risk getting rid of her completely."

And if that happened, it would be a shame, because even from the beginning it had been obvious that they had the potential to be a whole lot more than friends. But he would not go there with a partner, not again. He'd made that mistake with Andrea, and it had damn near torn his world apart.

The study door opened, and he turned around. Lyssa, looking pale and drawn, peeked in.

"Gabriel," she said warmly. "How nice to see you."

He smiled. Ever the lady, even at three in the morning. Not that he saw her much in the early hours of the morning—if he had, he might have noticed the changes in her behavior a whole lot sooner. Might have suspected something odd was going on. "Liar. Hope we didn't wake you."

Her smile was as pale as her face. "No, I was puking my guts out and heard your voices. Is everything okay?" She glanced at the two of them anxiously.

"Everything's fine, Lys." Gabriel glanced at his brother and saw the worry etched on his face. He knew then that Lyssa was in more trouble than Stephan was letting on. Knew that it wasn't *just* their relationship that was having problems. He very much suspected that something was wrong with Lyssa's pregnancy. And it seemed he wasn't the only one refusing to confide in his brother—but that was *his* fault. If Gabriel wanted to change the relationship with his brother, then he would have to be the one to bend first. Only he wasn't sure that was even possible after so many years of keeping everyone at arm's length.

"Can I get you anything?" she continued softly.

"Yeah. Go back to bed and get some rest." Gabriel met his brother's gaze. "I can contact Karl later this morning, if you like. See what he recommends."

At the very least, he should have something to stop Lyssa's vomiting. If she lost any more weight, the child she carried would weigh more than she did.

"I'd appreciate that." Stephan rose from the sofa and placed his half-finished whiskey on the table. "I'll see you out."

"I know the way by now. You take care of Lys."

Stephan gripped his shoulder, squeezing lightly. "See you tomorrow, then."

Gabriel nodded and walked away. On the front

steps, he stopped and looked up at the stars. He wasn't ready to go home, nor did he feel like going to the office. The breeze tugged at his hair, throwing dark wisps across his face. Sometimes the answer to a problem could be found only when the mind was free from the clutter of thoughts.

It was a good night to surf the breeze, to relax and just enjoy the freedom of the skies. Changing shape, he let the wind tuck under his wings and rose swiftly into the starlit sky.

SAM DREAMED AGAIN OF JOSHUA. This time, he ran ahead of her, up the moonlit slope—a phantom she could see but not hear. When he reached the crest, he flopped on the grass, staring up at the stars.

She lay beside him, puffing like an express train, but Joshua breathed so softly she could barely even hear it.

"The Southern Cross," he said, pointing to a kite-shaped formation. "A symbol of freedom."

"Not our freedom." Only at night were they free to roam, and only then when the moon was down.

"People died on that symbol. And they will die again." He hesitated, and she felt his shrug. "Soon."

She stared at him. His face was remote, cold. She hated that expression. Feared it. "What do you plan?"

"Revenge. Freedom for us both."

"They will never let us go."

He smiled, but there was nothing pleasant about that smile. Just as there was nothing pleasant about the fire that sprang to life on his fingers. She knew *exactly* what that fire could do. "They will have no choice."

She shivered, then sat up and rubbed her arms. "I don't want anyone to die, Josh."

He didn't answer. She looked at him and a smile touched the corners of his lips. "You don't know what you want."

Yes, she did. A home. A mom and dad. Friends. A normal life. Everything she didn't have now.

"Dreams that can never be achieved. Not with what we are."

"And just what are we, Josh?"

She woke with a start, her heart racing even as the question seemed to reverberate through the darkness. For several seconds she didn't move, but simply stared up at the ceiling. Just who the hell was this Joshua she kept dreaming of? Someone close, of that she was certain. Maybe a brother or a friend. Someone from the time she couldn't remember, the years between her birth and her arrival at the state-run home.

But if these were true memories, and not some form of subconscious yearning, why were they coming back now? What had happened in the last few months to crack the wall that had hidden her past?

As usual, she had no answers to her questions. Sighing, she threw the bedcovers to one side and climbed out. It was nearly eight-thirty. Time she got moving. Given Gabriel's terseness last night, he'd probably put her on report if she was late for work.

She grabbed a coffee, then got ready, barely catching the nine-thirty tram into the central business district.

Her dim little hole at the SIU certainly hadn't improved any in the brief time she'd been away. She threw her bag across the back of the chair and sat down.

"Computer on."

Izzy's image flicked to life. "Good morning, sweetness. Have a good trip in?"

"Absolutely wonderful." There was nothing nicer than being wedged between a guy reeking of garlic and a woman who tried to pick her up. "How'd the searches go?"

Izzy sighed dramatically. "Do you know how many people have purchased Heat in the last month? Two thousand four hundred and eighty."

Sam raised her eyebrows. Given the hype surrounding the perfume, she'd expected the figure to be much higher—although, having tested the stuff herself, she could understand. There was nothing particularly outstanding about the fragrance—at least to her untrained nose, anyway. "Any chance of cross-referencing those people? I need to find a doctor."

The purple boa swung into action. "You do like delving into haystacks looking for needles, don't you, sweetie?"

"Favorite pastime. Just do it."

"As long as time is something you have plenty of."

Right now, it was the *only* thing she had plenty of. "Got another search for you, as well."

"Well, hallelujah!"

"I want you to search SIU records for multi-shifters with twin sisters. And do a separate search for multi-shifting quacks while you're at it."

"By quacks, I presume you mean the medical profession?"

"You presume correctly."

"Human or animal?"

She raised her eyebrows. She hadn't thought of that—there was nothing to say a vet couldn't have the knowledge to cut up a human efficiently. "Both. And cross-reference the results against the Heat results; see if we come up with any similar names."

"Your wish is my command."

She snorted softly. Izzy's tone was anything but compliant. "You found any history on the four men in the photo?"

"I certainly have."

"Show photo and results onscreen."

Izzy disappeared, replaced by the photo Sam had found in Peter Lyle's apartment. It came as no real surprise that the four men had been in the military and worked alongside Peter Lyle at Hopeworth. Hal White, the oldest of the four, had died a month before Lyle's murder. The other three—Roy Benson, Jake Cooper and Liam Haynes—were listed as retired. Their pensions were generous, even by military standards.

"Any details on Hal White's death?"

Izzy reappeared. "Checking police files."

If Izzy had gone directly to police files, Hal White's death was listed as something other than natural. While she waited for the results, she leaned back in her chair and massaged her temples. If this damn headache didn't go away soon, she might have to visit a doctor herself—something she normally tried to avoid.

"Hal White's file remains open, sweetie. Cause of death unknown."

Interesting. Maybe it was fate that two of the five

friends had been murdered within a month of each other. Then again, maybe it wasn't. "Grab a copy of the case report for me. And send the current addresses of the three remaining men to my wristcom."

"Proceeding. Anything else I can help you with?"

"Yeah, the results for the priority-one search."

"Results being displayed."

There wasn't much to see. Of the four men listed on the birth certificate, only one—Mark Allars—was still alive. Interestingly, he lived only one block away from Roy Benson, one of the three remaining men in the photograph. None of the women were still alive. All eight had worked at the elusive Hopeworth.

She tapped a finger against her lips. "Do we have photos of any of these people?"

"Nothing available on file."

"What about their life before they joined the military?"

"Nothing available there, either, sweetie."

She raised her eyebrows. There should have been school and medical records, at the very least. "Why not?"

Izzy gave an exasperated sigh. "I'm a computer, not a mind reader. How would I know?"

"Have you tried asking Hopeworth for details?"

"No, and I wouldn't back your chances of getting an answer if I did."

Neither would she, but she had nothing to lose by trying. "Put in a formal request for information on these eight, as well as the four men in the photograph."

"Requesting."

"Good." Sam pushed her chair back and rose. "If

you happen to get any results back from the other searches, forward them to my wristcom."

"Consider it done, sweetie."

"And check out a car from the pool for me."

Izzy tapped a chicken-like foot for several moments. "Car nineteen on standby."

"Thanks, Izzy."

"Have a nice day," Izzy said, before the screen went blank.

Sam snagged her bag off the back of the chair and headed down to the car pool. An attendant handed her the keys and a pass-out to sign. She scrawled her signature across the bottom, then threw her bag into the back of the car and climbed in.

After joining the late morning traffic, she cruised through the city streets, headed for Kensington. Roy Benson, like his other three friends, lived in a suburb befitting the image of an independently wealthy retiree. Only Peter Lyle had made an attempt to hide his wealth—though not very successfully, given he had million-dollar paintings all over his walls.

It took her twenty minutes to get to Kensington. She stopped under the shade of an old plane tree, then climbed out and studied the two-story building across the road. It wasn't, as she'd expected, a house, but rather a retirement home—and an expensive one at that, if the gold fittings on the front door were anything to go by.

She collected her bag, slammed the car door closed, and walked across the road. She'd barely reached the steps when heat flashed across her skin—a white-hot rush that exploded her senses outward.

A kite was close—so close its evil itched at her skin and turned her stomach.

Her gaze darted upward. The kite was on the roof somewhere, moving to the left. She'd have to find the stairs and get up there . . . But the thought was cut off as glass shattered.

A second later, the screaming began.

SIX

GABRIEL GLANCED IMPATIENTLY AT HIS watch. Joan Hartwell, the postwoman who'd delivered the mail to the doctor thirteen minutes before she'd been murdered, should have been back from her rounds by now. He hoped she was just late and not the victim of some careful after-the-event cleanup by the murderer.

He crossed his arms and leaned a shoulder against the wall. Around him, machines hummed, sorting through the mail, watched by disinterested men and women of various ages. No one talked—probably they couldn't be bothered, given the noise and the fact that they all wore ear protection. A lonely job, and not one he ever would have opted for. The lack of human interaction would have driven him crazy. Despite what his twin seemed to think, he wasn't a loner. Not by a long shot.

"Oi! Agent Stern!" He glanced around. A big man in a sweat-stained brown shirt pointed toward the back door. "Joannie just came in."

Gabriel waved his thanks and headed toward the

back. Joan Hartwell was a weedy-looking woman with short black hair and pockmarked skin.

"Heard you were looking for me," she said, opening a locker that had seen better days. "What can I do for you, Agent Stern?"

"Just a routine follow-up. You heard about Dr. Brandon being murdered yesterday?"

Joan nodded. "Yeah, shame that. She was a nice lady."

"When you delivered the mail yesterday, did you see or hear anything suspicious?"

The woman shook her head. "I wasn't even at work yesterday, so I didn't deliver anything."

Gabriel frowned. "The security tapes very clearly show you delivering the mail."

"Then your security tapes have been tampered with. I was home all day. Ask the husband—that useless bit of manhood took the day off to look after me."

"Do you know who took over your mail run, then?"

"Ask the boss." She waved a hand vaguely in the direction of the offices.

"Thanks for the help," Gabriel said, unable to keep the slight edge of frustration out of his voice.

Joan nodded. "No prob."

Gabriel headed up the stairs and found Joan's boss—a small, harried-looking man who gave him the name of Joan's replacement, then blithely informed him that she hadn't been seen since her shift yesterday. Gabriel swore softly and went back to his car. After punching in the code for auto-drive, he set the course for SIU headquarters. Then he leaned an arm against the window, blindly watching the traffic slide by. The killer was a multi-shifter; that much was obvious. But maybe, just maybe, she was also a rare shifter-changer hybrid.

He scrubbed a hand across his jaw and then reached across to the onboard computer.

"Access the sweep report for Emma Pierce."

"Identification required."

"Assistant Director Stern. Badge number 5019."

"Voice patterns correct. Report online."

Emma Pierce had died of a massive heart attack. There was no evidence that the attack was anything but natural. Interestingly, the autopsy also showed that Emma had no ovaries. Tests indicated they'd been surgically removed somewhere between twenty-five and thirty years ago.

Which was when Emma was still a part of Hopeworth. Maybe the killer knew Emma. Maybe she knew the reasons behind the removal of Emma's ovaries. Maybe these killings were some form of revenge.

Though why attack four people who were barely a gleam in their mothers' eyes twenty-five years ago?

Unless, of course, their parents were somehow connected to Hopeworth and what had been done to Emma Pierce. Though that didn't make much sense, given that with the first two victims, at least, Emma Pierce was listed as their birth mother . . . unless, of course, those four people had come from eggs harvested from Emma's ovaries.

He read through the rest of the report. Cellular and DNA samples taken from clothes and other personal items in the second bedroom indicated that the boarder was closely related to Emma. Probably her sister, her mother, or even her daughter. Yet Emma was reportedly an only child, and both her parents died in a car crash when she was three months old. Her ovaries had been removed at some point in her late twenties, and while she certainly *could* have had children before that happened, there was no record of it. And certainly no record of any implant procedure later on in her life that would account for her being listed as the mother of all four victims. Which didn't, of course, preclude the possibility of Emma's eggs having been harvested before their removal and implanted into a surrogate.

But what did Hopeworth have to do with it all? What he needed was someone who knew a whole lot more about that place—someone like Mark Allars, who wasn't only a childhood friend of his father's as well as one of the names listed on Sam's certificate, but also a man who'd spent thirty-five years working at Hopeworth.

And it might be damn interesting to see the old man's reaction to Sam.

He reset the auto control for Kensington, then got out the wristcom and dialed Sam's number.

THE SCREAMS WERE COMING FROM the second floor. Sam flashed her ID at security and ran for the stairs, taking the steps two at a time. By the time she reached the second floor, all the nursing home's residents seemed to be milling in the corridor. Many more screams had joined the first, and the sound was almost deafening.

"SIU, folks. Please clear the area!" She had to shout to be heard above the din, and even then it did no good. Everyone ignored her—or perhaps they had their hearing aids turned down to cut out all that noise.

She pushed her way through until she reached the room at the far end of the corridor. Inside, the kite had sheeted its victim. Two nurses were gamely attacking the creature with brooms, alternatively sobbing and screaming for help.

"SIU, ladies. Step away!"

The two women looked up, relief etched across their faces when they spotted her. When both stepped away, she fired the stun gun at the creature's head.

It looked up and snarled, but she kept firing. The creature rose, shaking its head as it backed toward the window. Then it turned and jumped out. She ran over. The creature was fleeing for the nearest tree, white flesh billowing in the breeze.

There was a fire escape to the left of the window. She clambered out, then hesitated, glancing back. The nurses, their faces still white, were beginning respiration on the victim. Given the bloody condition of his face and chest, she didn't hold out much hope, but at least they were trying, no matter how gruesome the task was.

"I'll call an ambulance," she said, and immediately did so.

"Thank you," one nurse said. Her expression said it all; for all intents and purposes, the victim was dead. But that wouldn't stop her from at least trying. Sam nodded and ran down the rusting metal stairs. Her wristcom vibrated, indicating an incoming call. She glanced at it, saw it was Gabriel and groaned inwardly. The man had a knack for catching her at the wrong moment. She hit the answer button.

"What?" She jumped past the remaining five steps

and hit the ground running. The kite had taken to the treetops, jumping from one to the other like some great white bat.

"What's wrong?" Gabriel's voice, instantly on edge.

"A kite just attacked one of the four men in the photograph I took from Lyle's."

"Where is it now?"

"Heading west up Racecourse Road."

"Where are you?" His voice had a resigned note. He obviously had a pretty good idea of where she was.

"Right on its tail, figuratively speaking."

"I see you now."

He did? Why the hell was he in Kensington? A gray Ford slowed to a stop beside her and the door flung open.

"Get in," he ordered.

She did. After securing her seat belt, she leaned forward and watched the kite jump across the treetops. "It appears to be heading for the racecourse."

"It probably has some type of escape route there."

"I thought you said these things were brainless. And that they were only active at night."

"Obviously, we were wrong—on both counts."

"Are you admitting that the SIU doesn't know everything?" she said, slipping a note of shock into her voice.

His quick glance suggested he was not amused. She grinned and continued to watch the kite. If any of the pedestrians noticed the monster above their heads, they gave little indication. Nor did the passing traffic seem to see it. Maybe such monsters had become an everyday event, or maybe people simply thought it was a sheet tumbling in the breeze.

The creature leapt over the race ground's fence and disappeared from sight. Gabriel swore, then spun the wheel and aimed the car straight at the nearby gates.

"Hang on," he said, almost as an afterthought.

The engine roared as the car accelerated. As the gates loomed close, Sam closed her eyes, braced her feet and hung on grimly to her seat belt. The car slammed through the gates, the impact smashing the front of the car and throwing her forward, then back, as the air bags popped. Gabriel swore as the car skidded sideways and came to a jarring halt. "Can you still see it?"

She couldn't see a damn thing above the white balloon of the air bag. Sam opened the door and climbed out. The kite was still running through the trees, its white body dappled with shadows.

"I see it."

"Good. Catch."

She looked around in time to see him toss a laser rifle her way, then slam the trunk shut.

"Aim for its neck," he said. "Cutting its head off is the only way to kill it."

Just like a vampire, she thought bleakly. Maybe they *were* some sort of vampire offshoot.

They tracked the kite through the parking lot. The creature was running on all fours, and it was amazingly fast. She ran flat out, but she could barely keep up with Gabriel, let alone the creature.

"Listen," he said. "Can you hear that?"

Who could hear anything past her labored breathing and pounding footsteps? But she frowned, concentrating, and after a few seconds, caught it—the soft *whump, whump* of rotor blades. A helicopter, approaching fast. "Sounds like someone's coming to collect their pet."

"Maybe we should let them, then."

"I thought SIU policy was to kill on sight."

"It is, but these things keep appearing. I think it's about time we learned from where."

The kite stopped and stared skyward. Gabriel halted behind the cover of several old elms. She stopped beside him and tried to catch her breath. So much for thinking she was fit. Maybe she'd better start heading back to the gym.

The helicopter came into sight—a long red and silver bird that gleamed in the afternoon sunlight. She shaded her eyes and stared up at it. Was that some sort of cannon hanging out the side of the helicopter?

"Fuck, they're going to shoot it." Fear burned through Gabriel's voice. He flung an arm around Sam's waist and pushed her to the ground, holding her tight as he covered her body with his.

Behind them, all hell broke loose. Asphalt and dirt fired into the air, and then a wave of heat burned over them, thick with the smell of burned flesh. Sam threw her arms over her head and cowered under the protection of Gabriel's warm body. Another bomb exploded, closer this time. Huge clumps of black asphalt rained around them. Gabriel's shudder ran right through her, then she gasped as a sharp twist of pain ran along her calf.

Then nothing. For several long minutes, they simply lay there. The sound of the helicopter faded into the distance. All she could hear was the crackle of flames as they licked through the trees behind them, and the thunder of her heart, beating in rapid time with Gabriel's.

"You okay?" he whispered, his breath tickling warmth past her ear.

"I think so. You?"

"A rock has torn a hole in my jacket, but other than that, I'm fine."

She smiled. He sounded more aggrieved about the jacket than he did about the fact that he was probably cut as well. He rolled to one side, allowing her to sit up. Obviously, beheading wasn't the only way to kill kites. Blowing the shit out of them worked fairly well, too. Two gaping wounds now marred the parking lot—one where the kite had stood, and the other just before their row of trees. The old elms had no doubt saved their lives.

Gabriel tapped his wristcom and called in the fire brigade as well as an SIU cleanup team. When he'd finished, she motioned toward the craters.

"Someone didn't want to risk anyone following their pet."

He nodded. "They must have been watching with binoculars. Interesting that they chose to blow up the kite rather than us. They must have an abundant supply of them."

"Now *that's* an ominous thought!"

He rose and held out a hand and she let him pull her to her feet, her fingers almost lost within the heat of his.

"So, what happens now?" She gave his hand a light squeeze, then pulled hers away.

"Normally, we'd go back to headquarters and fill in the required mountain of paperwork."

She raised an eyebrow. "I sense a 'but' coming here."

"But I think it's more important right now that we go visit old Uncle Mark."

She frowned. "Who's Uncle Mark?"

"Mark Allars."

Anger rose, and she had to clench a fist against the sudden urge to whack him across the ear. "You *know* him?"

His gaze, when it met hers, held absolutely no expression. She might as well have been staring at granite. "He's an old friend of my father's."

"And you kept that from me? Knowing Allars was one of the names on my birth certificate?"

"You told me not to push you."

"But I didn't tell you to hold back vital information!" She stopped and shook her head. "My future lies in my past; you said that yourself. You keep saying you want me to discover who and what I am, yet you hold back something like this, something that could provide a vital clue. Why?"

"Because if you were ready to know, you would have done something. How long did that certificate sit in the drawer before you gathered the courage to even do a search on the names?"

"You tell me. You obviously went through my drawers to find it."

His gaze slipped from hers. "I was looking for a pen to write you a note."

A note she never got. "Why? Did the email go down that day?"

He shoved his hands in his pockets and turned away. The left shoulders of his jacket and shirt were torn, revealing several cuts. Blood oozed down his lightly tanned shoulder blade.

"Maybe," he said, after a moment, "I just wanted to say hello in person."

"More likely you were ready to berate me for not finishing some inane task you'd set." She glanced over her shoulder as the wailing sirens drew abruptly closer. Two fire engines had entered the parking lot. Behind the trucks came two gray Fords.

"I'm not always a bastard, Sam."

No, sometimes he could be infuriatingly nice; at other times, just infuriating. Then there were the times when he just looked at her, as if contemplating a fantasy he would never allow . . .

The two Fords pulled to a halt in front of the stand of trees. Three men and a woman climbed out. Gabriel walked across and chatted to them for several minutes, then came back, carrying two plastic bags.

"Here's a pair of pants to change into." He tossed her a bag. "I want that leg seen to before you do, though. You're bleeding fairly heavily."

She glanced down. Her right boot was covered in blood, yet she hadn't even felt any pain. It was amazing what fear and anger could do. "Whose clothes are we borrowing?"

"No one's. I asked Sandy to pick something up."

"Sandy being the blonde, I gather?"

"Yes."

"So how does she know my size?" She didn't bother asking how Sandy knew *his* size. That was patently obvious.

"I told her you're roughly the same size as her." His voice was as cold as the look in his hazel eyes. "She's got a medi-kit in the car. Get over there and let her look at that wound."

"Immediately, sir," she said, and saluted him.

His gaze narrowed and he muttered something she couldn't quite catch before turning away. *Good,* she thought. It was about time she started getting some of her own back. She walked over to the second car. Sandy was your average model type—leggy, a figure to die for, and sapphire-colored eyes. Stunning, in other words—though the term "bitch" also lingered in Sam's thoughts.

"Agent Ryan," Sandy greeted her, a warm smile touching her full red lips. "You'd best sit down while I tend to that wound. You're losing a fair amount of blood there."

Sam felt her hackles rising and couldn't understand why. The woman was being nice, for Christ's sake. Maybe *that* was the problem. It was something she wasn't entirely used to—especially given her partner's behavior of late.

She sat on the backseat and pulled up her pant leg. "I'll survive."

Another white smile flashed, revealing teeth that were as perfect as the rest of her. Sandy knelt, medikit in hand. "Yeah, I suppose you're used to it, being Gabe's partner."

Gabe. Not Stern, not even Gabriel. Gabe. "You two are friends, I gather?"

"Old friends," Sandy agreed, without looking up.

No dark roots, she thought. Either the dyeing techniques had improved dramatically or the woman was a natural blonde. "Do you still go out?"

"Occasionally. When we've both got free time."

Which confirmed what she'd thought earlier. And shot her theory that Gabriel was little more than a hermit who lived for work to hell. "That's nice."

"It usually is," Sandy agreed, glancing up.

The look in her eyes left Sam in no doubt that she was referring to horizontal rather than vertical pursuits. And somewhere deep inside, a vague spark of jealousy stirred. This woman saw a side of Gabriel she probably never would—but it was a side she *wanted* to see, and with a fierceness that was totally surprising.

Of course, to have a chance of seeing *that* side, she'd have to either stop being his partner or stop constantly sniping at him. And she wasn't sure which was the lesser of two evils.

"You can change in the car, if you like. I'll make sure the men don't bother you."

Like that was going to worry her, especially after ten years of sharing locker rooms with the men in State. But she nodded. Sandy picked up the medi-kit and shut the door, then sauntered across to the fire trucks to join Gabriel and the three other agents.

The pants turned out to be a pair of black denim jeans that fit like a glove. She wondered how Gabriel had guessed her size so precisely, because she and Sandy definitely weren't the same size. He'd certainly never got into *her* pants, and waist size wasn't something she'd felt inclined to mention. She threw her dark gray slacks into the bag, then climbed out of the car.

Sandy had finished tending to Gabriel's wounds and was currently standing shoulder to shoulder with the man. They made a good-looking couple, Sam thought, and she resolutely stomped on the desire to march over there and wedge them apart.

Instead, she leaned against the trunk of the car, crossed her legs to take the weight off her injured calf and waited. Gabriel finally walked over about ten minutes later, but not before giving Sandy a nice little kiss on the forehead.

God, anyone would think the man meant more to her than just an attraction that was never going to lead anywhere.

"Just got a report from the home—Roy Benson didn't make it," he said, stopping several feet away and regarding her somewhat warily.

"No surprise, given he'd had half his face and chest sucked off."

"Yes." He hesitated, then added, "Ready to go?"

She waved a hand. "After you."

He didn't move. "Sandy's just a friend."

"Look, it's really none of my business, is it? Let's just go."

He regarded her for a moment, then nodded. "We're taking Sandy's car. Mine's probably too bent to drive."

Just like its driver. The retort tingled on the tip of her tongue, itching for release. But if she annoyed him too much, he was likely to give her some inane task and send her hiking back to headquarters. She climbed into the front seat and slammed the door instead. Slamming doors was undoubtedly childish, but right then she was feeling particularly childish.

He started the car and headed back to Kensington. A third gray Ford sat outside Roy Benson's retirement home—obviously, Gabriel had called in a cleanup team to tend to the second kite attack. She wondered why. Surely it was a task he would normally have forced her to handle, especially given that it might be connected to Lyle's murder.

He drove on. Mark Allars lived a block away from

the retirement home in a single-fronted Victorian-style house that was probably worth a fortune, despite its run-down appearance. She studied the building as she climbed out of the car. The small front yard was filled with gate-high weeds, and the window to the right of the door was boarded up with wood. It looked abandoned—until you looked up and saw the state-of-the-art satellite dishes sitting on the roof.

The gate creaked when Gabriel opened it. Sam limped through and knocked on the door.

"Who the hell is it?" a rough voice demanded.

She raised her eyebrows and glanced at Gabriel.

"He's your average, cranky recluse," he said, then raised his voice slightly. "It's Gabriel Stern. Charles's son."

Footsteps shuffled toward the door. Seconds later it was flung open. An old man stood before them, wearing blue pajama bottoms and a battered, smoke-stained sweatshirt. His feet were bare, his toenails yellow and a good inch longer than his toes.

He leaned forward, peering at Gabriel with red-ringed, watery eyes. "So it is. Fancy that." Then his gaze turned to Sam and recognition flickered through the rheumy eyes. He stiffened, his knuckles white as he clenched the door.

"You," he breathed softly. "You're dead. They said you were dead!"

SEVEN

Sam glanced briefly at Gabriel, then back to Allars. "I have to say, I don't feel dead."

The old man blinked, and then he smiled. "You don't look it, either." His red-rimmed gaze went back to Gabriel. "What game are you playing here, son?"

"Mark, this is my partner, Sam Ryan."

Allars studied her for a moment. "No relation to Meg Moore, then?"

Hope leapt. Meg Moore was one of the four women listed on Sam's birth certificate. "I might be. I'm not really sure."

"Interesting. You look the spitting image of her." He hesitated and leaned close. His breath was a lethal combination of whiskey and salami. "Except for the eyes. Meg had real pretty green eyes."

Gabriel touched the old man's arm, drawing his attention away, and Sam took a deep breath of fresh air.

"Mark, do you mind if we come in?" he asked. "We have a few things to discuss with you."

"Sure thing, son. Just don't mind the mess." He stepped back and opened the door wide. "First door on your right."

Sam limped in after Gabriel. The air in the old house was a combination of staleness, sweat and old person. Dust lay thick on the baseboards and telephone table, and in the hallway, spiders hung in ropes from the ceiling. The old man obviously spent most of his time in the living room, because the dust and webs were absent there. Instead, newspapers and betting slips were scattered all over the coffee table and small sofa. A TV dominated one corner, and a comfy old recliner sat several feet back from it, one arm lined with remotes.

Gabriel swept the newspapers lying across the sofa into a pile, then stacked them in one corner. Sam sat down in the cleared space. Gabriel sat next to her, his thigh brushing hers, sending little tingles of electricity up her spine. She ignored it, though part of her wanted to confront it—confront him—about the awareness and what could be happening between them. If he ever let it.

Damn it, what was so wrong with her that he didn't want her as a partner and wouldn't consider her as a potential lover?

Allars shuffled across to the recliner. "Now, what can I help you with, son?"

"Emma Pierce. You recognize that name?"

"Sure thing. She worked at Hopeworth, same as Meg and me."

"What on?"

Allars smiled slightly. "Secrets Act, son. Even now, I can't talk about it."

"Can you remember who else you were working with at the time?" Sam asked quietly.

"It's just the body that's gotten old, girlie, not the mind." He hesitated, rheumy eyes distant. "Let's see—in my project there was Meg, Mike Shean, David Wright, Jeremy Park, Alice Armstrong, Rae Messner and Fay Reilly."

Sam crossed her legs, not just to ease the ache in her calf, but to keep in check the sudden rush of excitement. Those names were all on the birth certificate. Finally, she'd found someone who might know something.

"And Emma?" Gabriel asked.

Allars shook his head. "No. She was several years younger than us. That was a completely different project."

"Different how?" Gabriel's voice held a touch of impatience. "And don't quote me that 'secrets' rubbish. You haven't worked at Hopeworth for a good twenty years, and the project's probably obsolete by now."

Allars's smile was jovial, but there was something almost cunning in his eyes. "You'd be surprised."

"Mark, four people have been murdered in the last week. The only connection we have between any of them is Emma Pierce and Hopeworth. We have to find out what Emma was involved in. It may provide our only real hope of finding the murderer."

Allars's gaze was assessing. "Why don't you put in a request to Hopeworth itself?"

"I have," Sam said, and Gabriel gave her a brief look of surprise. Why, she had no idea, when it was the logical next step. "But you and I both know I'll only get the runaround. We need to catch this woman before she kills again, and we need you to help us."

"I like you, girlie. You've got guts."

Sam raised an eyebrow. "Does that mean you intend to help us?"

"I'm not sure that I can." Allars shifted slightly, bumping one of the remotes onto the floor. "But what's in it for me if I do?"

"Maybe your life."

Allars's rheumy gaze met hers. In it, she saw a shrewdness that spoke of a sharp intelligence. The aging body was definitely no indication of the mind trapped inside.

"Now what makes you say that?"

"Do the names Hal White, Peter Lyle and Roy Benson mean anything to you?"

"Yeah. Benson lives a block away."

"Lived," Gabriel corrected bluntly. "He was murdered about an hour ago."

The old man raised an eyebrow. "And you're thinking I might be next?"

"We don't know, Mark. Nor do we know if the murder of White, Lyle and Benson is related in any way to our serial killings."

"But they could be?"

"Maybe."

The old man sighed. "Lyle, White and Benson were three of the eighteen scientists involved in our project."

"What about Cooper and Haynes?" Sam asked.

Allars nodded. "Them, too."

So did that mean someone was going after people who worked at Hopeworth? And how did the death of Emma Pierce and the murder of the scientists link to the serial killings? Because Sam was sure they were linked. It was just too much of a coincidence for both these killings to be happening at the same time.

She leaned on the arm of the sofa and covertly massaged her temple. Her headache had sprung into high gear again. Maybe it was working in sympathy with her calf, which had at least died down to a muted ache. "What project were they working on?"

"In truth, I can't really say. It was real hush-hush. All I know is that it went by the code name Penumbra."

Penumbra? *Where in hell did the military get these names?* "How were you involved?"

Allars smiled. "I was a lab rat, much the same as the others. I provided cell samples, semen samples, stuff like that."

If Hopeworth was taking cell and semen samples, they were obviously delving into genetics. "For what reason? Isn't Hopeworth a weapons development center?"

"Yeah, they are. But there's all kinds of weapons, girlie."

Meaning Hopeworth was developing human—or rather, nonhuman—weapons?

Gabriel rubbed a hand across his chin, his expression thoughtful. "Were the other seven people involved in your project shifters as well?"

"No, I was the only shifter. David was a changer, Meg a werewolf and Alice a vampire. I'm not real sure about the other four. I didn't really have a lot to do with them."

Or he didn't really want to talk about them, for whatever reason. She tried a different tack. "What about the other scientists on the project? You said there were eighteen in total."

"Most died some fifteen years ago. A massive fire took out half of Hopeworth, and what wasn't destroyed by the fire was taken out by a quake. There were half a dozen other projects destroyed as well, I believe. I think Cooper and Haynes survived, but I have no idea where they might be nowadays."

She remembered her dreams, remembered the fire that had danced across Joshua's fingers, and a chill ran down her spine. Were the two connected? Was she—were they—Hopeworth brats?

"Hopeworth still stands, so the quake and fire obviously didn't destroy everything. Surely they had backups?"

"That's the thing no one can figure out. There was a good fire prevention system in place, but none of it worked. Everything was destroyed. The buildings, the computers, every scrap of data on Penumbra— backup systems, storage areas, everything—including the personnel who were in the buildings at the time. Nothing escaped."

"Nothing except five men." If the motive was revenge, why leave five alive? She glanced at Gabriel. "Maybe someone's making amends for a past miss?"

"But why wait fifteen years? It makes no sense."

"That it doesn't, lad. Especially when whoever set fire to Hopeworth managed to get in and out without ever being seen. If they could do that, they could finish it off properly."

"Could it have been an inside job?"

"Doubtful. Everyone in Hopeworth is microchipped. Every move is tracked."

Someone had microchipped her. Was that confirmation that she'd been a part of Hopeworth?

"Were there many families at Hopeworth?" Gabriel asked, obviously following her line of thinking.

Allars snorted. "Hopeworth is no place for kids, believe me."

"Then why do they employ an obstetrician?"

The old man shrugged. "The military has many strange ways."

"What about you, Mark?" she asked. "Did you ever have kids?"

Allars's smile held more than a little bitterness. "I couldn't. Some of the tests they did on us back then made us sterile. They compensated us, of course, but I know the women—and Meg in particular—were real resentful."

There was an edge in his voice that made her ask, "Just how well did you and Meg know each other?"

"We might have gotten married if we hadn't been in the military. Marriages between personnel weren't allowed. Once we'd left the military, things seemed to change." The old man shrugged, yet the sudden grief in his eyes belied his casualness. "Meg changed. She just wanted to be friends. We lived together, you know, here in this house."

"What about Emma Pierce, then?" Sam asked, feeling sorry for the old man. His life certainly hadn't gone the way he'd planned—but then, neither had hers. And at least *he* could remember his life. "Where does she fit into all this?"

"Emma was a friend of Meg's. She came to Hopeworth about three years after us."

"What sort of project was she involved in?"

Allars shrugged and dug a handkerchief out of his

pajama pocket to wipe his watery eyes. "We didn't really share information. It was code-named Generation 18, and I do know that everyone involved was either a shifter or a changer."

"Did they take cell samples from Emma, as well?"

Allars snorted. "They took a damn sight more than cells. They took her damn ovaries."

Sam blinked. "They *what*?"

"Yeah, real nice of them, wasn't it? Emma wasn't aware of it until much later, of course. At the time, all the women were on medication to prevent ovulation, anyway."

"But how could you not know you'd undergone major surgery like that? Surely there would have been a scar, at the very least."

"They were cutting into her, and the others, all the time. Taking little samples of skin, pieces of this, pieces of that. It was part of the job. Emma had volunteered to be a lab rat, like me and Meg. The pay and living conditions were top rate, even for Hopeworth. But so were the costs, as we later discovered."

"What price did you pay, Mark?" Gabriel's voice was soft and held a hint of compassion. "Besides losing Meg, I mean?"

"I'm barely sixty, and look at me. Shifters have a life span almost double that of humans, and here I am, ready for the scrap heap. But I'm luckier than some. Many developed cancers. Meg—" Allars hesitated, his gaze drifting to a photo on top of the TV of a gray-haired woman. Sam could see nothing of herself in that photo, despite Allars's earlier statement. "Meg developed skin lesions all over. It wasn't pretty and it wasn't quick." He hesitated and wiped his eyes again. "I never saw her die, you know. The military came and took her away from me."

"What about Emma?" Sam asked softly, and rubbed her aching head again.

"She had a rare muscle cancer. Ate away at her until she couldn't walk. She could barely even move."

Gabriel drew a small container out of his pocket and pressed it into Sam's hand. Painkillers, she saw with surprise. So much for covertly rubbing her forehead. "Thanks," she murmured.

He nodded, his gaze meeting hers briefly before returning to Allars. "So who looked after Emma when she lived at Melton?"

"Her sister, of course."

"Emma Pierce was an only child."

Allars snorted. "The only child who survived the accident, but definitely not the only child. Rose had heart trouble and was in the hospital at the time. The family was on their way to see her when the accident happened. Both became wards of the state and were adopted separately. The two sisters never caught up with each other until Emma was at Hopeworth, and by that time, they couldn't admit to the relationship. Em would have been thrown out had they known she had relatives."

Sam frowned at him. "Why would having relatives make any difference?"

"Hopeworth policy. I guess they wanted to make sure no one could sue them if the tests went wrong." A shudder ran through Allars's slight frame. "Which they did, quite frequently."

"Can you tell us anything about the sister?"

"Not really. But she was the spitting image of Em,

that's for sure. Looked about the same age, too. I only met her the once."

"I don't suppose you have any idea of her adopted name, or where she lived?"

Allars shook his head.

Gabriel swore softly. "And you really can't tell us anything else about the project Emma was on?"

"As I said, we didn't dare talk about what we were involved in. But why don't you go have a chat with Haynes or Cooper, if either of them is still alive?"

"Were they involved with Emma?" she asked.

"Those two—as well as White, Benson and Lyle— were the men in charge of Generation 18."

"Then we'd better get to them before our murderer does," Gabriel said, and immediately tapped the interface of his wristcom.

Sam studied Allars for a moment. The old man was staring at the photo again. He had the look of a man who'd seen more than enough of one lifetime. The look of a man who waited for death.

Then she frowned, remembering what he'd said earlier. "You said the military took her away. Do you know why?"

He shrugged and wiped his eyes again. "Precautionary measures. They said the lesions could be contagious."

"But how did they know about them? Did either you or Meg tell them?"

He studied her for a long moment, his rheumy gaze intense. "No. We didn't."

And yet the military had known. Either the house was wired, or Meg and Allars had been. She was betting on the latter. "Would you mind standing up for a moment?"

The old man considered her request, then nodded and climbed slowly to his feet. She rose and lifted his grimy sweatshirt.

"What you looking for, girlie?"

She raised a finger to her lips. His gaze narrowed slightly, but he nodded. Maybe it was a stupid precaution, especially after all they'd asked, but right now, it was better safe than sorry. Besides, Allars was the one who'd said all military personnel were microchipped—and if they were chipping employees, why not ex-employees involved in important projects?

"I'm looking for something to squash that great big spider about to run up the arm of your chair," she said, just in case there *were* listeners.

She carefully pinched the skin along his left side, working her way up toward the armpit. His flesh hung loosely from his skeletal frame, indicating he'd lost a lot of weight recently. Perhaps premature aging wasn't the only issue he had.

Then she found it—something round and hard just under the skin near his armpit. She glanced at Gabriel.

"What?" he said.

"Want to pass me one of those newspapers? The ones here are too flimsy to squash that spider with."

He raised an eyebrow but did as she bid before approaching Allars. She showed him the lump and then removed her fingers.

Gabriel pressed the old man's flesh. "Quite ugly, isn't it?"

"Nasty," she replied. She grabbed the rolled-up paper and thumped the arm of the chair with it. Remotes jumped and rolled off onto the floor.

"Hey, watch them things," Allars said. "They're expensive to replace."

She glanced at him. "Missed it. You got anything in the kitchen we could use?"

His gaze met hers, his expression shrewd. He knew she wasn't talking about fly spray. "Yeah, in the cupboards, under the sink."

She left the room and went in search of the kitchen. It lay at the far end of the house. Dirty dishes were piled in the sink, but otherwise the kitchen was relatively clean. She found a sharp knife, then grabbed a pot. After putting the knife into the pot, she filled the pot with hot water. Lighting the stove, she leaned a hip against the sink and waited for the water to boil and clean the knife.

Crossing her arms, she stared out the window. The old man's property was on a slight slope, and from the kitchen you could see the traffic on the nearby road.

Though it was early afternoon, a steady stream of cars rolled past. The constant, droning hum would have driven her mad had she lived here, but perhaps the old man liked it—and the reminder that he wasn't entirely alone in this world.

When the knife was sterilized, she hunted around for some antiseptic and a Band-Aid, then headed back to the living room. It barely took a minute to remove the chip from the old man's armpit. The cut wasn't very deep. Like hers, the chip had been planted close to the surface. She patted away the blood, dabbed on some antiseptic and stuck a Band-Aid across the incision.

Gabriel dropped the knife back into the pot of water and held the microchip up to the light. It was bigger than the one they'd found in her—about the size of a small pea. He scanned its image with his wristcom, then dropped the bug to the floor and crushed it under his heel.

"You mean them bastards have been listening to me all these years?" Allars said immediately.

"I'd say so," Gabriel said. "How else would they have found out about Meg?"

"Bastards." The old man squinted at the circuitry remains on the floor. "But why would they bother doing something like that? They forced me into retirement, for Christ's sake. Why would they want to keep track of me?"

"Maybe they were worried that some aspects of the tests they performed would have negative effects later in life." Gabriel got a small bag from his pocket, then knelt and swept the remaining bits and pieces into the bag. "Of course, destroying the chip will warn them that something is wrong."

"That's how they knew about Meg," Allars murmured.

"And maybe even Emma," Sam suggested. Though why would they take Meg from Allars's care and simply leave Emma to die? She glanced at Gabriel. "Did you find a chip in Emma?"

"It's not something we would normally look for," he said. "I'll get them to check."

Sam nodded, then picked up the knife and water and headed back to the kitchen. On the road below, a green army truck slowly cruised past.

Her heart leapt. It couldn't be a coincidence, nor could it be a reaction to the microchip being destroyed. The military were fast, but they weren't *that* fast. Either they'd been intending to pick up Allars anyway or they'd swung into action the minute she and Gabriel began questioning him. And that might mean the old man knew more than he was currently telling.

She waited, watching the traffic roll by. Eight minutes later, the truck did another drive-by. She walked back to the living room and went over to the window. Through the grime-darkened lace, she could see a military green Ford parked in the shade of a tree two houses down.

"We have company." She stepped back, out of sight. "One out front, and one out back."

"Damn, they moved fast." Gabriel looked at the old man. "Do you want to go with them or not?"

Allars snorted. "I've spent half my life with them, lad, and look what it's done to me. I don't want to spend what's left with them."

"Then you'll come with us." Gabriel dug the keys out of his pocket and dropped them into Sam's hand. "Take the car around to the back street and meet us there."

"There's a truck around the back, cruising past every eight minutes."

"Wait for the next pass, then give me a call."

She nodded, grabbed her bag and headed for the door. Not looking at the Ford down the street, she climbed into the car and started it up. The green Ford didn't follow as she moved off. They wanted Allars, obviously.

She turned left and stopped in the shadows of a gum tree. Four and a half minutes later, the truck rolled past the far end of the street.

She quickly dialed Gabriel's number. "The truck's just gone past. I'm moving into position now."

"I'm on my way."

She turned onto the main street and cruised down to Allars's back fence. A minute dragged by, then the fence rocked and several palings were torn away. Allars squeezed through the gap, followed quickly by Gabriel. He helped the old man into the backseat, then he climbed into the front.

"Where to?" Sam turned the car around to avoid running into the truck on its next drive past.

"We get away from this area as fast as we can. Then you take Mark to a safe house, and I go get Haynes and Cooper."

"Why aren't I taking Mark to the short-term-stay apartments within the SIU?" She glanced at him, frowning. "And I thought you ordered teams to pick up Haynes and Cooper?"

"I did, but Haynes is located close to here. It won't take long for the military to realize Mark has flown the nest, and Haynes will be their next target, so it's better if I get there first, just in case."

"And the reason we're not taking Mark back to headquarters?"

He glanced at her. "I really don't think it's wise to put the scientists with their lab rats. Mark's got a whole lot to be angry about."

"He's also old, and almost blind."

"But still only sixty. Don't let the feeble exterior fool you."

She grunted and put her foot down, speeding away from the area. If they wanted answers, they had to get to Haynes and Cooper. And she had a bad feeling time was running out.

*   *   *

GABRIEL GLANCED SKYWARD AS HE climbed out of the car. The wind was freshening and the clouds hung low. He hoped the impending rain would hold off until he got to Haynes. He hated flying in foul weather.

Gabriel bent and met Sam's gaze. "When Mark's safe, I want you to go back to headquarters and go through the search results. There has to be some link between the murders other than Emma and Hopeworth."

"Will do," she said. Though Sam's voice was tightly controlled, he could feel her annoyance at being given another desk job. But this time, he wasn't doing it in a deliberate effort to get rid of her. The simple fact was that she couldn't fly and he could. Had it been the other way around, he would have gladly let her go retrieve Haynes. Dealing with cranky older men was not his favorite pastime.

He closed the door and she sped off, tires squealing. He shook his head and called the SIU, checking the location of the two teams picking up Cooper and Haynes. Cooper had been retrieved, but the Haynes team were caught in traffic and half an hour away. He sent through an order for them to use their sirens and get there fast. Then, after hanging up, he shifted shape and soared skyward, but the wind buffeted his wings, making any sort of speed difficult. He half-wished he hadn't spent most of last night airborne. His muscles started to ache long before he'd reached the halfway point.

When Mulgrave finally came into view, he dove down, skimming the treetops, looking for Haynes's house, but he wasn't the only one. A military vehicle cruised slowly down the road. He could see two men inside, the passenger holding a street directory open on his lap. It might have been a coincidence, but he doubted it. Especially since similar vehicles had been sent after Allars. The fact that they were close meant there was no time for finesse. With a flick of one wing, he swung left, diving down to Haynes's well-kept redbrick home. He lined up with the kitchen window and arrowed directly at it.

Glass shattered, flying everywhere. He changed as he hit the floor, and rolled back to his feet. Though hawks had relatively thick skulls, the impact left him a little dazed. He shook his head, trying to clear his thoughts. Shards fell like rain from his hair, chiming softly as they hit the tiled floor.

"What the hell . . . ?"

A tall, thin gentleman wearing glasses walked into the room. Gabriel smiled in greeting, then swung a clenched fist. The blow took the older man on the chin and knocked him out cold. Gabriel caught him before he hit the floor and swung him up over his shoulder. Luckily, the guy didn't weigh all that much. Then he headed out the back door. A dog barked loudly to his left, running back and forth along the fence line. He ignored it, heading for the rear of the property and the adjoining backyard. After ducking behind the cover of a tin shed, he peered over the fence. No dog, and no sign of movement from the house.

He carefully hoisted Haynes over the fence, then quickly followed. After lifting the man back up, he ran for the front of the property. The gate was shut but not locked. He opened it and casually walked out into the street. There was a bus stop several houses down. Gabriel headed for that and eased the man into the seat. Holding him upright with one hand, he dialed the SIU with the other.

"Christine, get the team assigned to Haynes to pick me up at my current location ASAP."

"One moment, please."

The older man had begun to stir. Gabriel got out his ID, showing it to the man as he opened his eyes.

"I don't care who you are," Haynes growled. "What right do you have to come busting into my home and abducting me?"

"We've reason to believe your life may be in danger, sir."

"And you couldn't tell me this in my house?"

"No, sir." Gabriel glanced up the street. It wouldn't take the military boys long to discover Haynes wasn't home. No doubt they'd then turn to the tracker.

"Unit four is thirty seconds away, Assistant Director."

"Thanks, Christine."

As the wristcom disconnected, a dark gray Ford turned the corner. Gabriel waved it down and returned his attention to Haynes.

"I apologize for my methods, but we don't know who's behind the threats and didn't dare take a chance with your safety. Lyle, White and Benson have all recently been murdered, and we've reason to believe both you and Cooper are next."

"We all worked together," Haynes murmured, face pale.

"We're well aware of that, sir." Gabriel gripped the older man's arm, helping him up as the Ford pulled to a halt beside them. Haynes climbed in. Gabriel slammed the door shut, then walked around to the other side.

"Where to, Assistant Director?" The driver, a red-haired, freckle-faced youngster, asked.

"Headquarters." Gabriel glanced at the driver's dark-skinned partner, recognizing him from a recon trip they'd done several years ago. "How's that knee, Ford?"

The man smiled. "They have me teaching recruits how to drive. Scarier than missions, sometimes."

Ford had taken several bullets in his left knee when a mission went sour. Though doctors had replaced the shattered joint, he'd been left with a permanent limp. At only thirty-five, he'd been too young to retire, and too young to send to the vaults. The way he'd sent Sam to the vaults. Gabriel ignored the momentary stab of guilt. "Do you still carry that knife in your boot?"

Ford smiled. "Yeah. It comes in handy when the recruits get uppity."

The youngster driving grinned. Obviously, knives and dour instructors didn't worry him. Gabriel returned his attention to Haynes.

"We're taking you to SIU headquarters. You should be secure there until we find out who's behind these murders."

Haynes scrubbed a hand across the back of his neck. "What about Cooper?"

"I've sent another team out to retrieve him."

"I still don't understand why you couldn't have told me this at home. I would have gone with you willingly. So why knock me out and haul me away?"

Gabriel wasn't about to tell him the truth, especially if the military were listening in. "Because I believed we had very little time to play with."

Haynes grunted. "I left the damn heater on at home. It'll probably burn the place down."

Gabriel glanced at Ford. "Can you secure Mr. Haynes's place once you drop me off?"

"Yeah. No problem."

"Thanks," Haynes muttered.

Gabriel nodded, then leaned back in the seat, watching the traffic roll by. It didn't take them long to reach the city and SIU headquarters. The red-headed driver swung the car into the underground parking lot and stopped next to the elevator.

"Nice driving, kid." The youngster looked seriously insulted at the compliment, and Gabriel half-smiled and looked at Ford. "Be careful at Haynes's place. You could have company."

Ford's brown eyes narrowed slightly. "What type?"

"Kite." He hesitated. Though there were scramblers down here that should prevent their conversation being overheard, he didn't want the powers-that-be behind the chip to know that the SIU was well aware of what was going on—at least where the microchips were concerned. But, by the same token, Ford needed to know there might be trouble. In the end, practicality won out over wariness. "The military might also be present."

"Treat them as hostile?"

"Unknown."

Ford nodded. Gabriel climbed out and walked around to assist the old man out of the car and into the elevator. He swiped his security card through the elevator slot and pressed B25. Not only did that floor have short-term apartment cells, but it also possessed the latest in both electronic and psychic deadeners. The military would not be able to hear or track them.

The elevator swept them downward. When the doors opened again, Haynes made a surprised noise.

"It looks like an upmarket hotel," he murmured, as they walked out onto the plush mauve carpet.

"It is, in many respects." Gabriel strode toward the desk. "We've found over time that people cooperate more fully if you look after them."

Haynes gave him a sidelong look. "And if they don't . . . cooperate?"

Gabriel met his gaze. "Then we make them."

Haynes's gaze narrowed at the threat. Gabriel looked at the security officer. "Mr. Haynes needs a room. Full service."

The blonde nodded. "Room 25-4 is ready."

"Thanks. And tell me when team nine brings in Jake Cooper." He hesitated and glanced at his watch. "Has Agent Ryan reported in yet?"

The blonde pressed the com-screen. After several seconds, she looked up. "No, sir."

"Let me know when she does."

"Yes, sir."

Gabriel escorted Haynes down the corridor. Like the rest of the cells on the twenty-fifth floor, room four was divided into three areas—bedroom, living room and bathroom. There was no need for a kitchen, as meals were provided. Every room was monitored twenty-four hours a day.

Haynes dropped down onto a well-padded armchair and regarded Gabriel somewhat stonily. "Now that we're here, are you going to tell me the truth?"

Gabriel swung a chair around and sat down, resting his arms on the back. "I told you. We believe your life is in danger."

"And like I said, you could have told me that at

home. You brought me here for a reason, Assistant Director."

Gabriel raised an eyebrow. "Are you aware that the army put a tracking and listening device in your side while you did service at Hopeworth?"

Haynes snorted. "Yeah, it was policy. But that was twenty-five years ago. They removed it when I retired."

"We have reason to believe they didn't."

Haynes stared at him for several seconds, brown eyes sharp. "Are you saying the military are trying to kill me?"

"No, I'm not. But I have reason to believe they'd do whatever it takes to prevent you from helping me."

Haynes crossed his arms, a hint of confusion in his expression. "I don't know what you mean."

"Does the name Emma Pierce mean anything to you?"

"Emma Pierce." Haynes frowned. "She . . . worked with us in Hopeworth."

"She was one of your test subjects," Gabriel corrected. "On something called Generation 18."

"How did you know that? No one's supposed to know about those projects."

Those projects? How many attempts to manipulate nature had there been? He wondered how many of them had been successful—and what exactly they'd created. A kite-monster, perhaps?

"I've been talking to Mark Allars."

"Allars?" Again the frown flicked across Haynes's thin features. "The name seems familiar."

"It should be. He was one of your lab rats on something called Penumbra."

"Damn fool." Haynes shook his head. "The military will kill him for speaking to you, you know. Just like they'll kill me if I say anything."

So the military *were* willing to murder to protect their secrets. Interesting. "This room is fully shielded. They won't ever know."

"It won't matter."

"Why not?"

"Because the mere fact that you've brought me here will be enough."

"Better here than out there. As I said before, Lyle, White and Benson have recently been murdered—and by a creature I doubt is natural." He watched the realization dawn in the older man's eyes. "If that's true, the military might well be after you already."

"But that makes no sense. I mean, the projects were shut down years ago!"

"But the Hopeworth staff are still experimenting, aren't they?"

"Very likely."

"So what if some of those projects have been revived? The people in charge might not want any word about what happened in the past to leak out."

"They wouldn't fear that, because most of us can't speak about them."

"Why not?"

Haynes tapped his head. "Because they tampered with our memories when we left the military. I can't tell you anything truly vital because the information was removed and blocked."

"Was it just the scientists who had the memory alterations?" he asked, wondering why Allars seemed to remember so much.

Haynes nodded. "There was no real reason to alter the memories of the test subjects, as they didn't know all that much about the inner workings or logistics of the projects."

"Mind if I test just how thorough the erase was?" When Haynes shrugged, he added, "Tell me about Penumbra."

Haynes frowned. "Nope. No can do."

"Lyle, Benson and White, along with you and Cooper, are the only survivors from the fire that destroyed the Penumbra project—is that true?"

Haynes nodded.

"From what Allars said, it sounded like an inside job."

"Impossible. We were tagged and watched, twenty-four hours a day."

"What was Penumbra?"

"I can't say . . . I can't."

"The five of you also worked on Generation 18, that right?"

Haynes nodded. Yes and no answers were outside the limits of the blocks, it seemed.

"Emma Pierce was one of the test subjects?" Again a nod. "From which you took her ovaries?"

Haynes looked uncomfortable and dropped his gaze from Gabriel's.

"Generation 18 test subjects were either shifter or changers. What were you hoping to achieve?"

"Hy . . . Hyb . . ." Haynes scrubbed a hand across the back of his neck, his expression uncomfortable.

"Hybrids?" Gabriel finished. Haynes nodded.

So the military were trying to develop shifter-changer hybrids—something that occurred only rarely in the natural order of things.

"What about Penumbra? What were you trying to create there?"

Haynes could only shrug. The conditioning was stronger for that project than for the more recent one. Gabriel wondered why.

"Did the Generation 18 project succeed?"

A brief, sharp nod, and a hint of pride in the old man's eyes.

"How many successful crosses did you achieve?"

The other man shrugged. Either he wasn't sure of exact numbers or he couldn't say.

"Were there many failures?"

"All experiments have failures."

"What happened to them? Did they all die, or did some live?"

Another shrug. Haynes either didn't know or didn't care. Maybe both.

"Would the military have farmed the failures out for adoption?"

"I don't know. I was not privy to that sort of information."

Gabriel rubbed his chin. Emma Pierce had entered the military and had lost her ovaries to Generation 18. Given that she'd entered the military in her twenties, she was unlikely to have had children before then—not if having any family at all would have disqualified her as a test subject. And yet, the first two victims listed Emma Pierce as their birth mother. They *had* to be rejects from the project. The question was, why did the military have them adopted rather than simply killing them? If they were worried about security, surely death would have made more sense.

"Is it possible that one of the hybrids has gotten loose and is going after her less successful sisters?" A hybrid certainly fit the puzzle pieces in the doctor's murder, at least.

Haynes somehow managed to force an answer. "Tagged . . . Alarmed."

So if not a rogue hybrid from Hopeworth, then who? Was it Rose, the sister no one had known about?

He glanced at his watch again. Half an hour had passed. Sam should be back by now, and hopefully she had finished the search. He wasn't going to get much more from Haynes until the conditioning had been neutralized.

"I think you'd better rest for a while." Gabriel rose and walked to the door. "I'll send someone back with some food."

Haynes nodded and picked up the remote near the chair. He was taking his confinement well—maybe a little too well. Gabriel walked down to the security station. "I want a breakdown team assigned to Mr. Haynes. And get him something to eat."

The blonde nodded.

"Has Agent Ryan checked in yet?"

"No, sir. Not yet."

He swore softly and glanced at his watch. An hour and a half had passed since he'd left her. More than enough time to deposit Allars at a safe house and get her butt back here. Unless, of course, something had gone wrong. He strode over to the elevator. He'd call the safe house and see what was going on. And if she didn't have a real good excuse for her tardiness, he'd banish her to the vaults permanently. At least that was one way to ensure she was safe.

SAM GLANCED AT HER WATCH. An hour had passed since she'd left Gabriel. Given his desire to get rid of her, he'd no doubt hit her with an official warning about her tardiness. Three warnings and you were out, she'd been told.

She slammed the door shut and ran down the stairs. Allars had been almost impossible to accommodate. He'd insisted on the latest in TV and satellite connections, and, because of his inability to walk very far, had required an apartment with few steps. Unfortunately, most SIU safe houses tended to be in buildings that had no elevators—simply because a would-be assassin might make more noise climbing stairs than taking the elevator. In the end, she'd told the watch team to carry him up to his room.

Why the hell Gabriel simply didn't house him in the short-term accommodations back at headquarters was beyond her. Sure, Mark might well be pissed off at Cooper and Haynes, but she couldn't see him providing any real threat to the two men. But keeping them separated *did* make sense when it came to *not* keeping all their eggs in one basket. There was no saying to what lengths the military just might be willing to go to protect their secrets; maybe even as far as bombing the building. Which might have seemed over the top, except for the fact that the military might be behind the creation of the kites—and they'd blown their creature to smithereens rather than letting it get caught.

The brown-eyed security officer near the front door looked up from the monitors as she approached. "Is the grump settled in okay?"

"Yeah. Give him whatever he wants—within reason, of course. And don't fall asleep, Murphy. We don't want the military getting their hands on him until we've had time to question him some more."

"How likely is it that the military will try to spring him?"

That depended on several factors—what the military thought Allars might tell them, how much they knew about the SIU, and how quickly they could hack into SIU programming and get a list of current safe houses. "We don't really know. But your priority is getting him out of here if it happens."

Murphy nodded, and Sam swiped her ID through the slot. The front door opened and the wind gusted in, thick with the promise of rain. She lifted the collar on her jacket and headed out to her car.

Rain spotted across the pavement. She raised her face, enjoying the feel of the cold droplets against her skin. There was something almost soothing about it.

"Samantha."

She froze. The voice was deep and warm, yet it held a hint of caution. It was the voice of a man who'd once saved her life. The voice of a man who wanted Gabriel dead.

The voice of a man who was neither friend nor foe, but something in between.

EIGHT

SAM TURNED AROUND SLOWLY. THE hirsute stranger leaned against the building's brick wall, half-hidden by the shrubs and bottlebrushes that overhung the pavement.

"Just who the hell are you? And why do you keep popping up?"

The stranger smiled, though how she knew this, she wasn't entirely sure. She couldn't see his mouth through the forest of beard.

"When you are ready to know, you will find the answer here." He pressed a grimy hand over his heart.

She raised an eyebrow. "What are you? Some kind of mystic?"

This time she did see his smile. "Some days I believe I am. We must talk, Samantha. There is a small café just around the corner that serves excellent coffee."

He made a sweeping movement with his hand, indicating she should precede him, but she didn't budge.

"Tell me one good reason why I should go with you."

The stranger regarded her for a moment, brown eyes intense and somewhat sad. "The answers you seek will not be found through the man in this building."

She glanced briefly at the building. "What do you know about Allars?"

"I know he cannot help you." He hesitated and crossed his arms. It was an oddly defensive gesture. "At the very least, you owe me ten minutes of your time, Samantha."

She owed him a hell of a lot more than that, because he'd saved her life. But that didn't mean she had to trust him.

"Ten minutes, then."

He nodded, then smiled when she motioned for him to go first. She fell into step behind him. Despite his disheveled, unwashed appearance, there was nothing of the streets in his walk. He had the stride of a soldier—purposeful, balanced, and powerful.

A man ready to move, to fight, at a second's notice.

The café came into sight. The stranger chose a table under the awning, out of the rain. He sat down with his back to the street, letting her take the chair near the wall. Not that she felt any safer for it. She had an itchy feeling that this man could kill her faster than she could react.

Once they'd placed their orders, she leaned on the table and regarded the stranger steadily. "So what did you want to talk about? And how do you know so much about me?"

Her hirsute friend leaned back in the chair. He looked relaxed, almost sleepy, but she knew it was all an act. She could see the tension around his eyes, if nowhere else.

"We are two of a kind, Samantha. Two halves of one whole."

"What is it with these riddles? Can't you speak plain English?"

He smiled again. "When you are ready for the answers, you will see them—in your dreams and in your heart."

She licked her lips. This man knew about her dreams of Joshua. Maybe he was even responsible for them. "What are you doing to me?"

"I'm doing nothing. I'm merely watching and waiting to see what side you fall on. To see if you found what you started searching for so long ago. Though I think, perhaps, the answer is already clear."

"Not to me." She leaned back in her chair, smiling as the waitress placed her coffee on the table. "Why did you say Allars can't help me?"

"Allars was little more than a piece of meat the scientists were using. He was one of eight. He was told nothing and knows nothing—despite the presence of his name on your birth certificate."

This man knew too much about her. And though he could read her thoughts, she sensed he wasn't doing that now. "How do you know about the certificate?"

"I sent it to you."

"No, you didn't. Jack did."

His eyes were as shuttered as his face, yet she could almost taste the wariness in him. Its touch was so strong she might have named it fear in any other man.

But this man didn't fear. Didn't care.

And how the hell she knew that, she couldn't honestly say.

"Yes, I know." He tilted his head to one side. "You cared for him, didn't you?"

She dropped her gaze. "He was my friend." Or at least, she had thought he was—but that had turned out to be another great lie in the story of her life.

"And now?"

"Now I have only my work." And a partner who didn't want her.

"Sometimes it is better that way."

Only a workaholic or the dead would think that. But her private life was not something she wanted to discuss with this man.

"Jack said he got that information from Sethanon. Are you Sethanon?" If he was, she should be shooting him rather than talking to him. Especially when Sethanon was the number-one villain on both the SIU's and the Federation's hit lists.

"Sethanon is not a name I ever gave myself."

Truth or lie? She couldn't tell, and that worried her. "Allars told me he was involved in a project called Penumbra. That four of the eight involved were a changer, a shifter, a vampire and a werewolf."

"And the other four were psychically endowed. Mike Shean was a strong telepath and empath. Jeremy Park was a fire-starter. Rae Messner's gift was psychometry, and Fay Reilly was an emotive."

She stared at him. "How the hell do you know that?"

"Simple. Because I was there."

"You were one of the scientists?" She couldn't help the incredulous note in her voice. She could believe he might have been in the military, but a scientist? No way. This man was a killer, born and bred.

But then, with what she was beginning to learn about Hopeworth, maybe that wasn't so far off the mark.

He laughed—and it was an oddly familiar sound that scratched at the back of her mind.

"Not a scientist. Not even a test subject."

"Then what?" If he'd been involved with security, surely he wouldn't have known so much about the project.

"Samantha, you have all the answers you need. All you have to do is look for them."

"So, we're back to the riddles again." She sipped at her coffee. It was strong and sweet, with just a hint of hazelnut.

"Your favorite, I believe," he said softly.

This time he *was* reading her thoughts. She put her coffee down and leaned back, crossing her arms. "Tell me your name."

He hesitated. "I go by many names these days."

"Give me your birth name, then."

He looked away, but not before she'd caught the hint of anger in his eyes. "I was never given a name at birth. The names I have are ones I've collected over the years."

"Give me a name, or I get up and walk away."

His hesitation was briefer. "Call me Joe Black."

"What are you, a funny man? Joe Black was the name Death gave himself, in that movie."

He shrugged. "You asked for a name; I gave it to you. When you have no name of your own, you steal others that appeal. And that one appeals."

"Okay, then, Mr. Black—"

"Joe," he murmured.

"Mr. Black," she continued, ignoring his almost bitter smile. "What do you know about Jake Cooper and Liam Haynes?"

He sipped at his coffee for a minute. "Both worked on the Penumbra project. And both worked on Generation 18."

"What can you tell me about Generation 18?"

"Nothing that your partner doesn't already know."

He said the word *partner* like it was a curse. She raised her eyebrows slightly. "Why do you want him dead when you haven't even met him?"

"That would take longer to explain than we have."

She frowned. "And what makes you so certain Gabriel knows anything about Generation 18?"

"Because the logical step after the first three murders is to pick up and question the two remaining scientists. And Stern is nothing if not logical."

"How do you know about the murders? And how do you know that there are two men remaining?"

"I'm a mystic, remember?"

"Yeah, right. Maybe you'd better accompany me downtown for some questioning."

"Do not push me, Samantha."

Though there was no threat in his voice, no threat in the way he sat, fear surged and Sam swallowed. This man could reach out and kill her without even moving. Could snuff out the flame of her existence with merely a thought. How she could be so certain about something like that, she couldn't really say. But she *was* certain.

"If you wish to find some answers," he continued, "look at the pin I gave you."

The pin? The one he'd given her when he saved her

life? She frowned, trying to remember where she'd put it. Somewhere in her desk drawers, she thought. "Do you mean answers to the murders, or answers about myself?"

"Perhaps it would be a start for both paths." He drained his coffee in one gulp and rose.

"We shall meet again, soon," he said. "In the meantime, be careful. Your abilities will not protect you from the kites if you get too close."

"The kites? What do you know about them?"

A smile ghosted across his face. "I made them," he said, then raised his arms to the sky. His body shimmered, then began to blur, briefly resembling putty being molded by unseen hands. Then he leapt skyward on black wings.

A crow. The harbinger of bad news. The messenger of death. An oddly fitting choice for the stranger.

Could he be believed when he said he'd made the kites? She'd sensed no lie in his words, and yet it hadn't seemed the entire truth, either.

And that made a whole lot of sense, didn't it?

Snorting softly, she finished her coffee, then picked up the bill and paid it. She glanced at her watch. Another hour had passed. Gabriel was going to kill her.

It took half an hour to get back to headquarters. By that time, her head was pounding again. She went straight to her dark little hole.

"Computer on." She threw her coat over the back of the chair and sat down.

"Afternoon, sweetness. How's your day been?"

"Just peachy. You got those test results back yet?"

Izzy swung her boa, her expression a little startled. "My, we are a bit abrupt right now, aren't we?"

Sam rocked her chair back against the wall and

rubbed her eyes. Now her damn com-unit was telling her off. These things were definitely becoming *too* human. "Sorry, Izzy. I've got a bitch of a headache."

"Perhaps you should see a doctor."

There was something almost coy in Izzy's voice. She opened her eyes and stared at the pink fuzz-ball. "And can you recommend one?"

"I can recommend five, actually. Funnily enough, they've all bought Heat in the last month."

"Izzy, you're a doll. Did you cross-reference the results with our records?"

"Certainly did, sweetie. There's one match. Our doctor is a changer, but that's it, I'm afraid. Definitely no sister."

She tapped her fingers against the desk. The murderer was definitely a shifter; that much they knew. But that didn't explain how she was getting in and out without being seen. There was something else, something they were missing. "Make an appointment for me to see her."

"You might want to reconsider that. The doctor in question is a vet."

"Then I'll find a dog to take along. What about the Jadrone search? Is that finished yet?"

"I've been working my butt off here, darlin'. Of course it's finished."

"Was Emma Pierce listed?"

"No. But Harry Maxwell was."

"What?" Sam let her chair thump back. If Harry had a legal prescription, why did he need an illegal supplier? Had his need for the drug grown stronger than his legal prescription would allow?

"That's right, sweetness. Also listed were Raylea Burns, Anna Jakes and Dr. Brandon."

Along with Harry Maxwell, all victims of their serial killer. Sam rubbed her forehead. "Are these recent prescriptions?"

"Yes, though all four had been taking the drug since their mid-teens, from the look of it."

"Do a check on the prescribing doctor. And get me his address."

"Consider it done, sweetie."

"Thanks." Sam watched the purple boa rotate for several seconds. "Izzy, are any of the four on file as being shifters?"

The boa twirled a little faster while Izzy searched the records. "Not a one."

Then why the hell were they being prescribed Jadrone? Especially at such a young age? "Get me the autopsy results for Jakes, Burns and Brandon."

"Onscreen."

The three reports tiled onto the screen and Sam quickly read through them. No evidence of Jadrone had been found in the toxicology or blood reports. So why were they being prescribed the drug if they weren't actually using it?

"Izzy, who performed the autopsies?"

"Warren Michaels."

"Get him on vid for me."

Izzy tapped her foot for several seconds, then disappeared, replaced by a dark-haired man in his midforties.

"Agent Ryan," Warren Michaels said. "What can I do for you?"

"You handled the serial killer autopsies, didn't you?"

"Yep. Why?"

"I just found out that all of them were being prescribed Jadrone. Would you have any idea why?"

Michaels frowned and scratched his shadowed chin. "If they were taking it, I found no evidence of it."

"So I read. And yet all of them had been prescribed the drug since puberty, from what I can gather."

"I can't see why. They weren't shifters." He hesitated and frowned. "There was an unknown substance in their toxicology results, one we haven't been able to pin down. And I did notice severe bone degradation in both Maxwell and Jakes."

"Is it usual to be unable to identify substances?"

"No, not unless it's something new to the market. We're still searching, and may yet match it."

Then she'd keep her fingers crossed for a result. "What sort of degradation was there? And how might it be connected to Jadrone?"

"Shifting puts severe stress on the body's organs, particularly bone and muscle. As the shifter gets older, the bone and muscles become less pliant, more brittle. Arthritis and other associated diseases become a real problem. In a shifter, this doesn't normally happen until they are well into the mid–one-fifties, one-sixties. Even in humans, it doesn't normally happen until your late sixties." He paused. "Jadrone was administered to shifters to keep the pain at bay and slow degradation."

"Is there a history of this sort of degeneration in either Jakes's or Maxwell's family?"

"That we don't know."

She frowned. "Why?"

Michaels snorted. "They were adopted, the same as

Burns and Brandon. Don't you read follow-up reports?"

The edge of derision in his voice stung. "Obviously not." Nor had Gabriel mentioned that fact. "Let's presume there's no history of this in their background. What else might be the cause?"

Michaels shrugged. "Random chance? It happens. Kids as young as five get arthritis, you know."

Yeah, but their killer wasn't attacking kids as young as five. There was some sort of pattern here, but one they couldn't quite see yet. "What about the other two?"

"Minor degradation. A little more than what you'd expect for their age, but nothing extreme."

"Did you do a cellular analysis on the four?"

"No need to. They were human."

"Then do it. And tell me what you find."

Michaels raised his eyebrows. "By whose authority are you ordering this?"

"Assistant Director Stern's." She looked up as the man in question stepped into her office. He raised an eyebrow and walked the two steps over to the desk.

"Sorry, Agent Ryan," Michaels was saying, "I can't order that sort of investigation without permission from the man himself."

Gabriel placed a hand on the back of her chair, his face close to hers as he stared at the com-screen. "Then you have it, Michaels. Please proceed."

Michaels nodded and signed off, and Gabriel sat back on the edge of her desk. "What did I just authorize?"

"A cellular analysis on our four victims."

He crossed his arms and regarded her for a minute. The intensity of his gaze made her want to squirm like some errant ten-year-old facing a headmaster. And that, more than anything, annoyed the hell out of her. What was it about this man that got to her so easily?

"Really? Why?"

She tilted her chair back, her knee brushing against his and sending warmth surging across her flesh. But he didn't move, so nor did she. "All four were being prescribed Jadrone, and yet they were not on record as being shifters."

"Jadrone has no effect on humans."

"Exactly. And yet Maxwell was a junkie who got high on it regularly, and he and the others had been prescribed it since their teens. I think we need to find out why."

He frowned. "I agree. But there was no mention of Jadrone being found in their systems."

"Which makes me wonder why—especially with Maxwell. He was a junkie for years, and had severe bone degradation. It's unclear whether the Jadrone is at fault or something else."

"Are you doing a trace on the prescribing doctor?"

"Izzy's handling it now. Why didn't you mention that all four victims were adopted?"

"Why were you going through the files? You're supposed to be handling the kite murders."

"And the kite murders might well be connected to these murders." She studied him for a moment, then added, "You can't have it both ways, chum. Either you allow me to do my job properly, letting me follow all leads, or you confine me to this little box and the inane paperwork you keep dredging up, and get someone else to do the investigating."

"You'll do what I tell you to do. And right now,

that's investigating the kite murders—nothing more, nothing less."

His face was remote, his eyes cold. She felt like strangling him. God, the man was aggravating! As he no doubt intended.

"Why are you here, Assistant Director? Planning to leave me another nice note, were you?"

His arms flexed, as if he were clenching his fists. "You left the safe house more than an hour ago. Where the hell were you?"

"Having coffee with a friend."

"You don't have any friends."

"Obviously not." An edge of bitterness crept into her voice. She took a deep breath and crossed her legs. Warmth still tingled where their knees had touched and she scratched at it irritably.

"That's not . . ." Gabriel looked away from her gaze. "Next time, report in first."

"Yes, sir." This time she resisted the urge to salute.

His anger still washed over her, and she shuddered and leaned back, trying to get some fresh air.

Concern flitted briefly through his hazel eyes. "You okay?"

"Yes. Fine." She rubbed her forehead briefly. She really had to go see a doctor. Not only about the headache, but the weird sensations that kept washing over her.

Izzy chose that moment to reappear. "You have a five-fifteen appointment with the animal quack, sweetness."

"Thanks, Izzy."

Gabriel gave her com-unit a somewhat disgusted look. But then, he wasn't into cartoons. Or com-units with character. "You're visiting a vet? Why?"

"My dog's sick." She'd be damned if she'd tell him the truth. He'd probably go interview the vet himself and leave her here in this shoe box doing another inane task.

"You don't have a dog."

"I will tonight."

He studied her thoughtfully. "The cross-check came up with her name, didn't it?"

"Yeah." She rubbed her forehead again and waited for the axe to fall.

He was silent for a few seconds. Then he sighed and rested his palms on the desk. "When are you going to see a doctor about that headache of yours?"

Consideration when she'd expected an axe was definitely cause to be wary. "What do you mean?"

"I mean you've had that headache for the last few days. I think it's time you got it checked out."

"I will." She barely kept her irritation in check. Lord, it was bad enough that he was ordering her around at work. Now he was trying to run her private life, as well?

"When?"

"Soon."

Gabriel shook his head and looked at the com-unit. "Izzy, make an appointment for Sam with Dr. O'Hearn at the Collins Street clinic."

"Sorry, sweetie, but you're not the boss in this shoe box."

Surprise and annoyance flitted across Gabriel's features and Sam smothered her laugh. She would have hugged the cyber character if she could have. "Who's Dr. O'Hearn? SIU employed?" If he was, she was staying well away. An SIU doctor meant Gabriel could access her records, and he knew more than enough about her already.

He shook his head. "No, but she collaborates with both the Federation and the SIU. She's a specialist in nonhuman medicine."

Sam snorted softly. "So you could get access to my medical files?"

"Not with Dr. O'Hearn, I can't. She's a total stickler when it comes to patient confidentiality."

"Then why are you sending me to her?"

"Because she's not only the best, she's also the only one who might truly be able to help you."

Because they didn't know what was she was, other than the fact that she was not entirely human. She glanced at the boa-twirling fuzz-ball. "Do it, Izzy."

"Right away, darlin'."

"Tell Dr. O'Hearn I recommended you. She'll forward the bill to the Federation."

She raised an eyebrow. "I'm not a part of the Federation."

He crossed his arms. "You could be, if you wanted to."

"What's this, a recruitment attempt?" And why now, a good month after she'd found out about the Federation?

He shrugged. "No. Just something for you to think about."

"Why? I don't know a thing about the Federation, apart from what you've told me."

"I've already told you the important stuff."

"You gave me a brief background. That's hardly the same as knowing their current goals."

He shrugged. "If you're interested, let me know."

She considered him for a moment. His face, as ever,

was neutral. It was hard to judge whether he was actually serious or not. "I thought you were trying to get me out of your life."

His smile seemed almost bitter. "I don't want you out of my life—quite the opposite, in fact. I just don't want you as a partner. It's nothing personal."

Yes, it was—at least to her. And if he did want her in his life, then what role would she be playing if not a partner? A friend? It certainly couldn't be as a lover—not if his determined lack of reaction to her physically was anything to go by. Or was he merely reacting that way because she *was* his partner? Did he perhaps believe in not combining work and play? Or had he, she thought, remembering his first partner had been a woman, tried it once, and sworn never to do it again after losing her? *That* was most certainly the answer, though why she was so certain she couldn't say. It was just a conviction she felt deep inside.

She just wished he'd trust her enough to confide in her. Maybe then she could make him see how stupid he was being. But until he said something, she couldn't.

Izzy twirled onto the com-screen. "There's a call from a General Frank Lloyd on vid-screen. You want to take it?"

Sam glanced at Gabriel. He slid off the desk and stood near her chair—close enough to see the screen but out of direct line of sight.

"Patch it through, Izzy."

General Frank Lloyd came onscreen. "Agent Ryan, I presume?" His voice, like his appearance, was powerful.

She nodded. "What can I do for you, General?"

"I need to know why you have requested information on these thirteen people before we can go any further."

"We have a number of murder victims that may be linked with Hopeworth. They're certainly linked with an Emma Pierce, who worked at Hopeworth for a number of years. In fact, Emma Pierce may be the mother of at least two of the victims."

The general's sharp blue gaze narrowed slightly. "I see." He rested his elbows on the desk in front of him, fingers interlaced. "I'll be in the city this evening, attending the opera. Perhaps we could meet afterward?"

Gabriel grabbed a pen and paper, quickly scribbling. She glanced at it. "I've heard there's a very good restaurant in the South Bank—Han's, I believe it's called. Shall I make the reservations?"

"Around eleven should be suitable."

She nodded. "See you then, General."

The screen went dead.

"Well, well," Gabriel murmured. "A call from a general, no less. Your request for information certainly raised a few alarms."

"Have you heard of the general before?"

"No. But a Dr. Frank Lloyd attended the birth of both Raylea Burns and Anna Jakes."

Sam raised her eyebrows. "The same man, you think?"

"It's too much of a coincidence, otherwise."

"Why meet at a restaurant? Why not at Hopeworth? Or even here?"

Gabriel shrugged. "Neutral territory, perhaps? I doubt they'd let us near Hopeworth, anyway. The place has a level-ten security clearance."

Which meant top of the tree. Not even Stephan's autocratic Byrne persona would get in there.

"I gather you intend coming with me tonight?"

"Yes. I'll contact Han and arrange for us to be in the Dragon Room." He hesitated. "The restaurant is quite upmarket. Nothing casual allowed, I'm afraid."

She raised an eyebrow. "The last time I was there, I was dressed decidedly casual."

"Yes, but Han's wasn't officially open." He hesitated, then looked away. "I'll pick you up at nine-thirty."

"It's a date, Assistant Director."

He flashed her a grim look, and she smiled and watched him walk from the room. Sometimes, he was extraordinarily easy to rattle.

And that, just maybe, should be her line of attack. Damn it, there was something between them, and he had to be aware of it. Rather than sit back and wait for him to make a move, as she usually did when it came to men, maybe she needed to take the reins and lead the way. The worst that could happen was that he'd say no.

And as he was already doing that in other areas, what was one more rejection?

"Izzy, do a search through the personnel files. I need to find an agent who has a dog or a cat in need of vaccination shots that I can borrow."

"Searching now, sugar."

Good. Her next major worry was finding an outfit to wear tonight. Something subtle but stunning. She might not be able to stop Gabriel from thrusting her from his life—be it professional or personal—but she sure as hell could make him regret it.

Tall, curvaceous blondes weren't the only ones who could look like sex on legs.

SAM GRABBED THE BOX RESTRAINING the growling cat and climbed out of the car. Heat tingled across her skin, standing the small hairs at the back of her neck on end. Then her senses exploded outward, tasting the secrets within the clinic.

There was a woman inside who was not only a changer, but one who somehow felt unclean. And *not* in the unwashed sense.

Frowning—unsure why she was sensing *some* changers and shifters, but not others—and certainly not understanding what the hell her senses were trying to tell her, Sam headed inside.

After filling in a bunch of forms, she sat down. The cat, safely parked two seats away, had a claw through one of the airholes and seemed intent on shredding the seat.

"Dr. Francis will see you now," the receptionist said after a few minutes.

Sam collected the box, ensured the killer claw was pointed away from her body, and walked through the door indicated by the white-haired receptionist. Dr. Francis, like the woman out front, was in her mid-fifties. She wore what Sam called a power suit under her unbuttoned white coat—a tight-fitting, nononsense outfit that acknowledged her femininity but said hands off. Her hair was a rich chestnut, and undoubtedly dyed. Her face was natural, unmarred by makeup or face-lifts. A woman proud of her looks and her age.

A woman whose very presence itched at Sam's skin.

"And what can we do for you and Kahn today?" The vet's voice, like her looks, was striking and powerful.

Sam placed the box on the table and carefully pulled the cat out. It continued to growl its displeasure. "He's overdue for his shots."

The doctor nodded and walked across to the cupboard. "I haven't seen either of you here before, have I?"

"No. We just moved here."

"Oh yes? Where from?" The doctor's voice was flat. Making small talk through habit, not interest.

"Elwood." Sam hesitated. The doctor slipped a white glove on and moved back to the table. "Park Street. You know it?"

"Lovely area," Dr. Francis murmured, bending to examine the squirming, hissing feline.

Sam regarded her steadily. No reaction whatsoever to the location or street name. She'd have to push a bit harder. "I used to think so. But a neighbor of mine was murdered the other day."

The doctor glanced up. The shock in her face didn't quite reach her eyes. "How horrible! Did you know him well?"

Sam raised her eyebrows. "Yes, I did. I have an interview with the cops tomorrow."

The vet continued to examine the cat. "Nasty."

"Yeah, I'm not looking forward to it."

"Nor would I. Kahn's in excellent condition."

"That's good. He's been a little off his food. Not impressed by the change of housing, I think."

"Just keep him inside a while and he'll be fine. Hold him down, will you?" She took a needle out of the cupboard. "Why do the police want to interview you?"

Sam grabbed the cat by the scruff of the neck. It responded by trying to twist around and shred her hand. "Routine, I think. I was just unlucky enough to be in the building at the time."

"Did you see anything?"

"No." She hesitated again and frowned. The doctor watched her almost too carefully. "Though I saw the postman arrive. I swear he had something live in one of the parcels. I could hear it scratching around."

"It's illegal to send animals through the post. They should hang the person who did that."

"They'll probably get a pat on the head and a warning not to do it again."

"Yeah, the courts don't seem to care these days." The vet injected the growling cat, somehow avoiding the razor-sharp claws it flung her way.

"That's it. If you both head back to reception, I'll write up the bill and send it out."

Sam nodded and put the squirming feline back into the box. It was easy to see why this particular cat hadn't had any recent shots. Kahn was definitely a killer. She just had to hope the box would hold up until she got him back to his owner.

She headed back to reception and paid the fee. All the while, the back of her neck itched. Someone was watching her. Someone with death on her mind.

After seat-belting the cat carrier into the backseat, Sam climbed into the front and tapped the wristcom. The SIU's digital receptionist answered on the second ring.

"Christine, could you patch me through to workstation 1934?"

Izzy appeared onscreen. "This is a new experience, sweetie."

"I'd hate for you to be bored, Iz. Listen, do a search on Dr. Francis. I want a complete history—and if she lives in an apartment, include surveillance tapes from her home if you can get hold of them."

"Will do. And you have a six-thirty appointment with Dr. O'Hearn."

O'Hearn certainly didn't waste time. Sam glanced at her watch. She'd have just enough time to return the cat and get there. "Thanks, Izzy."

"Have a nice evening."

Sam started the car and headed out of the parking lot. And all the while, the eyes watched, burning into the back of her skull.

NINE

GABRIEL LEANED BACK IN HIS chair and glanced at his watch. Seven-thirty. He wondered how Sam was doing with O'Hearn. He'd phoned the doc earlier, calling in a favor and getting Sam squeezed in. He just hoped O'Hearn could discover the reason for Sam's continuous bout of headaches.

"Search completed," the com-unit intoned.

Gabriel rubbed his eyes and then studied the com-screen. "Results?"

"All four victims were adopted from the same State care center. All four victims were placed in care on the same day."

Coincidence? Not likely. "Did you find the birth certificates for Harry Maxwell and Carmen Brandon?"

"Yes."

"Who's listed as the mother?"

"Emma Pierce."

So Emma *was* the link. "Is there a complete list of all children handed into State care that day?"

"Searching. One moment, please."

Gabriel tapped the desk and watched the blank screen. And couldn't help thinking a pink fuzz-ball twirling a purple boa would definitely be more interesting.

"Seventeen children were entered into the care of the Greenwood center that day."

He shook his head. Seventeen children and no one had thought that odd? "Get me the complete list of names, their adoption records, birth certificates and current location."

"List and adoption records onscreen. Searching for birth certificates and location."

The list was in alphabetical order, with the adoption details beside each name. Gabriel scanned through the list. One name, halfway down, jumped out at him. The air left his lungs, as suddenly as if someone had punched him in the gut. Miranda Jones, now Miranda Stern. His sister.

He reached for the wristcom and quickly dialed Stephan's secure number.

"Byrne speaking."

Obviously he wasn't alone in the office, or he would have used the vid-screen. Gabriel swore softly. "We need to find Miranda, quickly."

"Why?"

"I just discovered all four murder victims had Emma Pierce listed as their mother, and they were adopted from the Greenwood State Care Center. Miranda's one of seventeen children that came in on the same day."

"She's moved. Charles will know where she's at." Though there wasn't the slightest change in his voice, he could feel his brother's sudden alarm. Felt it because it was in him as well.

"Maybe not. The reason Miranda moved in the first place was the almighty argument she had with him."

"Give him a call, then let me know. This meeting will be finished in ten."

"Will do." Gabriel hung up and quickly dialed his old man's number.

"Stern residence."

His father's familiar, suntanned features came online. Though close to a hundred years old, he barely looked fifty. His skin, like his still-black hair, showed little sign of aging. It was only when you looked deep into his green eyes that you saw the truth. They were the eyes of a man who'd seen too much death, too much destruction, for one normal life span.

"Father, I need Miranda's new address and phone number."

The welcoming smile faded. "What's wrong?"

"Stephan's updated you on our current investigations, hasn't he?"

Charles nodded. "Several days ago. There wasn't anything we'd consider a Federation matter, though, so it wasn't in-depth."

"I've just discovered a link between our murder victims. They were all fosterlings at the Greenwood State Care Center. Miranda came into care the same day as the others."

"And you think she's in danger?"

"I sure as hell don't want to take that risk."

Charles rubbed his chin. "I haven't heard from her in over a week."

That didn't surprise him. Miranda could hold a

grudge with the best of them. She'd once gone two
months without saying a word to *him*—just because
he'd had the audacity to call her date an idiot, which
she had been, as Miranda had admitted later.

"What about Mom?"

"She's still in New York. Flights out of Kennedy
have been delayed by storms. I'll phone her and see.
If not, Jessie will know."

Jessie was his oldest sister, and she had been something of a surrogate mother to the much younger
Miranda. "I want full protection on her."

"That goes without saying. I'll contact you when I
have the address."

The vid-screen went blank. Gabriel leaned back in
his chair and scrubbed his chin. He didn't like this.
They might not know where Miranda was, but that
didn't mean the killer wouldn't. She'd been ahead of
them every step of the way so far.

The com-unit beeped. "Director Byrne on vid one."

"Display."

Byrne's familiar features came online. "How'd you
do?"

There was a slight buzz overriding Stephan's voice.
He had the scramblers up, just to ensure no one listened in. "He didn't know, and Mom's still overseas."

"I thought she was due back yesterday."

"Yeah, she was. He's contacting Jessie."

"She'll know." Stephan ran a hand through his
hair. "I can't go look myself. I promised Lys I'd be
home early tonight."

"Nor can I. Sam and I have a meeting with a General Frank Lloyd of Hopeworth Military Base at
eleven."

Gabriel glanced at his watch. And if he didn't get

moving, he'd be late to pick up Sam. He wanted to ensure they arrived at Han's well before the general. He had an uneasy feeling about this meeting. Given the security surrounding Hopeworth's activities, the general had been too quick in agreeing to meet them.

"Hopeworth? How does that tie in with the murders?"

"Emma Pierce used to work with them. She was listed as the mother of all four victims, even though Hopeworth took her ovaries for tests. From what we've learned, Hopeworth's been experimenting in genetics."

"I've heard whispers of that over the years. Nothing concrete, though."

"I'd like to know if the kites are a by-product of their experiments."

"We would have been advised, especially given the spate of recent attacks."

Somehow, Gabriel doubted that. The military were not inclined to admit to mistakes, just to get rid of them. "Have we got enough manpower available to put watch teams on the remainder of the Greenwood fosterlings?"

"I'll have to pull some teams off other work, but yeah, we can manage. Send the list through and I'll arrange it."

The com-unit beeped. "You have a call on vid-line two, Assistant Director."

"Hang on a minute." Gabriel switched lines. His father's features reappeared. "Did you get hold of Jessie?"

"Yes. Miranda's living in a house out in Strathmore. Jess and Alain are heading over there now."

Alain was Jessie's shapechanging husband of six

months, and, quite literally, a bear of a man. "You told them to bring her back to the compound?"

"Kicking and screaming, if they have to."

"Let me know what happens."

The old man nodded. "Take care, son."

Gabriel switched back to Stephan. "Jess and Alain are picking up Miranda."

"Good. At least she'll be safe at home. You have any idea how the murderer is getting in and out of the victims' homes yet?"

"I've several ideas. Nothing concrete yet."

"Well, you'd better start finding something concrete. Our killer seems to have accelerated her schedule."

Like *that* was something he wasn't fully aware of. He held back the surge of annoyance. "I'll send the list through now. The quicker we can get surveillance teams on these people, the better it will be."

"Keep me informed."

"I usually do." The retort held a hint of hostility. He scrubbed a hand against his jaw. Getting angry with his brother wouldn't achieve anything. "How's Lyssa?"

"The herb Karl suggested is working. She only threw up once last night."

At least that was an improvement. "Send her my love. I'll be in touch."

He broke contact and glanced at his watch. Ten to eight. He'd better get going. He collected his jacket and headed down to the car.

An hour later, he ran up the stairs to Sam's second-floor apartment. He'd showered and changed, but he still felt like shit. What he needed was a good night's sleep. Something that wasn't likely to happen until they caught the murderer.

"Door's open," Sam yelled from inside.

He raised an eyebrow. It could have been anyone coming up those stairs. Maybe he'd have to sit her down and explain the basics of security—though as a former cop, with over ten years' experience, she should know all that. He pushed the door open and entered the apartment. It was starker than he'd remembered. The walls were bare of paintings, and she'd yet to replace the shelving and knickknacks lost in the bombing. He wondered whether she still had all the books in the bedroom.

"You're late," she said, her voice coming from the direction of the bathroom.

"Working on the case." He walked across to the window and stared out over the ocean. If he ever moved, it would be for something like this. Something right opposite the sea. The wash of waves across the sand was hypnotically soothing.

"Anything new?"

"Yeah, the four victims entered the Greenwood State Care Center on the same day as thirteen other kids. How'd you do with Dr. Q'Hearn?"

"She took some blood and skin samples. I have to go back tomorrow at eleven." Sam came out of the bathroom and walked toward him, and he felt his breath come short.

She wore what was becoming a standard uniform for her—a jacket and shirt, this time teamed with a knee-length skirt rather than pants. Only there was nothing conservative, or even normal, about *this* little dark gray number. Both the jacket and skirt appeared to be made from Contour, the latest in textile development. It clung like a second skin, displaying every curve with loving detail. The skirt was slit on one side to her thigh, revealing plenty of tanned leg.

She looked stunning. Sexy. And it sure as hell would be difficult to see her in *any* suit the same way again. He cleared his throat. This was not a good development. Not when he was trying to ignore his attraction to her.

She collected her purse from the coffee table, a smile touching her full, red lips. It was then that he realized she'd done it deliberately—had dressed to shatter his reserve and get some reaction.

"The cut on your leg has healed rather nicely," he said lamely.

Indeed, it was little more than a pale pink scar. She definitely healed way too fast. The three scrapes he'd received across his shoulder had barely scabbed over—and as a shapechanger he healed a good two or three times faster than a human. He'd have to call O'Hearn and mention it.

"Yeah, it has. Shall we go?"

He waved her ahead of him, locking her door and following her down the stairs. But he kept his eyes on the shining beacon of her red-gold hair rather than the enticing sway of her hips.

They drove to the city in silence. It was neither uncomfortable nor tension-filled, just the easy silence that existed between two people who understood each other well. Even if they were still relative strangers—something he had no intention of changing while they were still partners, no matter how sexy she was, no matter how comfortable he felt with her.

He found street parking and they walked the block

to the restaurant. Han's eldest son, Michael, made his way across to them as they entered.

"Hey, Uncle Gabriel, how's it going?"

Gabriel smiled and shook the big man's hand. Like his father, Michael towered over him by a good four or five inches and was almost twice as wide. "How are Danni and the kid?"

Michael beamed. "We finally decided on a name. Katie Jane, after Danni's mother."

"About time. I was beginning to think she'd have to choose her own name when she went to school. Michael, this is my partner, Samantha Ryan."

"Whoa! If I knew partners could look like this, I would have joined the force." He grinned and stuck out a hand. "Pleased to meet you, Samantha."

She grinned. "Please, call me Sam."

"Dad's put you both in the Dragon Room. You have sole ownership tonight."

"Thanks." Gabriel glanced around as two more people entered the restaurant. It looked like Han was having another good night. Already the place was so crowded you could barely move between the tables. He'd have to buy Han an extra-large bottle of bourbon for doing them such a huge favor. "We'll make our way there. You look after your customers."

Michael nodded. "Dad'll be with you in a few minutes."

Gabriel lightly placed his hand against Sam's back, guiding her through the tables to the private function room near the back of the restaurant. The holographic dragons played across the ceiling as they entered, the creatures diamond bright in the candlelit darkness.

"Lord, I still can't get over how real they look," she murmured, a smile touching her full lips.

Gabriel watched a sapphire-blue dragon flame a butterfly that danced near its tail. Warmth washed over his face, followed quickly by a hint of acrid smoke. The butterfly emerged from the flames unscathed, and the dragon looked miffed. "Han's always working on the holographs. His aim is to make them as real as possible."

A golden dragon dove for Sam's head and she ducked, then smiled ruefully. "He's just about achieved that."

Gabriel motioned her toward the table set up in the middle of the room. She sat at one end. He sat to one side of her, but the table was small enough that his knee brushed hers. The touch sent warmth rushing to his groin. He might not be willing to admit his attraction to his partner, but his body sure as hell had no such inhibitions. Just as well he was sitting down.

A door opened near the back of the room and Han loomed out of the shadows, his smile almost lost under the bushiness of his mustache.

"Gabriel. Samantha. It is good to see you both."

Gabriel clasped the big man's hand. "You, too, old friend. Thanks for giving us the room when you're so busy."

"For you, anything. I have the deadeners on full. No one will eavesdrop on your conversation."

"Good. The general should be here by eleven. Just keep an eye out for me. I don't really trust him."

Han nodded. "Do you want a drink while you wait?"

"Just ice water for me, thanks," Sam said.

"Are you sure? I do make the best cocktails in town, you know."

Sam grinned. "I'm still on duty. Water will do."

Han looked at Gabriel. "And you, my friend? Are you playing by the book?"

"The SIU would go into shock if I did. I'll have a beer, thanks."

Han nodded and walked away. Sam interlaced her fingers and leaned her chin on them. The ring of smoke around the blue of her eyes gleamed like ice in the candlelight, but there was nothing cold about the smile that teased her lips. A moment later, her bare foot slid up his shoe and under his pant leg. The skin-to-skin caress had his muscles—and other parts of his body—jumping in delight.

"Why don't you trust the general?" she asked.

When had her voice gained that sexy edge? "I just have a feeling about the man. He agreed to this meeting far too fast."

"Maybe he just wants to help."

Her foot was sliding up and down, up and down, and he was beginning to find it extremely hard to concentrate.

"The military is not known for its helpful nature," he said dryly. "He's got his own agenda for agreeing to this meeting."

"Then why come here? Why not somewhere more secure?"

"Han's is as secure as you can get, and the general might just relax his guard here."

She nodded. Then Han walked in, and her foot stopped its teasing. Gabriel wasn't sure whether to be relieved or annoyed.

"Thanks, Han," he said, once the big man had placed their drinks on the table.

"I have ordered a tray of savories for you both." A hint of amusement ran through Han's voice. "Complimentary, of course."

"Thanks," Gabriel repeated, and knew he'd get the third degree from his friend later. But what could he say? That his temporary partner was pushing boundaries in a way she'd never pushed before? That while he was attracted to her, he had no intention of heading down that path while she was his partner?

Han left. Sam raised her glass and slowly sipped. Moisture glistened like tears on her mouth. God, it would be so easy to reach across the table, to wrap his arm around her neck and kiss those droplets away.

But he could not. Dared not.

She raised an eyebrow, and for a minute he wondered if she'd somehow caught his thoughts.

"So, what do we talk about until the general gets here?"

"How about the weather?" he said, keeping his voice bland.

She smiled that smile again, and heat twisted through his veins. "How about we talk about us?"

"There is no us," he said gently, even though he wished it could be otherwise. "Not while we're partners."

"Then you're not denying the attraction between us?"

"Only a fool would do that. And while I may be many things, a fool is not one of them."

Amusement warmed the silver in her eyes. "I'm tempted to disagree with that statement."

He smiled. "Undoubtedly."

"So, is this reluctance to get involved with a partner the reason why you're trying to ditch me? So you can feel free to play?"

He hesitated. It was tempting, *very* tempting, to go down the same route, to play the bastard card yet again. But he just couldn't do it. And maybe if he *was* honest, she'd understand his reasons and stop pushing. "In truth, no. I have a habit of killing partners. I don't want you—or anyone else—to join the list."

She nodded, and he had the odd feeling she wasn't exactly surprised. "Then this 'no involvement' rule is one you've had from the beginning?"

Again he hesitated. "Not really."

She raised her eyebrow. "Then you *have* been involved with a partner?"

"It went badly," he said, "and I realized my mistake. Hence the rule."

"How badly?"

"She died." He paused, not wanting to get into a discussion about an event that had happened long ago, even if that event still haunted him today. "I can't make that mistake again. I *won't*. While you're my partner, nothing will ever happen between us."

"And if I happen to ask for a transfer? What then?"

Then he'd definitely be tempted. But to what end? As much as part of him longed for something deeper, his changer half—the half that had already lost its soul mate—wasn't looking for anything more than a casual relationship, and that was exactly what he had with Sandy. Free and easy, with no commitment or restraint on either side. And in the brief time he'd known Sam, he'd learned one thing—she wasn't the casual type.

"And are you considering asking for a transfer?"

"At this point, no."

"Then it's a moot point, isn't it?"

His wristcom chose that moment to ring. Almost gratefully, he answered it.

Stephan's grim features greeted him. "There's been another murder."

Something clenched in Gabriel's gut. *Surely not Miranda.* "Where?"

"Up in Greenvale. The neighbors reported hearing two women screaming. The local cops have called us in."

Tension flowed from his body. Greenvale was nowhere near Strathmore. "So it's definitely connected to our serial killings?"

"From what they said, yes."

"Damn." Gabriel glanced at Sam. "There's been another murder. Are you able to handle the general alone?"

"I've been a cop for ten years. I don't think an interview with a general is beyond me."

He wasn't worried about her interviewing techniques; he was worried about leaving her alone with a man instinct told him they couldn't trust. He looked back at the wristcom. "I'll head there immediately. Have you heard anything about Miranda?"

"No. I called the old man, and he's still waiting to hear from Jess and Alain. You?"

"Nothing." If he didn't hear something soon, he'd call Jess and see what was going on. "You home?"

"Yes. Call me if anything happens."

He meant Miranda-wise, not case-wise. "Will do."

Gabriel disconnected and met Sam's gaze. "Miranda's

one of my adopted sisters, in case you were wondering."

She smiled slightly. "One of? How many do you have?"

"Four adopted and two full sisters." And one dead brother, he thought grimly. Lord, he did *not* want to lose anyone else. He guzzled the rest of his beer and stood up. "I have to go. Be careful with the general. Remember, he probably has his own reasons for being here."

She nodded. "I'll give you a call and let you know what happened."

"Do that." He dug the car keys out of his pocket and dropped them into her hand. "Take my car. You can pick me up in the morning."

She nodded, and Gabriel walked from the room. Han was in the process of heading into the kitchen and stopped in surprise.

"You're leaving your pretty lady so soon?"

"She's not *my* pretty lady—or my anything else, for that matter."

Han's smile was disbelieving. "I saw you together, my friend. Lie to yourself, if you wish, but I have seen the truth."

"What you've seen is the natural attraction of a man for a beautiful woman in a formfitting outfit. Half the men in this restaurant looked at her that way."

Han's smile was gentle, almost mocking. "As you wish, my friend. What can I do for you?"

"Keep an eye on her for me. As I said, I don't trust the general, but I have to leave."

"She will come to no harm in my restaurant. I shall monitor them, if you like."

"I like. Thanks, Han." He clapped the big man on the shoulder and quickly left. In the shadows of the bridge, he shapechanged and headed for Greenvale.

SO MUCH FOR DRESSING TO *kill,* Sam thought, watching Gabriel's retreat. Even if he had admitted his attraction, he'd actually taken about as much notice of her as he would have a gnat doing the cancan.

She leaned back in her chair and toyed with her drink. As a seductress, she'd been a miserable failure. Beyond his initial surprise, he'd given no reaction, and made no comment about how she looked. Nor had he had any obvious physical reaction to her caressing him suggestively with her toes.

Maybe he really did prefer tall, leggy blondes to short, slender redheads.

She sipped her water and stared at the dancing dragons. After a while, a waitress came in and placed a platter of hors d'oeuvres on the table. She nodded her thanks and glanced at her watch. Ten past eleven. The general was late. She hoped he wasn't reneging. The evening would be a total waste if he did.

As if on cue, the door opened. Han came into the room, followed by two men. Heat tingled a warning across her skin.

The general wasn't human, nor was the man who accompanied him.

"Would you gentlemen like a drink?" Han asked.

"Two coffees," the general replied, his tone almost offhand.

"Two coffees it is." Han's gaze touched hers. "I'm only a call away if you need anything else."

She nodded. It was good to know Han was close.

There was something about these two men she didn't trust, and it was more than just the warning itching her skin.

Somewhere, sometime, she'd met the general before. There was something horribly familiar in the way he walked.

The two men sat opposite her. The general's companion was in his mid-twenties, with red-gold hair and green-gray eyes. He could have been Harry Maxwell's brother. Could have been *her* brother.

Maybe he was.

If Hopeworth was playing with genetics, and if she was somehow connected to Hopeworth, then anything was possible.

"Samantha Ryan, I presume?" the general said.

She took a sip of water and nodded, and the general glanced at the man beside him. "My attaché, Duncan King."

The younger man held out his hand. For a second, Sam regarded it warily, then she reluctantly clasped it. Power shot through her fingertips—a power that was similar to the kind of energy that she felt in storms, and yet somehow different. It was a little "earthier" than the ethereal energy of the storms.

One other thing she noticed was that part of the power that surged between them had a sucking feel—as if he were a drain and everything was swirling toward him. King was psychic, and he was attempting to read her. She tore her hand away.

The general's eyes narrowed slightly. "You mentioned a murder case on the phone. Are the thirteen men you requested information on suspects?"

"No, but they may be victims." She scratched her

palm under the table. Her hand burned where King had touched her.

"Ten of the thirteen men are dead. Why would you consider them possible victims?"

So the general knew about the recent kite murders. Knew, too, that the other seven men were dead. "We have two separate murder cases involved here. Benson, Lyle and possibly White were killed by a vampire-like creature we call a kite. We believe Cooper and Haynes are the next likely victims."

"Which is why the SIU currently has both under protection?"

She nodded. "We thought it best for their safety."

The general's smile suggested he didn't believe that excuse. "And the other eight people you requested information on?"

"Their names came up during our investigations into a recent series of murders." She hesitated, meeting King's icy gaze. "All the victims were in their mid-twenties, were adopted from Greenwood State Care and had red hair. Just like your friend here."

"I see." If he detected her slight lie, he gave no indication of it. "Then you have heard of the Generation 18 project?"

She raised her eyebrows. Gabriel was right—the general was just a little too eager to talk about military secrets. He had an agenda of his own, and if the heat washing a warning across her skin was any indication, it boded her no good.

"It's been mentioned, yes."

The general leaned back in his chair. "By whom? Allars or Haynes?"

He was direct, if nothing else. She shrugged lightly.

"We pieced together details from what they've both said. Which wasn't much, believe me."

"Nor should it be. One was little more than a lab rat, and the other had behavior modifications." He hesitated, as if waiting for a reaction.

She crossed her arms and returned his gaze steadily. After a few seconds, he continued.

"The first eight people on your list—Allars included—have nothing to do with Generation 18."

A point she already knew, as Allars had already told her that those eight—the names on her birth certificate—were test subjects rather than scientists. And that they'd been involved in a project called Penumbra. But for his safety, and maybe even her own, it was best to pretend ignorance. "Then what were they involved in?"

The general considered her for a moment. "Have you ever heard of the Penumbra project?"

She didn't bat an eyelid. "No."

He continued to stare at her, his expression neither believing nor disbelieving, just blank. As if, in that moment in time, there was absolutely no one at home in the general's mind. King had a similar blankness. Were the two conferring mind to mind?

"Those men," the general said eventually, "worked on both projects."

"But they weren't the only scientists involved, surely?"

"No, there were others." He gave her a cool smile. "They're long dead, though, so of no concern to either you or your investigation."

A waitress came in, carrying two coffees. Sam waited until she left before continuing. "From what we can gather, Emma Pierce was a part of the Generation 18 project. Is that true?"

"Yes."

"Then what, exactly, was Generation 18?"

The general picked up his coffee and sipped it slowly. Then he reached for the tray of savories, sampling several. Obviously trying to decide just how much to tell her.

"King, here, is a product of Generation 18."

So he *was* Maxwell's brother—or, at the very least, his test-tube brother. She raised an eyebrow. "So Hopeworth is breeding children?"

"Special children, with special gifts. Not all weapons are mechanical, you know."

The hint of pride in his voice rolled revulsion through her. Tiny children growing in a bloodless, emotionless vacuum, pawns to the military's whims? What madness was that? No wonder King acted like a robot. He'd probably had any sense of humanity hammered out of him. "And the seventeen children placed into Greenwood twenty-two years ago?"

"Failures. Nowadays, we place them into care."

Meaning that in the past they'd been discarded with the other rubbish? God, what sort of monsters were these men? "Why were they considered failures?"

"Because they were born human."

And that was a failure? That they'd even managed to survive made them successful. "But why farm them out for adoption? Why not keep them in the military environment? Surely even mere humans could find a place in Hopeworth?"

His smile was cold. "If we wanted human soldiers,

we could recruit them. Besides, we don't have the facilities to raise children."

Yet they had the facilities to raise their "gifted" children. What was the difference? "Then why were the failures being prescribed Jadrone? The drug has no effect on humans."

The general raised an eyebrow. "The SIU has better information than we thought."

Meaning such information would be buried deeper in the future. "The autopsies revealed severe bone degeneration in both Jakes and Maxwell. Why would that be?"

The general exchanged a glance with King. The younger man's eyes went curiously blank again, and then life returned as he glanced back to the general. It was almost as if the general was asking permission to explain.

Maybe that explained King's presence here—he was the link back to base. Which might also mean every word they said was being monitored.

But how, if Han had the scramblers up?

The general met her gaze again. "Though our failures could not shift or change, they still carried the genes. By manipulating them in the manner we did, we accelerated some of the problems that shifters face."

"But only two of our four victims had the degeneration."

He nodded. "It depends on which genes were matched. Some got lucky."

Or unlucky, depending on your view. "Then why were the two without the degeneration being prescribed Jadrone? The drug is dangerous when used long term, and it kills changers outright."

"We discovered a mix that hybrids can take with no ill effects."

She wondered how they'd discovered it. Wondered how many had died in agony before they did. "Do you know if there's a drug in development that can take Jadrone's place?"

The general exchanged another glance with King. "No. Why do you ask?"

"Harry Maxwell was addicted to Jadrone. Yet a week before he was murdered, he gave up cold turkey. His supplier said he'd found something to replace it."

"I know of no such drug."

Was he lying? She wasn't sure. Either way, it was obviously time to change the direction of her questions.

"Why do at least two of our victims have Emma Pierce listed as their birth mother when Hopeworth took her ovaries, and therefore all chance to have a child herself once she'd left the military?"

The general smiled. "You've certainly done your research, young lady."

"I'm trying to save lives, General. We think someone is going after your failures."

"It could just be coincidence."

The look in his eyes told her he didn't believe it was. "Answer the question, General."

He smiled. *A crocodile toying with his prey,* she thought.

"We never did anything without the permission of the people involved. In Generation 18, the sacrifice was one they made willingly."

Not if what Allars said was true. "Then why was Emma Pierce listed as birth mother to at least two of your failures when in truth the children were conceived and raised in a test tube?"

"Because, in a sense, she *was* their mother. If the eggs from her ovaries resulted in successful births—and by this I mean children evolved from the initial procedure that reached full term—then she was listed as birth mother on the certificate."

Given a woman's ovaries carried all the eggs she needed to see her through her years of menstruation, it left open the possibility of there being hundreds of children out there who owed their existence to the unknowing Emma. It also meant that there could have been literally thousands of children who began their journey to life only to have it snuffed out by natural causes or the military's whim.

Her heart ached at the thought. But maybe it hurt more simply because she could never have children of her own. "And the seventeen children placed into Greenwood? Were they the only failures from the project?"

"The only ones that survived, yes."

"How many of them can Emma call her own?"

The general hesitated. "Nine, I believe. But surely that is something you can discover yourself."

She smiled. Of course she could, but it was easier to ask directly. "What about successes? How many of those belong to Emma Pierce?"

"Five."

"Are they still with Hopeworth?"

"Yes."

And would be forever, if the general's tone was anything to go by. "How were people like Emma selected for these projects?"

"They volunteered. We had criteria, of course."

"Was one of those criteria to have no family outside of Hopeworth?"

The general began to tap the table lightly. It was the first sign of annoyance she'd seen in him. His stern features were as impassive as ever.

"People join Hopeworth with the knowledge that, once accepted, it becomes your life. Only with retirement can you walk away. The 'no family' policy is more a general policy for Hopeworth itself than one related to the projects."

From what they'd learned, even retirement was no guarantee of escape. "Did Emma Pierce have a sister?"

"No. Her family was killed in an auto accident when she was a child." He hesitated, staring at her bluntly. "As you surely know."

"We do. Only Allars swears Emma had a sister. He claimed to have met her once."

"Impossible." But his quick frown told of his uncertainty.

"Why was Emma chosen for the project?"

"As I said, she volunteered."

"Yeah, but surely all volunteers are not automatically selected."

His quick grin conjured more images of crocodiles. "No. Emma Pierce had the right qualities."

"Those being?"

The tempo of his finger tapping increased. "Her father was a shifter, her mother a changer. Emma herself could do multiple forms of both."

She stared at him, uncertain at first whether she'd heard right. "What do you mean, she could do both? I thought hybrids were extremely rare."

"Hybrids *are* very rare; I think the figure is something like one in a billion births. But Emma's abilities were rarer still."

"And that's what Generation 18 was creating? Hybrids capable of multiple identities and abilities? Did the project defy the odds?"

"We were more successful than the quoted figure, yes."

So the military had hybrids at their disposal. Her gaze went to King. Hybrids with psychic abilities. "Why wasn't Emma listed as a hybrid?"

The general's smile was disdainful. "Because those who do the testing don't know what to look for. Generally, the hybrid is stronger in one area. Emma was listed as a changer simply because that was her strongest ability."

Which meant, more than likely, that Emma's sister had also escaped the net. They had a definite suspect. Now all they had to do was find her—and stop her.

"Is it possible for one of your hybrids to have escaped and be killing her less successful brothers and sisters?"

"No. As I'm sure you're aware, everyone at Hopeworth is tagged. All movements are monitored. Even mine."

She nodded. "The question had to be asked."

"I'm sure it did." He leaned back in his chair, regarding her through slightly narrowed eyes. "You have very unusual eyes, young lady."

The tension level jumped several degrees, though why she wasn't entirely sure. She took a long drink of water and nodded. "A few people have commented on that."

"Inherited from your mother or father?"

"I was placed into State care as a teenager. I have

no memory of my parents." Her smile was grim. "As I'm sure you already know, General."

He flashed his reptilian smile again. "I admit to doing a little checking myself."

"Why?"

"I thought you might be one of our rejects. I wondered if, perhaps, the programming had slipped and you were using this case to learn more about Hopeworth. Something similar happened recently with another project's reject."

So Hopeworth knew how to reprogram babies. The place was definitely the stuff of nightmares. "I was not a Greenwood kid."

"No. And we never did use the Ashwood center."

He'd definitely done more than a little checking if he knew she'd been in Ashwood's care. She took another sip of water to ease the sudden dryness in her throat. Was it just nerves, or had the temperature jumped by several degrees?

"There *are* natural redheads in this world, General," she remarked, voice dry.

"Oh, I agree. But your hair is not just red. It is more a red-gold, and in certain lights—this candlelight, for example—appears molten. It is something of a signature for our creations."

She glanced at King. "Molten" was an apt description for his hair. "Coincidence, General."

"Maybe."

His tone suggested he didn't think it was so. "General, I'm nearly thirty. Too old for the Generation 18 project by about five years."

"I'm well aware of that. There were other projects, of course."

"Like Penumbra?"

"Penumbra was our only true failure." The finger tapping hesitated slightly. "Though sometimes I wonder . . ."

He glanced briefly at King. Again, she had the sudden impression of information being exchanged, though neither man moved or spoke.

The general pushed back his chair and rose. "I don't believe there is much more we can help you with."

Meaning there wasn't much more he *intended* to help her with. She nodded. "Thank you for meeting me, General. You've cleared up a few problems."

"Yes, it's been most . . . interesting. Please call if you need anything else."

If she needed anything else, Gabriel could do the calling. "I will."

He nodded, and walked from the room. Tension flowed like water from her limbs, and she took a deep breath. She hadn't realized just how uneasy the general had made her feel.

She took another deep breath, then she doubled over in the chair as cramps knotted her stomach. Cursing softly, she grabbed her bag and stumbled to the restroom.

And discovered, at the grand old age of nearly thirty, she was getting her first period.

TEN

GABRIEL DUCKED UNDER THE POLICE tapes and walked toward the house. The red and blue lights of the emergency vehicles washed across the white walls of the two-story building, providing color to an otherwise lifeless-looking landscape.

At this house, unlike the houses surrounding it, the owner had gone for the minimalist look—no trees, no grass, just white concrete to every corner. It was a landscaping trend he hoped didn't catch on.

He showed his badge to the gnarled-looking police officer manning the front door, then walked inside. The smell of blood hit him immediately. Its odor was rich and sweet and almost fresh. Obviously, the murderer had been violent again.

The scent led him into the kitchen, where Warren Michaels and his autopsy team were already present. Warren himself was near the body, and annoyance flickered through Gabriel. His brother must have called them in, even though he knew Gabriel preferred to be first at the scene; it was easier to imagine what had happened without the interference of others.

The CSM hovering in the middle of the room spun round. "Identification, please."

"Gabriel Stern, SIU," he intoned, absently flashing his badge.

The first victim lay halfway between the cooking units and the counter. Her body was all angles, like a doll some child had broken and abandoned, and her red hair was darkened with blood. Blood also gleamed darkly on the white tiles, and it had splashed against the glass-fronted cooking units. The victim had put up quite a fight before she'd succumbed.

He knelt next to Michaels. "Anything new?"

Michaels snorted softly. "Yeah, the whole method of killing. She's getting more violent each time." He pointed to the purple bruising around the woman's neck. "She strangled her until she was unconscious, and then stabbed her several times before gutting her. We're dealing with a very sick person here."

Or an extremely angry person. "How did the killer get in?"

"Glass door in the dining room."

"Forced?"

"No. Can you believe they'd left it open? In this day and age?"

He smiled. Michaels had obviously never made a similar mistake. "No tray of cigarette butts this time?"

"She barely had time to escape. She must have been going out the back door as the State coppers were breaking in the front door."

"Where's the second victim?"

"In the upstairs bathroom." The com-unit Michaels

held beeped. "ID confirmed on this one. Margaret Jones."

Which *wasn't* one of the names on their list. "Have her parents been notified?"

"A unit is being sent there now."

Gabriel nodded and rose. Red droplets led away from the body of Margaret Jones, back into the entrance hall. There was a small cluster near the base of the stairs, as if the murderer had stopped and looked up. Perhaps the second victim had come out to investigate the noise, only to see the bloodied killer and her knife.

But if that were the case, why retreat to the bathroom rather than heading for the nearest window? Even if she'd broken a limb in the jump to the ground, she might well have lived. The killer wasn't likely to come after her in the middle of the street.

Gabriel continued up to the second floor. There was another gathering of droplets at the top of the stairs, indicating the killer had stopped once again, perhaps to listen. Which, in a sense, contradicted the idea that the killer was angry. Someone in the middle of a blood rage wasn't this cautious.

So why *was* she becoming more brutal with each murder?

He headed toward the first doorway, which turned out to be the main bedroom. The pillows bore the indentations of two heads, and the rumpled state of the queen-sized bed gave evidence to the fact that not a lot of sleeping had been going on recently.

He moved on. The next room was another bedroom, which was in the process of being turned into an office. The bed was still present, but it was squashed in one corner while desks, chairs and filing cabinets—all new and still wrapped in plastic—filled the middle of the room.

The killer hadn't bothered to stop in either room, because the droplets moved on, evenly spaced. Gabriel frowned. The killer must have injured herself in the fight downstairs, as the blood was too consistent to be dripping from a knife.

He finally came to the bathroom, and realized the second woman must have fled here because the door had a lock. The wood bore heel marks, and the catch had been torn from the frame. A second CSM hovered in the doorway. Gabriel showed his ID and stepped past it.

Only to stop cold.

The second victim was his sister, Miranda.

SAM DIALED GABRIEL'S NUMBER, BUT all she got was a busy signal—something she'd been getting for the last half-hour. She frowned at her wristcom and wondered what else she could do to contact him, because something was wrong. He wasn't in danger, but something was definitely wrong. There was an ache close to her heart—an ache that was his, somehow echoing through her.

She studied the car's onboard computer for several seconds, wondering what she should do—go home, as he'd ordered earlier, or try to find out what was happening? Really, it was a no-brainer. How could she sleep knowing something was wrong? She punched Gabriel's address into the computer.

As the vehicle spun around and headed back to the city, she leaned back and watched the traffic roll by. That was the nice thing about these auto-drives. You could be as tired as all hell and it didn't matter. The auto-drive would get you to your destination regardless of the condition you were in. Though if the satellites ever malfunctioned, there was likely to be the biggest damn accident in recorded history. Sam yawned hugely and closed her eyes. It seemed she'd barely gone to sleep when the car pulled to a halt and beeped softly.

She climbed out and looked up. There were no lights on in Gabriel's apartment. She climbed the steps and leaned on the buzzer for several seconds. No response. Frowning, she stepped back, staring up. If he was still at the murder scene, why wasn't he answering his phone?

She got back into the car, tapped the wristcom, and tried his number again. Same result—busy. Maybe his phone was charging. She dialed SIU. Christine answered on the second ring.

"Christine, Agent Ryan here. Can you check and see if AD Stern's wristcom is working?"

"One moment, please." She turned away from the screen. The overhead lighting caught her hair, turning the black strands a rich dark blue. They'd certainly worked on making her realistic, Sam thought. Wisps of hair swayed with every move, and if you looked hard enough, you could see her breathe.

"AD Stern's wristcom is currently off-line."

"Turned off?"

"Yes."

In the time she'd known him, that phone had never been turned off. "Who's on the cleanup team at Greenvale?"

"Agents Michaels and James."

"Could you patch me through to Michaels?"

"One moment, please."

Christine disappeared, to be replaced a few seconds later by Warren Michaels's drawn features.

"Agent Ryan. What can I do for you?"

"I'm looking for AD Stern. He still there?"

"He left about forty minutes ago. Why?"

She hesitated. "He asked me to report in. I'm just trying to find him."

"Tried his wristcom?"

"No, I thought I'd call you first, just to piss you off."

Michaels raised an eyebrow, a slight grin twitching his mouth. "Yeah, dumb question, I suppose. I guess you've tried his home number too, in which case, I can't help you."

She bit her lip. Gabriel was fine when he'd left her at Han's, which meant something must have happened on the way to the murder scene or at the scene itself.

"Did anything strange occur while he was there?"

Michaels snorted and rubbed his eyes. "If you can call discovering your sister was one of the victims strange, then, yeah, I guess it did."

"*What?*"

"Yeah. He was shaken, as you would expect. Left pretty much immediately after."

She rubbed her eyes. "You got an official ID?"

"Yeah. Miranda Stern, current address fourteen Hillsyde Street, Strathmore."

Miranda, the sister he'd been desperate to find. Her name must have been on the list of Hopeworth adoptees. Christ, what a mess. "Who's listed as next of kin?"

"A Jessie McMahon."

"Got an address or number?"

"Yeah, hang on a sec."

An almost fierce look of concentration came over his face. After a second, Jessie McMahon's address and phone number appeared on the screen. While she had no right to call Jessie, she would if Gabriel remained unreachable.

"That go through okay?" he said. "I hate these things."

She grinned. "It came through perfectly. What about the murders? Anything different from the first four?"

"Yeah, she's getting more violent. She tried drugging her first victim, only it didn't work. Both women put up a good struggle before they died."

"What was the entry/exit point?"

"She came through an open back door and left through the bathroom window as the cops were breaking in the front door."

"What was the first victim's name?"

Michaels glanced down for a second. "Margaret Jones."

Who *wasn't* on their list of possible victims. Meaning, more than likely, she'd simply been in the wrong place at the wrong time. Either that, or their killer was going off on another tangent.

"Other than the violence, was there anything different in the murderer's actions?"

Michaels scratched his chin. "Well, she had no time for a ciggy, that's for sure. But she didn't with the doc, either." He hesitated, then frowned. "And she injured herself this time. Right hand. And pretty badly, if the constant flow of blood is any indication."

"When you do an analysis on the blood, could you send me the results?"

"Sure thing."

"Thanks, Michaels." She hung up, then redialed SIU and got put through to Izzy.

"This is becoming a habit, sweetie. Don't you ever sleep?"

She rubbed gritty-feeling eyes. "Not lately, I don't. Iz, did you finish the search on Dr. Francis?"

"I surely did. She was born in New South Wales in 1987, the third child of a Meg and John Francis."

Which made her sixty years old. Only slightly older than she'd guessed. "No relation to Emma Pierce, then?"

"No, honey child. Afraid not."

Damn. Every clue they'd had pointed to Emma's elusive sister. If Dr. Francis wasn't the sister, how was she connected to the case? She *was* connected; of that Sam was sure. "Were you able to acquire the surveillance tapes from her building?"

"Yes."

"Any visits from anyone connected to this case?"

Iz twirled the boa for several seconds. "Max Carter and Harry Maxwell were regulars until the time of Harry Maxwell's death."

She raised her eyebrows. Max had moved from his lair? How, given his sheer size? "What hospital is Max holed up in?"

"St. Vincent's."

"His condition?"

The boa twirled again. "Critical but stable."

"Great. Iz, can you do a search of the case files and grab the list of children placed into Greenwood's care?"

"Got it, sweetie."

"Patch it through to my wristcom, will you?"

"Consider it patched."

The wristcom beeped, indicating it was receiving information. "Thanks, Izzy."

"Have a nice night, sweetness."

She hung up, then glanced at her watch. It was nearly two in the morning. The hospital wasn't going to let her interview Max at this hour, no matter how vital it might be. She'd have to wait several hours. All she could really do now was head home and get a few hours' sleep.

SAM WOKE WITH A START. Her heart thundered with a rhythm that spoke of fear. Heat crawled over her skin, warning of danger. She glanced at the time. Four fifteen. She'd been home for nearly two hours, and asleep about half that.

She stared into the darkness that filled the living room. She'd fallen asleep on the sofa, as she did most nights. The TV had turned itself off, and the only sound to be heard was the wind sighing through the window she'd left slightly open.

So what had woken her so abruptly?

She wasn't sure. Frowning, she rose and headed to the bathroom. But halfway there, she heard it—a slight beep outside her front door. An inconspicuous sound unless you knew what it meant. Someone was using a key-coder to break into her apartment.

The sensation of danger crawled over her skin, so intense it burned. But before she could move, the door handle turned. She stilled, barely daring to breathe, and hoped like hell the shadows would hide her.

The door opened slightly. A figure appeared, dressed in black, features covered by a mask. A woman.

She hesitated in the doorway, then threw something toward the bedroom. It landed with a soft thump, the impact obviously cushioned by the thick carpet. The woman stepped back and closed the door.

Sam stepped toward the object on the floor. It was round and metallic, and it had numbers that glowed into the darkness. Numbers that were counting down from ten . . . nine . . . eight . . .

A bomb. *Another* goddamn bomb. And she'd only just had the place rebuilt after the last one . . .

She dove for the window, as she had last time. There was little other choice. The bomb beeped and then exploded. Heat sizzled across her bare feet as she crashed through the window. Glass and flames followed her into the night as she tumbled down to the ground two stories below. Only, like a cat, she somehow landed not only on her feet, but unhurt. She wasted no time on reflecting how or why this was possible, running instead for the front of the building.

A car engine roared to life. She cursed and pounded around the corner. Lights cut into the darkness. She threw up her arm to protect her eyes, then she realized the lights were drawing close. The engine roared and tires squealed as the driver accelerated—directly at her.

She threw herself sideways, but not fast enough. The car swiped her side, and pain leapt like fire through her body. She hit the concrete with a grunt. Darkness surged through her and she knew no more.

GABRIEL LEANED BACK IN HIS chair and rubbed his eyes. They ached, like the rest of him ached—and his heart most of all. But there was no time to rest, no time to contemplate *what if.* Not until he caught the bitch who'd murdered his sister.

Behind him, his father paced, his strides long and somehow furious. Grief was something that hadn't fully hit the Stern clan yet. Anger, and the need to find Miranda's killer, were uppermost in everyone's mind.

Which was why they were here. Though the Federation's headquarters was supposedly on Collins Street, this small bomb shelter was its true heart—one of a dozen built within the city during the new millennium, when the Race Wars were at a peak. The shelter was a two-story-deep complex that housed the Federation's information-gathering center. The SIU might pride itself on having an extensive network system, but the Federation had operatives in every government, every union, and every rebellious group currently on record. Though officially the Federation was not terribly active these days, it kept its finger on the pulse and was ready to intervene whenever and wherever needed.

Right now, those resources were concentrated on finding his sister's killer.

The door behind them opened. Gabriel glanced around. Stephan walked to the table and dropped a sheaf of papers on the glass-topped desk.

"That's everything we could find on Hopeworth

and its projects." He collapsed into a chair and rubbed his eyes. Though family members currently manned the center, the image Stephan retained as the head of the Federation was the image the world knew—black hair with green eyes rather than blue. This was the Stephan who was the image of their father rather than his true self, Gabriel's nonidentical twin. Even here, in the true heart of the Federation, they had to be careful. "Our contact in Hopeworth wasn't able to help. Security has been tightened since these murders began."

Gabriel raised an eyebrow. "Since they began? Did he say why?"

"A security breach the day before the murders started, apparently."

"Someone got into their system," he mused. "That's how the killer found out about the Generation 18 adoptees."

"And probably why the general was so anxious to meet with you. He wanted to know how much SIU knew."

Gabriel nodded, and glanced at his watch. "I'll call Sam at seven and see how the meeting went."

Stephan's gaze narrowed. "Why not call her now?"

"Because it's four in the morning, and she deserves to get a few hours' sleep before I start hounding her again."

"Miranda is dead. Doesn't finding her killer take precedence?" There was an almost accusatory note in Stephan's rich tone.

Gabriel clenched his fist and somehow restrained the urge to launch across the table and slug his brother. "I know Miranda is dead. I found her, remember?"

"Enough, both of you." Charles slapped a palm down on the table. The sound ricocheted through the abrupt silence, as sharp as a gunshot. "Fighting among ourselves is not the answer. And as much as I want to find this murderous bitch, I agree with Gabriel. What young Samantha has discovered can wait until morning. I have a feeling that we have all the clues we need right here."

He nudged the case reports with a finger. Gabriel stared at his twin for several seconds and saw the anguish and guilt in his eyes, which was no doubt a mirror of his own. Like him, Stephan felt he should have done more to prevent Miranda's murder. He sighed and reached for the top folder. "We've been through these. There's nothing here."

Charles pulled a chair out and sat down. "How is the killer getting in and out of the murder scenes?"

"I think she's a hybrid; one we haven't got on record."

Stephan raised an eyebrow. "The tests are pretty intensive. It's doubtful that we missed one."

"But it's only in the last ten years or so that our tests have become so precise. Before that, it was hit-or-miss, with most hybrids being allocated shifter or changer status, depending on which was their stronger trait. Emma Pierce was fifty-six. So was her sister. There's no record of Emma coming in for tests since puberty."

Stephan frowned. "If she was part of Hopeworth, that's not surprising. As for the sister, we haven't been able to find anything on her yet."

"A little too convenient, don't you think?"

"Erasing records is not something an everyday hacker can achieve—not without setting off alarms."

"If they got into Hopeworth, we're dealing with someone a little more skilled than your average hacker."

"True." Stephan rubbed his chin thoughtfully. "You know, it might also indicate someone who has regular access to records. How else would they get into the system without raising alarms?"

"A government employee?" It was certainly a distinct possibility. As Stephan said, anyone without clearance hacking into the file system would have raised alarms. It was doubtful such a person could have erased data so completely without getting caught.

"You might even be looking for a cop," Charles said, his deep voice somber. "They have access to all manner of records, and who would have a better understanding of how to avoid detection at a crime scene?"

Gabriel frowned. "If our killer was a cop, her hybrid status would have been picked up in the six-month checkups. As you said yourself, the tests are pretty extensive."

"They never picked up Sam's extra chromosome," Stephan said, "so it might just be possible they'd miss this. Race is not something that is checked every six months, unless the officer has noted his or her desire to become a vampire."

"True, but still . . ." Gabriel hesitated as the door opened.

Jessie walked in and dropped several sheets of paper on the table. "We traced the birth certificates for every one of the Greenwood adoptees. Emma Pierce is listed as birth mother for nine of them." She hesitated, tears suddenly welling in her green eyes. "The killer is working straight down the list. Miranda . . ."

She broke off. Stephan stood, gathering her in his arms and holding tight. Gabriel reached for the papers. Emma Pierce's children were highlighted. Miranda was number five of nine. He looked up.

"Then we know the next victim. Jeanette Harris is number six on the list."

Charles smiled grimly. "Get protection on her right away."

"Already done," Stephan said. He handed Jessie a handkerchief, then met Gabriel's gaze. "If our killer is a cop, she'll know about the safety measures we've taken."

"It won't stop her. She's a hybrid. If she's in animal form, more than likely our people won't even see her." He hesitated. "But Sam might be able to."

Charles studied him through narrowed eyes. "Why do you say that? I thought she didn't have any talents."

No talent or too much talent? He was beginning to think it was the latter. "Test results to date indicate no psychic inclination, but I've seen her in action. In certain situations, she can sense the presence of other nonhumans. She sensed the shifter who'd attacked Finley in the labs, for instance, even though no alarm had been given."

"And didn't she sense the fact that Mary was a vampire long before either of us were aware of it?" Stephan said.

Gabriel nodded. "And yet she *didn't* know you were a shifter and that Martyn was also a vampire."

"As if she could sense the evil in people more than

what they were," Charles murmured. "How very interesting."

"And useful, if that is the case," Stephan said. He glanced at Gabriel, his gaze hardening. "Assign her to Jeanette Harris immediately."

Gabriel stared at his brother for several seconds, then reached for his wristcom. In that instant, pain hit—a sledgehammer that belted him sideways. He hit the floor hard, clutching his head, desperate to break the connection running fire up the left side of his body and into his brain.

"Gabriel!" Fear and confusion ran through his brother's voice.

Hands grabbed him, touching his neck, feeling for a pulse. Darkness welled, a tide that threatened to overwhelm him. "I'm okay. It's not me," he managed to gasp out.

"Sam?" Stephan's voice, close by his side.

He somehow managed to nod. In that instant, as fast as it had come, the pain eased, becoming a muted throb in the back of his mind. He took a deep breath, shook off his brother's grip and struggled to his feet.

"What the hell was that all about?" Charles demanded, his lean face pale.

"It appears Gabriel and Sam have formed a telepathic bond of some kind," Stephan said. "What you just saw is him experiencing what has happened to her."

Though Stephan's voice was tightly controlled, Gabriel nevertheless felt his twin's anger. It was as if the link being forced with Sam had somehow unfettered the link with his brother. Neither of which he wanted.

He tapped his wristcom again and quickly dialed

her home number. No answer. He tried her wrist-com, and got the same result. "She's not answering."

"I'll arrange for a team to go and check her apartment." Stephan's phone beeped. He moved away slightly and answered it.

Jessie touched Gabriel's arm, catching his attention. "You can use the link to find her, you know."

He met his sister's compassionate gaze and knew she could taste the worry in his mind. Jess had taken after their mother, and was both an empath and a clairvoyant. "What do you mean?"

Her quick smile was sad and, in some ways, an echo of the almost bitter smile Stephan had given him last night. "Your connection with this woman must be strong if a link has been forged despite your determination to avoid all such bonds." She hesitated and tucked a wayward brown curl behind her ear. "If you open fully to the bond, you can use it to track her down."

Once opened, never closed. He didn't want that sort of closeness with anyone ever again. Coping with the death of a loved one was bad enough in itself, but when you could feel it within every pore and fiber of your being . . .

"Andrea was a long time ago," she said softly.

A long time, yes, but still not forgotten. In the worst of his dreams he could still feel the bullet that had torn through her heart and shattered his world. Could still feel the hand of death as it reached for her soul.

Jessie touched his face gently, like a mother calming a frightened child. "Such fear was perhaps understandable when you were younger, Gabriel, but it is way past time you accept what has happened and move on with your life. Blocking the world out is never the answer—and you have hurt Stephan more than you can ever imagine."

He glanced at his twin. "I know. But blocking him out has become such a habit that I'm not even aware of it anymore."

"Until this Sam of yours came along."

"She's not *my* Sam." Why did people keep calling her that? *Shit,* the truth was, they barely even knew each other. "She's my partner—and if I have my way, won't even be that for much longer."

Jess raised a dark eyebrow. "Are you denying your attraction?"

"When you can read the truth in my mind?" He smiled a little grimly. "I'm not that foolish. But it's an attraction I have no intention of following through on. I don't want to lose another partner."

"Such things cannot always be controlled, Gabriel. As evidenced by this bond you're forming."

"If I can cut my twin from my thoughts, I can cut an unwanted connection with Sam, believe me."

Her smile became a little sad again. "You will end up a very lonely old man if you're not careful, Gabriel."

He briefly cupped her cheek with his palm. "How will I end up lonely when I have a sister who'll nag me senseless?"

"You're hopeless, little brother." She leaned forward and placed a light kiss on his cheek. "And soon you will learn to watch what you wish for."

Gabriel glanced up sharply. She met his gaze with a cryptic smile and stepped back as Stephan approached.

"That was headquarters." His face was grim. "Sam's apartment has just been bombed. Again."

Jessie gasped softly. "Is she all right?"

"A question Gabriel can no doubt answer."

He ran a hand through his hair. "She's alive. She wasn't caught in the bombing—that much I know."

"Then you'd better figure out how to find her. She's probably our best shot at stopping this murderous bitch fast." Stephan glanced across the room. "Meantime, Dad and I will search the State Police recruitment records and see if we can find anything suspicious."

He watched the two men leave the room and then looked at his sister. "How do I use the link to find her?"

SAM GROANED AND HELD HER head. There were a thousand tiny madmen in there, all intent on beating drums out of sync with each other. The headaches she'd experienced before had nothing on this. The noise created by the madmen vibrated through every nerve, every cell—it even seemed to gain form and dance around her. Her whole body thrummed to the beat of its tune. Then slowly, she realized the noise was real, not imagined. And she realized she was not alone.

She lifted her head. Dr. Francis, the vet she'd taken her borrowed cat to, stood four feet away, her arms crossed and a contemptuous look on her face. Behind her, though cloaked in darkness, Sam could make out a series of tumbledown brick walls. No light broke the darkness, and the air had a stale smell. All around them, noise hummed. Machinery, she realized. They were on a building site.

But what kind of site operated in the middle of the night?

"You should be dead," Dr. Francis said. Her voice was still polite, still disinterested. "First you managed to overcome a lethal dose of Jadrone, and then you somehow survived a car accident that would have killed most."

"*You* were the budgie in Max's office," Sam murmured. The men in her head were beginning to find some rhythm, making a semblance of thought possible. "Why did you think Jadrone might stop me?"

"Because a colleague of mine said it would." A smile fluttered across the doctor's brightly painted lips. "She can sense others of our kind, as you also appear able to do."

If she and her colleague thought Sam a changer, that at least explained the dose of Jadrone. "Your colleague's name wouldn't happen to be Rose, would it?" When Dr. Francis merely smiled, Sam added, "So why did you try to kill me? And Max?"

"Max was nothing more than a weak fool." Contempt dripped from the doctor's voice. "He would have told you of our partnership, would have implicated me in Harry's murder. With Max all but dead, I thought I was safe until you showed up at the office."

So the doctor had known who she was and had simply played along. She must have followed her to O'Hearn's and then home. Obviously, the doc had no idea that Harry's murder was tied in with a serial killer. Maybe she didn't read the newspapers.

Sam tried to ease the ache in her left leg by shifting

her weight slightly and realized she couldn't even move. Her legs were wrapped in something cold and heavy. Chains.

Fear rose, but she thrust it away. There was no time for fear, only escape. And if she didn't do that soon she would die, of that she was certain.

"How were you involved with Harry?"

"He was nothing more than another test subject."

"For your new drug?" she guessed. "An addictive and expensive replacement for Jadrone?"

"Yes. One that helps shifters without the hallucinations."

"So why not sell it through regular channels? It'd be a huge hit on the open market."

"Because it is not without its problems, and it's deadly to both changers and humans. A drug like that would take years to get approval, if it ever did." Dr. Francis hesitated, and a siren blasted through the hum of machinery. "Time for me to go. You, I'm afraid, must remain here. But don't worry, you won't have to wait long for death—twenty floors of an old high-rise are about to come crashing down upon your head."

At least that explained the predawn activity. If the old tower was anywhere near a large number of office buildings, the demolition team would have been given clearance to work only between midnight and dawn.

"The chains that contain you are silver-coated," Francis continued. "You cannot change shape until you escape them, my dear. And by then, death will be falling around your ears."

"You won't get away with this. The SIU doesn't take kindly to someone killing their operatives." She had no idea whether this was true or not, but, hell, it sounded good.

"By the time they find out you didn't die in your apartment bombing, you will be dead and I will be long gone."

The doctor stepped back and raised her arms, and her body blurred, briefly resembling putty being squeezed into a too-small tube. Then she became a budgie and flitted away through the darkness.

Sam glanced down at the chains. The two ends ran off into the darkness, one to her right and the other to her left. They were connected to hooks in the wall that kept the chains taut. All she had to do was un-latch one and she'd be free.

She lunged sideways. The chains around her waist bit deep, and breathing became difficult. She ignored it and tried to flick the end of the chain off the hook on the wall. It didn't even budge. Cursing softly, she sat back up and grabbed hold of the chain. Taking a deep breath, she pulled back as hard as she could.

A muffled thump ran through silence, followed by a thick wave a dust. She coughed, and glanced up. A shudder ran through the ceiling above her, and cracks began to appear—spider-like lines that raced from the edges toward the middle.

Fear surged. Time was running out. She swore and pulled back on the chain again. The hook on the wall shifted slightly. Another muffled thump ran through the silence. Dirt and plaster began to rain down on her.

"Come on, you mother, come *on*!"

The hook came free with a sudden pop and sent her sprawling backward. At the same time, another muf-fled thump ran across the shattering darkness, closer this time. The ceiling above her groaned. The spider-like lines intermingled and the whole ceiling dropped.

She screamed and threw herself sideways. But the chains still restricted her movement and all she could do was throw her hands over her head and pray for a miracle.

ELEVEN

GABRIEL HIT THE GROUND RUNNING. One section of the old high-rise had already been demolished. Dust rose in a wave, stinging the night sky with the scent of decay and death.

He wrenched open the door to the command center. The two men inside turned around, surprise evident in their expressions. He flashed his badge. "You have to stop the demolition. We have an agent trapped inside the building."

"I can't. It's automated."

He grabbed the man's shirt and dragged him close. "Listen very carefully. I have an agent trapped inside. I want the demolition stopped, and I don't care how you do it."

"Okay, okay," the man stuttered. "We'll try."

"Don't try. Just do it." He thrust the man away from him, grabbed the flashlight that was sitting on a bench and headed back outside.

Another muffled explosion ran across the silence. The old building seemed to shudder, and then the west wing came down in an almost graceful silence. More dust rose into the sky.

He swore and ran for the central building, the area that had once housed the building's basement. That was where she was.

The main doors were boarded shut, but several well-placed kicks soon fixed that. Dust rolled out to greet him, as thick as the darkness beyond the doorway.

He coughed, and turned on the flashlight. Another explosion rolled through the night, followed quickly by a muffled scream.

Sam. As yet unhurt by the falling debris.

He picked his way down the shattered corridor, heading for the emergency exit sign that gleamed brightly in the beam of the flashlight. The stairs beyond were a tangle of wood and jagged plasterboard. He shone the light upward. Part of the ceiling had collapsed. It wouldn't take much to bring the whole lot down.

He continued on. Dust caught at his throat, making him cough, and the air became stale, almost hard to breathe.

"Gabriel?" Her voice rose from the darkness, full of sudden hope.

"Here." He swung the light to the left. Her voice had come from beyond the row of disconnected walls.

"I'm trapped," she said. "Hurry."

Another explosion ran through the darkness. He swore and wondered why the fools in charge hadn't stopped the demolition. Surely they could throw a power switch. With no power, there would be no computer to regulate the charges.

Plaster and brick began to rain from the ceiling, deadly missiles that drew blood every time they hit. He ran through the maze, dodging and weaving the best he could. The flashlight danced across the darkness, briefly illuminating shadowed corners. None of them held Sam.

"Talk to me, Sam!"

"Here!" she said.

She was close, so close. He kicked his way through a doorway. "Again."

"On your right, through the door, I think."

There were two doors on his right. Letting instinct take control, he booted open the second of the two. The light picked out her dust-covered face.

He knelt by her side. The ceiling had half collapsed, covering her in plaster and wood. But that wasn't what held her. Chains did. Anger rose, swift and hard. The would-be assassin had better hope he wasn't the one who caught her.

"You okay?" He pushed the debris away from her body, grabbed the end of the chain and began to unwind it.

"Fine," she said. "How did you find me?"

He met her gaze briefly. Confusion and relief mingled in her smoke-ringed blue eyes. She wasn't aware of the bond she'd forged. *Good*. Perhaps he'd be able to close it before it got too strong.

"Long story." He unwound the chains from her legs and tossed them to one side. "Can you move?"

"I think so." She grabbed his hand and pulled herself up. No sooner had she put weight on her left leg than it collapsed under her.

He grabbed her before she could fall back down. "Looks like you've done some damage to your leg."

He slipped an arm round her waist, taking her weight—what little there was of it. "Let's get out of here."

She didn't argue. They made their way back to the stairs, their progress agonizingly slow. Though she made no complaint, her pain stabbed at the back of his mind.

Another muffled thump ran across the darkness. A shudder ran through the bricks around them, and the dust became thick enough to carve. The flashlight's bright beam flared against the soupy swirl, unable to penetrate more than a yard or so.

They struggled up the stairs. Behind them, it began to rain bricks and wood, gently at first, but increasing in volume and strength. The building was coming down. Gabriel swung Sam up into his arms and ran like hell for the front entrance. The collapse was a tidal wave that raced behind him. He could feel the strength of it pushing at his back, urging him to fall. Plaster and wood crashed around them, and the dust was so thick he could barely breathe, let alone see.

He stumbled past a mound of wood and bricks and out the front door. A deep groaning filled the silence—the final scream of a dying building. He kept on running.

The old building came down with an almost silent sigh, and a sudden rush of wind battered at him, thrusting him to the ground. He twisted as he fell, so that he cushioned Sam's body with his own. For a few seconds, all he could hear was the thunder of her heart, and all he could feel was the warmth of her body pressed against him. And all he wanted to do was keep on holding her, because it felt so right, so real, somehow.

The two men scrambled out of the control room.

"Jesus, man, are you all right?"

The sandy-haired worker he'd threatened stopped several feet away. Which was just out of reach. "Yeah. Call an ambulance, will you?"

"I'm okay," she murmured, struggling against his hold on her.

He released her and she rolled away from him and sat up. Though she made no sound, her teeth caught her bottom lip. Beads of sweat broke out across her brow.

"Sure you are." He took a handkerchief from his pocket and began wiping the dust from her face. Her left cheek was badly scratched, and blood oozed down to her chin. "Tell me what happened."

"I pissed off that budgie again." She took a deep, shuddering breath. "And I'm gonna sell my damn apartment. People keep insisting on bombing it."

He half-smiled at her indignant tone. "Are we talking about the budgie that tried to shit all over you in Max's office?"

"That's her. Otherwise known as one Dr. Francis. Ex-colleague to one Max Carter, and would-be supplier to Harry Maxwell."

"But no relation to Emma Pierce?" he guessed.

"Unfortunately, no. She's not our serial killer, just a would-be drug mogul who hasn't taken the time to see the bigger picture. She *is* working with someone who I suspect might be Rose, though it wasn't confirmed. But I'm going to take great delight in throwing Dr. Francis's well-manicured butt in prison, I can tell you."

He grinned. "I almost feel sorry for Dr. Francis."

Her grin briefly echoed his. "Sure you do." Then

she hesitated, her smile fading as her gaze searched his. "I'm sorry to hear about your sister."

An ache cut through his heart. An ache he'd been trying so hard to ignore. "How did you find out about it?"

It came out more abruptly than he'd intended, and she raised an eyebrow in surprise. "You weren't answering your phone, so I called Michaels to see what was going on. He told me."

"Why were you calling in the first place?"

"You asked me to report in, remember?" She leaned back on her hands and studied him for a moment. "Why the third degree?"

He thrust a hand through his hair. He hadn't meant to be so brusque, but he didn't want the whole world knowing about his sister's death, either. Not until the Stern clan had time to deal with her loss, time to say goodbye. "Sorry. I guess I'm not ready to talk freely about her murder just yet."

"Especially with me, I suppose."

Her words were a whisper he barely caught, and her expression suggested a loneliness as deep as anything he'd ever experienced. He half reached out to comfort her, but then he dropped his hand. This was what he wanted, he reminded himself fiercely. And more than ever, he wanted her to remain safe.

Silence reigned as they waited for the ambulance to arrive. He itched to get back to searching for his sister's killer, but he wasn't enough of a bastard to simply walk away from Sam before she'd received medical attention.

After a few minutes, she ran a hand across her bloody chin and asked, "How did you find me?"

He shrugged. "The locals took note of Francis's car

as it sped away from your building. We traced her here."

"Really?" There was disbelief in her face and in her voice. "Then how did you know which building I was in?"

"It was the only one left standing. I took a chance."

Her gaze searched his face. "Why are you lying to me?"

"I'm not." A siren finally sounded in the distance. He glanced past her, watching the red and blue lights of the ambulance draw close. "The ambulance is here."

"I want to go home, not to the hospital."

"Your home's been bombed, remember?" He brushed a strand of hair from her forehead.

She jerked away from his touch, expression annoyed as she glared up at him. "I don't care."

"Okay. But let the doctor examine you first."

"Fine." She crossed her arms and stared at him mutinously.

He knew her silence would last only until they were alone. Then she'd want answers—answers he had no intention of giving.

The ambulance officers trotted across the grounds, medical bags in hand. Sam bore their ministrations in silence, though he could feel her annoyance, a wave of heat that washed past his mind. Having opened the link to find her, he could now feel her emotions as easily as he breathed. Touching her thoughts was only a matter of reaching out . . . but he had no intention of playing with that sort of fire. He'd shared such a link with Andrea. Once was more than enough.

"There's severe bruising around the hip and torso

area, but otherwise, you seem okay," the ambulance officer said. "You might want to go to the hospital as a precautionary measure—"

"No, I'm fine, really." Sam flashed Gabriel an I-told-you-so look. "I'll just go home and rest."

"It would be better if you had a thorough check at the hospital first—"

"No," she said, more firmly this time. "I'm fine. Honestly."

Neither of the two officers looked happy, but they packed up their bags and walked back to the ambulance.

Gabriel called a cab, then held out his hand, and Sam hesitated only briefly before accepting his assistance. She was still wobbly on her feet, no matter how fit she claimed to be.

The cab came within minutes. He helped her inside, climbed in beside her and punched her address into the onboard computer. Despite his earlier thoughts to the contrary, she asked no further questions. Maybe she'd finally given up.

It took half an hour to reach her apartment. Several SIU gray Fords were parked out front, but the police vehicles had gone. No lights shone in any of the windows above or below her apartment—perhaps the neighbors were getting used to being woken by bomb blasts in the middle of the night.

They made their way up the stairs. Sam showed little emotion as she stepped through the shattered doorway to her apartment.

He watched her limp to the bedroom, and then he moved across the living room to the window. Yet again she'd escaped a bomb blast by diving out into the night. He stopped and stared at the pavement below. At the very least, she should have broken a limb in a fall like that. But her bruising had come from the car, not the fall.

It would be interesting to see what O'Hearn came up with.

He turned from the window as two SIU men, bags in hand, filed out of the bedroom.

"Anything to be found, Burton?"

The big man shook his head. "The bomb was incendiary, as you can see by the flame damage. It was meant to kill rather than cause structural damage."

"Send me a full report as soon as you can."

The big man nodded. Gabriel tapped his wristcom and ordered a pickup on Dr. Jane Francis. Then he walked into the bedroom. Sam stood in the middle of the room, staring at the mess of soggy boxes almost blindly.

"Sometimes I wish I could step back in time," she said, her voice a little distant and etched with pain. "Just go back to a time when my partner was my best friend, and I was just a plain old orphan, not some kind of freak."

Her pain ran through him, a living thing he could almost taste and touch. He ached to reach out, to hold her. *Remember Andrea,* he told himself sternly. *Don't get involved too deeply.*

"We all wish for things that cannot be," he said, his voice sharp. "Sometimes we just have to accept fate and get on with it."

She snorted softly. "Like you're getting on with it, Assistant Director?"

He frowned. "What do you mean?"

She didn't answer, simply shook her head and

picked her way toward the window. "What do you want me to do about Dr. Francis?"

"I've ordered her to be picked up. She'll be charged with attempted murder. You'll have to write up the report as soon as you can." He hesitated. "Was she responsible for bombing your apartment?"

Sam nodded. "Do you want a written report on my meeting with the general as well?"

"Yes, but you can give me the basics now, if you like." One thing was for certain—he wasn't sending her to watch over Jeanette Harris. She'd been through enough for one night.

She crossed her arms. To anyone else she might have looked calm. Casual, even. But her anger washed through his soul and burned him with guilt.

"Nine of the seventeen children placed into Greenwood's care have Emma listed as their birth mother. She, and more than likely her sister, was a hybrid shifter-changer. One who can take on multiple forms of either."

"I'd already guessed we were dealing with a hybrid." Although he certainly *hadn't* guessed that the hybrid might be capable of multiple animal as well as human identities. *That* was unheard of. Or so he'd thought.

"Did you also know that the purpose of Generation 18 was to design psychically endowed hybrids for the military to use as weapons?"

So Hopeworth was mucking about in the genetic sandbox. Maybe the kites *were* one of their creations. "Anything else?"

She was silent for several heartbeats, staring out the window. "I think there'll be trouble with the general in the future."

Her voice was almost subdued. He frowned. "What do you mean?"

"Why did the general agree to meet with us?"

"You requested information."

"Information you found out without the general's help. He told me nothing, really. But he thought I was one of the rejects trying to get information on where I came from."

His confusion deepened. "Why would he think that? You're too old, for a start."

"He said it was my hair color. Apparently, it's something of a signature in their projects."

If she'd come from one of their projects, it would certainly explain the birth certificate with eight names on it. But the general seemed to know the exact location of all his rejects. Why wouldn't he know if she was one of them?

"If you're one their rejects, you have nothing to worry about." Hopeworth had showed no interest in the Generation 18 rejects.

"But what if I'm not a reject? What if I'm something else entirely?"

"From what I can see, you're either a reject or in Hopeworth. What else is there?"

"I don't know." Her voice was so soft he barely caught it. "But I've a feeling I'm going to find out."

She rubbed her arms and he clenched his fists, fighting the urge to walk across the room and comfort her.

"I've got to go," he said abruptly. "I want you to do a search through our records. See if there have been any official requests for information on our Generation 18 rejects."

"That's something you could order your computer to do in a minute flat, Assistant Director."

Which was true enough. But he had to find some way to keep her out of the line of fire, however temporary. "A computer can't follow up and have an informal discussion with the requester's captain or director."

She looked around at him, one pale eyebrow raised. "You think the killer might be a cop or agent?"

"There's a good chance. The only way she could have found these seventeen people so quickly is through official channels. No alarms were raised, so the records weren't hacked into."

"And if I find anything?"

"Contact me or Stephan. Under no circumstances are you to go after her yourself."

"Edging me out again, huh?" She shook her head slightly. "I never took you for a coward, Gabriel. I guess I was wrong."

His anger rose, swift and hard, and her eyes widened. Maybe she wasn't as unaware of the link as he'd thought.

"Better me being a coward than you being dead." He hesitated and ran a hand through his hair. "Damn it, just do what you're told. I can't deal with this now."

"And you won't deal with it later," she murmured.

He smiled grimly. She knew him too well. "My wristcom is on. Contact me if you find anything."

"I've already said I would."

He stared at her for several seconds longer, taking in her slender form, the almost defiant way she stood. Like hell she'd contact him when she found anything. But short of tying her to a chair to keep her safe, there was nothing he could do. "Make sure you lock the door when I leave," he said, then turned and walked from the room.

SAM SCRUBBED A HAND ACROSS her eyes and wondered where the hell her brains were. Antagonizing Gabriel would only make him more determined to get rid of her. *If* that was even possible.

He appeared on the street below and climbed quickly into an SIU car. She wondered where he was going, as it was pretty obvious he had no intention of going back to SIU. For half a second she thought about following him, but she knew that would only get her into deeper shit. And she was in enough of that now.

She sighed softly and turned away from the window. Though her bones ached with exhaustion, she knew sleep would elude her. Not that she could sleep here anyway. What the fire hadn't destroyed, the water had. The insurance company was going to love her for making another claim so soon.

She walked through to the living room and locked the front door. The bomb's damage had been confined mainly to the bedroom. Parts of the living room had been scorched, but it was more water damage out here. The books she'd salvaged after the first bombing had borne the brunt of the second. It was doubtful she'd be able to save anything this time.

She walked into the bathroom. After taking a quick shower, she filled a large overnight bag full of clothes, collected her toiletries and the few jewelry items she had, then left.

And she had no intention of coming back, unless it

was to clear out the rubbish and hand over the keys to the new owner.

Half an hour later she walked into her office.

"Computer on," she said, dropping her bags on the floor beside her desk.

Izzy's image flicked to life. "Morning, sweetness."

"Iz, I want you to run a check on the seventeen Greenwood adoptees. See if anyone besides myself and AD Stern has requested information on them."

"It might take a little while."

"Time is something I have plenty of." Sam leaned back in her chair and rubbed her eyes. The first thing she'd better do was find a new place to stay. Somewhere secluded, perhaps. At least if she was bombed again, there'd be no neighbors to disturb.

"Could you also dig up an accommodation guide for the Melbourne metro area?"

"Onscreen, sweetie."

She spent an hour scanning through the list and arranging appointments, and then she grabbed a coffee and several painkillers in an attempt to ward off the growing aches in her stomach and head. No one had ever told her having periods was so damn painful. But then, her education in that regard had come from computerized health books, not from a mom who could impart the *real* facts.

Izzy reappeared on the com-screen. "Search results in. There's only been one other request for information, I'm afraid."

One was all they needed. "Who?"

The purple boa twirled for several moments. "One Michael Sanders, State Police."

"Michael? Not Michelle?"

"Yep."

The killer was female; that much was certain. Still, that didn't mean this Michael wasn't an accomplice. He was certainly worth talking to.

Not that *she'd* be talking to anyone but Sanders's boss. "Iz, make an appointment for me to talk to Sanders's captain, then send the information to AD Stern's wristcom, and cc it to Director Byrne. Mark it urgent."

"Consider it done, sweetie."

"Thanks."

She leaned back in her chair and propped her feet on the desk. Her eyes ached beyond belief, and everything else seemed to thump. It was nearly eight in the morning. Time, perhaps, to catch a nap. Certainly she was in no danger of being caught. Gabriel was the only one who seemed to know the location of her broom closet.

"Iz, turn off the lights and lock the door, will you? And cancel any screen calls. I don't want to be disturbed unless it's urgent."

The room went dark. She closed her eyes.

And dreamed.

She stood in the middle of an empty room. Whiteness surrounded her, so bright it made her eyes water. Though the room was empty, she was not alone.

He was here.

Though she couldn't see the hirsute stranger, his presence filled the room—a powerful, unseen shadow that circled slowly around her.

"Why have you called me?" she said.

"It is you who have done the calling, Samantha. I merely answer."

"*Then show yourself.*"

He smiled, a sensation that ran like fire through her mind. "*When you are ready to see me, you will.*"

"*More riddles.*"

"*No. A truth you are not ready to accept.*"

It made no sense. Nothing this man said made any sense.

"*Tell me your problem, Samantha. Is it the kites?*"

"*No.*" She hesitated. "*Did you send the kite after the five scientists?*"

His smile rippled through her like shadowed sunshine. "*No. I may have helped make them, but I do not always control them. Not yet.*" He paused. "*You will regret saving the scientists.*"

"*Why?*"

"*Because of their past. They deserve no future for what they have done. Their death is long overdue.*"

"*It all ties in with the mysterious Penumbra project, doesn't it? You're the one who originally tried to destroy it.*" She hesitated again. "*It's my duty to protect Haynes and Cooper, you know.*"

He said nothing for a long moment, but his thoughts continued to circle. She could almost see them, a blaze of unhappiness as bright as the sun.

"*Though I rejoice their deaths, as I said, I am not the one killing the scientists.*"

"*Who, then?*"

"*Hopeworth has realized that their reconditioning is not as strong as they thought. You are not the only one Allars has talked to.*"

"*If Hopeworth was behind the murders of the scientists, why, then, did they send those cars out to collect Allars and the others?*"

"*Because it's far easier to make people disappear once they are behind the walls of Hopeworth.*"

That, at least, made sense. "*If our murderer has talked to Allars, why wouldn't she have killed him? Especially since Haynes and his mates were on the project that Emma was involved in?*"

"*Sometimes it is better to leave a foe alive.*" He smiled. "*Of course, it could also be that he was neither creator nor spawn.*"

Maybe. "*Is that why you've left Gabriel alive? Because sometimes it is better to do so?*"

"*In this case, most definitely.*" The fierce sunshine of his unseen smile rippled through her again. "*Stern plays an important part in our future. As much as I want to destroy him, I can't.*"

Our future? She and this stranger had some sort of future together? Now, that was a scary thought.

"*These questions are not the reason you called me here, Samantha. What really troubles you?*"

"*I'm selling my apartment.*" Why she came out with that, she wasn't entirely sure. It was a guess, maybe. This stranger seemed to know an awful lot about a past she couldn't remember. Maybe he'd also know an awful lot about the apartment she'd inherited.

His essence stopped moving. A slither of surprise ran round her. "*That is your choice, of course, but can I ask why?*"

She tilted her head and contemplated the shadow that was Joe Black. "*People seem to like bombing it. You gave it to me, didn't you?*"

"*Perhaps.*"

"*Why?*"

"*Because I could.*"

Annoyance spun around them. Hers, not his. "Why can't you just drop the riddles and give me a direct answer?"

"Why are you so afraid to seek the answers?"

She frowned. "What do you mean?"

"I gave you a clue, Samantha. A key that will unlock some answers and solve at least one riddle. You have not yet sought the lock."

"The pin," she said, remembering it.

"The pin. Seek its image and you will find your murderer. You will also find the first stepping-stone to your past."

"If you know so damn much, why don't you tell me?"

"Because you will never believe me. Some things we must find for ourselves."

His presence faded, and with it went the bright room. She woke with a start, then rubbed a hand across her eyes and glanced at the clock. Eight forty-five. She hadn't even been asleep an hour. Sighing softly, she reached into her desk drawers and searched around until she found the pin. It was an abstract man and woman, standing side by side, one dark, one light. A gift from her hirsute friend when he'd saved her life about three months earlier.

She leaned forward. "Iz, scan this for me." She held the pin up to the electronic eye on the upper corner of the com-screen.

Izzy reappeared, boa whirling lightly. "Scanning, sweetness." A blue light ran the length of the pin.

"Run a search on the image. I want the name and address of every company that uses it."

"Will do."

"Thanks. And can you get me the personnel file for Michael Sanders?"

The file appeared onscreen almost instantly. She raised her eyebrows. "That was fast, Iz."

Izzy reappeared, somehow managing to look mighty pleased with herself. "I put in a request for the file when you asked for the search results to be sent to AD Stern. Just in case."

Sometimes, the artificial intelligence they'd installed in these things was scary. "Good thinking, Iz."

"Thanks, sweetie."

Michael Sanders was a baby-faced man who looked to be in his early thirties, with a slender build and thinning brown hair. It was only when you looked at his eyes that you realized he was not as young as he first appeared. Those eyes, a brilliant, unfathomable green, were the eyes of a man who'd seen, and done, too much.

He had a clean slate, both as a police officer and in his private life. Good arrest record, lived alone, no wife. His parents were killed when he was a baby, but there was no mention on file about who had raised him after that. Relatives, presumably, though there was no next of kin listed.

So why didn't something feel right?

"Iz, I don't suppose you could dig up whatever info and photos we have on Sanders's parents?"

"Looking for needles again, are we?"

"Could be." She frowned and stared at his photo. Those eyes just didn't belong in that face. "And dig up anything you can find on the accident that killed them."

"I may have to search through insurance reports. It might take a while."

"I've got the time, Izzy, believe me." But whether the next reject did was another matter entirely.

After a pause, Izzy announced, "I found their driver's license photos. Not the best quality, I'm afraid."

"Enhance and display."

"Can do."

Two photos appeared onscreen. Michael Sanders looked nothing like his parents, nor did he have any siblings she could compare him with—he was an only child.

"Display Sanders's birth certificate, Iz."

"Onscreen."

Bingo. Michael Sanders was adopted. His birth mother and father were one William and Barbara Ryan. "Iz, see what you can dig up on these two." She pointed to the two names.

The boa began to whirl. "I'm starting to stress here, darlin'."

Sam grinned. "You'll live."

"Three companies found using a design similar to that logo I scanned."

"Display."

The names appeared onscreen. There was a textile manufacturer and a plastic surgeon, neither of which was what she was after. But the third name probably was; it was an adoption agency.

What were the odds that *that* adoption agency was the one Michael Sanders was adopted through? Whoever this Joe Black really was, he seemed mighty aware of just what was going on. But did that make him a friend or an enemy?

She didn't know. But she had a suspicion that he

was neither; that the connection between them was deeper, more mysterious—and more dangerous—than anything like mere friendship.

"Information found on adoptive parents, Frank and Margaret Sanders."

"Hit me with it, babe."

"Frank Sanders was born in Sydney in 1955 and worked with the Metropolitan Fire Brigade. Margaret Sanders, née Johnson, was born in Melbourne in 1956 and worked as a waitress while attending night school. She became a doctor and worked at the Royal Women's Hospital. The two married in 1990, after Frank Sanders transferred to Melbourne. They adopted a child, a five-year-old girl named Rose Pierce, in 1995."

She stared at the screen, wondering if she'd heard right. Rose Pierce? The elusive sister of Emma Pierce? Why, then, was Michael Sanders listed as their son? "Anything else?"

"They were killed in an automobile accident in 2020."

Which was the year Michael Sanders was born. She frowned. "They adopted only the one child?"

"According to the records, yes."

She rubbed a hand across her eyes. This didn't make sense. If they adopted only Rose, why, then, did the records list squeaky-clean Michael as their son?

"We got anything on Rose Sanders, then?"

"Searching."

At least they now knew the reason why the initial search for Rose Pierce had come up blank—though the adoption *should* have come up.

Unless, of course, someone had deliberately buried

the information. It was only due to her search on
Sanders's parents that she'd even discovered Rose
Pierce.

"What agency was Rose adopted from, Iz?"

"Goes by the name of Silhouettes."

A chill ran down her spine. That was the same
adoption agency that used the pin's logo. Joe Black
had pointed her to Rose, *not* Michael. He obviously
knew a hell of a lot more than he was letting on. "Get
me a warrant, Iz. I want to go through their files."

"Warrant on the way, sweetie. No current information on Rose Sanders available."

She frowned. "What do you mean?"

"Her driver's license lapsed in 2040. There's been
no record of utility payments since then. No credit
transactions recorded. No usage of Medicare card."

"No death certificate?"

"None issued or recorded."

Interesting. Rose dropped out of sight about the
same time that Sanders graduated from the police
academy. How the two were connected, she wasn't
sure. But they *were* connected; she was sure of that.

"Warrant approved, sweetness."

"Good. Grab the adoption records and do a scan
for Rose and Michael Sanders."

"Can do." The boa twirled for several minutes.
"Record for Rose Pierce onscreen."

Sam looked through the documents. There was
nothing out of the ordinary. Rose was placed into
Silhouettes' care when she was twelve months old,
after being in the hospital for several months. A
search for relatives had come up with no one. Rose
stayed at the state-run home until adopted by the

Sanders family. "Print me a copy of the ID photo, will you?"

"Printing. No records are available for Michael Sanders."

For some reason, she wasn't entirely surprised. She glanced back at Rose's file. The officer in charge of the adoption was one Mary Elliot. Sam frowned—that name was familiar, though she wasn't entirely sure why.

"I found a police report for the Sanderses' accident, sweetie."

"Read it out loud, Iz. My headache's back."

"If you work yourself as hard as you work me, I'm not surprised."

She grinned. "Just read the report, Iz."

"The Sanderses' car was run off the Great Ocean Road and had plowed into a tree at high speed, killing both of them instantly. Several witnesses had reported seeing a red four-wheel drive hit the rear of the Sanderses' car just before the accident. The four-wheel drive was later recovered in Warrnambool."

"Stolen?"

"Yes. There were no prints beyond the owner's in the car."

"Did the witnesses ID the driver?"

"The description was deemed too vague. A big man with red-gold hair was all that the witnesses were able to provide."

A cold sensation crept over Sam's skin. Red-gold hair—the signature of Hopeworth's children. Maybe the military *had* discovered Rose's existence, and rather than jeopardize their precious project, they'd tried to destroy Rose and her parents.

So who had looked after Michael? Rose? "Did you find anything on Michael Sanders's birth parents?"

"Not a jot, sweetie."

"There has to be something on record."

"Sorry, sweetness. There's no record of a William and Barbara Ryan having a son named Michael born in 2020."

"But how is that possible? Background checks are a part of enlistment. With such a discrepancy in his records, he should never have been cleared to join State."

The boa twirled. "I'm not the recruiting officer. Don't ask me."

Sam rubbed her chin. "Did anything untoward happen around the time of Sanders's supposed birth date?"

Izzy tapped a knobby foot for several seconds. "Headlines onscreen, sweetie."

After flicking through several pages, she found her answer. A fire had swept through the hospital in which Michael was supposedly born. Though no one had been killed, most of the records and computing systems had been destroyed.

She leaned back in her chair. If she were a gambler, she'd put money on the fact that the fire had been deliberately set. It was just a little too convenient.

"Iz, search through Emma Pierce's file. See if there's any mention of when she retired from the military."

The bony foot tapped again. "March 2040."

Basically the same time as Michael Sanders's appearance. Coincidence? Probably not.

"Does Mary Elliot still work for Silhouettes?"

"She retired five years ago. She currently resides at the Greensborough Home for the Aged."

If she was in a home, then the odds of her remembering anything of note were not good. Still, it was worth a chance. Sam grabbed her handbag and placed the photo of a young Rose Pierce inside. "Book me a car, Iz. If anyone's looking for me, I'll be with Mary Elliot."

TWELVE

GABRIEL GLANCED AT THE CLOCK for the umpteenth time. He hated stakeout duty. Hated sitting alone in a car watching a dark apartment—especially when there was a murderer at large who could easily slip through their carefully laid net.

Jeanette Harris had been spirited away to safety. In her place was an SIU agent, a multi-shifter who'd assumed Jeanette's form. The apartment itself was wired, and no one would get in or out without raising an alarm.

Yet he had a vague suspicion it wouldn't be enough.

He scratched the back of his neck and looked around. A paperboy pedaled slowly down the street, flinging papers haphazardly at each house. Sometimes they landed near the front door, but more often than not, they landed deep in the bushes. The kid gave him a cheerful grin as he passed, and the next paper soared over the front fence and rattled against a window. The faint sound of curses could be heard. The kid chortled as he pedaled away.

Gabriel smiled and glanced back at the apartment building across the road. Nothing had moved. The black dog still sat guard near Jeanette's front door, and the sparrow hawk was lost amongst the shadows within the branches of the gum tree. Two more SIU agents, in human guise, watched the back.

If the murderer was a cop, she'd know of the precautions taken both here and with the remaining adoptees. If she had any sense, she'd back away and bide her time.

But something told him that wouldn't happen. The increasing urgency and violence in each successive murder pointed to a killer well aware that the SIU was closing in on her.

His wristcom beeped twice into the silence. He flicked the answer button. "Stern here."

Stephan appeared onscreen. "Did you read the file from Sam?"

Gabriel pressed a button and saw the second call was from her. "It's just arrived."

"Apparently the only request for information on the adoptees, outside yours and hers, came from one Michael Sanders."

Sanders. The State Police officer with the strange eyes. "Have you requested that he come in for an interview?"

"Yes, but he's off duty and not home. I've got a team watching his apartment."

"Good." He glanced at the rearview mirror and frowned. The paperboy had disappeared. Odd, given that this was a cul-de-sac and the only way out of the street was the way he came in. "Call you back, Stephan. I've got to check something out."

He hung up and climbed out of the car. For a moment, he stood still, listening to the sounds of the morning. The wind was chilly and thick with the scent of rain. The flow of traffic from the nearby Western Freeway was a steady hum, as were the usual morning noises as people woke and readied for work. The only thing missing was the trill of birds waking to greet the dawn.

Given the early hour, they shouldn't be silent. And usually, the only reason they did fall quiet was that there was a predator near—or something that looked like a bird but wasn't. Gabriel reached again for his wristcom. "Briggs, Edmonds, keep alert. Something's happening."

"Will do."

He headed down the court. Two houses from the end, he found the kid's bicycle, thrown under a large tree, with papers scattered everywhere.

The house, a two-story, slab-style building, showed no sign of life. The windows were dark, and he couldn't hear any movement. Frown deepening, he walked down the driveway and around to the rear of the house. Again, nothing.

He scratched the back of his neck irritably and returned to the street. Jeanette Harris's apartment block looked undisturbed and silent. He shifted shape and rose skyward.

To his hawk senses, the wind was a rich plethora of smells and sound. Toast burned two houses down, mingling with the rich aroma of coffee and the almost-too-powerful scent of rotten meat from the overflowing rubbish bins in the house just below. A mouse ducked for cover as he flew over some bushes, the creature's shrill shriek music to his ears. Beyond that came the startled cry of a budgie from a nearby tree.

Budgies—wild budgies—didn't actually live in suburbia. He circled toward it.

Blue feathers exploded from the tree as the budgie rose skyward, wings pumping frantically. He circled. If this budgie was the hybrid they were after—or even the missing Dr. Francis—then its sudden flight didn't make sense. All it had to do was sit quietly in the tree and he probably wouldn't even have seen it. His hawk sight was keen, but he wasn't capable of seeing past the thick, dark canopy of the treetop.

He watched the budgie's flight for several more seconds, then slowly winged after it. Every sense he had suggested this bird was a changer, and therefore more likely Dr. Francis rather than their hybrid—just as everything suggested this sudden retreat was a setup that smelled worse than Stephan's gym shoes in summer.

Still, he had little option but to follow. He'd tried once before to catch a felon in his claws and had almost killed the man. Hawk claws were meant to rake and kill, not gently capture. Of course, killing might be considered justifiable in this case, but he wanted answers as well as her death. He needed to know why she was killing people like Miranda—people who had done nothing more than being born.

They winged their way along the Western Freeway and across to the industrialized suburb of Altona before the budgie finally began to descend.

He circled, watching the small blue bird arrow through a broken side window of what looked like an abandoned factory.

The smell of a trap was so strong he could practically walk on it. He drifted down, watching the factory, trying to see if there was anyone else about. Two cars were parked around the back of the building, which meant the budgie could have a friend waiting below. He circled down, shifting shape as he neared the ground.

The hood of the black Ford was warm to the touch and had been driven very recently. The other car was cold, suggesting it had been here for a while.

The wind tugged at several loose sheets of metal along the factory's roof and whistled through the many gaps in the walls. The building had been abandoned for some time. Why, then, were the murderous budgie and her friend here?

He pressed the locater switch on his wristcom, then drew his gun and slowly approached the door. The handle turned somewhat stiffly, and the door opened with the slightest of creaks. He moved inside, dropping to one knee to present less of a target, and quickly scanned the darkness. The windows that weren't broken were caked with dirt and cobwebs, and the few beams of light that managed to filter through them did little to break the blackness. He could barely see more than a few feet ahead.

He rolled his shoulders slightly, trying to ease the tension. Once his eyes had fully adjusted to the darkness, he moved along the wall. There were several large shapes across the other side—offices, by the look of them. There was also what looked like a set of stairs, leading down into a deeper pit of darkness.

He'd find the budgie there, instinct suggested, but he'd also find the trap.

He checked the two offices, but they held nothing but a scattering of broken furniture and years of dust.

If there was anything in this old warehouse to find, it was definitely on the floor below. He stopped in the doorway of the second office, studying the stairway to his left.

He *should* call for backup, but in this thick silence, his voice would carry all too easy. He could text, of course, but he'd never really mastered the art on the wristcom, with its tiny keyboard, and it would take him longer than he suspected he had. They had to know he was here. If he didn't make a move and appeared to be waiting for help, they'd surely leave. He couldn't cover all exits, couldn't stop two of them, and while he could fly fast, it was doubtful he'd be able to out-fly a car intent on losing any pursuer. Meaning he might lose his only opportunity to get close to this murderer. He had no idea what game she was playing right now, but he had a feeling it was one he had to see to its end.

He edged down the stairs. The darkness wrapped around him, so blanket thick that he could barely see the steps. The wind didn't extend this far, and the still air smelled old.

When he reached the bottom step, he stopped. Though he could hear no sound, awareness washed over him. Someone stood close.

He swung, sweeping with a booted foot. His kick sliced through the thick darkness but connected with nothing more than air.

A malevolent chuckle ran around him. He moved right, keeping his back to the wall and his gun set on stun and ready to fire.

Sound whispered across the silence. Footsteps, moving through the darkness. The back of his neck began to itch again. The air stirred and he dove away, catching a brief glimpse of a knife as it sliced through where he'd stood only seconds before. He hit the ground, rolled back to his feet, and fired.

The pulsating light of the laser briefly illuminated a bloated, red-veined face, but the stranger moved far too fast and the shot missed. Footsteps slithered away.

Not the budgie, he thought, but someone else. He backed to the wall. Breath stirred the silence, its rhythm rapid, as if full of terror. Or excitement.

Another footstep scraped across the silence, this time only yards away. He dropped to a crouch and crept forward. The harsh breathing continued, each intake of air a whisper of pain. Once again this wasn't the budgie, but her friend with the bloated face.

He rose and swung his fist. It connected with a wall of flesh that felt as solid as a brick wall. A stomach, not a chin. The man had to be huge.

There was a grunt of pain and then air stirred. He ducked. The knife sliced past his chest, the tip of steel nicking one of his shirt buttons. Obviously, they were trying to hurt rather than kill him.

He stepped back and fired the laser. In the brief flare of light he saw a bulbous nose, mismatched eyes and ragged, flapping lips, all on a figure over eight feet tall. The man looked like a cross between a giant and an ogre.

The shots hit the stranger's shoulder. The big man grunted and stumbled away, right arm flapping uselessly. Gabriel sighted the laser on the sound of his footsteps and fired again.

The man hit the ground with a thump and didn't move. Gabriel listened to the silence for several seconds, wondering where the hell the budgie was, then moved cautiously forward. A human form loomed out of the darkness. The stranger was a mountain, even lying down. Gabriel nudged him with a boot. He didn't move.

This close, he could see the rise and fall of the stranger's chest—giant bellows that struggled to work. Gabriel frowned. It almost seemed as if the weight of his flesh pressing down on his lungs was too much to move. He might die if he remained in that position for very long. The air stirred, warning him of movement behind him. He ducked, but not fast enough. Something smashed into the side of his head and the lights went out.

SAM DUG OUT HER ID and showed it to the nurse manning the reception desk. "I need to see Mary Elliot."

The nurse frowned. "Mind if I ask why? Mary's not in the best condition, nowadays."

Sam put her ID away. "What's wrong with her?"

"Short-term memory loss, stroke." The nurse hesitated. "She's still regaining speech and mobility."

Damn! Why was it that every lead they seemed to get was compromised in some way? "I need to see her, if it's possible. We think she might be able to help us with a case. If she begins showing any signs of stress, I'll leave."

"Make sure you do. I don't want her upset." The nurse pressed a button on her desk. Seconds later, another nurse appeared. "Lisa, take Agent Ryan to see Mary, please."

Sam nodded her thanks to the receptionist and followed the second nurse down the corridor. The rooms were all locked. Apparently, they were taking no chances on an inmate walking free.

The second nurse stopped at a door about halfway down. "Mary, like most of the patients in this wing, tends to live in the past. They have no concept of current time or events, and if we let them wander at will, they'd become dazed and confused."

And it was a hell of a lot easier on the staff if they weren't free to roam, Sam thought grimly. "Thanks," she said, as the nurse opened the door.

The woman nodded. "Just buzz when you want out."

"Will do."

The door closed behind her. The room wasn't the glorified prison cell she thought it would be. Huge windows lined one wall, overlooking a garden that was a mass of flowers and trees. Several of them did at least open to let in fresh air, but the gap wasn't large enough for anything more than a bird to get through. Certainly, Mary wouldn't have been able to escape that way. The remaining walls were a buttercup yellow and lined with brightly colored prints. There wasn't much furniture, but what there was added to the cheerful feel of the room.

A thin, gray-haired woman sat statue-still on the sofa, apparently mesmerized by the children's show on the television. Sam walked over and sat beside her. There was no reaction.

"Mary?" she said softly.

The woman turned around. For a second, there was little life in her blue eyes; then she blinked and the right side of her face lit up in a smile.

"Josephine!" Her words were slightly slurred, but

not beyond understanding. "As I live and breathe, fancy seeing you after all these years!"

What were the odds of getting mistaken for someone else twice in as many days? Sam dug out her ID and showed it to Mary.

Confusion ran across the old woman's face. "You're not Josephine?" Her gaze darted from the ID to Sam's face.

"No. My name is Samantha. I'm a police officer."

"You look like young Josephine did."

And maybe she did. If she was a product of Hopeworth, then it was very likely that there were others out there who resembled her. But right now, it wasn't a point worth arguing. "Mary, do you remember working at the Silhouettes Adoption Agency?"

A smile tugged the right corner of the woman's mouth. "Yes. I worked there for many years. Lovely place. Lots of bonny babes to look after."

"Do you remember a child named Rose Pierce?"

"Rose Pierce," the old woman mumbled, face locked in a frown. "The name does seem familiar."

Sam dug the photo out of her handbag and handed it to her.

The old woman studied it for a few minutes before a smile touched her lips. "Rosie Pierce," she murmured, gently touching the child's image with one gnarled finger. "Now, there was a strange one."

"Strange how?"

"We could never settle her as a babe. She kept screaming and reaching out for something—though we never did figure out what. Not until later, that is. And, of course, no one wants to adopt a child that's always crying."

"She was in the hospital for many months, wasn't she?"

"Yes. We got her from the hospital, once it had been confirmed that her parents were dead and there was no living relative to look after her."

"Why wasn't she sent to the same adoption agency as her sister?"

The old woman frowned again. "We didn't know about the sister—not until later. And by then, it was far too late. The sister had been adopted and her new parents weren't interested in a second child."

"How did the separation affect Rose?" She'd heard tales of twins sharing emotions, thoughts, and even pain, no matter how many miles stood between them. Was it possible that Rose, even at such a young age, had that kind of connection with her sister?

"She was such a dear little thing, but so serious. As soon as she could talk, she wanted to know where her sister was. We couldn't settle her, no matter what we tried."

"Wasn't she only twelve months old when she came to Silhouettes?"

"Yes, but the bond of the twin is sometimes very strong." Mary hesitated, blue eyes sharp. It was hard to imagine this woman being anything but in full control of her memories. "But you should know that, Josephine. You're a twin, are you not?"

"My name is Sam. I showed you my ID, remember?"

"Did you?" Confusion flitted across the good half of Mary's face. She rubbed her forehead wearily. "Sometimes my memory is not so good."

"You're doing just fine, Mary." Sam patted the old

woman's hand gently. Her skin felt like rough paper. "Tell me about Rose's adoption by the Sanderses."

Mary sighed. "They were such a serious couple. Not the sort our little Rosie really needed. She was too serious herself—she needed to laugh, needed someone who would bring her out of her shell."

"Did you advise against them adopting Rose?"

"Yes." She sighed again. "But Mrs. Sanders fell in love with her, and in the end that was the important thing. Little Rose needed lots of love."

Sam raised an eyebrow. "Why? Was she traumatized by the separation from her twin?"

"In a sense, yes. But she was having serious identity problems by the time she hit three."

Identity problems at three years old? Most kids could barely speak at that age, let alone have concerns about who or what they were. "What caused Rose to have these problems?"

"She was a shifter," Mary said, and patted Sam's hand. "Most shifters have identity problems when they find their alternate shape at such a young age, but in Rose's case it was compounded by the fact that she could take any form."

"So she was a multi-shifter?" Just like her sister.

"Yes. But also a female-to-male shifter."

She stared at the old woman, wondering if she'd heard right. Female to male? If hybrid shifter-changers were considered extremely rare, then what were the odds of someone being born a female-to-male shifter? "That's not possible."

"I didn't think so, but there it was, happening to little Rosie right in front of me."

"But . . . how?"

The old woman shrugged. "There are some people

in this world who claim to have been born in the wrong bodies—males trapped in female forms, and vice versa. Maybe that's what happened to Rose— only she could do something about it."

"Her male form—did he have a name?"

Mary considered the question for several seconds. "Michael. I think she called him Michael."

Michael Sanders, she thought grimly. Their young cop with the old eyes. Gabriel would want this information straightaway.

Sam stood. "Thanks for all your help, Mary."

"You're welcome, Josephine." She hesitated, tilting her head to one side. "How's that brother of yours?"

"Mary, I don't have a brother," she said gently.

Confusion clouded the old woman's face. "Yes, you do. Joshua. A sprightly lad with a mass of red hair."

A chill ran down her spine. *Joshua.* The boy she'd dreamt about nearly every night. She licked suddenly dry lips. "Mary, I think you're confusing me with someone else. My name is Samantha, not Josephine."

"So you've changed it again. I can't keep up with you two." She sighed softly. "I wish those damn doctors had given you all names instead of numbers. Hell of a lot easier on the rest of us."

The chill increased. Hadn't Joe Black mentioned something about being only a number and never having a real name? She sank slowly back to the sofa. "Mary, when did you know Josephine and Joshua?"

"Years and years ago. I was in the military before I retired and became a nurse at Silhouettes, you know."

"And Joshua and Josephine—they were twins?"

The old woman smiled, her eyes distant, lost in the years. "And the liveliest of all my charges. I guess that's why you managed to survive at all."

She rubbed her arms. "Survive? Then many didn't?"

"Oh no. So many bonny babes were lost." Mary hesitated, sniffing back a tear. "That's why I left, you know. I couldn't stand to see all the dead children."

"And Hopeworth let you leave?" From what she'd learned about the place, she'd have thought no one would be let loose until they had exhausted their usefulness.

"They had no choice. The project was destroyed." Her gaze met Sam's, blue eyes shining with tears. "Until you walked into the room, I thought both you and Joshua were dead."

Allars had mentioned that the Penumbra Project had been destroyed by fire. Coincidence? Somehow, she doubted it. Joe Black had sent her to Silhouettes, with the warning that she would find the first stepping-stone to her past. Silhouettes had led her to Mary. Was the old woman that stone? Or was she so lost in the past that she was confusing reality with fantasy?

"How old were Joshua and Josephine when you last saw them? Children change a lot as they grow up, Mary, so how would you recognize Josephine if she *did* walk in the door?"

"Children change, yes, but not the Hopeworth kiddies. They always looked the same, no matter what the age. They just filled out, gained muscle and length." Her gaze rose. "And you all had the same color hair. There's no mistaking that color, you know."

General Lloyd had said much the same thing. And if Mary was right, and she *was* one of Hopeworth's children, then her features, like theirs, hadn't altered all that much in the thirty years she'd been alive. It was a somewhat chilling thought.

"What was the name of the project you worked in, Mary?"

"I . . . I can't remember." She rubbed her forehead with gnarled fingers. Tears ran silently down her weather-worn cheeks. "It hurts if I try to remember."

Behind them, the door opened. A nurse stepped into the room. "Enough questions, Agent Ryan. Mary's heart rate just leapt alarmingly. We can't afford to let you stay any longer."

Sam silently cursed, then rose. "I'll come back another time."

Mary caught her hand, squeezing it gently. "Please do. I don't get very many visitors nowadays." She hesitated and frowned, looking around the room in sudden confusion. "This isn't my home. Why am I here?"

The nurse motioned Sam to the door, then she squatted down in front of the old woman, gently taking her hand.

"Mary, you were sick, dear. You came here to get better, remember?"

The door swung shut on the nurse's soft words. Sam stood in the corridor and took a deep breath. It was hard to decide whether she'd found a clue to her past or simply more confusion.

What she needed was something to eat—maybe food would help her think more clearly. Then she'd better call Gabriel. She glanced at her wristcom, but at that moment, pain hit her, hammering into her brain. She gasped, felt her shoulder hit the wall, then slid to the floor, holding her head and fighting the wave of nausea and darkness washing through her body.

Footsteps came running. Hands touched her shoulders. "Agent Ryan, are you all right?"

As quickly as it had come, the pain left, leaving her with only a vague sense that something was wrong. She took several deep breaths and nodded. "Yeah. Sorry about that. The sudden movement must have set off my headache again."

The reception nurse frowned. "If the headaches are as bad as that, you need to go see a doctor."

"I am." She struggled to her feet. If these damn headaches were an indication of what she had to look forward to every month, she was regretting her wish to fully develop as a woman. It was certainly a case of watch what you wish for, because it might come true.

"Maybe you'd better sit down for a while," the nurse suggested, touching Sam's arm in concern.

But Sam shrugged the touch away. "I'm fine, really. I just haven't had breakfast yet, and I do have an appointment with a doctor at eleven." She glanced at her watch. It was nine-thirty now. Time enough to get something to eat before she headed into the city.

"Maybe you'd better not drive until you do eat. Just in case that headache comes back."

Sam nodded. "I'll walk down to the shops first. Thanks for your help."

The woman shrugged. "No problem."

Sam headed out to the main street and quickly dialed Gabriel's number. No answer. She frowned. Last time there was no answer, something had been wrong.

Something was wrong this time, too.

She studied the long line of shops in front of her and headed for Subway. Then she dialed SIU.

"Christine, put me through to Director Byrne, please."

"One moment, please." Christine reappeared in half that time. "Director Byrne is currently in a meeting and cannot be disturbed."

She swore under her breath. "Could you leave a message with his secretary? Let him know Rose Pierce is State Police Officer Michael Sanders."

"Message forwarded."

"Thanks."

She disconnected, then stepped into Subway and ordered herself a roll and coffee. By the time she'd finished both, it was time to head into the city.

Doctor O'Hearn's office was situated near the Spencer Street end of Bourke Street. Located on the thirteenth floor, it overlooked the old rail yards and the newly refurbished Etihad Stadium. It was the sort of view that cost millions, though she couldn't see why. She'd prefer a view over parkland any day.

She was ushered into the doctor's office almost immediately. O'Hearn was studying several reports on her desk, but she glanced up as Sam settled into the well-padded visitor's chair.

"Samantha. How are you today?" She leaned back in her chair, a smile crinkling the corners of her gray eyes.

O'Hearn was the motherly type—full-figured and kindly looking. But there was a hawklike sharpness in her eyes that suggested this was a woman who missed little.

"Fine, thanks. I finally figured out what was causing those headaches, though."

The doctor smiled. "Yes. Your hormone levels did indicate you were about to menstruate, which must have been somewhat surprising, given what you'd been told."

That was an understatement if she'd ever heard one. "Have you any idea why this should suddenly happen now?"

O'Hearn picked up one of the files and studied it for a few seconds. "Well, we did find some interesting anomalies in your test results."

No surprise there, given what Finley had already discovered. "Such as?"

The doctor considered her, gray eyes calculating. "What do you know about genetic coding?"

"Absolutely nothing."

The doctor smiled again. "Then I shall attempt to explain this simply. Each race has a set genetic code— though, of course, there are variations available within each code. Humans have one base pattern, shapeshifters another, and so on. But with you, your basic genetic coding has been spliced with the partial coding of at least two other races."

"Shapechanger would be one," Sam said, thinking back to what Francis had said about sensing others of her kind.

O'Hearn nodded. "And also shifter. But there's at least one other partial code we've not yet identified."

Sam raised an eyebrow. "If I have the coding of all these races, why am I not able to shift or change?"

"That I don't know. Nor do I know how this has happened, save that it does not appear to be natural."

Sam rubbed her arms. While the news was far from surprising, it was a confirmation that she didn't really want. Hopeworth was looking more and more like a possibility.

"Would having the mixed coding explain the developmental delay?"

"To some extent, yes. Both shifters and changers do not fully mature until they hit thirty or forty human years. It is nature's way of compensating for their extended life span."

Which was why most of the test subjects at Hopeworth were at least in their late twenties to early thirties. Sam rubbed her forehead. "Then why was I told at fifteen that I would never develop? Surely they would have picked up the shifter/changer coding as easily as you did."

"My tests are a little more intense than your average physician's, and I have spent a good part of my life focusing on the health and welfare of nonhuman races." A hint of pride crept through the doctor's warm voice. "I'm sure the physicians who examined you were good, but I'm a damn sight better."

And modest besides. "So you're saying they wouldn't have been able to pick up on the genetic abnormalities?"

"Why would they even look? You're listed as human on your birth certificate. They'd have no reason to search beyond that."

Especially not for an orphan, at a time when medical expenditure of any kind was being closely watched by the government. "What about these other sensations I seem to be getting? Being able to sense the presence of other races, being able to pick up my partner's emotions and, sometimes, even thoughts."

O'Hearn interlaced her fingers. "Most psychic abilities don't start to fully develop until the onset of puberty."

Sam sighed. "I was tested for psychic ability when

I entered the State Police. And I came up with a big fat zero."

"Yet you told me that in the recent tests done at the SIU, you came in neutral."

"Yeah. So?"

"Those tests were designed by Gabriel—and designed specifically to indicate whether or not a person has psychic ability. You either have them or you do not. No one comes in as neutral."

"But I did."

"Yes. And that would indicate a talent strong enough to evade both the psi-nullified environment of the SIU and the tests themselves."

"This is too weird." In the space of a few days, she'd gone from being a sterile, orphaned nobody to a multi-raced fertile woman with growing psychic talents and maybe even a brother.

"It certainly is a puzzle," O'Hearn agreed, "but one I think we can eventually solve."

Sam took another deep breath. No doubt the solving would involve more damn tests. "So what do you want to do?"

"First, I want your permission to request the test results from the SIU. I think they would complement my research. Who's the physician in charge there?"

"A man named Finley."

"Finley?" The doc raised a gray eyebrow. "He's one of the best in his field. I didn't realize he was working for the SIU now."

"He's been wanting to do more tests himself. So far, I've refused."

"Why?"

Sam shrugged. "Obstinacy, perhaps? Or maybe even fear of discovering the truth."

"Which is understandable. Sometimes it is better not to know."

Sam smiled grimly. "But there are things happening to me that I need to understand, and I can't sit on my hands anymore. Do what it takes to find out what the hell is going on in my body."

"Good girl." O'Hearn leaned forward and picked up the second folder. "I'll book some more tests and let you know the times. I'll also contact Gabriel and request the SIU test results." Then she hesitated, frowning slightly. "It might also be worthwhile if I work with Finley on some of these tests. He's more familiar with gene manipulation than I am."

"The SIU will probably have to approve it, but it's okay by me. Though Finley's not due back from leave until the eighteenth."

"We'll get around that." The doctor shuffled the two folders together. "I'll get onto this straightaway."

Sam stood. "I'll wait for your call, then."

O'Hearn nodded. "Don't worry, dear. You'll have your answers within a week or two."

A minute from now was not soon enough. Still, she'd waited nearly thirty years for some answers. Two weeks more wasn't going to kill her.

Then a chill ran over her skin. She couldn't escape the sudden notion that she was wrong.

Very wrong.

THIRTEEN

SAM SPENT SEVERAL FRUITLESS HOURS apartment hunting, then gave up and went back to SIU headquarters.

The real estate agent had given her a vague idea of what her apartment would fetch, and it was a sizeable sum. She'd be able to buy something close to the city, which would save her having to either buy a car or continue to put up with the overcrowded transport system each day. She only had to travel twenty minutes as it was, but that was more than enough.

She dumped her bag on the floor beside her desk and flopped back in her chair. For tonight, at least, she'd have to find a hotel.

"Computer on."

Izzy appeared. "You have a call, sweetness. From General Frank Lloyd."

"Fuck." Sam rubbed her eyes. The last thing she wanted, either now or anytime in the immediate future, was to speak to the general. She couldn't shake the image of a crocodile toying with its prey—that prey being her.

"Put him onscreen, Iz."

The general's powerful features appeared and a chill ran over her skin. This man would play some part in her future, and none of it would be good.

She rubbed her arms. "What can I do for you, General?"

"The question is more what can *I* do for *you*."

His smile made her skin crawl. "General, it's been a long day. Just get to the point."

He raised a bushy eyebrow. "Given your questions regarding the Generation 18 project, I thought you would be interested to know that we've discovered the identity of the man who hacked into our system."

And he'd only just discovered this name? Somehow, she doubted it. "It's not Michael Sanders, I suppose?"

The general frowned. "No. Orrin Whittiker."

He seemed to place an odd emphasis on the man's name. Was she supposed to know the man? "Who is?"

"A reject from a different project."

"Jesus, General, how many rejects do you have wandering the streets?"

"At last count, one hundred and forty-five. There could be one or two more I don't know about, though."

One hundred and forty-five rejected children? How many successes must they have had? And how many deaths? If what Mary said was true, then the latter number, at least, was very high.

"Do you keep track of all your rejects?"

"Oh yes. We can't afford not to."

Then Hopeworth had known about the murders.

Had known, but had done nothing. "Do you intend to pick up this Orrin Whittiker?"

"If we can find him, yes. But we thought, perhaps, it might be in both our interests if you were also looking for him. If you do get to him before us, we'd appreciate you handing him over once you have finished with him."

That was not up to her. "Only if you offer the same guarantee, General."

He smiled. "That I cannot guarantee."

So why even call her in the first place? Something was *very* off. Was this some sort of test? If Orrin had breached Hopeworth, he could certainly tell her more about that place than they might wish . . . unless that was the whole point. But why the hell would he want her uncovering more about Hopeworth, especially if she was one of their rejects? "What project was Orrin rejected from?"

"I cannot tell you that."

"General, I need to know what to expect when I go after this man."

The general hesitated, his eyes going curiously blank. There was no doubt that he was telepathic—and right now, he was obviously contacting higher authorities.

"Orrin," he continued, barely skipping a beat, "possesses an unusual height and girth. He is also extremely strong."

"What sort of unusual height are we looking at?"

"He's over eight feet tall, and at least half that wide."

She blinked. She'd be trying to arrest a man almost double her height? Like that was going to happen.

"What the hell were you trying to achieve with Or-rin's lot? Man mountains?"

The general's almost cynical smile suggested she wasn't that far off the mark. "We have his last known address, if you're interested."

"And .would it do me any good? Haven't you al-ready checked it out yourselves?"

"Not as yet. There is a team on the way, of course, but Hopeworth is farther away than the SIU and you are likely to get there faster. Orrin is best contained; by whom doesn't matter."

If he was best contained, then why hadn't he been earlier than this? The general was playing his own game here; she was sure of that, if nothing else.

"Then give me the address." It was a shame she'd never be able to charge the general and his military cohorts with obstruction of justice. They'd had this information from the beginning of the murders—of that she had no doubt. Yet they'd sat on it. Had sim-ply watched while people like Gabriel's sister were brutally murdered.

It was just as well that she wasn't standing face-to-face with the general. She'd be tempted to punch him.

"Orrin lives in the government housing estate in Melton. Twenty-eight Errol Street, to be precise."

She frowned. Emma Pierce had lived on that same street. "Thanks for the help, General."

He nodded and disappeared. Izzy reappeared on-screen. "Need anything, sweetie?"

"Yeah, request me a gun and a car."

"Feel like shooting someone, do we?" Izzy's foot tapped several times. "Stun or dual?"

She hesitated. If this man was as big as the general had suggested, she wasn't going to get caught having only a stun gun to defend herself with. "Dual, just to be safe."

"Request being processed."

"And see if you can get Gabriel Stern for me, will you?" She leaned back in her chair, watching the boa twirl.

"No answer, sweetie."

She frowned. This wasn't like Gabriel. Not when he'd said he'd leave the phone on. "Try Director Byrne, then."

Stephan's face appeared on screen. "Agent Ryan," he greeted, voice neutral yet somehow sharp. "What can I do for you?"

"I've just been in contact with General Frank Lloyd. He discovered the name of the man who hacked into their system and recovered the information on the Generation 18 rejects."

"Do you need assistance in picking him up?"

"If what the general said about his size is true, then yes, I will."

"I'll assign Briggs and Edmonds immediately."

"Thanks." She hesitated briefly. "Sir, have you heard from AD Stern? I've been trying to get ahold of him for several hours now."

"No, I haven't." Stephan rubbed his chin. "He was on watch detail at Jeanette Harris's place, but he went to investigate something else and hasn't been heard from since."

And Stephan was worried, though his face, like his voice, showed absolutely no emotion.

"Have you talked to the remaining teams? Do they have any idea where he might have gone?"

"Yes, I did, and no, they haven't. The two agents at the front of the building reported he climbed out of his car about five minutes after a paperboy had gone past, and that he walked up the street into a house. He was last seen flying away in his hawk form."

"No location indicator after that?"

"We investigated his last known location, with little result." He hesitated, leaning back in his chair. "I don't suppose you've felt anything?"

She hesitated. How much should she tell Stephan? In many ways, she didn't really trust him, simply because her desires and needs were of no consequence to him. The only thing he cared about was the Federation, the SIU and his wife. And in that order. "Not exactly, sir."

Something in his eyes suggested he didn't believe her. "If he hasn't reported in by this evening, I'll be in contact."

Her frown deepened. *That* sounded almost like a threat. "Yes, sir."

"Oh, and Agent Ryan?"

"Yes?"

"We got Dr. Francis. She's currently in holding, and will be charged with attempted murder, at the very least."

"Good." One crazy bird off the radar, one to go.

Stephan signed off and she leaned over to collect her bag from beside the desk. Time to go collect a man mountain.

AWARENESS RETURNED SLOWLY. AT FIRST, Gabriel felt nothing beyond the pounding ache in his head. Gradually, though, he became conscious of something sharp under his side, digging into his ribs. Became aware that his shoulders burned, as if stretched back too long and too hard. He tried to shift into a more comfortable position, but couldn't, mainly because he was trussed up tighter than a roast for Sunday's dinner.

He opened his eyes. The room in which he lay was enclosed in darkness. There were no windows, meaning there was no chance of light getting in or him getting out. The air was still, and it tasted almost foul.

As his eyes adjusted to the darkness, he found the door. Heavyset and metal, it looked like something you'd find on a commercial refrigerator. Then he looked around his prison again and saw the rails above him, hung with empty hooks. He was in a meat storage locker. No wonder the air held a mix of death and fouled meat.

He shifted his legs. The object under his ribs dug deep, biting into his flesh, and he swore and jackknifed away. It was glass, not stone or rubble, as he'd presumed. Probably the remnants of some drunk's cheap wine bottle. Judging by the amount of glass surrounding him, the drunk had spent a fair amount of time here. Obviously, the building in which the meat locker was housed had been abandoned long enough for street people to consider it a refuge.

Unless they were in the same building that he'd followed Dr. Francis into, the chance of immediate rescue was next to zero.

But the glass itself might provide a means to escape, if he could manage to grab a piece. He shifted his shoulders and arms, trying to work some slack into the ropes. After a good ten minutes, he had to rest. Whoever had tied him had done a damn fine job. He could barely breathe, let alone move.

The sharp tattoo of footsteps came from beyond the confines of his prison, and then the metal door screeched open. Brown leather boots appeared. He looked up and found himself staring into Emma Pierce's face. *The sister,* he thought. The elusive Rose Pierce.

"Good to see you're finally awake, Assistant Director." She stopped a good three feet away and stared at him with an expression that wavered between contempt and caution.

"What are you doing, Rose? None of this will bring Emma back. Especially not killing innocent adoptees."

Her smile was cold. "Especially when one of them was your sister, huh?"

Anger flashed through him, but it was useless, given the circumstances. He could no more attack her than he could fly right now. "What's the point of all this? We know who you are. We know who your next victims will be. You're insane if you think we're going to let you get anywhere near them."

She began to pace. Her walk was long and powerful, almost masculine. "You may think you're clever, AD Stern—and you certainly put two and two together far faster than I might have wished or hoped— but believe me when I say you have no idea exactly *what* I'm capable of."

Oh, he had a pretty good idea. The question right now, however, was why was he still alive? What did she intend to do with him? "Taking me hostage will get you no closer to your victims. The SIU doesn't bargain."

Her smile was a slash of contempt. "I know that. I have no intention of going down that road, anyway."

"Then what do you intend?"

"You'll see soon enough." She hesitated, studying him almost too intently. "What, no other questions?"

She wanted him to talk, though he wasn't entirely sure why. He could see no harm in obliging, though, especially if it gave him some answers. "Why are you killing these people? If you hold a grudge, it should be against Hopeworth, not the innocent by-products of their experiments."

"I have no grudge against the adoptees. I'm only carrying out my sister's final wish."

"Emma wanted her children dead?"

Bitterness ran across her face. "These aren't *her* children. They were never conceived by her, never grew to life in her womb. They're an aberration of nature, something that should not exist. So they must die, as Emma wished."

"How did Emma find out about the adoptees in the first place?" He was pretty confident Hopeworth wouldn't have told her.

"A chance encounter with a reject from another project gave us the clue, though I reckon Em might have had her suspicions anyway. We formed a pact with the reject. We helped him, and he helped us."

"Then why cut out the wombs and ovaries in the women, or the penis and testes in the men?"

For a moment, Rose didn't answer. She paced the floor behind him in long, aggravated strides. "Do you know what it is like to be a twin? To share your twin's every thought, every desire and every anguish?"

His smile was grim. He should, but he didn't. Perhaps he would regret it one day, but for now, he was happy to continue blocking Stephan.

"I spent half my life physically locked away from my sister," Rose continued softly. "It didn't matter, because even as a child, all I had to do was reach out and she was there, in my mind, ready to comfort or talk."

So, even as babes, the two had known about each other. "What kept you apart as you got older? Hopeworth?"

Rose came back within sight. Her face darkened. "The bastards sucked her dry, and then they spat out the husk. They didn't care what happened to her once they'd finished with her. I was the one who had to pick up the pieces. I was the one who had to see and feel her agony as the cancers *their* treatments and explorations had left her with ate away her body." She hesitated and clenched her fists. "I was the one who had to watch her die and feel her relief as death sucked her soul away."

And the experience had obviously left her more than a little off-center. "Why didn't you bury her, Rose? Why not offer her the dignity in death that she couldn't get in life?"

"Because once the soul has gone, the body is only a lifeless shell. It doesn't matter what happens to it."

Rose and Emma where born shifters, and yet they obviously had none of the beliefs that were ingrained into most shifter families. Maybe it was because they'd been adopted at such a young age and raised by humans. But even humans buried their dead. Gabriel shifted slightly, trying to ease the ache in his side where the glass had cut. His fingers brushed against something sharp. More glass. If he could grab it, he might just be able to cut the ropes and escape.

All he had to do was keep her talking and direct her attention elsewhere.

"It is a belief among my people that if the body is not properly interred, the soul cannot go on and be reborn."

Rose raised an eyebrow. "And sticking them six feet under is supposed to aid this rebirth?"

He smiled grimly. "Sticking them six feet under is nothing but a waste of good planting soil."

"Well, at least we agree on something." She turned away and continued her pacing. "Let's go back to your earlier question. Why do I cut up these innocents, as you call them, so badly?"

He raised an eyebrow. He'd asked that question a good five minutes ago. Had she just decided to answer, or was she simply trying to keep him talking?

"You told me Emma wanted them dead," he said. "But *you* wanted them to suffer. To suffer as much as your sister had suffered."

She stopped and regarded him in surprise. "Very good, Assistant Director. And yes, I wanted them to know what Emma had suffered to give them life. I wanted them to die suffering, just like her. But that is not the reason for doing what I did."

She turned away and resumed her pacing. He caught the shard of glass between his fingers and began to saw at the rope.

"You must understand something about Hopeworth—it never lets people go. Not completely. Everything Emma did, everything she said, Hopeworth heard. Even though she was useless to them, they couldn't let her go completely. It was the same with the adoptees, though not for the same reasons. By removing their eggs and sperm, I denied Hopeworth access to Emma's line, as well as finally ending any connection Emma—and those who'd come from her genes—had with that place."

"You can't be sure of any of that." Blood was slick on his wrists—he seemed to be cutting himself more than the damn rope.

"Yes, I can." Her sudden smile was bitter. "Emma was microchipped, you know. Hopeworth wanted to be certain of her location at all times. The adoptees didn't need it, however. They were bugged psychically."

Several strands of rope gave away, giving him a little more movement. Blood rushed to his fingertips, tingling painfully. He ignored it and kept on cutting.

"How can you bug someone psychically without them knowing?"

"The same way a thief can pick your pocket without you knowing. It just takes knowledge and timing."

If this were true, then Hopeworth might know a damn sight more about the Federation than anyone in the Federation wanted. Miranda had been privy to more than a few secrets.

"So Hopeworth has stealth-trained telepaths?" Which was harder to do than most people realized. The human population seemed to think telepaths could just read thoughts anywhere, anytime. In reality, it was nowhere near that simple. If it were, telepaths would be on a fast track to insanity. Besides, even the most psychically dead human could usually tell when he was being read—it was like walking into your house and realizing you'd been burgled. It was something you could just sense.

"My, you're not just a pretty face, are you?" Her

voice held a sarcastic edge. "Of course Hopeworth
has stealth-trained telepaths. They've been breeding
talents and God knows what else for close to fifty
years."

He met her gaze. In the green depths of her eyes,
intelligence mixed with madness. A deadly combination. "How do you know all this?"

"My reject friend told me. He'd been doing a little
investigating himself, trying to figure out where, and
what, he'd come from. He's stolen an amazing
amount of information from the military with them
being none the wiser."

If they believed that, they were fools. He had a suspicion very little escaped Hopeworth's attention.
"Your reject friend wouldn't happen to be that mis-
shapen giant I felled, would it?"

"And he's more than a little pissed off over that,
you know. I had to send him home and give him time
to cool down. Of course, I also had to promise that
he could kill you after I'd finished with you."

He snorted softly. "I'm sure you intend to kill me
anyway."

"Oh yes. But at least I would have been quick about
it. Orrin savors the suffering and the blood. It feeds
some need in his soul."

Which was as good a reason as any to be well and
truly out of here by then. Another strand of the thick
rope snapped loose. Time. He just needed more time.

"Sounds to me as if you should be attacking Hopeworth more than the innocent by-products of their
experiments."

She gave him a cold smile. "We intend to, once I
fulfill Emma's dying wish."

The woman was definitely mad if she thought she

could go up against the might of Hopeworth and win. "And how does Dr. Francis play into all of this?"

"She's been a useful ally when it comes to getting access to people and drugs. She's also a very useful decoy. She led you into my trap pretty successfully, don't you think?"

Yes, she did, and more the fool him for not following instinct and staying at the house. "What did *she* get out of the situation?"

"Test subjects for her Jadrone replacement. Of course, I did have to kill them afterward, but I don't believe that worried her."

"So what do you intend to do with me now?"

"You will help us more than you can know." Rose regarded him steadily for a moment. "Shall I show you how?"

Amusement mingled with the madness, and his gut clenched. Whatever it was, it wasn't good.

Her body began to shift, to mold itself into a new form until what stood before him was his own image. Rose wasn't just a shifter. She was what they'd long thought impossible—a cross-gender hybrid.

"So what do you think, Assistant Director?"

Her voice was his. So that was why she hadn't minded answering his questions. She wanted to hear how he talked, the inflections in his voice, the way he used words.

"I think you're mad." Mad enough to get away with it. He sawed desperately on the last few strands of rope. He had to stop her here, *now,* or the adoptees would die. The agents watching them wouldn't question his sudden appearance or his need to check each adoptee personally. They were all too used to his eccentric ways.

She smiled. "I don't intend to hold the disguise long. Just long enough to get to the rest of the adoptees and kill them."

"You'll never find them."

"Your computer doesn't have their location? I very much doubt it."

It did. And as good as her disguise was, she'd probably get past the voice and eye scans. If he got out of this alive, he'd have to talk to Finley about finding another way to secure vital information.

She glanced at her watch, which, like her now too-short clothes, hadn't changed. "Time runs away from me, unfortunately. As much as I enjoyed our little chat, I now have to go. Be good, Assistant Director. I'll be back in a few hours."

She turned and walked to the door. The last of the rope strands fell from his wrist and he jerked upright as Rose opened the door. He threw the rope to one side and lunged for the door.

It slammed shut in his face and he punched the metal in frustration. Her laughter ran around him, fading as she walked away.

SAM CLIMBED OUT OF HER car and studied the house opposite. The redbrick, single-story house with a metal picket fence and well-tended garden looked no different from its immediate neighbors.

Only it was. Evil resided inside.

She rubbed her arms, then reached back into the car to collect her coat. The wristcom buzzed against her side. She slipped on the coat and answered the call.

"We're in position, Agent Ryan."

"Give me five minutes, Briggs, then move in around the back." She glanced down the road, studying the gray Ford parked several houses down. She pointed toward the side of the house and saw an answering nod from inside the car. Taking a deep breath, she walked across the road and opened the front gate.

The front curtains moved. Evil had been watching.

She climbed the front steps and pressed the doorbell. When there was no response after several minutes, she banged her fist against the door. "SIU. We know you're in there, Mr. Whittiker. Please come out."

Briggs and Edmonds climbed over the front fence and edged down the side of the house. She fisted the door again. "I have a warrant for your arrest, Mr. Whittiker. Please, come out, or I'll be forced to break in."

Again, no response. She drew her weapon, took aim at the lock and fired. The door smashed back against the wall. The head of the armory hadn't been kidding when he'd said the gun would stop an elephant. The damn thing hadn't even been set to full.

She edged into the shadows lurking in the hall. There was a door to her immediate left and another farther along the hall to the right.

Evil waited near the right door.

"Stop playing games, Orrin, and come out." She ducked into the left-hand doorway.

Footsteps moved away. He was trying to circle around behind her. She turned and studied the room. Heavy drapes shrouded the window, keeping the room locked in darkness. And yet she could see as clearly as if it were day. A vid-screen dominated the far wall. In the center of the room were several old chairs, separated by a coffee table. To the left of these was another doorway.

It was to that door that evil headed.

She walked across the room and stood in the obscurity of the far corner. After several minutes, she heard a whisper of breath. He was close, so close.

She waited. The air stirred again. Orrin appeared, mouse quiet as he ducked through the doorway and padded forward. For a moment, she could only stare. His damn fists were bigger than her entire head. He was beyond huge.

She widened her stance and aimed her gun. "SIU, Orrin. Put your hands on your head and do not move. I'll shoot if you do."

He hesitated. Fear and anger sizzled through the darkness, slamming into her. She reeled back into the wall, trying to keep her balance through the sudden dizziness, unsure what was happening but aware that the giant was somehow responsible.

Orrin dove for the window. Though tears blurred her vision, she pulled the trigger. Energy sizzled through the darkness and struck the giant's thigh. Orrin yelped, but somehow managed to climb to his feet and keep on running. She tapped her wristcom.

"Orrin's on the street, running west."

The dizziness cleared as she ran out of the house. She leapt the front fence and pounded down the street after Orrin. But she was taking three steps to his one and losing ground fast.

"Orrin, stop, or I'll shoot."

He put his head down, arms pumping as he tried to run faster. She fired a warning shot over his head. It did no good.

She aimed at his legs and fired. The shot took him

in the thigh again, and this time it brought him down. The ground shook as he hit. She stopped several feet away. He lurched toward her, trying to grab her feet. She danced away, the weapon primed and ready to fire again.

Edmonds and Briggs joined her. Even then, it took all three of them to handcuff Orrin and get him into the back of the van.

She slammed the door shut and wiped the sweat from her forehead. "Take him back to headquarters and get his leg seen to, Briggs. I'll meet you there."

The older woman nodded. Sam watched the van drive away, then called Gabriel. Still no answer. Uneasiness stirred anew. Something was very wrong. She scratched her head, turned and walked back to her car.

For now, there was nothing she could do. If Stephan didn't know where Gabriel was, what hope did she have of finding him?

She drove back to headquarters. After dumping her handbag in her office, she made her way down to the holding cells. Briggs and Edmonds were waiting in the corridor.

"How is he?"

Briggs shrugged. "He's loud, ugly as sin and the rudest bastard I've ever met."

Sam smiled. "I meant his wound."

"To be perfectly honest, I hope it festers and causes his leg to drop off." Briggs turned her face to the side. A bruise darkened her skin, stretching from just below the eye down to her chin. "I'm lucky to escape with just this. He knocked Thornhill through the front doors. Cut him up pretty badly."

Thornhill wasn't an agent she'd met as yet. "Will he be okay?"

"According to the docs, yes."

At least that was something. Sam glanced at Edmonds. "And you?"

The big man smiled. "By the time he got to me, security had swarmed. They sedated him and brought him straight down here."

The cell door slid open and the doc stepped out. "The wound is fine. His temper is not, however. I've given him another dose of sedatives and ordered him chained up. Under no circumstances are you to undo those chains. Not if you value your life."

"Any prospect of him breaking free?"

The doc hesitated. "Under normal circumstances, I'd say no. But that man is far from normal."

Wasn't *that* the truth. She glanced at Briggs. "You two keep close watch. If he does happen to achieve the impossible, fire every stun gun you've got."

Briggs frowned. "But we'll hit you."

"I like my chances with the stun gun better." And with that, Sam headed into the cell.

Orrin glared at her. He had the sort of face only a mother could love. One eye seemed to ride higher than the other, and his nose was bulbous and lumpy, reminding her somewhat of cauliflower. His lips were flabby, flapping loosely whenever he moved. His bald head shone in the artificial light. A few strands of hair clung just behind his ears, and these—a bright red-gold in color—stuck out like chicken feathers, thick and bristly.

Briggs was right. This was one ugly son of a bitch. She walked around him and checked the restraints. So far, they showed no stress, though Orrin was constantly flexing the muscles along his shoulders and arms, trying to work free.

She walked back to the front and stopped, hands behind her back. "What can you tell me about Rose Pierce?"

He hawked and spat. The yellow mass landed near her left boot, but she didn't move. "We know she's responsible for the deaths of five people. What we're not sure of is your involvement in those murders."

He made no response, but simply continued to glare. His eyes were a muddy brown and full of anger, full of hate. She'd seen that sort of hate before. It wasn't aimed at her in particular; it was just a hate of anyone in a position of power. Government, police and, in particular, the military.

And that's the angle she needed to attack from.

"We got your details from a General Frank Lloyd. Seems they've been watching you for quite some time."

He jerked slightly. "They don't know nothin' about me. You're lying."

His lips were like jelly, and continued to wobble after he'd finished speaking. It was a dreadful sight. No wonder Orrin was a mass of anger—he'd probably grown up the butt of everybody's jokes.

"On the contrary, it was the military who gave us your name and address. They know you've been breaking into their system. They know it was you who stole the Generation 18 records. They've requested we hand you over to them once we've finished."

"You do that, and I'm dead!"

She raised an eyebrow. "Do you think I care?"

Orrin regarded her balefully. "Why are you doing this? You're one of us. You should understand."

She crossed her arms. "One of what, Orrin?"

"A reject. A castoff."

"And that's what you are? A military castoff?"

He nodded. "You think nature is this cruel? This face is man-made. And the bastards deserve to die."

On that, she had to agree. "Then why attack other rejects? Why not attack the military themselves?"

"I needed help. That was the price."

"Whose price, Orrin?"

He opened his mouth, then shut it and continued to glare at her.

She tried a slightly different tack. "You know, Orrin, if you don't cooperate, we'll have nothing to hold you with. I'm afraid we'll simply have to hand you over to Hopeworth."

He scowled. His bottom lip dropped, almost touching the end of his chin. It was not a pretty sight. "You can't do that. You know they'll kill me."

"And why would they want to kill you, Orrin? You just said you were a reject."

"A reject who knows too much about their projects. They've wanted to get their hands on me for some time."

He was obviously paranoid, if not psychotic. "Orrin, Hopeworth has known all along where to find you. They could have picked you up at any time."

"Not true." But he licked his lips and regarded her a little fearfully.

"Very true, I'm afraid. Hopeworth bugs its rejects, you see." She stepped forward and pressed two fingers against his side. "Feel that lump? It's a microchip capable of transmitting voice and location."

Orrin growled. He lunged forward, teeth bared, and Sam jumped back out of reach. The chains creaked as Orrin's full weight fell against them. They held, but she wondered for how long.

"You lie," he hissed, flexing his massive shoulders again. "They would have picked me up if they had known."

She shrugged. "Maybe you rate yourself a higher threat than what they actually think you are."

"I know things."

"So do I." She started pacing, more to settle her rising nerves than anything else. "I know for a fact that Hopeworth has been monitoring both the rejects and the retired scientists. I know for a fact that they've been aware of your involvement in the murders for quite some time. I know that each of the victims evolved from eggs taken from Emma Pierce. I know Rose Pierce is responsible for those deaths. I also know that Rose Pierce and Michael Sanders are one and the same person."

"You know nothin'."

She stopped and quirked an eyebrow. "I know that the military want to get their hands on you. I know that you don't want to go. But unless you start cooperating, I have no choice but to turn you over to Hopeworth."

He snarled, his arm muscles tensing as he flexed his shoulders. She watched warily, certain the chains wouldn't hold much longer.

"You help me, I'll help you," he said, after a few minutes.

She resumed her pacing. "Is that the sort of deal Rose offered?"

"Maybe."

"In what way do you think you can help me?"

"Rose has insurance. One of your own."

Alarm slivered through her. That was why no one could get hold of Gabriel. Rose had him.

"The SIU does not bargain for the life of its operatives."

"No? Then he dies." Orrin shrugged, but the gleam in his eyes was malicious.

Sam stepped closer. "If you know what is good for you, you'll tell us where he is—right now. The SIU is not bound by the same rules as the police. We play a whole lot rougher, believe me."

Orrin snorted. "Like I'm really afraid."

"Well, that's a shame." She glanced to the mirrored wall on her right. "Briggs, get a break team in here immediately, please."

"Will do." The metallic edge the speakers gave Briggs's voice could not disguise her enthusiasm.

The big man frowned. "What's a break team?"

She crossed her arms. "What does it sound like, Orrin? You had one chance to play fair, and you declined. Now we get nasty."

He lunged against the chains again, his teeth snapping. His canines were sharp, she noted. Almost as sharp as a vampire's. "You won't get nothin' from me."

"We'll see." She glanced at the wall again. "Buzz me if he changes his mind and decides to talk, or when the break team finishes."

"Will do," Briggs repeated.

Sam walked from the room. Out in the corridor, she stopped and took a deep breath. Tension oozed from every muscle. There was something about the big man that made her skin crawl, and it was more than just the sense of evil. It was as if he were something that should not exist—something obscene, like the kites.

She glanced at her watch and decided to get a coffee. The coffee machines in the building produced a black substance that tasted little better than dishwater, but right now she didn't feel like walking down the street to get something better. She wanted to be on hand when the break team started in on Orrin.

She headed up to the foyer. It being a public area, the machines there tended to offer better quality dishwater.

Only everyone else in the building seemed to have had the same thought, because by the time she got down there, the damn machine was out of coffee. She thumped it in frustration, then punched the button for hot chocolate. Better than tea, she supposed. She was watching it pour when Gabriel walked through security and headed for the elevators.

Orrin had been lying. Odd that she hadn't detected it. She grabbed her chocolate, almost burning her fingers as the hot liquid splashed up over the sides of the plastic cup, and hurried after her partner.

"Gabriel, wait!"

He continued walking, but he looked over his shoulder. There was no recognition, no emotion, in his eyes when his gaze met hers.

Heat crawled over her skin, whispering secrets to her mind. She stopped abruptly. Hot chocolate splashed over her hand again, dripping across the pristine tiles near her feet.

This wasn't Gabriel.

This was a shapeshifter, taking his form.

FOURTEEN

SAM DROPPED THE CHOCOLATE IN the nearby bin and drew her gun. "AD Stern, please stop right now."

The shifter looked over his shoulder. Surprise flitted through the familiar hazel eyes, then he dove into the nearest elevator.

She cursed and ran for the doors, but they shut a whisper too soon. She punched the call button and watched the floor indicator. The shifter was heading to the lower levels—probably to Gabriel's office.

A second elevator appeared. She punched the floor number and paced the confines of the cab as it began its descent.

Why would a shifter come in here imitating Gabriel? What would Gabriel have that would be important enough for someone to take such a risk? Truth was, she didn't know. At no time in the last month had he brought her into his confidence, and the only case she'd really been involved with was the rejects.

She stopped. It wasn't just *any* shifter; it was *Rose*.

She was here to get the location list of the remaining rejects. The woman had to be stark raving mad to take such a risk.

And yet, she'd made it past security without a hassle. She might even have gotten past Sam had it not been for her weird ability to pick out certain races.

The elevator stopped and Sam squeezed through the doors before they'd fully opened, running into the foyer. The shifter was halfway down the hall, heading for Gabriel's office.

"AD Stern, please stop right there."

The shifter turned and fired. Sam dove to her left. Laser fire sizzled down her right leg, and she yelped. The smell of burning material mingled with the stench of crisped flesh. *Her* flesh. The bitch had the laser set on full.

Ignoring the deep-set throbbing in her leg, she rolled to her feet and squeezed off several shots. The shifter ducked into the nearby hall, firing as she moved. The shots hit the wall inches above Sam's head.

Sam scrambled forward as a strident alarm shattered the silence. Footsteps pounded toward them. The shifter appeared, gun aimed, and Sam dove to one side. A blue-white beam sizzled half an inch from her stomach, striking the wall behind her. Metal melted, oozing downward.

She rose on one knee and fired again. Again the shot missed the fleeing shifter. She cursed. Security appeared from the hall to her left, weapons raised.

"That's not AD Stern," she said, pointing to the fleeing shifter. "Take her out immediately!"

"Agent Ryan, please put down the weapon."

"For Christ's sake, didn't you hear what I said? That is *not* AD Stern! Stop him immediately!"

Footsteps echoed in the silence. The shifter, running away. And the morons in security uniforms were letting her go. She swore and rose.

"Put down your weapon," the security officer repeated, "or I'll be forced to shoot."

There was no understanding in the officer's dour features, no realization of the evil he was letting loose. All he saw was an agent firing at a superior officer. She had no doubt he'd shoot if she fired her gun again.

She dove for the hall anyway. As she hit the ground, she sighted on the fleeing form and fired. The shifter jerked, her squawk decidedly unmanly as she stumbled into the wall. Then a laser burned into Sam's body and agony swept her into unconsciousness.

GABRIEL PACED THE CONFINES OF his prison for the umpteenth time. There had to be some way out of this box. There *had* to be. He couldn't let Rose get into the system and find the new addresses for the adoptees. She had to be stopped!

He had no doubt that she would get into his office. The SIU, for all its security, hadn't really considered the problem of multi-shifters taking on the form of their operatives. His only real hope lay with Sam and her odd ability to sense the evil in people.

Only he'd pissed her off so severely lately that she was likely to avoid him—especially given his lack of reaction to her none-too-subtle seduction attempt.

He punched the wall in frustration and it buckled under the force of his blow. Hope stirred, and he leaned forward for a closer look. Several of the rivets were missing in the strips holding the metal sheeting in place. Daylight gleamed through the small gaps.

This section of the refrigerator must have been built on top of existing walls—walls that had once been plasterboard. Over the years of abandonment, the plaster must have disintegrated, leaving only the insulation and the metal sheeting of the refrigerator itself.

This was his escape. He stepped back a pace, then booted the wall. The pinpricks of daylight became brighter. He kicked it again. A fist-sized gap appeared along the left-hand side.

But as he raised his leg for a third try, pain hit him, flashing fire down his leg. He grunted and dropped to his knees, clutching his thigh and trying to regain his breath.

Fire hit again, this time his shoulder and side. Agony seared his brain and burned through his body. Then it was gone, leaving him shuddering and gasping for breath.

Sam had been hit. How or why he didn't know, but she was hurt, and badly. He had to get out of this damn prison.

He climbed slowly to his feet. The wall gave way after half a dozen more kicks, peeling back like dented butter. The room beyond was small and dust-laden. The two small windows to his right were barred, though the glass had long gone. Not even his hawk form would fit between the bars.

He climbed through the wall and walked to the door. It was locked. He stepped back and kicked it. The lock broke after the fourth boot, and the door slammed open. The hallway beyond lay wrapped in dusk. Light filtered in from the strip of glass high above, and dust, stirred by the door opening, danced lazily in the sunbeams.

He couldn't hear any movement, but the sudden prickling sensation along the back of his neck suggested he was no longer alone.

Rose was back. He had to move.

He ran to the end of the hall and cautiously opened the door. It led into the factory proper—a huge space filled with little more than dust. A roller door dominated the wall to his left. Beside it was a second door. From where he stood, it was impossible to tell whether it was locked or not.

His footsteps echoed in the cavernous space. Though he could hear no other sound, the sensation that Rose drew close burned. Keeping near the walls, hoping to be less obvious in the dust-laden shadows, he made his way around to the door.

The handle turned when he gripped it. He opened the door and looked out. The room beyond was a loading bay. A second roller door at the far end stood open. Beyond it, he could see thunderous skies.

He rubbed the back of his neck. Though he couldn't see her, Rose was close. Watching. Waiting. It didn't matter. He had to take the risk. He had to try to escape while he still could.

He shifted shape and flew toward the open roller door. Movement caught the corner of his eye. Rose stepped out of the shadows, weapon raised.

He pumped his wings, flying as hard and as fast as he could. He felt rather than saw the report of the laser, felt the heat of the shot burn toward him. He flicked his wings, soaring up and sideways.

The shot sizzled past him, burning a bullet-sized hole in the metal wall. He arrowed through the door and into the freedom of the storm-clad skies. Footsteps raced behind him, and then a second shot burned through the air.

Again, he dove away, this time to his left. He wasn't fast enough. The shot tore through his wing, exploding through flesh and bone as easily as it had the metal wall. Agony fired through his brain. Then he was tumbling, careening out of control, back to the earth and Rose's waiting arms.

FOOTSTEPS ECHOED THROUGH SAM'S BRAIN, the rhythm of barely restrained anger. It was a beat accompanied by a muted throbbing in her shoulder and leg. Waking was not something she wanted to do—not if the throbbing was any indication of the pain that awaited on the return to full consciousness.

But she had little choice. Someone was shaking her good shoulder, demanding that she wake.

She forced one reluctant eye open. A woman's face swam into view. It was a strong face, a pretty face. A face that would take no shit.

Oddly enough, it reminded her of Gabriel.

Why, she had no idea. The woman's hair was dark brown and curly, her eyes almost catlike and mint green in color. But it was in her eyes that Sam could see the kinship, if nowhere else. Her gaze was at once sympathetic, demanding and hostile—a look Sam had seen all too often in the warm hazel depths of Gabriel's eyes.

"Who are you?" she asked.

The woman raised a dark eyebrow. "A direct, lucid question when you should be screaming in agony. Interesting."

"Would screaming in agony get me an answer any quicker?" Truth was, she probably *would* be screaming in agony if she didn't have the feeling that it wouldn't matter one jot—not to this woman, and not to the man who paced so angrily beyond her line of sight.

"Probably not." A smile that was impossibly white flashed briefly. "My name is Jessie McMahon."

No wonder she could see a similarity to Gabriel—the woman was his sister. No doubt the angry pacer was Stephan. "Where am I?"

"At SIU headquarters, in holding cell number nine."

Which was probably the most secure area in the whole of the SIU. Even if Sam screamed her lungs out, no one would be the wiser. The room had more shields than Parliament, and was generally reserved for the most dangerous criminals.

What a laugh, when all *she'd* done was try to stop an enemy. They were the ones who should be locked up, since they were the ones who'd undoubtedly let the enemy go.

"Why aren't I in the damn medical center?" Her voice came out cracked, harsh. She swallowed, but it didn't ease the burning dryness in her throat, though a dry throat was the least of her problems. She stank of burnt flesh, and her whole body ached—even if in a lackluster way. But once the numbness from the laser burns wore off, she would be screaming in agony.

Jessie's smile was cold. "Because, my dear, you tried to shoot my brother. You're lucky it was security firing at you and not anyone else."

Like Stephan, she surmised. Anger washed over

her, a wave of heat that momentarily echoed in Jessie's cat eyes.

"God, have you two any idea what you've done?"

Jessie grabbed her hand, her grip like steel, her skin like ice against the heat of Sam's flesh. "We stopped you from killing my brother."

Sam laughed harshly. She couldn't help it. These people supposedly dealt with the supernatural all the time, yet they were willing to believe the obvious without questioning.

"I bet you haven't even bothered looking at the tape, have you? You dragged me down here and just can't wait to beat the so-called truth out of me." She tilted her head back a little, but she still couldn't see the man who paced behind her. "Well, the truth is, I've had enough of you people. I fucking quit."

"You can quit after you've told me why you shot at Gabriel." Stephan's voice was unemotional, yet it sent a chill down her spine all the same.

"You're incredible." She tried to wrench her hand free of Jessie's, but couldn't—because her arms were strapped down, as were her feet. "Go view the tape and see if you can't guess the goddamn answer yourself."

"We've both seen vid-footage. And all we're actually sure of right now is that Gabriel has left the building and can't be contacted, and that you shot at him. Security shot you when you ignored their order to lower your weapon."

"And did you bother rewinding far enough to see him shooting at me first? Did you hear me tell security it wasn't AD Stern, but a shifter? Did you bother going far enough along the tape to hear the girly scream he emitted when I actually hit him?"

Stephan finally came into her line of sight. Though his face was emotionless, his blue eyes were stormy with anger. "How do you know it was a shifter? He passed all the security checks."

"Meaning you didn't view the tapes properly." She snorted softly and shook her head. "I would have thought that you, of all people, would not have let emotion cloud your judgment."

"Just answer the damn question."

"The shifter who took Finley's form in the labs a month ago passed all security checks, too, but that didn't make him the real Finley."

Jessie regarded her intently. "Why do you think it was a shifter and not Gabriel?"

Sam frowned. "I don't know. It's just something I sense sometimes."

"Gabriel did mention this ability, remember?" Stephan shared a brief glance with his sister, then his gaze returned to Sam. "Why didn't you alert security first?"

Because *that* would have been the smart thing to do. She blew out a breath. "I didn't stop to think. She was heading for Gabriel's office, probably to get the relocation list of the adoptees."

Stephan's gaze narrowed slightly. "You keep saying 'she.' Why?"

"Because the shifter in question is Rose Pierce, also known as Michael Sanders, State Police officer. I *did* send that information to you." She hesitated and watched the realization dawn in their eyes. "Yeah, your sister's killer. And you just let her walk away in your rush to get me to the torture room."

"We are not torturing you," Stephan growled.

"Then what do you call not offering someone with

severe laser burns medical help? A picnic in the park?"

"Security, get medical help in here right away."

Sam smiled grimly. One point for the innocent victim.

"How can this woman be a cross-gender multi-shifter?" Jessie glanced at her brother. "That's not possible, is it?"

Stephan frowned. "I certainly didn't think it was."

"Well, at least one person has it," Sam muttered. The fire in her leg and shoulder was beginning to fade against the deeper burning in her left side. If medical help didn't get here soon, she *would* be screaming.

Stephan met her gaze again. "You're certain it wasn't Gabriel?"

"Yes. And if your security people had done their job properly, you would have had Rose confined, not walking free. You might even know where Gabriel is right now, rather than continuing this aimless conversation with me."

His brief smile was grim. "Ah, but see, you're going to help us find Gabriel."

She blinked. "I think you just lost me."

Stephan resumed his pacing. "Jessie is not only both an empath and clairvoyant, but she also teaches the use of psychic abilities. You and Gabriel have formed a connection—a bond, if you like. He has used the link at least once to find you. You are about to return the favor."

She shook her head. "I don't—"

Stephan took four strides and leaned down, his face inches from hers. Anger radiated from every pore, and she met his stormy gaze and swallowed. There was no compassion in this man's eyes, no humanity. The only thing he cared about was his family, and she had no doubt he would kill *anyone* who threatened his family's safety in *any* way.

"You will do this." His voice was soft, without inflection. He didn't need it. His eyes held enough violence to spark a war. "You will find my brother, whatever the personal cost. You owe him your life, and you *will* return the favor."

"Stephan," Jessie warned softly, touching his arm.

He swung away and resumed his pacing. There was a savageness in every action, a raw brutality that had not been evident before now. Was this the real Stephan, or was it merely a by-product of his worry for Gabriel?

She suspected the answer might lie somewhere in between the two.

Jessie touched her hand again. Sam met her cat-green gaze.

"I showed Gabriel how to use the link. That's how he found you at that demolition site."

"Then thank you for saving my life, but that doesn't mean I can return the favor."

"Yes, it does. The link would not have formed if one or the other did not have the capacity."

"But I don't have the capacity. Ask *him*." She pointed her chin toward the pacing Stephan. Even that small movement sent ripples of pain down her body. Her stomach turned, threatening to rise. She swallowed heavily. "He's seen the test results. I came in negative."

"You came in neutral," Stephan corrected. "Not the same thing."

"I've never attempted anything like that. I wouldn't even know where to start!"

"As Stephan said, that's why I'm here." Jessie's gaze was shrewd, calculating. "Are you willing to try?"

As if she had a choice? "What do you want me to do?"

"Close your eyes." Jessie's soft voice took on an almost hypnotic quality. "Concentrate on the darkness and the sound of my voice. Take deep, slow breaths."

She closed her eyes and took a deep breath. Pain ripped through her, as sharp as a knife. She swore vehemently. "Get me some damn painkillers or I'm out of here."

As threats went, it was pretty lame—not only because she was strapped down, but because her leg was as numb as her arm, and any sort of quick movement would be nigh on impossible anyway.

"No," Stephan said, his voice abrupt, harsh. "Painkillers will dilute your ability to concentrate."

She glared at him. She was really beginning to dislike the man. Yet it was easy to see why he, rather than Gabriel, ran both the SIU and the Federation. "So does pain, buddy, believe me."

Jessie squeezed Sam's fingers lightly. "This won't take long, as long as you concentrate. Then we can let the medical help in."

Meaning they were going to keep her in confinement until they'd thoroughly checked her story? *Bastards*. And that fact, if nothing else, hardened her resolve. She'd meant what she'd said before—she'd had enough of these people. She wanted out, wanted to go back to the State Police. At least there she'd be treated a little more fairly—even if she *had* shot her partner.

"Let's get on with it, then." She closed her eyes and tried to ignore the throbbing aches in her body.

"Bring Gabriel's image to your mind. Concentrate on it."

She frowned and did as Jessie asked. Gabriel's image swam through her mind, its focus blurred, distant.

"Concentrate," Jessie whispered. "Imagine your mind as a hand, capable of reaching out and touching him."

Sweat trickled into Sam's closed eyes, stinging. She tried to ignore it. Gabriel's image went in and out of focus, as if viewed with some ill-adjusted lens.

"Reach for the image, Samantha. Reach out and touch him."

"I can't," she whispered. There was some sort of barrier between them, preventing her from reaching across. A fence of her making, not his.

"Focus on the image, Samantha. Focus until you can feel his presence within every fiber of your being. Then let your mind touch his."

She concentrated on the blurred image, willing it to become clear. Sweat trickled through her hair, along the side of her face. Abruptly, the image became focused, and she was there, sharing his mind, his thoughts. His eyes.

The ground sped underneath them. They arrowed toward a doorway, heart pumping as fast as their wings. Behind them, the air shuddered with sound. Heat sizzled. They soared upward. The shot hit the wall, spraying metal through the air. They flew through the doorway and into the open skies. Freedom, if they could get clear fast enough. Another shot. Again, they dodged. But this time the shot hit, exploding through wing and muscle and bone.

Agony surged through every fiber and tore her mind from his. She screamed, then darkness hit and she lapsed into unconsciousness.

When awareness returned, it was again to the sensation of someone shaking her shoulder.

It should have hurt, but it didn't. She frowned. ·Gabriel had been shot, not her. He was alive; that much she knew. For how much longer was anyone's guess—and there wasn't one damn thing she'd seen that could help them in any way.

"Samantha, open your eyes and look at me," Jessie demanded, her voice cracked with worry.

She opened her eyes and said, "He was shot while trying to escape. That's all I know, all I saw." All she felt.

"Fuck." Stephan thrust a hand through his hair. "There has to have been something you saw that can help us find him."

"He was in a warehouse of some kind. It was abandoned."

"Which leaves us with probably a thousand choices citywide," Jessie commented, her expression worried as she glanced up at Stephan. "How much manpower can you muster?"

"Not nearly enough, quickly enough," Stephan muttered, and resumed his pacing. "Even if we pull in the Federation operatives, it'll still take hours."

In which time Gabriel could have bled to death if he didn't get medical help. The phone rang in the brief silence.

Stephan grabbed the receiver almost savagely. "Byrne here."

He listened quietly for several minutes and then said, "Get all available teams down there immediately, but don't move until I join them."

He hung up and swung round, his expression an odd mixture of anger and surprise. "Why didn't you tell me you'd ordered a break team for Whittiker?"

"When did I have the chance? I was shot and dragged down here for questioning. I don't believe I was given much of a chance to say anything." She hesitated, more to keep her growing tide of anger in check than anything else. Stephan was not someone whose bad side she wanted to get on. "Why? Have they got an address out of him?"

"Yes. A warehouse in Altona." He pressed a button on the side of the phone. "Security, cancel the medics and take Agent Ryan straight down to medical. I want a twenty-four-hour guard placed on her."

"Gee, nice to know that I'm trusted."

Stephan barely glanced at her as he walked toward the door. "Until I check out your story thoroughly, you will remain under guard."

And if they didn't find Gabriel at the warehouse address Orrin had given them, she was in big trouble. That much was obvious.

The door opened. Three gray-clad security officers strode in.

"Barnes, I want full identity tests taken on anyone entering the building."

Barnes, a big man with craggy features, frowned. "That'll cause a bit of hostility, sir."

"I don't care. Just do it."

Barnes nodded and stepped aside as two medical officers came in, guiding a gurney between them.

"I'll let you know what happens," Jessie said to

Sam, then rose and stepped away as the two doctors approached.

One shoved a needle none too gently into her arm. Thankfully, it was her numb arm, she thought wryly. After a few seconds, the throbbing aches that assailed her body began to ease and her eyes grew heavy.

The doctors picked her up and placed her onto the gurney. The last thing she saw was Stephan handing Jessie a laser rifle as he walked from the room.

SHE DREAMT AGAIN OF THE white room. This time Joe's shadow was less indistinct, more man-shaped than merely a blot of darkness.

"*You called to me again. Why?*" *His voice held just a hint of annoyance.*

She shrugged. "*It's not as if I do this consciously. It just happens.*"

"*Nothing just happens, Samantha. You reach out because you wish to talk. But your timing right now is not the best.*"

"*Why? What does a street bum have to do that is so important?*"

His amusement washed over her. "*Who said I was a street bum?*"

"*That's the image you present to the world, isn't it?*"

"*It is. But I am not what I appear. You'd best remember that.*"

The soft warning sent a chill down her spine. She knew nothing about this man, who, conversely, seemed to know so much about her. She didn't even know if she could trust him. And yet, he'd saved her life, had given her somewhere to live when she most needed it and had come to this room when she called—even if she wasn't aware that she had called.

His sigh was a breeze that stirred past her hair. "What troubles you?"

"I did a search on the pin. It led me to Mary Elliot."

"Did it, now?" There was no surprise in his voice. He'd obviously known all along where it would lead.

"She kept confusing me with a woman named Josephine. Kept insisting I had a brother named Joshua."

"And do you?"

His shadow swirled slowly around her. Though he appeared relaxed, she could almost taste his tension.

"I have dreamt about Joshua, but I don't know who he is." She studied the shadowed form in front of her for a second. "Just as I don't know who you are. You might be Joshua, for all I know."

"I might. I might not."

"And the answer will be found in here," she retorted, lightly touching her chest, just above her heart. "When I am ready to find it."

She sensed more than saw his smile. "Took the words right out of my mouth."

"What a surprise." She stared at the ceiling for several seconds. Though the bright light was harsh, it did not hurt her eyes or make them water. "Am I a product of Hopeworth?"

His essence stilled. "I have said before that I cannot provide you with answers. You must seek them yourself."

"Cannot or will not?"

"Will not."

She nodded. He knew more than he would ever tell; that much was obvious. "I met with a General Frank Lloyd yesterday."

"I know."

"How do you know?"

His smile swirled around her. "As I said before, I know more than you comprehend."

She didn't bother raging against his obtuse answer, simply because it wouldn't get her anywhere. "I have a feeling the general and I will meet again."

Joe's shadow began to move. Agitation stirred the still air. "Be wary of the general. He sees more than most men."

"That's because he's not exactly a man, is he?"

Joe hesitated. "No, he is not. He is a product of Hopeworth, born and bred to do the bidding of the military. He is not someone you want anything to do with."

She rubbed her arms. On that, at least, they agreed. "I may not have any choice in the matter."

Concern churned around her. "You had a premonition?"

"Maybe."

"Then get the hell away from here. Leave the state, if that's what it takes."

"I can't. At least not until I know my partner is safe."

"Your partner? The man who has been trying to get rid of you?" He made no attempt to disguise the derision in his voice.

"Yeah, that one." She shrugged. "He saved my life. Now his life is in danger."

"Then find him and get far away from the general."

"Finding him is the problem. His sister seems to think we have formed some sort of mind bond, but *when I tried to find him through it, all I got were his emotions and pain."*

Joe didn't answer immediately, though his essence continued to swirl around her. "Your talents are only now truly developing—and as yet, no one can be really sure which way that development will head. One thing is obvious, though. It will not be standard."

She raised her eyebrows. "Another riddle?"

"No. A simple truth." He hesitated. "Maybe this linking with Stern, at least on your side, is one springing more from emotional than rational thought. Perhaps your ability is empathic rather than telepathic."

"And yet, here I am, talking to you."

Again she felt his smile. "This is very different. This is something neither of us can really stop or control."

"Why not?"

"The answers will—"

"Yeah," she retorted. "I know the rest of the rhyme, so don't bother."

"If you wish to find your partner, leave tonight and go to where he was last seen."

She frowned. "Why tonight?"

"It storms."

"Yeah? So?"

Impatience ran around her. "Just go, and you will see. For now, I must go."

His essence, and the white room, fled. She woke suddenly. Rain pelted against the window to the right of her bed. Lightning cut across the night, and the power of it stirred the air, filling her soul. She breathed deeply. Every pore seemed to tingle with the storm's energy.

From beyond the doorway came the sound of footsteps, a tattoo that was both angry and impatient. Jessie appeared. Water dripped from her burgundy coat, splashing across the tiles as she walked over to Sam's bed.

"What happened?" Inane question, when all she had to do was look into Jessie's eyes and see the answer. They hadn't found Gabriel.

"We found his wristcom, but nothing else. There was no clue as to where they might have gone."

Sam rubbed her forehead. Joe had told her to go to the warehouse. Though she had no idea why, she wasn't about to doubt him. Not when Gabriel's life might be at risk.

"Where's Director Byrne?"

"Interviewing Whittiker again."

She almost felt sorry for Orrin. Almost. "You have to take me to that warehouse."

Jessie frowned. "Samantha, you're in no condition—"

"Yeah, right," she snapped back. "Like you were so concerned about my condition down in the holding cell."

Jessie had the grace to look uncomfortable.

"Do you want to save your brother or not?" she continued.

"Of course I do. But you can't even walk."

"That was hours ago. I'm better now." Even if she wasn't, she had no intention of mentioning it. She owed Gabriel—though certainly not any of his damn relations—and she intended to repay that debt. Then she'd be free to leave and get back to a normal life, with normal people.

But could anything ever be normal when her discovery of her true nature was only just beginning? Deep down, she suspected not.

Indecision rolled across Jessie's face. "Stephan's ordered that you be kept here. That under no circumstances are you to be allowed to leave."

Obviously he had plans to cross-examine her again if Orrin failed to deliver. "I think I may be able to find Gabriel, but I need to get out of here now. I can't wait for Stephan."

"I'm not SIU. I can't countermand Stephan's orders."

"Then call him. Tell him if he wants to find his goddamn brother, he has to trust me, and he has to release me."

"I don't think he'll listen."

"Try."

Jessie nodded and walked from the room. Sam stripped the covers away and swung her legs over the edge of the bed.

Her right leg, from thigh to knee, was a scarred, red mess. But at least it was a healing scarred, red mess. Though the skin pinched slightly when she moved, it didn't seem to restrict her. Nor did it hurt. She rotated her shoulder. Again, though there was a definite tightness in the skin, she could move it without pain. How was this possible only a few hours after being shot? She didn't know, and right now she didn't really care.

All that mattered was getting to Gabriel before time ran out.

She padded across the cell to get her clothes, the

tiles cold under her feet. She dressed quickly, then went back to bed—just in case one of the med staff walked in before the clearance came through for her to be up and about.

But come through it did.

Ten minutes later, she walked out of the building and into the power of the rain-swept night.

FIFTEEN

GABRIEL WOKE TO THE SOUND of pacing—short, vicious steps that spoke of anger and frustration more eloquently than any words.

He lay on the floor of an office of some kind. The star-shaped base of a chair sat less than a foot away from his head. Beyond that, he could see the sturdy metal legs of a desk. The carpet underneath him rubbed almost harshly against his skin, and it was a practical gray color. It was the sort of hard-wearing carpet they used in state-owned buildings and in housing developments.

That he was no longer in the warehouse was obvious. He shifted fractionally, trying to see the rest of the room. Bad move. Pain shot through his body, a red wave of heat that left him not only gasping for air but soaked in sweat.

The tattoo beat of violence hesitated and then headed his way. Boots appeared before him, wavering in and out of focus. He squeezed his eyes shut, trying to shake the sweat from his vision, then opened them again. The boots were still there. Black and practical. The kind worn by the State Police force.

He looked up. Even that slight movement forced new rivulets of sweat to run down his forehead.

Rose stared down at him, her eyes as dark as the night-dark window at her back. "Good to see you're finally awake, Assistant Director."

Despite the cheerfulness of her tone, the fury in her eyes suggested all had not gone well.

"I wish I could say the same."

Her smile was thin, bitter. "The arm hurts a little, does it?"

She nudged it with the tip of her boot. Pain tore through his body, and he gritted his teeth against the scream that tore at his throat. He glared at her through the drips of sweat. "Bitch."

"Yes, I am." She laughed and turned away. "You didn't tell me about your partner, Assistant Director."

Something cold ran through him. Rose had shot Sam. "You didn't ask."

"True." Rose leaned against the front of the desk, contemplating him silently for a few moments. "What is she? I was under the impression she was a changer, but her survival of the Jadrone suggests a shifter of some kind. One who is sensitive to others of her kind."

"Something like that." It was obvious from the annoyance etched into Rose's features that Sam *had* managed to stop her, and had been shot for her efforts. At least she wasn't dead—he would have known if she were.

"It's unfortunate, you know, as it calls for a change in plans."

And he was supposed to be sorry about that? Anything that sidetracked this woman's mad schemes *had* to be a good thing. "Try my shape again. You never know. You might get through a second time."

"I am not a fool, Assistant Director. Please don't treat me like one."

There was no point in replying. He carefully ran his fingers up his injured arm until he found the laser wound. The cut felt clean, but his arm was definitely broken. Which was no real problem, because his shapechanger bones healed extraordinarily fast. He just had to set the bones straight, and the healing would begin. He could also feel an ominous damp patch under his right shoulder, but he had no idea where that blood was coming from.

"You stated before that the SIU does not bargain for its operatives," she said. "You'd better hope that you're wrong, because it's your only chance to live."

"Then there's no chance at all." Nursing his shattered limb with his right arm, he rolled fully onto his back. To say it hurt would be an understatement, but he needed to see where he was. The room was small, and the only exit points were the window behind the desk and the two doors, one opposite to where he lay and the other close to his left. He could hear no sound beyond this room. Hopefully, it meant it was just him and Rose here.

"I want Director Byrne's silent number," she continued.

He gave it to her. If she thought to get around the automatic tracing by using Stephan's silent number, then she was very wrong.

He waited almost impatiently for her to grab the phone. All he needed was for her attention to be diverted for a second or two, and he was up and out the door. His arm might be shattered, but he still had two good legs. And the desperation to survive was a mighty fine painkiller.

Rose picked up the laser near the phone and pointed it in his direction. "Move and you die."

She set the phone to speaker and dialed the number he'd given her. After several rings, Stephan's familiar voice came online.

"Byrne here."

"Director Byrne. How nice to finally speak to you."

There was a brief silence. Though the trace was automatic, he knew Stephan was now ordering a second trace to start, this time involving satellites to track the exact location.

"Who is this?"

Rose glanced at her watch. As a cop, she'd know the call would be traced, but he doubted if she knew it could be tracked via satellite as well. That capability was a well-kept secret.

"I think you know who this is, Director. Shall we cut to the chase?"

"What do you want, Rose?"

"You know what I want. I have something to offer in exchange."

"You must know we do not make exchanges for the lives of our operatives. We can't afford to."

"Then you condemn him to death."

The silence seemed to stretch forever. Gabriel nursed his arm and wished, for the first time in his life, he knew what was going on in his brother's mind. They both knew the rules—they both knew the risks of being caught in a situation like this. Both knew that, in the end, there was no real choice.

But had it been *him* on the other end of the phone, he would have found some way to give them another choice.

"Let me speak to him," Stephan said eventually. "I want to know if he's still alive."

"Oh, he's alive. Bleeding, sweating and silently cursing me, but he's definitely alive." She motioned toward the phone with the gun. "Speak to the man, Assistant Director."

"Here, sir," he said.

"Situation?"

Rose clicked the safety off the gun. A soft whine filled the room as the laser powered to full.

He took heed of the warning. "As she said."

"Enough," Rose cut in. "I want an answer, Director, and I want it fast."

"Look, I haven't the power for a decision like this. I need to go higher."

Rose glanced at her watch again. "You have precisely two hours. Then he dies."

"Just make sure he lives until you get my damn—"

Rose hit the receiver, cutting him off. "Four seconds until the trace was complete. That will really piss him off, don't you think?"

Maybe. Maybe not. It depended on how fast the satellites got into action.

Rose reset the laser. "I'm afraid there's a lot more to do, the least of which is ensuring you don't bleed to death within the next couple of hours. Can't have my insurance policy expiring before its proper time, now, can I?"

The woman was certifiably crazy. "It's not something I want, I can assure you of that."

She gave him a thin smile. "No doubt," she said, and squeezed the trigger.

Gabriel swore and rolled away from the beam. His injured arm hit the floor, and agony exploded. Then the second burst of laser fire hit, sweeping him into unconsciousness.

SAM STUDIED THE WAREHOUSE THROUGH the Mustang's rain-washed window. Even with the headlights on high beam, the building was little more than a hunched shadow in the stormy night.

"I can't see what coming out here is going to achieve," Jessie said, leaning on the steering wheel to peer through the windshield. "We went over everything already. There's nothing here to find."

"Maybe." But she had to try, at the very least. "You'd better wait here. No sense in both of us getting wet."

Jessie's gaze was dubious. "You're sure you're okay?"

"Yeah." Sam opened the car door. The wind snatched it from her hands, flinging it fully open. She winced. "Sorry about that."

Jessie shrugged. "There's a flashlight in the glove compartment. Grab that."

Sam did, even though she didn't really need it. With all the lightning, the night was almost as bright as day. She climbed out and slammed the door shut. The wind tore at her hair, blowing it in all directions. The rain sheeted down, sluicing off her coat and soaking into her boots. Yet in the wildness, there was power. She could feel it running across her skin, crackling across her fingertips. She breathed deeply, drawing that energy inside, feeling it surge through every pore, every fiber, although she wasn't entirely sure how this would help her to find Gabriel.

She walked toward the warehouse. The wind howled through the shattered windows lining the front of the building—an eerie sound that had goose bumps fleeing across her skin. Mixed with this moaning was the high-pitched scream of metal as the wind tore at the roofing. It sounded like the dead being tortured.

Shoving her hands in her coat pockets, and half-wishing she'd brought some gloves, Sam made her way down the side of the building. It briefly protected her from the full force of the wind, though the night was still bitterly cold. Thunder pealed in the distance. She began counting the seconds, but she had barely gotten to three before jagged lightning split the night sky. The center of the storm was only a mile away. Whether this would make any difference to what might happen, she wasn't sure.

She reached the back and came out of the protection of the building. The wind slapped against her, forcing her to stagger several steps before she regained her footing. Lightning tore through the sky again. In the residual brightness, she saw the ramp and loading bay. This was it. This was where Gabriel had gotten shot.

She walked forward slowly, not toward the loading bay, but away from it. He'd been flying when he was hit, striving upward to escape the loading bay. He wouldn't have come down close to it.

Overhead, thunder rumbled again. The power of the storm echoed through her—a force that filled her, completed her, in a way she couldn't even begin to understand or hope to explain. When she clenched her hands, sparks danced across her knuckles, a visible sign of the energy coursing through her being.

It scared her. Terrified her. But if this power helped her find Gabriel, then she'd use it and worry about the consequences later.

She splashed through puddles, following the rain-slick pavement toward the rear of the property. Hopefully, there she'd find a clue that Stephan and Jessie had missed.

The fence line came into view. The double gates leading out of the property were padlocked. She turned left and walked along the perimeter, following instinct and hoping it wasn't leading her astray.

Again, the sky rumbled. In the following flash of lightning, she saw something flapping wildly in the wind-torn darkness. A piece of material, caught in the fence.

She splashed quickly through the mud. The material was dark gray and felt like silk. The sort of material Gabriel favored in his jackets. She tore the strip free and rubbed it between her fingers. He must have snagged his jacket on the fence as he fell. She hoped his jacket was the only casualty.

Thunder reverberated. Its power shuddered through her, and energy, as bright as the lightning itself, sparked again between her fingertips, this time dancing over the small strip of material.

Power hit her with the force of a hammer. She grunted and dropped to her knees, splashing mud into her face. But she ignored that and clenched the material tight, struggling to breathe under the weight of the energy running around her, through her.

Images struck—jagged pieces of information that

knifed through her mind. A suburb full of redbrick houses. A street name. A factory perched between two supermarkets. A "For Sale" sign out front, bearing the number 52. Gabriel, pale and unconscious, stretched out on a gray carpet.

The power faded, leaving her trembling and gasping for breath. She shuddered and swiped the muddy water dripping from her nose. What the hell was that? And how had Joe known it would happen? Jesus, she had to find out just who he was and how he knew so much.

But right now that was not her main priority. She struggled upright, the material still clenched in her hand. But with most of the night's power having left her system, it was little more than a sodden strip. Even so, it was proof that he'd been here, proof that she'd found what they could not. A clue. A possible hope.

As she made her way back to the car, she tapped her wristcom and quickly called the SIU.

"Christine? Patch me through to Director Byrne."

Stephan came online. In the background she could hear strident alarms. "What do you want now, Agent Ryan?"

For the first time since she'd met him, Stephan actually looked, and sounded, stressed. "I know where he is, sir. I'm heading there now."

"The address?"

She gave it to him. "I wouldn't call in too many reinforcements, though. Might inflame the situation."

"The situation is already inflamed. She gave us two hours." He hesitated, glancing down. "Forty-five minutes ago. And Whittiker has escaped."

That was not a good development. "Escaped? How?"

"We don't know, and we can't find him."

"He'll be heading to the factory to meet up with Rose and help fulfill his end of the bargain."

"Maybe. I'll meet you there, Agent Ryan." He hesitated again, blue eyes sharp with anger. "Under no circumstances are you to move in until we get there, understand?"

"Yes, sir." Whether she actually obeyed was another matter.

Stephan grunted and signed off. She climbed into the car.

"I'm going to soak your seats, I'm afraid."

Jessie waved a hand. "Forget it. Did you find anything?"

"I certainly did." She grinned and punched the address into the onboard computer. "Let's go rescue your brother."

JESSIE HALTED THE MUSTANG IN the supermarket parking lot two doors down from the factory. Sam shivered. Even though the car's heating was on full, she still felt as cold as a snowflake in a storm. At least she'd discovered one thing tonight—this damn coat wasn't exactly waterproof. At least not when the rain was more like a torrent than a gentle shower. Her sweater was sodden underneath.

She peered through the waterfall running down the windshield, trying to see the factory. A solitary light glimmered in front of the building, but against the force of the storm, it did little more than illuminate the small patch of ground directly beneath it.

She glanced at her watch. It had taken them half an hour to get here. That gave them forty-five minutes before Rose's deadline ended. If Stephan didn't get here soon . . .

Headlights glimmered through the rain. The car cruised past the factory, not slowing until it reached the parking lot entrance. It turned in and came to a halt beside them.

She climbed out of the Mustang. The wind cut through her sodden coat, as sharp as a knife. She shivered again and shoved her hands in her pockets. Not that it helped much.

Jessie stopped beside her. "Bitch of a night," she said, as she wrapped a rubber band around her hair.

Stephan climbed out of the gray Ford. "It might play to our advantage," he said. "With the force of the wind, it's doubtful Rose will hear any noise we might make."

"Orrin will." Sam didn't know why she was so certain of this. "Did you bring any backup, sir?"

Stephan nodded. "Briggs and Edmonds. They're making their way around to the back of the building."

"Let me go in and scout the situation. If Orrin's there, we'll have to get rid of him first."

"Definitely not—"

"With all due respect, sir, we haven't the time to stand here and argue. Orrin will hear you, but he won't hear me." Not with the storm and the night as her ally. She held out her hand. "Give me an earphone and just trust me."

"I don't care to risk my brother's life—"

"Stephan," Jessie interrupted softly, "it's Gabriel's only chance."

He glanced at his sister and then handed Sam the earphone. "I want a running commentary, and I want you to call us the minute there's a problem. Understand?"

She tucked the small device into her ear and nodded. "I'm not stupid enough to tackle Orrin alone, believe me."

"Good." He reached into his pocket and withdrew a Holcroft laser. "Take this with you."

The laser clung to her palm like a second skin and she felt safer. "Thanks."

She turned and walked toward the factory. The wind tore at the gum trees along the fence line. Leaves and twigs littered the footpath, becoming miniature boats as they were caught in the rush of water streaming toward the gutters. At least the tree canopies protected her from the worst of the rain. She climbed the waist-high fence at the front of the building and stopped, letting her gaze roam across the dark factory.

Thunder rumbled across the night. Power surged, dancing through her soul. Energy again leapt across her fingertips, warming the chill from her flesh.

But through the power came the sensation of evil. Orrin was inside the factory, keeping watch near the back. The softer bite of evil that was Rose's presence came from near the front of the building. Obviously, her best bet was to enter from somewhere near the middle.

Once she reached the meshed gate, she shoved the laser in her pocket, grabbed the links and began to climb. Her coat caught on one of the top rungs, tearing as she swung over. Water dripped past the sodden neck of her sweater, chilling her already cold flesh. She cursed softly.

"Problem, Agent Ryan?" Stephan's voice breezed through the earphone, cold and efficient.

"No, sir," she answered, keeping her voice low so that Orrin didn't hear. "Just tore my friggin' coat."

"We'll buy you a new one. You near the factory entrance yet?"

"I'm approaching the side door now, sir."

She splashed through the puddles and up the stairs. The side door was padlocked. She picked up the lock, studying it in frustration. *Just great*. She didn't have her pick with her, and if she shot her way in, it might alert those inside.

She studied the long building. In the brief flash of lightning, she saw windows high up. Too high for her. Unlike Gabriel, she hadn't the option of flight— nor were there any trees close enough to use as a ladder.

Her gaze returned to the lock. Thunder rumbled, and once again the force of the storm surged through her body. The energy tingling across her fingers became a bright, blue-white flame that danced across the lock, encasing it in fire.

In a heartbeat, it was little more than dust in her hand.

The flame muted again, but it didn't completely disappear. She stared at the blackened scraps in her hand. What sort of psychic ability was *that*?

She didn't know, and right now she didn't care. Not if it helped free Gabriel.

She raised her hand, letting the wind scatter the lock's remains. Then she carefully opened the door. The passageway beyond was dark and narrow—not the sort of place she really wanted to get caught in. There was absolutely no fighting room.

But she had little choice. Orrin still stood guard near the back. Rose was near the front. Gabriel was probably somewhere between the two.

"Entering the factory now," she said, closing the door carefully behind her.

"See if you can find Gabriel and get him out of there. We'll take care of the rest."

That was just fine by her. She'd never had a death wish, and Orrin was not someone she ever wanted to confront.

She eased forward, her fingers wrapped so tightly around the laser that her knuckles practically glowed. The air smelled stale, old, and a steady, moaning creak filled the silence—the wind tearing at the loose roofing.

The passage curved around to the right and opened onto a set of stairs. Sam stopped, listening. The awareness of evil stirred through her. Orrin still stood guard near the back of the building, but Rose was on the move. Sam's sense of her flowed across the darkness, moving steadily closer. Had Rose heard the door open? Did she suspect something was wrong?

Sam had no idea, nor was there any use worrying about it. She had to get off these stairs and out of Rose's way before she appeared. Right now, it was better that she avoid being seen—at least until she'd found Gabriel and knew he was safe.

And once she knew that, she was more than willing to back away and let Stephan vent his anger. Would Orrin and Rose survive that? She very much doubted it.

She edged quietly down the steps, stopping again at

the bottom. Thunder vibrated through the air. The
following flash of lightning briefly illuminated a vast,
empty space. She looked up. Skylights were regularly
spaced along the roofline. She'd have to watch that
she wasn't caught in the open during the next flash. It
would be just her luck that Rose would walk by at
that precise moment.

Once on the factory floor, she headed left, keeping
to the deeper shadows under the stairs. Sound stirred
the silence—the scuff of a heel against concrete. She
squatted in a corner, waiting.

The sense of wrongness flooded the night, making
it difficult to breathe. From the hallway to her right,
a woman appeared. Rose, obviously, as she was the
image of her dead sister.

"Orrin?" the woman said. Though it was barely a
whisper, Sam heard her clearly. Perhaps it was the
night and the power of the storm. Perhaps it was just
the emptiness of the factory allowing her voice to
carry so well. "I'm heading up to check the side
door," the woman continued. "If you don't hear from
me, presume the worst. Kill Stern and get the hell out
of here."

Damn. Once Rose walked up those stairs and discovered the unlocked door, she'd know *someone* was
here. Sam had to find Gabriel and get him out of here.
Fast.

Rose drew close and Sam's skin crawled. The stink
of the other woman's evil was almost suffocating.
She didn't move; she barely dared to breathe. Rose
grabbed the banister and hesitated, her gaze sweeping the shadows in which Sam hid. Sam's breath
caught, and she tensed.

After a moment, Rose moved on, her footsteps fading away as she disappeared down the hallway above. Sam had, at best, a few minutes left to find Gabriel.

She ran across the factory floor, heading for the rear of the building and Orrin. Gabriel had to be near the giant somewhere.

She came to a door and opened it cautiously. Another hallway. She stepped inside, stopped, then reached into her pocket for the strip of material. Sparks leapt across her fingertips, firefly bright in the darkness.

Gabriel was two doors down and to her left. She padded forward. The door wasn't locked, nor did it appear alarmed. An ominous sign, because it meant they were sure Gabriel couldn't escape.

She quickly stepped inside and closed the door. It was the office she'd seen briefly in her visions—small and cramped, with cheap, dingy gray wall-to-wall carpet. Gabriel lay near the desk, not moving but breathing.

She waited, listening to the silence as she studied the room. There had to be something here, something that would warn them if Gabriel woke up. Surely they wouldn't be foolish enough to think the ropes that bound him would hold him.

Or maybe they *were* that foolish. Maybe Rose was delusional *and* overconfident.

She knelt by Gabriel's side. His skin was pale and clammy, his breathing rapid. Shock, she thought. He shouldn't be moved, but she had no choice. She pressed the earphone. "Found him."

"Alive?" Stephan's voice was tightly controlled. He'd feared the worst.

"Yes. Unconscious, though."

"We're moving in."

And Orrin was moving out. The giant had sensed her, though she had no idea how. But then, if she could sense him, why wouldn't he be able to sense her, especially if they were both products of Hopeworth?

One thing was obvious, though. She couldn't stay here. To do so would risk Gabriel's life. Rose wouldn't kill her insurance policy unless she had no other choice. Sam would have to do the one thing she'd been trying to avoid—confront Orrin.

"Orrin's on the move. I'm going to try and lead him away from Gabriel. Have Briggs and the others wait near the back entrance."

"Be careful."

A totally unnecessary warning. She rose, then hesitated. She couldn't leave Gabriel here unprotected. Rose obviously wasn't sane. Why *wouldn't* she come back here and kill Gabriel, just for the hell of it?

She quickly undid the ropes binding his arms and legs but she left them looped, so that to the casual glance he still looked bound.

Then she touched his cheek, pinching it gently. "Gabriel, wake up."

He groaned, eyelids fluttering. She pinched harder. Right now, there was no time for niceties. Not when Orrin was drawing close.

"Gabriel, wake up, goddamn it."

He did. Pain burned bright in the hazel depths of his eyes. His gaze was unfocused, and he blinked several times, struggling to stay awake and regain some semblance of alertness.

She couldn't wait for that.

"Here, take this." She shoved the laser into his hand. "Protect yourself. The ropes are undone. I'm going to lead Orrin away from this room. Stephan's on his way. Leave if you can."

He blinked owlishly and she wondered if he'd heard anything she'd said. Sweat dripped into his eyes, and the stink of burnt flesh was heavy in the air. His shattered arm was obviously bad. So, too, was the cut he'd sustained on the fence, if the wide circle of blood near his shoulder was anything to go by.

Still, if he hadn't bled to death by now, he probably wasn't in danger of doing so within the next five minutes.

His eyes started to close again and she touched his cheek gently. "Gabriel, stay awake. Stay alert. Orrin's on his way. Wait till he has checked this room, then get up and run."

If you can. Because he showed no sign of real understanding. She bit her lip, rose and walked across to the internal door. It led into another office. She slipped inside.

Outside the factory, lightning flashed—something she heard and felt rather than saw. Energy crawled across her skin. Stephan was closing in. So was Orrin. His lumbering steps reverberated through her brain, as sharp as the evil that stung the stale air.

This room also had two doors. She took the left, simply because Orrin approached the other. It led into another corridor. She turned right. The back door had to be down here somewhere. If she could find it and open it, Briggs and Edmonds might be able to help her take out Orrin before Rose was alerted to the fact that something was wrong.

Sam came to another door and opened it to find another set of stairs, this one leading down into a wide, dark room. A roller door dominated the wall opposite. A smaller door was beside it, padlocked and bolted from the inside rather than the outside. Briggs had no chance of getting through that without blasting her way in and telling the world of her presence in the process.

In the hallway behind her, a door opened. It wasn't so much the sound she heard as the stale air stirring. Orrin hunted.

She descended the stairs and ran to the outer door. The sparks dancing across her fingertips leapt to the padlock the minute she picked it up. Within seconds, it was dust.

If she'd had the time to be frightened about this new ability, she would have been. But right now, Gabriel's safety mattered more than anything else—including her fear.

She pulled open the bottom dead bolt and reached for the top lock, but it was too high and she couldn't get anywhere near it. Cursing, she swung around, looking for something to stand on.

And saw the door near the top of the stairs open.

SIXTEEN

SCENT STIRRED AROUND HIM. SAM'S scent. Vanilla and cinnamon, such a warm and enticing mix. Like her. He opened his eyes, blinking several times before his vision swam into focus.

He was still in the office, still on the floor. His arm was numb. Sadly, that numbness didn't extend to his back, where it felt as if every muscle was being torn apart. Even the mere act of blinking made his gut churn uneasily.

Sam wasn't in the room. But she had been; otherwise he wouldn't have smelled her.

Or was it merely wishful thinking?

No, he could feel her closeness, as surely as he could his heart. And she'd left him a laser. It clung like a limpet to his palm.

Where had she gone? And why?

Rose, he thought. She was hunting Rose. He had to find her—and help if he could.

He rolled onto his back, and a dozen fresh aches assaulted his body. Sweat beaded on his forehead and dripped down the side of his face. For an instant, darkness loomed. He would have welcomed the fall back to unconsciousness except for the sudden realization that if Sam was here, she would need his help. She couldn't cope with the likes of Rose alone.

He grabbed the edge of the desk with his good hand and, gritting his teeth, slowly, carefully, eased himself upright. But his legs wouldn't take his weight and buckled beneath him. His knees hit the floor, his back scraping against the desk as he fell sideways. A scream tore up his throat, but it came out as little more than a sharp hiss.

When the room stopped spinning, he tried again. This time he made it. He wiped the sweat from his eyes, then staggered across to the door, where he stood, trembling like a newborn just learning to walk. As much as he needed to change shape to repair his arm and stop the bleeding, he couldn't. Not when he was in this sort of state. It was all he could do to remain conscious.

The door opened into a corridor. Two doors to choose from—the right one was closer. He didn't have much strength left, and he didn't know how much longer he could keep going. So he headed right.

The door led into a deeper darkness, and he had the feeling of a vast emptiness. There were no sounds beyond the creak of loose roofing. He stepped out. Overhead, lightning flashed, briefly illuminating the room. He was in a factory of some kind. There were stairs directly in front of him, leading up.

He staggered across the emptiness and grabbed the banister—had to, because otherwise he would have fallen. His heart felt like it was ready to tear out of his chest, and the darkness whirled around him. He took several deep breaths and slowly, carefully, began to climb.

Footsteps whispered across the night. He stopped, listening. They were coming to the top of the stairs and heading directly toward him. It wasn't Sam. He would have known if it were. So it was probably Rose.

He held his ground, simply because he had no other choice. He couldn't move with any sort of speed, and Rose would hear him if he tried. It was better to remain where he was and hope for the element of surprise.

He clenched his fingers around the laser and waited. The steps drew close—a beat of violence that ricocheted across the night.

Rose appeared on the top step. She began to descend, then stopped abruptly. There was a click and light flooded across his face, momentarily blinding him.

"Well, well. Here I am expecting an intruder, and I find you instead. How did you escape the ropes?"

"Double-jointed."

He squinted, trying to see her silhouette against the brightness of the flashlight. He dared not use the laser until he was certain of her position. Surprise would give him only one shot, so it had better be a good one.

"Why don't you just turn around and head down the stairs? I can't have my insurance policy running around injuring himself. Orrin wouldn't be pleased."

"You're fuckin' mad, do you know that?" Which probably wasn't the sanest thing to say, given the situation.

"Why, thank you. That's the nicest thing you've said all day. Now move."

He pressed the safety off the laser. "And go meekly to my death? I don't think so."

"Assistant Director, don't be a fool. I have a gun, and I'm not opposed to shooting a hole the size of a football field in your knee. Dragging you across the floor would be a pain, though, so I'd really prefer not to."

From the hallway behind her came a second whisper of sound. A door creaking open. Her gaze hardened. "It appears we have a visitor after all, which leaves me with little choice. I can't have you wandering around unattended, now, can I?"

He raised the laser and aimed for the flashlight. The bright beam went out. Rose yelped and then swore. He threw himself sideways. His back hit the banister and agony exploded. Laser fire bit through the night, burning into the step he'd just vacated. Another burst of laser fire lit the darkness, its source the hallway beyond Rose.

There was a thud, then Rose's body fell past him, landing in a broken pile at the base of the stairs.

He looked up. Stephan, still in his Byrne disguise, appeared out of the darkness, a laser by his side.

"And the lesson from tonight is never to attack my brother without first looking over your shoulder for me." He squatted next to Gabriel, eyes grim despite his half-smile. "The bitch didn't deserve to die so quickly, of course. How are you feeling?"

"Like shit. Help me up."

"I don't think that's a—"

"Damn it, Stephan, don't argue. Sam needs help."

"Then let me and Jessie handle it."

"The way you let the SIU handle this? This is not a responsibility the director should be handling."

"I'm not here in my capacity as the director."

"I realize that. Now help me up."

Stephan gripped his arm and steadied him as he rose. Pain tore across his back. For a minute, it felt as if someone was shoving red-hot pokers into his backbone, clear through to his gut. He hissed and blinked the sweat out of his eyes.

"Brother, you're useless to everyone like this. Let us handle it."

"Would you, if it were Lyssa?"

Stephan regarded him steadily. "Lyssa's my wife. We're talking about your partner—a woman you've been trying to get rid of."

A woman who was dead if he didn't get moving. "Yeah. So just shut up and help me down the stairs."

ORRIN STEPPED ONTO THE LANDING. Sam couldn't see him; the night hid him as surely as it had hidden her earlier. But she could feel him, feel the stink of his evil.

"I knew you were one of us." His voice jarred the night, edgy and somehow out of tune with the power that flowed through the darkness.

She backed away from the door. If she could get to the deeper shadows, maybe he'd lose her . . .

"I can see you, you know. I can see you as clear as day. It's one of the advantages of our gift."

"What gift is that, Orrin?" If he could see her, why couldn't she see him? Why could she only sense him?

"The gift of darkness. The ability to ghost, to become one with the night."

No mention of the power within the storm. No mention of the firefly dance of energy that could shatter locks as easily as she breathed.

Perhaps Orrin thought to keep it a surprise. Perhaps he didn't even know about it. There was no way of knowing if her apparent ability to disappear into shadows was in any way linked to his. They might not even be talking about the same type of ability.

But Orrin had come from Hopeworth. The more she delved into her past, the more obvious it was that the military base was her birthplace. The gifts Orrin spoke of were a cousin to her own; of that she was sure.

"Vampires ghost, Orrin, and you're no vampire."

The giant walked down the stairs and she backed away, her gaze sweeping the large room, searching desperately for some sort of weapon. It was no use running. Orrin was almost twice her height and would catch her in no time.

"No," he replied. "But their DNA runs through me. And I *will* taste your blood before this night is out."

Like hell he would. Damn it, how close were Briggs and the others? Or Stephan? She still had the earphone on—maybe she should just shout for help. But that would warn Orrin and Rose that the others were out there, and if Orrin's behavior was anything to go by, that was something they weren't aware of yet. For Gabriel's sake, she had to play this solo.

Besides, there was no guarantee that even with the help of Briggs and the others, they'd be able to take the giant out. Not when he had the night as his ally. To be able to shoot someone, you had to be able to see him.

Orrin reached the bottom step and stopped. Though she couldn't see his smile, she could feel it.

"Nowhere to run here, little girl. Just one big room with only the two exits."

Her back hit the wall. She edged along to the right. "You can't cover both of them at the same time, Orrin."

"I don't need to. I move fast—faster even than you."

"You can't know that." Though she had a suspicion that he could. After all, if it was possible for her to taste evil, why couldn't it be possible for him to know instinctively what she could and couldn't do?

But if that were the case, why wasn't he saying anything about the power of the storm?

Her foot hit something and metal scraped harshly across the concrete. Orrin laughed.

"You think that little metal pick is going to hurt me?"

Shoved deep in some unlikely orifice, yes, it probably would. She quickly picked it up. Orrin's so-called pick was a good three feet long and as heavy as sin. It should make a rather nice dent, even in a head as thick as Orrin's. *If* she dared get that close.

He stepped toward her. Heat crawled over her skin, whispering secrets. Orrin was, as he'd said, kin to the vampires, but one who could walk through the day without fear. A dhampire, one who drank blood not out of necessity, but purely for enjoyment.

She hefted the metal rod, holding it in front of her like a staff. Why hadn't she sensed Orrin's true nature earlier? Was it because the daylight hid his vampire half, or was it more a case of these new abilities coming into focus because of the storm's power?

"Why not simply turn yourself in, Orrin? At the moment, you're guilty of little more than being an accessory. A few years, max, in prison. Piss easy for a man like you."

"And Hopeworth? You think I don't know they'll swoop in and get me?"

"You have a real fixation with Hopeworth, haven't you?" She balanced lightly on her toes, ready to run given the slightest hint of movement from Orrin.

"You're one of us. You should know what it's like, being poked and prodded and examined endlessly. I won't go back to it. I can't."

She frowned. He seemed to have awfully clear memories of something that happened when he was a baby. "That was a long time ago, Orrin."

"Twenty years," he agreed. "I was nearly ten when they dumped me. But I remember. And I will have revenge."

Not if she could help it. Not that she wanted to protect Hopeworth—far from it. Everything she'd learned over the past few days had only convinced her that they deserved everything Orrin had planned, and a whole lot more.

No. The problem was Orrin himself. His desire to kill was so strong she could almost taste it. He planned to play with her, planned to drink her blood until he drained her dry. Then he planned to do the same to Gabriel.

To stop him, she'd have to kill him. If she could.

He rushed at her, a gale force she felt rather than saw. She danced away and swung the bar with all her might. It connected against flesh with a sickening crack. The force of the blow shuddered up her arm and momentarily numbed her fingers.

He laughed. *Laughed*. He was as mad as Rose.

She backed away, gripping the bar hard, her gaze locked on his evil stain.

"You're good, little girl. Not many can match me for speed."

Gabriel could. No doubt Stephan could as well. She hoped like hell he was listening in—no, make that running to the rescue. It had been nothing short of madness to ever think she could play this game with Orrin. The giant was too fast, too strong.

"As you said, we have something in common. Give it up, Orrin, while you still can."

"You're all talk, little girl. And if you're waiting for those others to come to the rescue, I have to tell you, five is not enough."

Fear slivered through her. "What are you talking about?"

He chortled. "Those five heartbeats that draw close. I sensed them ages ago, though I have to admit I didn't feel you until you were really close."

Why? That was the question that needed to be answered, but she wasn't going to risk asking Orrin. The less the giant knew about her—or rather, her appalling lack of knowledge about her past and her skills—the better. "If you know they're there, you must know that you're never going to escape."

"They don't hold enough firepower to stop me."

"One laser set to the maximum is enough to stop you, Orrin."

"But I am one with the night. They can't see me. Only you can."

A point she'd mulled over not so long ago. "This is the SIU we're talking about here. You think they don't have weapons to bring down rat bait like you?"

He snarled—a sound that crawled across her skin, sending shivers up her spine. It was a malignant, angry noise.

"Then I'll just have to use you as a shield before I kill you."

"Not something I'm planning to let happen, I can tell you."

"Who said anythin' about choice?"

He rushed her again. Air surged from her left—a fist, looking for a target. She ducked and then swung the bar. Felt it caught in some gigantic vice before it was ripped from her hand.

She turned and ran. He didn't follow. *Playing with his prey, enjoying the hunt,* she thought.

She stopped at the far end of the room, her breath coming in short gasps that tore at her throat. From fear, more than exertion.

He flung the bar to one side. It hit the wall hard enough to leave a dent and clattered to the floor halfway between herself and Orrin.

"Come get your toothpick, girlie."

Said the spider to the fly. "No, thanks. I'm comfortable right where I am."

He sighed. "You really aren't playing the game right, you know."

She flexed her fingers, trying to ease the tension knotting her limbs. Energy tingled across her fingertips, firefly bright in the darkness. Maybe she really didn't need the bar. Maybe she had a weapon primed and ready to go.

If only she could figure out how to use it without getting too close to Orrin.

"Fire won't hurt me, if that's what you're planning with that lighter."

He'd seen the brief dance of flames across her fingers, obviously. Overhead, thunder rumbled. The storm was close, so close. She could feel the vibrations of it shuddering through her soul.

Orrin swept toward her again. She ducked away, but this time he was ready for it. His fist connected against her chin and sent her flying. She hit the concrete with a grunt, the air leaving her lungs in a whoosh. For a moment, stars fizzed across her vision.

Then she felt the wind of Orrin's approach. She scrambled upright and staggered away. He stopped.

"I haven't had a good fight in ages," he said, almost wistfully. "Perhaps I'll kill you fast at the end, just to show my appreciation."

"Gee, thanks." She gingerly touched her chin. Blood dripped from a cut a good two inches long. Orrin had to be wearing a ring of some kind.

"You're welcome, little girl."

Obviously he'd missed the sarcasm in her voice. Thunder rumbled across the night again. Every nerve ending seemed to respond to the call of the storm. Power tingled through her body, a wildness that burned at her fingertips, aching for release.

She clenched her hands and watched the stain that was Orrin. Again the air stirred. This time she didn't move, but simply stood watching and waiting. His evil rolled over her, a black wave of darkness that made her shudder in revulsion. His steps drew close.

At the last possible moment, she ducked. The wind of his punch stirred her hair. She reached up and grabbed his arm. Fire leapt from fingers—jagged pieces of lightning that raced up his arm and across his body.

She could see him, she realized. See the sudden flash of terror in his eyes.

He screamed as the force of her power flung him across the room. Then the lightning died, and weakness washed through her. Her legs collapsed from beneath her, and suddenly she was kneeling on cold concrete, gasping for breath, her whole body trembling with exhaustion. Whatever the power was, it had limitations—physical limitations. The force was a hell of a lot stronger than she ever could be.

Orrin hit the concrete with a splat that shuddered through the foundations. He groaned for several moments, the smell of burnt flesh heavy in the air.

Finally, Sam took a deep, shuddering breath and pushed upright. Now was the time to run for the stairs, to try to escape. She staggered forward, but Orrin rose. For a moment, he simply stood and watched her. His arm hung by his side, blackened. His eyes were dark, glazed and certainly no longer human. The vampire half of his soul had risen fully to the surface.

There would be no mercy for her now. Nothing but death, long and lingering, if she didn't get the hell out of here now.

The darkness cloaked him once more, and with a primeval scream of fury, he ran at her. She'd never make the stairs. As the realization hit, she swung away, running for the back door. Energy still tingled at her fingertips, a muted echo of the force she'd unleashed on Orrin. Perhaps it would be enough to shatter the top lock and open the door. She had to get help. She couldn't survive Orrin without it.

She leapt for the door and slapped a palm high up, fingers barely brushing the lock despite her leap. Fire danced across the bolt. There was a brief report, like gunfire, and then the bolt disintegrated.

Orrin closed in so fast she didn't have time to get the door open. She leapt sideways and hit the ground instead, thrust an arm against the wall to steady herself, then ran. Away from Orrin. Away from the door.

He gave chase. His steps echoed in her ears, drawing closer with every beat of her heart. Fear surged, as did the fire. It pulsated through her body, burned at her fingertips. But to use it, she'd have to stop, have to let him get close enough to touch her. And that could be fatal.

She neared the stairs again and thought briefly about climbing them. But he'd catch her at the door, and there was no room to fight on the landing itself. Nor could she afford to block the entrance, just in case Stephan or the others came to the rescue.

She ran past the steps, headed once again for the far side of the room. The thump of Orrin's footsteps drew closer, until it was almost all she could hear.

Wind stirred, a cyclonic force reaching out to grab her. She ducked to the right, felt his fingers tear down her arm, and headed back across the room, knowing she had little time left.

He caught her hair and wrenched her backward. She yelped and fought for balance, but he was far too strong. He threw her backward and she hit the floor with another yelp. Then he was on her, his weight crushing her chest and stomach, his fingers around her neck, squeezing hard.

Desperation burned through her. Her arms were pinned by his knees. She couldn't move. She struggled to breathe. Light danced before her eyes—starbright light that wavered in and out of focus.

She *had* to free her arms. The fire that burned through her soul was her only chance to live. She began to struggle, bucking her body, trying to shift his bulk enough to free her arm. One would do. One would kill.

He laughed, and the sound crawled across her skin. "Fight, my pretty. Fight while I watch you die."

She tried to reply but couldn't. Her breath was little more than short, sharp gasps. The dancing lights were getting brighter, and the darkness of unconsciousness threatened. She didn't have much time left.

The door at the top of the stairs opened. Footsteps whispered across the silence. Two sets—two men.

"Sam?"

Gabriel's voice. Etched with pain, but strong. Relief swam through her. At least he would live.

"Sam, are you here?"

Of course she was here. Couldn't he see her? Couldn't he see Orrin? Couldn't he see that the fucker had her so close to death?

She blinked. No, he couldn't. Orrin was cloaked in darkness. And perhaps she was, too.

She struggled harder, bucking her body, trying to dislodge the giant's weight or loosen his fingers. Orrin made no noise, and no acknowledgment of the two men on the landing. Either the bloodlust had made him oblivious to his surroundings or he just didn't care.

"Sam, I can't see you, but I know you're here somewhere. Where's Orrin?"

"Right here," she tried to scream, but it came out as little more than a weak gasp. Her lungs burned with the need for air. His fingers were digging deeper and deeper into her flesh. He'd soon crush her larynx.

Then he'd drain her, while her goddamn partner stood by and saw nothing but darkness.

The blue-white beam of a laser fire bit through the night, striking the concrete very close to them, and Orrin jerked in surprise. Sam bucked and managed to get one arm free from the weight of his knee.

Overhead, thunder rumbled. Lightning flashed— not only across the night, but right through her soul. Fire scorched through every nerve ending, aching for release.

Another laser beam bit through the darkness, close enough to touch. Orrin swore under his breath. Just for an instant, his fingers relaxed and she sucked in a great gulp of air.

"Gabriel, here!" she screamed, then slapped her hand against Orrin's thigh.

Power surged—a lightning flash that poured from her fingers to him. He jerked, mouth open in shock, as electric fingers of light swam across his body.

The storm-held power wrenched his weight from her, shattering his cover of darkness as it flung him across the room.

The laser light flashed again. Two beams, a deeper blue this time. Orrin landed near the base of the stairs, a gaping black hole where his face had been.

He was dead. Thank the gods, he was dead.

Relief stirred, but she didn't. It was all she could do just to gulp in great gasps of air. Her throat burned, as if his fingers were still around it, digging deep. But she'd survived. With the power of the storm, and a little help from Gabriel, she'd done the impossible.

She'd survived Orrin Whittiker.

Footsteps drew close and Gabriel appeared, his movements stiff and slow, like those of an old man.

His face was white and etched with pain. His hair was matted, black with sweat and stiff with blood.

He knelt beside her, then reached out to touch her bruised cheek. "I've seen you look healthier."

"And here I was thinking you'd never looked better." Her voice came out as little more than a harsh whisper. It didn't matter. She knew he'd understand her, even if no words came out.

He raised an eyebrow in surprise. "Oh yeah?"

"Yeah," she said. "You're alive."

A smile twitched his lips. "How did you find me?"

"With those psychic abilities I don't have."

His smile grew. With one finger, he gently traced the line of her cheek to her chin, his touch like fire against her skin. Awareness surged between them, and just for a moment, she saw the desire in his eyes. The longing. Then his gaze hardened and the warmth disappeared, right along with his touch.

Anger fired through her. She was sick of playing these games, sick of being shoved into a shoe box and being told to stay. Sick of his words and actions saying one thing, yet his *reactions* saying another. He didn't want her as a partner, and, truth be told, he probably wouldn't have her as anything else.

Fine, then. Let him win the war, if that was what he really wanted.

It was time she started taking control of her life. And part of that was not only finding her past, but creating a future as well. If Gabriel wanted no part of that future, then fine. It was time she accepted the fact and just moved on.

"Stephan's calling an ambulance for us both," he said, his voice all cool efficiency. "And organizing a cleanup team."

"Rose?" Her voice was still scratchy, but it was filled with barely controlled annoyance.

"Dead. Stephan shot her."

"Good." She rolled sideways and carefully climbed to her feet. The effort left her head swimming, and for several seconds she rested her hands on her knees and gasped for breath.

"What the hell are you doing?"

He reached out, perhaps to steady her, perhaps to stop her, but she jerked away from his touch and saw the flicker of surprise on his face. "I've told you before, I don't like hospitals. I'm going home." Or, at least, to the motel she'd booked into for the night.

He frowned. "You should get checked out first. Besides, what have you got to go home to?"

Nothing—the same as ever. And that was just something else she'd have to change. Placing her trust, and her need for friendship, in the hands of her partners had been nothing short of stupidity. And in the end, it had only led to grief. All her life she'd been longing for friends, for family. Maybe she couldn't do anything about the second desire, but she could certainly get off her ass and do something about the first. Life was there to be explored—and it was about time she started doing that.

It was a pity she hadn't realized that before Jack had come along. Though in many ways, he had perhaps saved her. She was no longer content to drift. She wanted—needed—something more out of life. "What does it matter to you what I have and haven't got to go home to?"

His gaze briefly searched hers, then he shrugged and said, "It's your life."

"That it is," she muttered, and turned away.

She could feel his gaze on her back, curious, and perhaps a little angry.

"Sam," he called softly after a few seconds.

She hesitated, and half turned around. "What?"

"Thanks."

In the hazel depths of his eyes, she saw the warmth, the longing, that he would never admit to and never unleash. In many ways, Gabriel Stern was just as imprisoned by his memories of the past as she was by her lack of them.

And there was nothing she could do or say to free him. The choice was his, and it had been made long ago.

"Forget about it," she said, and walked away.

If you loved *Generation 18*,
be sure not to miss the final book
in the thrilling Spook Squad series,
which will be out next month!

PENUMBRA

by

KERI ARTHUR

Here's a special preview:

SAMANTHA RYAN PLACED HER HANDS on the front of her boss's desk and said, "I want a transfer, not more of your damn excuses."

She knew that speaking to Stephan in such a manner wasn't the best idea, especially when he was the man in charge of both the Special Investigations Unit and the more secretive Federation—a man who'd ruthlessly do whatever it took to get the answers he needed or the job done. She knew *that* from firsthand experience; she'd suffered through his interrogation without the medical help she'd required after she'd been shot while trying to stop the shapeshifter imitating her partner—a man who also happened to be his brother.

Not that she thought he intended her any sort of harm right now. He had as much interest in finding out who and what she was as she did. But he certainly *could* make her life hell—though how much worse it would be than her current hell was debatable.

She leaned across the desk and added, *"Sir,"* a touch sarcastically.

Stephan Stern raised one blond eyebrow, as if mildly surprised by her outburst. An outburst he'd *known* was coming for months. "You know I don't want to do that."

"I don't honestly care what you want. This is about what *I* want." She pushed away from the desk, unable to stand still any longer. Damn it, she'd spent more than half her life with her head in the sand, cruising through life rather than participating, and she'd had more than enough. The time had come to get greedy—to think about *her* wants, *her* desires, for a change. And what she wanted right now was not only a more active personal life, but a working life that involved something better than a broom closet. "Transfer me back to State, let me resign or find me another partner. As I said, I don't care. Just get me out of my current situation."

Her angry strides carried her the length of the beige-colored office in no time and she turned to face Stephan. His expression was as remote as ever, but she'd learned very early on that Stephan was a master at hiding his emotions—and that his dead face was just as likely to mean fury as calm.

"I prefer to leave you with Gabriel, as I still believe you two will make a formidable team."

Sam snorted softly. "That has never been an option, and I think we both realize that now."

It wasn't as if she hadn't tried, for God's sake. But her partner was still going out of his way to exclude her from everything from investigations to chitchat. Access to the SIU's vast computer system just wasn't worth this frustration and unhappiness.

Especially since she was getting jack shit in the way of information about the past she couldn't remember.

Hell, her dreams were providing more information than the SIU's system. The only trouble was, how much could she actually trust the dreams?

And how much could she trust the man who constantly walked through them?

She didn't know, nor did she have anyone she could talk to about it—and that was perhaps the most frustrating thing about this entire situation. She *needed* to get a life. Friends. People she could trust and talk to. Hell, even a pet would be better than going home alone to a soulless hotel room every night.

"I prefer to give the situation more time." Stephan crossed his arms and leaned forward. "However, I do have another option that might suit us both."

Sam met his gaze. His blue eyes were sharp, full of cunning and intelligence. Stephan was a shark by nature—and this was the reason he, rather than his twin, Gabriel, ruled the SIU and the Federation.

Of course, that also meant she was beating her head against a brick wall where Gabriel was concerned, because Stephan was always going to look after his twin's interests first. Even if said twin didn't appreciate his efforts any more than Sam did.

She came to a stop in front of his desk and couldn't help feeling like a fish about to be hooked. "What might that be?"

"You remember Dan Wetherton?"

She nodded. "Last I heard, no one was sure if the body Gabriel found was the real Wetherton or a clone."

"Well, as it happens, it was the original."

Sam snagged the nearest chair and sat down, interested despite her wariness. "Gabriel and I theorized about the possibility of whole brain transplants making clones a viable replacement option, but officially—as far as I'm aware—it's still considered impossible to create a clone that exactly duplicates the mannerisms and thoughts of the original person. They may be genetically identical, but they are nevertheless different." She hesitated, frowning. "Besides, I read the in-house reports and tests done on the living Wetherton. He was declared human in all scientific results."

"And a clone isn't?"

She grimaced. Clones were human, no doubt about that. But whether that actually granted them *humanity* was a point of contention between the scientists and the theologians. "Having only met one clone, who was trying to kill me at the time, I don't feel qualified to answer that particular question."

Amusement touched the corners of Stephan's thin lips. "As it happens, the test results were altered by a party or parties unknown long before we got them." He picked up a folder from his desk and offered it to her. "These are the originals. Have a look."

From past experience she knew that it was pointless to ask how he'd gotten hold of the original papers. Stephan worked on a need-to-know basis—and generally, that meant the less everyone knew, the better. She doubted even Gabriel was privy to all his secrets.

Not that Gabriel himself was particularly open. Not with *her,* anyway.

She leafed through the information inside the folder. It included the genetic tests on both Wetherton and the clone, the coroner's report and Wetherton's medical history.

"Wetherton had cancer," she said, looking up. "Incurable."

"Which the current version no longer has."

She threw the folder back on the desk. "If you know he's not the original, why not simply kill him?"

"Because we wanted to know why he was cloned. And where."

"But not who had cloned him?" Did that mean they suspected the mysterious Sethanon was behind it all?

"As I said, we don't know the where and the why. But there is only one suspect for the who."

"But the military is experimenting with genetics. There's no reason why Wetherton can't be their boy."

"No, there's not."

His tone seemed to dismiss her speculation, and yet she had a vague notion that she'd hit upon the very issue that was troubling Stephan. Only, for some weird reason, he didn't want to acknowledge it. "And what about the replacement parts industry? Have you checked to see if they have started developing fully formed beings, or is that just too obvious?"

His expression became briefly annoyed. "We never overlook the obvious."

Of course not. She smiled slightly. Irritating Stephan might be akin to prodding a lion with a very short stick, but when she got even the slightest reaction, it was oddly satisfying.

"The black-market trade in cloned parts is booming," she said. Of course, it was fueled mainly by humanity's desperation to cheat death. An incredible number of people seemed willing to pay exorbitant prices to grow new body parts, so why not take it a step further, and attempt a cloning miracle? Not just a replacement heart or liver or whatever other part had failed, but a whole new body?

But humanity was more than just a brain; it was also a heart and soul. Medical science might be able to transfer flesh and brain matter, but how could anyone transfer a soul? Even if they could pin down what a soul actually was?

Not that rules ever stopped anyone—especially when there was huge money to be made.

And somewhere along the line, someone had succeeded in achieving at least part of the impossible—fully fleshed, viable clones who looked and acted like the original. Wetherton, and her ex-partner, Jack Kazdan, were proof of that. Although something *had* gone wrong with Jack's clone; it might have looked like him, but it had had serious problems speaking. But then, it had been given a shitload of growth accelerant, so it wasn't truly a surprise that it couldn't speak well. It had never really had the time to learn.

"His source is not black market. We're sure of that."

She studied him for a moment, then changed tactics. "Wetherton's just been made Minister for Science and Technology, hasn't he?"

Stephan nodded. "Two years ago he was trying to shut down many of the science programs, stating that the money could be better spent on the health care system. Now he's in charge of the lot."

"Why hasn't anyone questioned this sudden change of heart? Surely the press has noted it?"

"Noted a political backflip?" Amusement touched his lips again. "You're kidding, right?"

Point made. Flip-flopping politicians were such a fact of life that even the press had gotten tired of them. And the public at large simply ignored them, except when the flops directly affected their bottom line.

"What advantage would having a clone in such a position be for someone like Sethanon?"

"Sadly, we don't know the answer to that one yet."

Not until they caught Sethanon, anyway. And *he* had proven as elusive as a ghost.

"So you've had Wetherton watched?"

"We've had an agent in his office for the last two months, but she can't get close enough. Wetherton plays his cards very close to his chest."

If the man was a clone, he'd have to. One mistake and the truth would be out.

"What does all this have to do with my wanting a transfer?"

He smiled—all teeth and no sincerity. "The minister has recently received several death threats. He was given police protection, but the would-be killer has slipped past them on a number of occasions and left notes. The minister has now requested the SIU's help."

She regarded him steadily. "So who did you use to drop the notes? A vampire or a shapeshifter?"

Amusement flickered briefly through his eyes. "The original threats were real enough."

Yeah, right. There was just a little too much sincerity in his voice for her to believe that. "Am I the only agent being sent in?"

"No. You'll handle the night shift—it suits your growing abilities better. Jenna Morwood will do the days."

Morwood wasn't someone she'd met. "What's her specialty?"

"Morwood's an empath and telekinetic."

So she'd be able to see an attack coming by simply reading the emotions swirling around her—a good choice for this sort of work. "Are we the only two going in?"

"Yes." He hesitated. "Wetherton has requested that the night watch stay at his apartment when he's there at night. Since the first two threats were hand-delivered, I've agreed to his request. I want you to observe everyone he meets. Become his shadow and learn his secrets."

A huge task. "And the reason you're sending two female agents?"

Once again, that insincere smile flashed. "Wetherton appears less guarded around females."

"Meaning what? That he's likely to hit on us?"

"It's a distinct possibility. And before it's mentioned, no, I do not expect or want you to sleep with the man."

"Good, because I wouldn't." She hesitated, frowning. "Wetherton's made much of his caring, family-man image over the last few years. That doesn't quite jell with him hitting on anything with breasts."

"He and his wife separated not long after the original's death. Since then, he's bought a nice apartment on Collins Street and now spends most of his nights there. He's also been seen with an endless stream of beauties on his arms."

She frowned. Wetherton wasn't exactly a looker—though that in itself didn't mean anything. Some of the ugliest spuds in the world had immense success with the ladies simply because of the wealth they controlled, or their sheer magnetic power. But from what she remembered of Wetherton, neither of these was a factor.

"I'm surprised the press haven't had more of a field day."

"They did initially, but a politician behaving badly isn't exactly news these days."

That was certainly true. "I doubt whether I'll learn all that much doing night shift. Surely most of his business will be conducted during the day, no?"

Stephan smiled grimly. "Wetherton has a surprising number of business meetings at night—and usually at nightclubs, where it's harder to get a bug in."

"He'll be suspicious of me. He's not likely to trust me with anything vital."

"Not for a while. It may take months."

Months out of her life and her need to find her past. But also months away from Gabriel. Would absence make his heart grow fonder? A smile touched her lips. Unlikely. "What about time off? You can't expect either of us to work seven days a week."

He nodded. "You'll each get two days—though which two will depend on Wetherton's schedule. Generally, it will be the days he spends at home with his children. We have other arrangements in place there."

"Will the press buy our sudden appearance in his life? This sort of protection is usually handled by the feds, not the SIU."

"They won't question our appearance after tonight, believe me."

The dry coldness in his voice sent chills down her spine. "Why? What are you planning for tonight?"

"A spectacular but ineffectual murder attempt.

Wetherton may be injured, and will, of course, demand our help."

"So who's the patsy?"

Stephan shrugged. "A young vampire we captured several weeks ago. He'd been something of a political dissident in life, and his afterlife has only sharpened his beliefs."

And Stephan had no doubt been feeding his madness, aiming it toward Wetherton. Meaning this plan had been in motion for some time, and that this assignment was part of a bigger picture than he was currently admitting to.

Goose bumps ran up Sam's arms and she rubbed them lightly. Perhaps the vampire wasn't the only patsy in this situation.

"I gather the vamp will die?"

"He murdered seven people before we captured him. His death is merely a delayed sentence."

"What if he escapes?"

"He won't."

Sam shifted in her chair. "If Wetherton is up to anything nefarious, it's doubtful I'll be privy to it."

"No. There will be certain times you'll be sent from the room; this is unavoidable. To counter it, you'll bug the room."

"Most federal buildings have monitors. The minute a bug is activated, an alarm will sound."

"They won't detect the ones we'll give you. Our labs have specifically developed bugs that will function in just this sort of situation."

And no doubt developed a means of detecting them, too. "How long do you think I'll be guarding Wetherton?"

Stephan shrugged. "I can't honestly say. It could be

a month; it could be a year. Parliament doesn't convene again until the middle of next month. By then, you will be such a fixture in his life that no one will comment."

By then, she hoped Wetherton would have revealed all his secrets and she could get on with her life. Spending months in Canberra, yawning her way through endless cabinet sessions, was not something to look forward to.

She crossed her arms and stared at Stephan. He returned her gaze calmly. The uneasy feeling that he wasn't telling her everything grew.

"You're doing this to get back at Gabriel, aren't you? You want him to care."

"I'm doing this because no other agents have your particular range of talents. Your ability to detect evil could be vital in this case."

No lies, but not the exact truth, either. She sat back, feeling more frustrated than when she'd first entered Stephan's office. Guarding Wetherton was not the job she really wanted, but what other choice did she have? It was either this or put up with endless hours of mind-numbing paperwork in her shoe-box office in the Vault.

"How do I keep in contact?"

"You'll be wearing a transmitter that will be monitored twenty-four hours a day." Stephan reached into his desk and pulled out what looked like a gold ear stud. "This is the current model. It records sound and pictures. You turn it on and off by simply touching the surface."

"I don't have to get my ears pierced, do I?" She'd rather face a dozen vampires than one doctor armed with a body-piercing implement.

Stephan's smile held the first real hint of warmth she'd seen since she walked into his office. "No. The studs are designed to cling to human flesh. You actually won't be able to get them off without the help of the labs."

Just as well she could turn them off, then. She needed some privacy in her life, even if it was only to go to the bathroom.

"When do I start?"

"Tomorrow night." Stephan picked up another folder and passed it across the desk. "In here you'll find detailed backgrounds on Wetherton's friends, family and business acquaintances."

She dropped the folder onto her lap. There was plenty of time to look at it later. "You were pretty certain I'd take this job, weren't you?"

"Yes. What other choice have you actually got?"

Indeed. "And Gabriel?"

"Will be told you've been reassigned."

Which would no doubt please him. He'd finally gotten what he wanted—her out of his life. "And will I be? After this assignment is over, that is?"

Stephan considered her for several seconds. "That depends."

"On what?"

"On whether or not he has come to his senses by then."

A statement she didn't like one little bit. "You owe me, Stephan," she said softly. For ordering his agents to shoot when she'd been trying to stop the shifter who'd taken Gabriel's form. For the hour of questioning she'd faced afterward when she should have been in the med center. For saving his twin's life. "All I want is permanent reassignment."

His gaze met hers, assessing, calculating. "All right," he said slowly. "As I said, this assignment could take more than a year to complete. If you still wish a new partner at the end, I will comply."

She stared at him. He had agreed to her demands far too easily. She didn't trust him—and didn't trust that he meant what he said. But for the moment, there was little she could do about it.

"What happens if I need access to files or information?"

"You'll have a portable com-unit with you, coded to respond only to your voice and retinal scan. You'll also have priority access to all files, though a copy of all requests and search results will be sent to me."

She raised an eyebrow. Priority access? Whatever it was Stephan thought Wetherton was involved in had to be huge.

The intercom buzzed into the silence and Stephan leaned across and pressed the button. "Yes?"

"Assistant Director Stern to see you, as requested, sir."

"Send him in." He gave her a toothy smile that held absolutely no sincerity. "I thought you might like to say goodbye."

Gabriel was the last person she wanted to see. She could barely control her temper around him these days, and hitting a superior officer would only get her into more trouble than Gabriel was worth. And Stephan damn well knew it. She thrust upright. "You're a bastard, you know that?"

"No, I'm a man faced with two people who won't acknowledge that they are meant to be partners."

The door opened, giving her no time to reply. She clenched the folder tightly but found her gaze drawn to the tall man entering the room. His hazel eyes narrowed when he saw her.

But just for an instant, something passed between them—an emotion she couldn't define and he would never verbally acknowledge. And that made her even angrier.

"Sam," Gabriel said, his voice as polite as the nod he gave her.

"Gabriel," she bit back, and glanced at Stephan. "Will that be all, sir?"

A smile quirked the corner of Stephan's mouth. He hadn't missed her reaction. "Yes. For now."

Gabriel stepped to one side as she approached. It was probably meant to be nothing more than a polite gesture—he was simply making way for her to get past—but it fanned the fires of her fury even higher. One way or another, this man was always avoiding her.

She met his gaze and saw only wariness in the green-flecked hazel depths of his eyes. Ever since the factory shootout with Rose and Orrin nearly two weeks ago, he'd treated her this way. She wasn't entirely sure why. And in all honesty, it was time she stopped worrying about it. She had more important concerns these days.

Like finding out who she really was. *What* she really was. Like getting a life beyond the force.

She stopped in front of him and his scent stirred around her, spicy and masculine, making her want things she could never have. Not with this man.

"You win, Gabriel. You have your wish. I'm out of your life." She held out her hand. "I wish I could say it's been pleasant, but you sure as hell made certain it wasn't."

His fingers closed round hers, his touch sending warmth through her soul. A promise that could never be.

"You've been reassigned, then?" Relief edged his deep voice.

"Yeah."

He released her hand and her fingers tingled with the memory of his touch. Part of her was tempted to clench her hand in an effort to retain that warmth just a bit longer. But what was the point of holding on to something that was little more than an illusion? A desire that probably came from loneliness more than any real connection?

"Who's the new partner?"

There was something a little more than polite interest in the question. Were he anyone else, she might have thought he cared. With Gabriel, who knew?

Sam shrugged. "It's really none of your business now, is it?" She glanced back at Stephan. "I'll talk to you later."

He nodded and she met Gabriel's eyes one final time, her gaze searching his—though what she was looking for, she couldn't honestly say. After a few seconds, she turned and walked out, her fury a clenched knot inside her chest.

GABRIEL WATCHED HER GO AND the anger so visible in every step seared his mind, reaching into places he'd thought well shielded and far out of reach. Whatever this connection was between them, it was breaking down barriers not even his twin had been able to traverse, and raising emotions he'd long thought dead.

Which was just another reason to get her out of his working life. Whether or not she should then appear in his social life was a point of contention between the two parts of his soul. The hawk half—the half that had already lost its soul mate—wanted no strings, no ties, nothing beyond those that already existed, but the human half wanted to pursue what might lie between them. Wanted to discover if, given the chance, it could develop into something more than friendship.

Not that there ever would be a chance, if her anger was anything to go by. Which was precisely what he'd wanted, what he'd been aiming for over the nine months they'd been partners. So why did his victory feel so hollow?

He shut the door and walked across the room to the chair. "So," he said as he sat down. "Where has she been reassigned?"

Stephan leaned back in his chair, his blue eyes assessing. "She's right. It really is none of your business now."

"Don't give me that crap. Just tell me."

Stephan smiled, though no warmth touched his expression. It was that, more than anything, which raised Gabriel's hackles. Stephan was up to something, something he wouldn't like.

"She's on special assignment as of tomorrow."

Gabriel regarded him steadily. His brother was enjoying this. He could almost feel his twin's satisfaction. "Give, brother. What the hell have you done?"

Stephan steepled his fingers and studied them with sudden interest. "I've assigned her to the Wetherton case."

The Wetherton case? The one case she should have

been kept well away from, if only because of its possible links to both Sethanon and Hopeworth? "Get her off it, Stephan. Get her off it *now*."

His twin's gaze finally met his, filled with nothing more than a steely determination. "She is the best person for the job, whatever the risks."

"You haven't even warned her, have you?" Gabriel scrubbed a hand across his jaw. Christ, she could be walking straight into a goddamn trap, and there was nothing he could do to save her.

"She knows we believe Sethanon is involved," Stephan commented.

"Which is the least of our worries. Wetherton's and Kazdan's clones can have only one source, and we both know it. Neither the government labs nor the black marketeers have succeeded with personality and memory transfers. Hopeworth has."

"Or so our spy tells us. It's not something we've been able to confirm."

The Federation had attempted to place spies in Hopeworth on several occasions, but it was only in the last few months that one of their operatives had leaked this information—though so far it was only his word backing it up.

"I think Hopeworth basically confirmed their involvement when they maneuvered to get Wetherton's clone in charge of their budget."

"If they wanted their clone in charge of their budget, they should have got him assigned to Defense."

Gabriel crossed his arms. Hopeworth had fingers in both pies, and Stephan knew it. "Did you even mention Hopeworth to Sam?"

"It was mentioned. But we don't know for sure if Hopeworth is involved."

"Then did you at least tell her Sethanon is more than likely involved with Hopeworth?"

"No, because we have nothing more than a suspicion to back this up. We have no photographs of him. We don't even know if he truly exists. He is currently nothing more than a name."

"A name that has over thirty SIU and Federation deaths attributed to it. And I don't particularly want Sam's name added to that list." His voice was tight with the anger coursing through him. True, he'd wanted to lose her as a partner, but he certainly hadn't wanted to throw her to the lions, and that's basically what his brother had done. She would have been safer remaining his partner than taking this mission.

Stephan grimaced. "Nor do I, brother. Believe me. But we need to uncover the source of these clones. We need to draw Sethanon out, and we need to uncover whether or not he is involved as deeply with Hopeworth as we suspect. And the truth is, she's the best bait we have to achieve those aims."

"What about our source in Hopeworth? Has he heard any whispers about Sethanon?"

Stephan shook his head. "It's not a code name the military uses."

"Kazdan knew who he was, so others must. It's just a matter of uncovering the various layers of his organization."

"Which is why Samantha has been assigned to Wetherton. We know he's a clone. We know his name was on that list she got from Kazdan. We need to know what that list was, and what Wetherton had promised to do in return for life eternal. And why the original was deemed expendable enough to kill and clone and not directly exploit."

"But that still puts her too close to Hopeworth. That could be extremely dangerous."

Stephan leaned back in his chair and regarded his brother steadily. "Only if, as you presume, she is a product of Hopeworth itself."

"You've seen the initial reports from O'Hearn. You've seen the coding. Whatever Sam is, she's definitely not a product of natural selection."

"Yet it was Sethanon who assigned Kazdan to monitor her every move. Sethanon who appears to know just who and what Samantha is. You noted that yourself. Couldn't that mean he's responsible for her creation?"

Possible, but not likely. Gabriel didn't doubt that Sethanon wanted to use her, but if the man had been responsible for her creation, why would he take the risk of releasing her?

"Sam had a military microchip in her side," Gabriel pointed out. "The same sort of chip that we found in both the Generation 18 rejects and in Allars." She was also afraid of Hopeworth. Though she had never said anything, he could feel her fear as clearly as if it were his own.

"And yet our source in Hopeworth can find no record of her, though he can find records on every other reject."

"Maybe because her project was destroyed by a fire years ago."

"A fire would never destroy every scrap of information. Nor could it erase every memory."

"And yet everyone says that Penumbra was destroyed that completely."

"People still remember the project, Gabriel. They just don't remember her."

Mary Elliot, the nurse who'd worked on the project, apparently did, but she was just one of many, and a woman with a faulty memory at that. Partially thanks to Alzheimer's, and partially thanks to the military's habit of "readjusting" memories. Gabriel shifted restlessly in the seat. "What if she isn't a reject? What if she's something else entirely?"

Stephan raised an eyebrow. "What do you mean?"

He didn't really know. It was just a feeling. The extent of Sam's memory loss, the depth to which the truth appeared to be buried and the fact that someone was willing to bomb the SIU in order to destroy her test results—it all spoke of intent. It suggested that someone, somewhere, was protecting her from her past, whatever that might be.

He actually doubted that it was Hopeworth trying to conceal who she was, even if they were her creators. The military weren't that subtle. Besides, if Sam was one of their creations, they would never have let her go—especially not with the potential she was now showing.

"Look," Gabriel said, somewhat impatiently. "All I'm saying is that if Sethanon feared her enough to place a watch on her, we should not risk using her as bait in an attempt to catch the man."

"We don't even know if, in fact, it is a man we are after."

Gabriel leaned forward and glared at his twin's altered features. It was in moments like this—moments when he almost wanted to punch the cold smile from his brother's face—that Stephan's ability to shape-shift into the form of any male he touched became a problem. It was harder to restrain the urge to hit him when he wasn't wearing his own face. "Damn it, Stephan, don't play word games with me!"

Something flickered through his twin's blue eyes. Anger perhaps. Or regret. "Do you, or do you not, agree that we must learn more about Sethanon?"

"Yeah, but—"

"And do you, or do you not," Stephan continued, his voice soft but relentless, "agree that Sethanon's interest in Sam might be the lever we need to draw him out of the shadows?"

Gabriel rubbed his forehead. This was one battle he wasn't going to win—not that he ever won many against Stephan. "At the first hint of danger, I'm going in."

"Samantha can take care of herself. She's proven that time and time again."

But this was different. This was leaving her roped, tied and blindfolded in front of an express train. "I won't see her harmed."

Stephan smiled. "And here I thought you didn't care for her."

"I've never said that. All I've ever said is that I don't want her as a partner. That I don't want to see her dead."

"Have you ever considered the fact that this fear of losing partners is irrational, and that maybe you should seek psychiatric help for it?"

"Considered it? Yes. Acknowledge it? Yes. Am I going to seek psychiatric help? No." He met his brother's stony gaze with one of his own. "If I wanted to talk to anyone, I'd talk to our father."

"Because, of course, you couldn't talk to your brother." Stephan's voice was almost bitter.

Almost.

"My brother has a tendency to put the needs of the Federation and the SIU above the needs of everyone else—including his brother."

Stephan didn't immediately comment, just leaned forward and picked up a folder from the desk. "Here's the file on your new partner."

Gabriel ignored the offered folder and stared at his twin through narrowed eyes. "What do you mean, new partner?"

"I've told you before. All field agents, whether SIU or Federation, now work in pairs. There have been too many murder attempts of late to risk solo missions."

"How many times do I have to say it? I don't want a partner!" What was his brother trying to prove?

"Then you'll remain at your desk and leave the fieldwork to the agents in your charge."

He was tempted, very tempted, to do just that. But both he and Stephan knew that being confined for any length of time would make him stir-crazy.

Besides, he was more valuable to the SIU and the Federation in the field.

"Who have you assigned me?"

Stephan dropped the folder on the desk and leaned back in his chair. Though there was no emotion on his face, Gabriel could feel his twin's amusement.

"James Illie."

Who was the State Police officer they'd recruited after he'd made a series of spectacular arrests—arrests that involved one of the biggest vampire crime gangs in the city. He was good, no doubt about it.

The only trouble was, the man was a womanizer who was always on the lookout for his next conquest.

"It won't work." And Stephan knew it.

"Then make it work. And don't try dumping Illie in the dungeons. He'll bring in the unions the minute you try."

Wonderful. "Is this all you called me in here for?"

Stephan smiled. "No. There's been a break-in at the Pegasus Foundation that we've been asked to investigate."

"The Pegasus Foundation?" Gabriel frowned, trying to recall what he knew of the organization. "They won a military contract recently, didn't they?"

"To develop a stealth device for military vehicles, yes. But whoever broke in wasn't concerned about stealth devices."

"Then what were they after?"

"That's something you'll have to find out. All I've been told is that the person or persons involved managed to get past several security stations, three laser alarms and numerous cameras. It was only due to the fact that the intruder set a lab on fire that they were even aware someone had slipped their net."

"So we're saying that the person who started the fire is someone who can become both invisible and insubstantial? Is such a thing even possible?"

"We've never seen it before," Stephan answered. "But then, we've never seen a lot of the things we are now encountering, so who knows?"

"Was it just the lab that was destroyed?"

"That I don't know. They're not giving much away—not over the phone, anyway."

No real surprise there, given how easily phone conversations could be hacked these days. "So why were we called in? The Pegasus Foundation has more military ties than we have agents. Why not ask them to investigate?"

"It was the military who asked us to investigate." Stephan hesitated. "They asked specifically for you and your partner."

"So they want Sam." But if the military didn't know anything about her, why had they specifically asked for her to be included in the investigation?

"Who signed the request?"

"A General Frank Lloyd."

As Alice would say, curiouser and curiouser. "Sam met Lloyd at Han's." She'd been wary of the general and convinced they'd meet again. "You have to warn her about the military's interest."

"No, I won't." Stephan hesitated. "And neither will you."

Like hell he wouldn't. It was one thing to let her go; it was another to leave her blind. He crossed his arms. "What time is the Pegasus Foundation expecting us?"

Stephan glanced at his watch. "You're to meet with the director—Kathryn Douglass—at four thirty."

It was nearly four now. Then Gabriel frowned. "Kathryn Douglass? Why does that name sound familiar?"

"Because her name is on that list Kazdan gave to Sam."

A list that had marked potential clones and vampires, as well as assassination possibilities. "So which one was she? Clone, vampire or potential dead meat?"

"That we can't say, as there was no note beside her name," Stephan said. "Illie's requisitioned a car and is waiting out front."

Gabriel met his twin's gaze. "Thought I'd skip without him, huh?"

Stephan's smile touched his eyes for the first time. "I know you, brother. I know the way your mind works. Don't ever forget that."

Then he'd know Illie wasn't going to be a fixture in Gabriel's life for very long. If he'd wanted a partner, he'd have kept Sam.

"Then you'll know precisely what I'm thinking now."

Stephan's smile widened. "Yeah, and it's not polite to abuse a family member like that."

It was when your brother was being such a bastard.

Stephan's smile faded. "Keep away from her, Gabriel. She has a job to do, and I don't want you getting in the way."

"What I do in my own time is my business, not yours," Gabriel said, voice flat. "I'm warning you, don't ever try to control my personal life."

Stephan raised an eyebrow. "You have an obligation to both the SIU and the Federation, just as I have."

"Yeah, right." Gabriel turned and headed for the door. The Federation and the SIU could go hang if it meant letting Sam walk into a trap out of no more than ignorance.

He may have succeeded in getting rid of her as a partner, but that didn't mean he wanted her dead.

"Gabriel, I'm warning you. Leave her alone."

Gabriel stopped with his hand on the doorknob and glanced over his shoulder, meeting his brother's gaze. "Or you'll what? Censure me? Bust me down to field agent again? Do it. I don't really give a damn."

"This could be our one chance to draw Sethanon out!"

"That doesn't justify sending her in blind."

"Gabriel, I'm giving you a direct order. Do not go near her. Do not warn her."

"Then you'd better get my file out and add the black mark to it now, because that's one order I have no intention of obeying."

And he slammed the door open and stalked from the room.